A Revolution
of the Mind

A Revolution of the Mind

By MV Perry

First Heeler Books Edition

Paperback ISBN: 978-0-578-31404-4

Printed and bound by Bookmobile

Minneapolis, MN

Cover Art by Clare Nauman

www.clarenauman.bigcartel.com

Book Design by Simon Hartshorne

http://reedsy.com/hartshorne-simon

www.heelerbooks.com

twitter: @HeelerBooks

Printed in the United States of America

10 9 8 7 6 5 4 3 2 1

A Revolution of the Mind

MV PERRY

Dedicated to Mark Fisher.

"The current ruling ontology denies any possibility of a social causation of mental illness. The chemico-biologization of mental illness is of course strictly commensurate with its depoliticization. Considering mental illness an individual chemico-biological problem has enormous benefits for capitalism. First, it reinforces capital's drive towards atomistic individualization (you are sick because of your brain chemistry). Second, it provides an enormously lucrative market in which multinational pharmaceutical companies can peddle their pharmaceuticals (we can cure you with our SSRIs). It goes without saying that all mental illnesses are neurologically instantiated, but this says nothing about their causation. If it is true, for instance, that depression is constituted by low serotonin levels, what still needs to be explained is why particular individuals have low levels of serotonin. This requires a social and political explanation; and the task of repoliticizing mental illness is an urgent one if the left wants to challenge capitalist realism."

~Mark Fisher

"The harshest criticisms of any place come from
those who truly love and belong to it."
~Harper Lee

"The way to improve a problem is
to study its conditions."
-W.E.B. Dubois

"Even the children of the rich have to
choose a side in the class war."
-Ellen "Boo" Harvey

CHAPTER 1

December 2015

I stood in the cold, waiting for the elevated train, looking at the boxes and the crushed tall boys spread amongst the stones and the granite beneath the rails. As the train approached the platform, I dreamt about falling onto the tracks, interrupting my fate, and felt an ephemeral, injudicious release from the strain on my body and my mind; like a sedative in alcohol. This was a thought I held at most times of my life, unwillingly and unconsciously, just below the limits of my awareness. It became explicit whenever it could be manifested in a traitorous impulse, such as in this moment, or on many moments on the platform just before the train's arrival. It was my boogeyman of the mind, it came out sometimes when I looked at the knife in the kitchen drawer or the stack of pills on my dresser. I could have done a better job of confronting it, but avoidance was a pillar of my upbringing.

Not that I would ever act on this impulse, but it was there, and as the train came, I leaped gently away from the edge towards the center of the platform, cheerfully and easily despite the despair of the act. Like a microcosm of my life after I actually gave a damn about *living* it.

My mind was a great, unrelenting bastard, and as a consequence of that, I lived in defiance of my demise. It deemed no memory good, no moment too innocuous to avoid the wickedness of the beast. No statement was too meaningless, no matter from whom or in what context, not to be somehow turned into a condemnation of my existence. For that was the craft of the beast: to turn everything into the perception of hell.

After that leap backward, I smiled and exhaled. The absurdity of living while always wanting to die was on occasion funny to me, probably for the same reason that some old philosopher said that the harshest truths could only be expressed in jokes. My breath fumed ahead of me in the December night, along with the breaths of the others waiting for the train. In the sky above the gloss of the train, isolated snowflakes fell in and out of the light. I rested my weight against my right foot; my heel pressed into the crevice between two uneven piles of wood; my bag sagged over the side of my shoulder over my hip and my left leg bent into a thin contrapposto pose, like the statue of David; my books as my sling and stone to fell my American Goliaths.

I was the last to get on the train and took a seat alongside the wall. Mine was the seat adjacent to the pole, and I dug my shoulder into the metal for rest. I opened one of the flaps of the bag to retrieve a text on the psychiatric survivor's movement. It was deep in the bag, pinned between the fat protrusion of one overstuffed pocket and a handful of other books I keep for my spare moments. Amongst them: a frayed copy of the constitution and the federalist papers, the edition of the *S.C.U.M. Manifesto* with a wrist cutter on the cover, a political science study about the rise of Bill Clinton and the New Democrats, and *Notes From Underground*.

I was heading south through Evanston after meeting my old friend Lammie for a sendoff dinner before she moved to Colorado for a new job. The train was at half capacity, containing some Northwestern students and a few straggling passengers. The nearby corner reeked of urine, and the heating system's industrial hum droned in passenger space. At a stop, a loud, physically activated man entered the train and started talking to the train doors. He had a bunch of crap in triple-bagged grocery plastic, and I could smell him from my seat seven feet away. He shouted, in a rhythm all to his own, "God BLESS the U-S...of A! God BLESS the USA! Civil liberties WITHOUT the social re-sponsibility! Yes ma'am, civil liberties without social responsibility!

Give me diplomatic immunity or give me death! No prisoners here! Aw yea!" His odor was pungent and dreadful, as though he had crawled out of a trash fire, and I let him be, as I usually do when these types come on; that being said, I could neither ignore him nor help myself from bursting with laughter at his next statement. "Just whip it BABY! Just whip it RIGHT! Just whip it BABY! Whip-it alllll night!"

The lights of the trains swept across one another with the impression of spontaneous inertia, as though this ordered system had the quality of working in nature, like strange fish in motion, deep in the ocean. There was a brisk, routine transfer at Howard; everyone crossed the platform routinely, and nobody turned their heads towards the other commuters as they did so. The passengers boarded a sitting train on the other end of the platform and returned to the same positions as before, some lounged with their arms over the seats, and others with their heads tilted downwards at their phones or the floor. The percussive confrontations of the train against the rails grew louder than the indoor hum. The homes we passed in Rogers Park were adorned with seasonal bulbs, providing a light performance through the windows, with red, green, and white slurring across the glass.

Whatever musings I had to myself in the car ended as a man entered while talking brashly into his phone. He spoke cheerily about the details of his afternoon at his retail job, details that I would only treat with trite, formal significance in my own life, or with no consideration at all. It reminded me of something the poet Szymborska wrote about her sister, who could talk and talk and talk about what happened in her day as though the future of life rested on it, and it needed to be recorded and put into an encyclopedia. I always found myself around people who found energy and amusement in the littlest of things, and I regularly viewed them with drab contempt. I have also admitted, however, that this characteristic in others was what made them light and happy, and my lack thereof was a key component of why contentment eluded me interminably. My next thought about the man on the train was that he was high. He was certainly young enough for it, and glib enough. That was another thing that put my friends at ease that I could not enjoy: weed. I used to be able to spend an evening sharing a joint with a friend, watching a dumb film, or listening to rock music and being superficially awed by it. In the past few years, however, smoking marijuana had provoked dissociative experiences and audio hallucinations. I both resented and envied this passerby for his appearance of ease before a world that I had grown to find excruciatingly burdensome.

The train had rolled on, and I absentmindedly missed my home exit, riding the train one station further southbound than I had intended to go, to the Argyle Red Line. I did this a few times over the summer, unaware that I was too far off until I was hard on the street. Once, I wandered east of the stop and saw an intoxicated woman, stumbling and unresponsive to the Chicago police who were harassing her. I was younger then, and still in a more neurotic and innocent state of conflict between my home and reality. It was a burning hot Chicago afternoon—one that made the concrete boil in the air like heat over desert sand. A friend of the woman, a man perhaps in his late fifties, was trying to escort her home. The cops stood casually along the roadside, thumbs tucked into their belts and waistbands, jeering and chuckling. "Look at ya, you're blitzed in public!" one of them said in a piercing, amplified Chicago accent.

That was in Uptown, a hardscrabble neighborhood where the world changed with each block. It was one of the only melting pots in a city that otherwise claimed entire neighborhoods according to one ethnic identity. Uptown before my time had been marked by homelessness, deinstitutionalized mental patients, Latin Kings, poor blacks, and poor Appalachian whites. The

Wobblies also had a headquarters there, and while elements of this old Uptown remained, they were now constantly under threat of being displaced by a conservative alderman, the type of man who was at once a friend to real estate developers while also being a scourge to homeless people. "Don't feed them, you'll only reinforce their bad behavior!" he once addressed his ward.

The part of this mysterious Uptown that I was most interested in was the informal psychiatric community that inhabited the neighborhood after the fall of the asylums. When America emptied its hospitals, patients were given often only given a bus token before being sent on their way without a plan for them to go anywhere specific. In Chicago, that bus took them from Reed Hospital to Uptown via the Montrose bus. This practice was common in the US. To solve the madness problem in New York, politicians would put it on a bus and send it to New Jersey, and vice versa. Centuries earlier, the artist Hieronymus Bosch had painted the *Ship of Fools*: an iconic, proverbial boat of what were then called idiots, morons, and madmen, who had no captain and sailed nowhere.

When I eventually returned to the correct stop, Berwyn, I observed that the neighborhood just one CTA station removed from Argyle was notably more tranquil. The story of Chicago, city of broad shoulders and underground abortions, is a story of adjacent inequality. This fact is both homicidal and suicidal, for the same core reasons, though these take on vastly different forms of social ills, none of which are desirable, all of which are potentially fatal. I remember this each time I crossed Uptown's tent cities and its homeless citizens on Broadway or read about the political pressures of gentrification, only to then return to Andersonville, flourishing with its residential avenues, cobblestone alleys, and its single-family homes, which in the springtime have gardens so lush you can only see fragments of the individuals sitting in the yard through the leaves, and in the winter can rest just as picturesquely in the nature as snowfall. No CPD vans were sitting at the roadside, and the quietness of the neighborhood was quickly made apparent as I walked alongside a small, scattered crowd. For a moment, I had a creeping paranoia encroach upon the back of my head as the people behind me paced a step closer to me than I was comfortable with. I clutched my key tightly and tensed my arms in a preemptive defensive posture, and then loosened once again as the crowd disseminated into their buildings or streets.

In the blocks remaining on my walk, my disorientation intensified. I was at a point beyond fatigue and beyond sanity, and I saw distrust and threat in all things. The inanimate architecture of the city—the trees, the buildings, the gates, and the harmless little animals—stood before me as a mere façade, concealing deeper, more wicked truths. All of this acted in a conspiracy against me, looming towards me, ready to condemn and attack. My balance went off, and I felt my equilibrium veering toward my side. It was a struggle to maintain any sort of a center, physically, mentally, or otherwise. My consciousness became more vicious and I could not evade the thought that the truth of the universe was that I existed only to feel and be degraded, and this communicated itself through the happenings of everything around me.

In a moment of pseudo-solitude, I looked at the light-polluted sky through the anemic December branches, and the clouds, which were thin as exhaust from traffic. The miasma comforted my paranoia, and I felt more at home. When I was growing up, I spent many nights looking out through my bedroom window at my parents' house in the northern suburbs. The sky above the city was colored in a broad, murky orange, and faded into black about thirty degrees above the horizon, like a vast panorama of a Rothko painting.

That night in the city, with the silhouettes of trees and their naked branches pinned against the gray of the winter, the sky was gloomy and sick, and I felt more poignantly in tune with the time and place in which I was living, more cognizant of what it meant to exist at the literal end of times.

The doorknob to the lobby of my apartment building almost broke in my hand as I pulled on it, extending from its hinges so as to fall out of place altogether. I had been meaning to tell the landlord but never quite got around to it. Instead, I jimmied it back into a normal position and left the maintenance call for another time, or another tenant. My mailbox was full, but I never opened or read my letters. The building was old, and the stairs had a must like old tavern walls that had inhaled years of smoke. The woman below me had been diagnosed with borderline personality disorder, and at times my noise at night would wake her from a sleep that she could not regain without a midnight display of rage. Once she had chastised me viciously in the early morning when I did not realize that my delicate shuffling above her had the power to trigger an episode that powerful. I'd thereafter been careful each time I passed her apartment. We had never resolved the confrontation, and our basic pleasantries as neighbors always made me cautious, like one of us might snap.

I opened my apartment and dropped my backpack on the floor. It thudded into an otherwise silent room. I had left the heating off earlier in the day, and there was a chill in the unity, which suited the general array of the place. Most of it looked fit for a widow or a shut-in: I had, for instance, piles of old mail on top of one of my grandmother's hand-me-down tables, the ones she had obtained in a French market, and which I had damaged while moving in. I had collected over 500 books, stacked by genre—mainly mental illness, disability theory, gender, race, Palestine, history, political science, and literary essays—in the corner of the room. Lastly, there were a few sparse pieces of furniture, and I flung my limber body like unfolded laundry onto the form of the couch while I resigned to my depression.

I plugged in an old set of Christmas lights that I had arranged across my ceiling. I considered reading a book, but lacked the endurance for any sort of labor, and laid with my right arm pressed against my forehead. At some point, pressing my hand into my forehead became my response to depression when it was too thick and too foggy for me to respond to the world as quickly as I would otherwise be able. I didn't imagine it accomplished anything but a placebo effect; but then we had long operated with a system of drugs that did the same. My father, who I found unexpectedly compassionate to my plight, never understood why I did this every time I got bad. "I don't know, Dad, it helps me get by," I'd tell him. Other nights, Dad would suggest a positive-thinking exercise, or to get back on drugs, as though the only thing between myself and sanity were self-help exercises and a pill. Once I had gotten a diagnosis, I had been subjected to volumes of unsolicited advice from the people in my life, very little of which was worthwhile.

With these lights, these books, this exposed brick wall that I gazed at, and this little space I kept to myself, I suppose that was the same rationale for how I lived. It helped me get by.

Near midnight I went to my room and flipped on night music before bed: *Rothko Chapel* by Morton Feldman, a composer and piece I had been listening to a lot. My sheets were crumpled and cool, and I sat with legs folded on my bed while I broke fifty milligrams of Seroquel in half and swallowed it. After thirty seconds, I took the second half, just to take the edge off. The pills were contained in small, orange pharmaceutical capsules on the dresser beside my bed, stacked alongside old papers, cards, and envelopes, like a skyline over snowy ground. One of the exposed papers had a dark pencil sketch of tattoos that my friend Sally designed for me: one, a fire flower, a desert plant that blooms after fires; the other, a willow tree, like the one in my parents' backyard, both sad and majestic. Next to the designs was a draft of a suicide note I'd once written on a torn half-sheet of journal paper during a 3:00 A.M. madness. It simply read, *Sing Tavener at my funeral. Love, Boo.*

I bundled into my sleeping pose, ensconced in several layers of sheets, with frozen glass at my window as the sole incubation between myself and the outdoors. Again I thought about suicide, but only passively, as the thought came and went amongst other brusque, disheveled ideations. I grabbed the edges of the sheets tighter and curled my knees into my chest, cringing occasionally as a point of shame or insufficiency from my life came to mind.

I did not sleep for some time, and as my waking hours prolonged, a mental nihilism dominated me. First, it was in the form of great despair and vexation; then it became physical, throbbing through my veins and urging me to throw myself into a violent fit. Eventually, the convulsion settled, and I slept, but only for a couple of hours. During this rest, I had brief, lucid dreams of demons and mythical creatures, and in the middle of one of these nightmares, I woke into sleep paralysis and was immobile with fear and hallucinations of the very dancing, writhing creatures that I had in my dreams moving before me in my room. My walls were pulsating in red and blue colors, and the paralysis kept me contained in my bed until the visions wore off. Liberated once more, I plugged in my Christmas lights and stayed awake into the early morning.

Between dawn and 8:00 A.M. I got light rest. In the morning, I felt frail in body and spirit, like the delirium of a sick child home from school. The days after a night of that kind of tumult always felt like a branding iron after it's cooled in water. There was a resting period needed to return to normalcy, and it could take a lot of time. My phone alarm rang, disturbing my anxious silence. I turned it off, remained in bed, and focused my breathing deep into my diaphragm, slow and solemn. The back of my throat was dry, and my nasals were congested with crusty winter illness.

On my windows, the morning light gleamed into the ice of the glass, and against my instinct, I got up for the day.

I went to a pile of clothes (on top of old computer cords and bits of trash) at the edge of my room, and chose an arbitrary sweater, *Pennsylvania State University* across the front, from a selection of fabrics donning various other colleges I did not attend; a sweater I acquired while meeting someone in a blackout, previously belonging to a chest I do not remember and think nothing of. In my hallway, I turned the heat up to seventy-five degrees. I had little appetite for breakfast and felt repulsed by the idea of eating. In bad states, my stomach greets food with a feeling like a finger shoved down the throat, ready to regurgitate the intake on contact. I opened my fridge and peeked into the manufactured light. On the bottom shelf, I had a glass pan of pre-made oatmeal with crinkled foil wrapped over it that sat alongside several other foiled-over plates of half-eaten meals. I prepared a bowl of the oatmeal and warmed it in the microwave. Over forty minutes, I ate a single serving, and then set the bowl into my sink in a bath of water. That was the most productive thing I did in a morning otherwise spent traipsing, muttering, and staring into my apartment.

In the afternoon, I withstood a temporary panic and remembered that I had not taken my morning Effexor. Either that, or I had taken my morning dose and conceded to taking another dose to forestall the onset of vertigo, nausea, anxiety, and suicidal ideation that comes when one attempts to wean off of this manipulative substance. I continued to take Effexor not because it was of any benefit to me, but because I was scared of its withdrawals. In essence, I was addicted to it. My psychiatrist didn't know that these withdrawals happened to people who missed even a single dose. He said he did not learn of these withdrawals from the research; he had to learn of them by giving me the drug. There were many days when I could not get a quick refill.

Withdrawal would set in as an insatiable craving that occupied my chest, and I felt as though I could sprint down the center of the street until the jolt wore off. Then, later on, I would hear voices, or images would appear before me that did not exist in reality. I cared little for how that craving scratched against my skull and my throat, how the mind drifted into a flat place, and a hollow, fatiguing coat of air weighed upon me.

That evening I undressed, threw my clothes onto a pile on a chair in my room, and showered in preparation for Mark's visit. He had been in graduate school in Washington for business, and I had not seen him since the day after Thanksgiving—a day I count as one of the best of my life. It was a simple day, but since I had never actually had a romantic relationship before, it meant a great deal to me. In the morning, I picked him up from his parents' home in East Wilmette, and we drove to a bookstore in Evanston to get coffee and gifts for family. His presence was soothing enough to act through the cynicism I'd otherwise experience in hangover. I splurged at the store and got a collection of photographs from Uptown in the 1970s for myself.

Afterward, we fucked in my apartment three, maybe four times, virtually the only time I'd done that for hours. Towards the end, he was more spontaneous, unlike how he'd been before: gratifying, but conventional and risk-less, with all of the stroking and petting and positions that every American knows as routinely as a television lineup after dinner. And with a kiss afterward. By the third hour that afternoon, I positioned myself on top of him as I'd been many times before, and he grabbed my hips and pulled me forward, licking me while I grabbed my bed frame, unsuspecting, and now opiated in the moment. Then he stood, and I kneeled and did the same to him, and we flipped over and finished the act in one continuous, vigorous dance outside of time and thought. The trope is to have cigarettes afterward, but being a daughter of interior design, I cared too much for the stain that cigarettes would leave in the room. Instead, we shared an IPA from my fridge and listened to *Blood on the Tracks* in its entirety, all while lying nonchalantly, as people do while looking into the clouds in a field.

The thought of more of that invigorated me, but only momentarily. I brought my iPod speakers into the bathroom, played choral music, and fidgeted with the loose handle of my showerhead until the water reached a temperature in between the extremes. In the past, I'd made a point of intermittently applying water according to a principle of conservation. December in Chicago, however, is frigid, and so was my apartment, and I kept the stream of warmth running on the back of my neck, just at the point where the top of my vertebrae exposes itself, for nearly fifteen minutes. My gaze faded off into a point on the curve of my tub where some ugly bathroom spots needed to be rubbed out, and I tucked my arms around my knees, close to my chest, thinking the worst of everything.

I dried myself in the residual steam of the bath, with the rawness of the air just beyond the shower curtain meeting my exposed skin, and bringing me back into a chill. The music played on, and I hurried into slim corduroy pants and a black sweater in my room and shook the towel through my hair. I sat on the edge of my bed and browsed my laptop. The sun was down and the apartment was dim. My mattress squawked as I moved my weight around it. On social media, I saw a post from two nights prior that I do not remember writing, and could not decide if I agreed with upon revision. It read:

> *The root of sanism comes from the idea that civilization requires the absence of mental disturbances. As "mental illness" is supposedly the embodiment of these disturbances, it has been amongst our most neglected, feared, and ostracized conditions. There should be no doubt that this is reflected in our present society. There*

*should be no doubt that appearances of insanity still invoke a
sense of great apprehension, and that pretenses of sanity hold
unmerited allure.*

I had been reading Manning Marable at the time, who posited
that the root of racism was in economic exploitation, and I felt
compelled to make a comparable, grand statement about sanism,
though without documentation. In lieu of any real Mad academic
movement, virtually every idea I've developed on the matter had
been borrowed from a parallel thought regarding American racism. Was this Facebook declaration true? Possibly. A bit histrionic
perhaps, depending on the reading, but the climate lent itself to
loose expressions of trans-historical outrage. It may well have
been a quick restatement of Foucault and nothing more, and
who knew if that man had the definitive take on madness and
civilization. But then, nobody knew exactly what sanism was, or
where it stemmed from. I could say with great certainty that the
world of psychiatric disability was constrained by second-class
standards. That not all of those standards may have appeared
as a clear, belligerent form of social oppression to a secondary
observer, they nonetheless interacted with the individual in
such a way as to induce and sustain a lifeless, desperate, and
marginalized role in this world. If this did not technically qualify
as a form of oppression, at the very least it felt like something
we would define as oppression, if not something much worse.

Like other matters in the US, suffering was a communal
phenomenon made private. It ought to have been aired out
and understood as something that existed amongst social relations— between parent and child, person amongst peers, women
amongst men, white amongst black, boss amongst worker—and
yet it was removed from of this context and rearticulated as a
personal burden of genetically disadvantaged people. For lack
of a better phrase, "just deal with it" was the governing mantra.

Some could *deal with it*—that is, repress it—and did not speak to it outside of the trust of a few intimate confidants. Others had a more precarious, more vulnerable disposition to insanity, and the individualization of suffering came at a tremendous personal cost.

We were only at the tip of the iceberg with these ideas about madness, discrimination, and society, and it was beyond my authority to speak much more. We only knew a fraction of the depth of what has been done to Mad people in this world; what lay in the mass beneath the surface would have had Oedipus stab his eyes out a second time over. I had faith there were millions of other people who felt that way, but barring mass acts of bravery to make this a real point of social ferment, they would remain reserved, obscure, retraumatized, and detached from their collective potential to rewrite the culture they lived in. I tried to build something against that, Lord knows that I tried, but I found myself returning to where I started: solitary, bitter, separatist, psychotically depressed, and ready to die out of personal asphyxiation. I had to accept that the spiritual revolution was neither for me nor for my time.

Downward on my online feed, I saw an article about prisons, jails, and mentally ill people in Illinois. The state had reached a consent decree with the department of corrections, and the headline declared Cook County Jail, "The New Asylum for the Mentally Ill." The article opened, "Lawyers representing 11,000 mentally ill inmates in Illinois prisons have reached a settlement with the state in a long-running class-action lawsuit that alleged inadequate treated amounted to "cruel and unusual punishment." It carried on with the details of solitary confinement, and further into the article, there was a video interview with a survivor of that treatment. He spoke in a hasty, eerily dispassionate rhythm:

Mental health therapy consisted of... (expletive), there was no therapy. They'd chain you to a cement stump in a small rectangular room, with your arms tied to your feet so you're stretched back like a bow and arrow. You'd be on one end, the psychiatrist would be on the other, and an officer would sit in between and stare at you the whole time, and then, later on, he'd call you a (expletive) and things like that. 25 years, half of my life. On release, I was given no medication, no medical card, no nothing. I had to go cold turkey on those years of meds they were giving me. But I did have to get a rehabilitative evaluation for my parole, which entailed the possibility of civil commitment if they deemed me too mentally unstable. They were going to commit me to an institution for what they did to me. The PTSD I have right now is so bad that the whole thing comes back to me as I talk about it. The taste of the cell rolls over my tongue. I have the same nightmare every night, of trying to break my neck while I was in that cell. It's always like this. I sit and pick at my fingers until they bleed. I can't be around other people. I don't belong out here. I don't understand it. Everybody keeps offering me medication out here, but I don't want to be on medication. I want to figure out who I am. I want to go back to that cell and scream at it.

As I was watching the video conclude, my apartment doorbell rang suddenly and cantankerously. I went dumbstruck and grasped to find my bearings, as one does after a fire alarm. I went to my door and buzzed Mark inside. The stairwell leading up to my unit was thin and narrow, like an enclosed watchtower. I stood at the top of it and heard his steps against the fabric of the stairs in a drawn-out silence. I saw him more clearly as he lugged up the last flight, dressed modestly but handsomely. He wore a black rain jacket over a few other layers of clothing and carried a big paper bag with seasonal shoelace handles. He didn't look at me until he reached the top of the flight, where he stood before me, slow to embrace, and looked at me quietly. He lifted his arms at his sides, like light, open wings. I looked up at him and pressed my hands against his cold cheeks, and kissed him. "Hello, dear," I said. We then stepped back into my unit. The row of lights hanging across the ceiling pointed indiscriminately across my wooden floor, leaving patches of shadows and dull shade in between the spotlight on the ground. On the couch against my exposed brick wall, I sat next to him. My legs twisted towards him, and he sat squarely and reclined.

We exchanged gifts with one another. I placed a brick of a wrapped gift onto his lap and *oophed*. He made no guesses about what it might be and tore it open to see the glass casserole dish and cookbook I prepared for him, with recipes that were mostly plagiarized from a family cookbook. He seemed nonplussed or underwhelmed. Or perhaps I was reading into it. My parents always told me not to take gift-giving seriously, though I still felt I had disappointed him. He then offered me a crinkly, soft bundle with an envelope. I opened the wrapping to get a green scarf and opened the envelope to get a thumb drive. "It's some of the music I've been talking about," he said as I pinched the object and looked at him. It came with three printed pages from Microsoft Word, containing a list of artists and album titles. "Haas, Holliger, Ives," I read, looking over the list. "And I'm the depressed one, Mr. Mitchell?"

"You're welcome too, Boo." Then I kissed him, though his lips were tucked into his mouth.

"How was Evanston last night?" he asked.

"Good."

"And Lammie?"

"She's excited for Denver."

After a few minutes, I felt fretful and suggested we leave my apartment for dinner, so we left and walked to the L. The weather was moist, autumnal, and many degrees warmer than the day before. Some of the trees had leaves on them still, and the streetlights illuminated a coat of fog running through the branches just above us. We walked at a formal, busy pace, and Mark asked if I was excited to see my family.

"Yes, it should be alright," I said. Then I let my resentment get the better of me, and added, "Though my brother has of course gotten more racist the longer he has stayed at Notre Dame."

"Ah yes, Tea Party Kevin," he laughed.

"Being around him really pains me. I just can't do it without rolling my eyes and fighting with him. I ought to be able to get over it, but I can't."

We crossed Broadway Avenue after an ambulance ran a red light before us. The train station was a block ahead. "He's become even more swaggering and reactionary," I added. We entered the station, paid the fee, and stood at the platform.

"Boo, your brother was always that way," he said.

"Not to this extent. About a year and a half ago he made this weird announcement at dinner that he was a libertarian, almost like he was coming out as one, and ever since he's been going out of his way to talk about government and markets. It's like he takes whatever my father says, internalizes it, and bumps his chest with it. And when I visited his house in South Bend, he and his friends kept going off with all of these n-word jokes. It was all they knew how to talk about. I don't know what it's all about."

"The racist jokes?"

"No, the whole schtick. That whole campus is stuck in 1952. South Bend, God, what a great choice I made not to attend. And the sad thing is that he and his friends will all do well for themselves and get 100k jobs right off the bat, do seventy hours per week as consultants, and wind up in cocaine parties in River North. It doesn't matter whether or not they're racist. They'll advance all of the same."

"Sounds like a fun life, I must say," he said.

"Except for the part where he'll use it as leverage to talk down to me all of the time, and where it destroys any faith left in God," I corrected him.

At Jackson, we got off the Red Line and sidestepped our way through the subway station. A young man played a sophomoric guitar for bus money in the tunnel. He sat on his shoddy amp and jammed to the pentatonic blues, bending the high note of each of his phrases and sighing on the way down. The electricity of the instrument curved through the air of the tunnel, and in it, I heard all of the amateur rock fantasies of my old friends from high school. It made me smile lightly.

Mark was a few steps ahead of me and nodded at me from the stairs of the underpass to the Blue Line. I skipped my gait up to his place, and we walked downstairs beside one another. I paid almost no attention to the people we passed. The tunnel to the next train was unkempt, with stained, scratched walls of graffiti and McDonald's paper advertisements. Weathered homeless men sat against the tiling beneath the ads. We did not wait long for the Blue Line to arrive and entered a nearly empty car going west. Inside, there was a man across the car from us with a thick red beard and a heavy jacket, and next to him a thinner man with a sixteen-ounce can of Half Acre beer. The juxtaposition of these strangers looked quintessentially Midwestern to me, and I felt that I could imagine exactly where they would be going, and what their personalities were like.

Mark and I had not said anything to one another in minutes, but I was not bothered by this. We arrived in Logan Square, a neighborhood I did not usually frequent. This was partly because I had no life when Mark was not in town, and partly because my madness had distanced me from the people I knew who lived there. Additionally, it felt like a desperate extension of college: gentrified, alcoholic, chain-smoking, and homogeneous in age and taste. I went insane in this setting before, and I did not expect a different outcome for myself if I tried it again.

The restaurant we walked to was close to the L station. It had a five-dollar pasta and beer special that Mark had taken me to once over the summer, and which we wanted to go to again, though we arrived to learn that it was closed. I raised my fist aimlessly to the air, and shouted, "Those bastards!" while Mark scratched his head sheepishly, embarrassed about taking me to a date that did not exist. Instead, we went to a nearby wine bar. It was a modish venue, or tried to be, as too much of that superficially edgy neighborhood did. The cheapest glass of wine on the menu was seven dollars, which we both ordered, and then we squandered another twenty dollars on chocolate dates and rigatoni.

We laughed over the pretentiousness of the restaurant, and about how we would never be convinced to eat there with better knowledge. Mark lost himself in thought as he chewed one of his dates, of which there were only a few, despite the price. His mental presence seemed to be drifting from our table, and then he shook himself. The walls were decorated with international photographs, and after some light discussion about them, Mark started going off about how he wanted to go "off-the-grid" and open a coffee shop in a different country. I entertained his fantasy with suggestions regarding cannabis and amateur poetry for his shop. "Oh, but I wouldn't want it any other way," he said with a grin, bent with his elbow over his knee so I could catch a smell of his cologne, and feel, without actually touching him, the warmth of his chest.

We finished our wine out of monumental yet fragile glasses and took the train toward Daley Plaza. Each year, German merchants set up shop there and sold wooden carvings and knit sweaters at Christmastime. Mom brought me, Kevin, and our cousins there every December as a tradition. She'd grouse and talk to herself on the drive while she struggled for parking, and we all shouted childish things at her from the back seat. In the windows of Marshall Fields were displays of literary Christmas scenes. *A Christmas Carol* in one, *The Nutcracker* in another, and both had puppets moving within them like the Disneyland boat rides. I think Mom liked the idea of taking us to see the windows more than we enjoyed it ourselves.

That night with Mark, much of that innocence was absent. Picasso's iron sculpture stood forebodingly over this miniature town of convivial food and merchants, brooding like the heartless Chicago machine it symbolized.

There was a tent with steam coming out of the top where people went to be warm, and families huddling for pictures just outside of it with drinks and sausage in their hands. We went inside and bought spiced wine served in a small glass boot. After kicking the toes together, we drank. The tables were made of massive barrels with countertops, and I put my elbow on them for support while we sipped wine and talked. We soon got restless staying still, and perused the market. I bought a stein for Kevin, an effortless gift, and we meandered through the plaza a bit longer. There were sparse flurries of snow, and the warmth of the spiced wine and the homeliness of the food aroma put me into a mawkish place of mind, along with the Salvation Army bells and the saxophone jingles coming from the street corner.

We left and passed a woman in a wheelchair panhandling with a Styrofoam cup. The organization I was working with at the time technically worked on the homelessness system, but I knew nothing about it and had only recently made a point of stopping to talk to homeless people like I would anyone else. Generally, I made quick discussion, and gave the person a few dollars, sometimes a five or a ten, and then went on my way. The privileged were always a bit contrived when they first made a principle out of treating others as equals. The woman asked us for money and Mark said, "No," and walked ahead. My inertia followed him, but the gravity of my conscience pulled me to the woman, and I almost tripped as I awkwardly pivoted and turned my body toward her. I decided to give her charity and removed a wad of bills from my pocket that I had earned from my restaurant job. I seldom carried this much money on me, and I realized instantly that I only had tens and twenties—too much to give to someone on the street. Pocketing the wad, I returned to Mark and ignored the woman. Behind me, I heard her outraged voice, "Oh, look at all those tens and twenties, you shallow bitch." Her voice faded, and I forgot about her half a block later.

It was a bit after ten when we arrived back in Andersonville, an old person's night out. The weather was vaguely warm, and dirt was piled into the cracks of the sidewalk where snow and ice would usually be at that time of the year. Mark bent his arm and I put mine through it. My arm pressed into his ribcage, and I could sketch an outline of his bones through his fleece jacket. We went to a Belgian craft beer bar on Clark Street, that beautiful strip of life, and settled at two open seats at the counter. It was a bar I went to often, a thoughtful abode, unlike the obstreperous sports bars and clubs that the few friends I still saw spent their time in.

We ordered seasonal beers and joked about what it would be like to work there, and about the supposed beer acumen and pallets required to do so. Mark seemed more relaxed and gregarious, as if he was five drinks deep and joking with old friends at a bar. It consoled me, and I disclosed that I suspected that my seriousness as an individual discouraged him from behaving naturally, and was doing its part to drive him away. "No, your intensity is a good quality," he assured me, and for a moment my doubts were relieved.

After one drink, we walked the few blocks back to my apartment. We shuffled in front of one another while making trite conversation. The light above the door was on, the rest of the apartment was dark, and Mark put on string music from his library—loud, terse, profound music. It was a notch too loud, and I asked him to lower the volume, and we embraced one another again, then slept together in my bedroom. In our climactic motions, he pressed on top of me and tucked his face into the crevice of my neck and shoulder, and reached his arm through my hair to buffer my head as it bumped into the bed frame. Afterward, we reclined with my bedsheets spread clumsily across us. I looked outside the window at the shades of the trees against the sky over the neighboring rooftops. There was a sole candle lit on my dresser amidst all the mess I keep on top of it, and we made shadow animals in the glow of the wall next to us while we fell asleep, my two-fingered rabbit devoured by his five-fingered monster. Then I blew out the flame and fell asleep.

I spent Christmas day in post-alcoholic, decaffeinated ennui; the hangover of college, with my muscles wrapped into one another, my throat dry, my piss yellow, and my mind clamped into a tight and whiny place. The night before we hosted my father's side of the family, all fifty of them. On Christmas, we hosted my mother's side of the family, all fifty of them. I referred to the Harveys and the Vandenheuvels as Stoics and Epicureans, respectively. The Harveys were a family of Midwestern businessmen who saw work as life's foremost necessity, and who were prepared to emotionally counter any possible tragedy and then show no feeling when it occurred. Their sense of humor was oriented toward cynicism, brevity, and acerbic putdown; my father excelled in this craft. The Vandenheuvels were the Epicureans, known for the extra glass of wine and for leisurely if not longwinded talks that went nowhere. Both were heavy drinkers, and on Christmas Eve, as with every holiday, we got drunk.

I went for a jog after we opened gifts and had Christmas breakfast, and I wore only a light sweater and running shorts.

Nobody else was outside, and the atmosphere was still, open, and unimposing. There were long, green lawns in front of the homes, without even a patch of snow, and the golf course behind my parents' house appeared to be in spring condition. In a generation's time, December will be the cruelest month, breeding lilacs out of the dead land, mixing memory and desire of Christmases past. I indulged in some of that longing as I ran, nostalgic and remorseful for a less corrupted and infinitely more naïve place and time, with a sparkle in my eye for Northwestern, Georgetown, and, when really delusional, Princeton. I was younger then. To be forgiving, I understood how the allure of a neighborhood like this could encourage one's view towards grandeur. These homes had a halo effect that could last for generations. Children who had done close to nothing for themselves would be hanging around the country clubs they were brought up in, and their children would have access to them, too.

But I got older, far too old. I didn't see the shine like I once did. I saw the world of Gatsby, inhabited by people who were so deeply a part of the problem that they did not even know a problem existed, like Midwestern Louis XIV's and Marie Antoinette's singing modern variations on the theme of "Let them eat cake." The oligarchical comparison was no joke, either. Throughout my youth, my family got Christmas cards from the Bush family and the Romneys, which was nice. Art Laffer mentored my father in his formative years, and my father stood by his political influence for the entirety of his life, even as much of the world's future has been compromised as a direct result of it. To this, my father said nothing, because he denied its reality. I grew up going to parties with the man who obtained the Lewinsky dress onto which Bill Clinton ejaculated. He boasted about it at my parents' cocktail party before the story ever went national, when I was only six years old. My family went to dinners with the lawyer who represented George W. Bush in the Supreme Court case of the first stolen election of the new century. Being a lawyer, he insisted that everything about the election was clean. Being a Republican, my father believed him.

When I played girls' soccer, Bobby Kennedy's son coached my team, dressed in his Nantucket chic, with his rolled-up sleeves and his flowing hair. Although many people in the North Shore spoke with complete acrimony about the Clintons and the Obamas, the truth was that the same men who sat at the board during the British Petroleum spill, who surveyed its consequences and said, "So what?" were private equity and country club partners with the very couples and bankers who sponsored the rise of Barrack Obama at every moment of his career in Illinois. That was American capitalism: the subsumption of all things political to an exponentially opulent financial sector, defined simultaneously by a high capacity for cataclysm and an equally extreme lack of conscience or sense of personal accountability in disaster. As I grew, I had to let go of the belief that these putative progressives of the Democratic Party represented a real challenge to the slow death of the world, for these *elites for the people* were a mere extension of timeless class circles and were always susceptible to being a launching pad for the agenda of the Right. Comparatively, disdain for Democrats amongst conservative elites was little more than a petulant, partisan, and hypocritical matter of the culture wars, as the Obamas and the Clintons were more on their side than anyone else's. None of these figureheads opposed their foremost goal: the accumulation of private wealth and influence. They only offered a flavor of that goal which conservative elites found distasteful, as it did not center them in the fable of American exceptionalism.

And yet, eccentricities of the wealthy aside, none of these people were *bad people*. You would not think so if you stepped into their home, where you were welcomed, fed, served, and treated with careful manners. They were ordinary people, only with more breathing room to mistake untruth for truth and be rewarded for it. How, one might ask, could my father be both a decent man and one who sat at our kitchen table, mocked environmental science, and conflated activists with terrorists? The simplest and correct answer was because of money, the virus propelling this whole ordeal. Having realized all of that, I grew out of the values of my home and learned to see the world of Zelda Fitzgerald, lost within the cloud of wealth, whose words were taken by her husband and accredited to him, and who was later institutionalized and died in a fire. The foremost distinction between her time and posterity was that we stopped keeping our psychiatric institutions out in the open anymore. The asylums of our times were more diffuse and much harder to identify. People died due to similar states of madness, but in softer ways.

Through it all, I questioned, like a cursed daughter of the Old South, the depth and profundity of the contamination, whether or not I ever stood a chance to live without the ghosts, and whether or not a true reparation of the spirit, of mine or anyone else's, was even possible.

I jogged for about three-quarters of a mile and then walked with my hands hanging over my head and my legs chilled by the air. My balance fell off, and I dropped toward the side. Here and there a leaf scattered, then left in silence. I could hear dogs fighting in the distance. My mind was otherwise still, without a single thought to disrupt the walk on Christmas afternoon.

On a sudden turn, however, I became self-aware that I was at ease, and neurosis took hold. I became consumed within myself, over matters and irrationalities that had nothing to do with the run. I twitched my shoulders and ticked my head; I grimaced at the side of my face until it strained. I pinched my fingers together and gestured my forearms back and forth, talking to myself. To get out of this I sprinted, as though desperately running away from something, and then stopped because I looked like a fool.

I did this every few minutes in spurts that lasted for a block, and finished each blast with my hands in my face, breathing cautiously through the navel, hoping to reestablish composure.

The remainder of the walk home felt defeated. I strolled the rest of the way back, entered my parents' home through the back way, from the far side of their yard. The sky remained overcast and windless. There were pellets of deer droppings along the pavement, and the dog was exploring the other corner of the property. The soles of my feet, feeble after the running, rolled against the sodden dirt under the sparse autumn grass in the yard.

Inside, Mom was at the kitchen sink in her morning robe, her hair parted like she had not slept and her facial expression as plain as any other day, cleaning the wine glasses and dessert plates that the party the night before had used after the dishwashers were sent home. Her eyes were fixed on scrubbing the dishes, and while working, she said, "Oh, Boo, Aunt Mary wants to take you aside and talk to you tonight."

"About what?"

"She emailed this week about Claire. Apparently, she isn't doing so well in New York, and when Mary pressed the issue, Claire pushed back and got nasty. She brought Joan to talk to her once when things had gotten bad in college, but she thinks it might be better if you got involved."

"Well, I don't know anything about that, but I'm willing to talk."

I pulled a pint glass from the cupboard for water. As I cupped it in my palm, I reflexively thought about breaking it in my grasp and envisioned my blood flowing out of me. A moment later I was filling that same glass with water at the faucet.

In the family room, Dad and Kevin were watching *Christmas Vacation*. I fell gracelessly into the couch just in time to watch Randy Quaid and his timeless holiday pronouncement, "Shitter was full." A crass pleasure, but an important pleasure nonetheless.

On the commercial break, my father and brother flipped between sports documentaries and professional basketball so I took my glass and left. While I did so, Kevin made a snide and useless comment about being "above" the pleasures of television with the family. I almost turned to berate him for it, but Dad interrupted, and said, "Guys, please. It's Christmas." I could not blame him, either, given last year's Christmas fight about the non-indictment of Darren Wilson, which made Kevin feel as proud and vindicated as I'd ever seen him, and the previous year's blow-up about the Notre Dame girl who had killed herself after football players assaulted her. *She was bipolar, you can't say definitively say it was the rape that made her do it.* My brother was as free to entertain his delusions as I was.

I walked upstairs to my childhood bedroom. The stairs squeezed as I climbed them, and the dog scurried upstairs beside me and darted toward my room. The floor of my bedroom was disorganized with clothes, gifts, and wrapping materials, though on the whole things were far cleaner than in my apartment in the city. I still had to prepare gifts for the evening, yet I had used all of the masking tape the day before. I looked for a second roll in the drawer of my bed stand. It was full of old ticket stubs from high school and, underneath those, old psychiatric prescriptions, along with an empty bottle of Heineken.

My head started to ache and I lied down, covering myself in my old sheets. I put early sacred music on and fell into a half-sleep. An hour, perhaps ninety minutes later, I woke. It was hard to tell through the grogginess. I showered and dressed, and it was evening by the time I was ready. Downstairs, the lights were on during an hour of dwindling winter darkness. The marble shined in the kitchen, revivifying the Francophile décor in the room. My parents' home had high Victorian ceilings, broad rooms, more televisions than people, tightly ordered spaces that I was anxious to disturb, trinkets and miniatures from street markets across the earth, unopened wine from private investment parties, and a stately, removed ambiance that I coped with mainly through media entertainment and alcohol. It could host an art exhibit or a political fundraiser, given the proper arrangements, and it would feel completely appropriate.

The evening outside became black, and my mother's family began to arrive in small crowds. Dad greeted them and offered drinks, and they mingled through the first floor of the house. I had half of a Manhattan and talked with my relatives in a huddle beside the isle in the kitchen. My feet were warm on the marble tiling; my parents had a heating system installed so the floor would be warmed in the wintertime. When I finished the Manhattan, I poured a chardonnay and walked to the living room, where a fire burned at the end of the room and a polished grand piano stood. My cousins' toddlers were palming their hands on the keys, with spritely, three-to-four note clusters thudding and clanking from the piano.

Many of my other cousins were sitting around a table by the bay window overlooking the yard, which my mother had adorned with candles and plates that we only used for holidays. The temperature outdoors dropped, and you could feel the chill seeping into the room from the side of cracks in the window. I went and stood with my cousins; my wine glass four-fifths full. My cousin Marty approached with his hands in his pockets. "Drinking tonight?" I asked.

"I don't need alcohol to have fun, Boo."

"So that's a 'yes.'"

"Yes, eventually."

My older cousin Tina followed behind us. I hadn't seen her in years. She'd missed previous holidays while doing dissertation research in Western Africa, or the South of France, or somewhere. I was honestly not sure exactly what it was she did. She greeted me, and said, "Boo, my dear. How is life?"

I wanted to say, "Life sucks," but instead I said, "Life is good," reiterating one of those little white lies I go along with to prove my sanity to others. Tina then asked, "What are you doing with everything?"

I discussed tidbits of mental health policy with her, unable to wrap all the conceptualization on the issue that I had been developing into a straightforward pitch. Tina nodded while I talked. As I blathered, I forgot that I was even talking. My contemplation extended across the faces in the room, the cacophony of the chatter, the children giggling, and Count Basie's string orchestra playing Christmas carols from the speakers in the kitchen.

Then I found myself rambling on to Tina about what exactly it was I wanted, partly out of intimidation. Tina had spoken in conferences at some of the country's most renowned schools and was more poised than the rest of us. She crossed her arm at her torso, rested her other elbow on top of it, and held her glass of wine just under her chin while looking into me in a penetrating, intellectual way. I dipped my head and said, softly, "Well, what I want is very grand. I want the kind of networks for resistance and organizing for people diagnosed in psychiatry as we have for, say, young women, queer people, or people of color, if that makes sense. A new institution to catch people before they fall off, or feel that they must be silent and passive. A political platform and consciousness to join."

"Ok," Tina nodded. I felt she was analyzing me. "So, what do you have to do to get into that?"

"I don't know. I really don't know," I said. "I could be an organizer. I want to see people in the streets. I want to see people with psychiatric disabilities thinking and acting as a class. I want to see a whole library of knowledge created and made accessible to the average person. I want every type of scholar, artist, civic engager, and person to be asking about it. Historians, political scientists, sociologists, anthropologists, writers, just with an emphasis on the mind. I need people to understand it outside of the context of, say, psychiatry and psychology, not that those things are totally, um, totally unimportant, but I want to see recognition of the fact that the human mind is a machine of amazing experiences, even deeply oppressive experiences, and that we have to ask the questions about how the world has formed around this diversity of the mind, and what it has done and continues to do to those who aren't, how shall I say this, *mentally acceptable.*"

Tina nodded again, ambivalently. I could not tell whether her look was confused or if she was gradually understanding me.

"And why not psychology?" Tina asked.

I was drunk already. "From my experience, psychology programs are a modern-day M-R-S. Degree. Too many bougie girls who don't really care about crazy people. Besides, they aren't asking the same questions I am."

"Come on now, I think your experience is a little jaded," she said.

"It certainly is," I said, taking another sip. "Yes, you are correct. I've just been disappointed by too many people who clearly don't care two shits about the people they'll be studying or treating. The field has earned my distrust."

At that point, I retreated from my austerity to speak to a related point. "Anyways, as I was saying, what I really want is something very grandiose, like a major social movement. It's just, catalyzing that, even articulating the need for it, is a very difficult thing. I don't think the right questions have been asked, I don't think the right organizations have formed, and I don't think that the lefties who typically ask these sorts of questions have crossed that boundary yet. In fact, they're often disdainful of it. I've gotten used to saying, 'The same people who would geld a man for a racist transgression would say that he is mentally ill for being a racist.' And they say this and they have no concept of the contradiction at play. They don't really give a damn about the crazies, those hypocrites. Disability, especially psychiatric disability, is a dirty area to a lot of people, an unknown point. I haven't yet figured out what to do about it, and of course, I'm just one person who has no audience and no formal position, and who knows nobody who even talks about it. But I'd like to see something large, something that confronts our system of values as well as our social order and our politics. I just don't think the networks for doing that are there quite yet. Nor the consciousness, for that matter. There's potential, there's enormous potential, but galvanizing it is a very tricky thing. I think the best route for me at the moment is to continue to study and get out there in whatever way I can."

My brother approached the table. He too appeared several drinks deep. "What's up, family?" he announced in his young, commanding voice.

"Not much," Tina said, and then looked at me. "She was just telling us all about these brilliant ideas about mental health and society."

"Ah, yes," Kevin smirked. "How is your revolution coming, Boo?"

My brother, the great denier, the great agitator. The man who would readily write off the words, *Give me your poor, your hungry, your huddled masses*, and slap a massive bumper sticker over it: *America: Love it or Leave it.*

"Not now, child," I told him.

"Oh, please, tell us all about it again," he said.

"I've tried explaining things to you and you willfully brush it away each time. Piss off and go back to Notre Dame if you don't want to do anything but make people feel wrong, even when you're obviously the one in the wrong."

"What, shouldn't I think it's peculiar that you insist on these theories that you have no evidence for? Please, tell me how you're being held back, here in Winnetka, because people hate the mentally ill?" I looked at him with a restrained face. He continued in a mocking tone, "Psychos of the world unite!"

I took the bait, for I truly could not help myself. "Oh, why do you keep up this obstructionist shit on Christmas, of all days? Firstly, what theories? Secondly, the only reason you see no evidence to it is because every time I defend myself, you shift to a different subject entirely, or laugh and pretend it doesn't matter."

"Well, you make these comparisons to civil rights, when in fact there's no equivalence between any of that."

"I'm sorry, since when did you give a damn about civil rights?"

"There's nothing about having a mental illness that was anywhere near as bad as black people had it during the Civil Rights Movement. It's a preposterous claim."

"What claim? What are you going for here? I've never said that they were the same. I look up to past movements as a model. They're all I've got."

"That's not true, you say you want a civil rights movement for mental illness, but it's not the same thing at all. The two lots are apples and oranges. You're making the comparison to amplify your cause."

"Kevin, we are talking about people with *rotten apples* and *rotten oranges*. Whichever you'd get, you'd want to throw away. Exact parallels do not negate the point, especially not when coming from a private racist such as yourself."

There was a moment of conclusion. I was distressed, and part of the party around us had grown quiet, tentative, or agitated. I sat upright, breathed into my stomach, and tried to forget about it. Bing Crosby was singing *O, Holy Night* somewhere in the background.

"I just don't understand why you are so resistant to things you have such little exposure to," I said to him, with better holiday manners this time, but my brother had already moved on to a different subject with my cousins. He stepped aside to a circle of my male cousins, his chest open, to tell them his college stories. My cousins were thinner than Kevin, dressed in tweedy vests that my aunts had selected for them, and all held green beer bottles of St. Pauli Girl, Heineken, Stella Artois, and Rolling Rock. They laughed with their heads back at his impressions of the drunk guys that he was mimicking.

My mother announced dinner, and the family gathered its meals in a buffet around the kitchen island counter. My aunts had elaborate necklaces and velvet fabric dresses and my uncles had guts, fifty years in development, protruding at the bottom of their buttoned shirts. Each held my mother's china plates in front of them in preparation for serving. On the island, there were mashed potatoes, asparagus, glowing rolls of bread, and beef tenderloin. I forked a couple of pieces of red beef and ornamented the plate with small portions of the rest. There were six tables set up throughout the house, with bottles of red and white patterned over green tablecloths. Seating was chosen mostly along generational lines. My sole remaining grandparent, my mother's mother, sat in a wheelchair at the head of her table, where her grandchildren served her. She was plump in her age, with a soft white bob cut and a fur jacket. The foundation of her makeup seemed applied as thickly as crayons and her hands were bent at the knuckles with severe arthritis. When the Doc was alive, he would sit at the other head of the table, wearing a velvet jacket and an ascot and his big psychiatrist's glasses. We'd invite priests from Saint Francis Xavier parish to eat with us, and in his last years, Doc would forgo prayers before the meal, and slap people on the back of the head while their hands were folded. Father Sheridan asked him one year, "Jim, is nothing sacred to you?"

"No, Father," the Doc said. "Nothing at all."

I chose a seat at a table next to my grandmother's table,

alongside a couple of my cousins and all of the toddlers and children in the family. We spent the meal asking the children questions about their lives, focusing all of the attention on them, and trying to make games out of their brutally honest and ridiculous answers. The Doc had once said about having children at the table, "We don't know how to talk to ourselves, so we let the four-year-olds do the talking for us."

Kevin and my uncles were at the next table over. They were talking about Notre Dame football and their bowl game results, as though the subject merited careful analysis. Damned, damned Notre Dame. It was the Midwestern Vatican, in the worst sense of both terms. When they were done talking about football, they talked about Kevin's love life. "So, Kevin, why did you leave this girl Lindsey?" my uncle asked.

"The drugs made her less decent," Kevin said with food in his mouth, "which I must confess was part of the appeal in the first place." They laughed uproariously and high-fived him. It reminded me of the time when my cousins made the same response when they learned that not just one but two of my cousins dated the girl who got kicked out of my Catholic high school for getting an abortion.

I had a hilarious, albeit morbid, distraction a moment later when my cousin Charlie brought the Doc's ashes around the table, provoking people to "pull my ashes." The Doc loved that juvenile joke, where he'd offer you his finger, you'd pull it, and then he'd fart. And as for his ashes, the plan was to cremate my grandmother whenever she passed and then bury the two of them together someplace by Lake Michigan. Until then, the Doc's ashes were kept with my parents, in a plastic bag in a white box that used to hold frozen sausages and just happened to be the right size for my grandfather's cremated remains. Charlie's mom Vicky scolded him for this joke. "Charlie! Show some respect for the Doc!"

"Please, mom," he said. "He'd want it this way."

My aunt Joan walked around the table pouring more wine. She poured Sauvignon Blanc into my glass. "No, I'm alright," I said as she did so.

"No, you're not," she said and poured it to the top. That was also a joke we picked up from my dead grandfather.

We finished our dinners and sat around the tables, candles lit and bodies warm with food and booze. I overheard my mom talking about an alderman from the Back of the Yards ward who had recently condemned gang violence in his neighborhood. "How brave is he?" she said. "Props to him for standing up to those gangbangers and saying, 'Stop terrorizing our neighborhoods!'"

"Oh, the crime in the city," my Aunt Mary added. "That's why we should stay on the North Shore."

My father and my aunt Joan had also devolved into a political discussion, on the shooting of LaQuan MacDonald. A month prior, the city had released a videotape of the shooting, bowing to public pressure to do so. It was a fuzzy dashboard recording that showed a hyperactive police officer shooting sixteen bullets into a shaking young man with a knife, who had been contained and was standing away from eight other officers who had arrived on the scene before him. Nobody had been talking about anything else for a month. "What we need to know is what the mayor knew and when he knew it," my father said to Joan while I eavesdropped from the other table.

My unmarried uncle from Minnesota brought a date to dinner, and this was the first time she had met the family. Eager to hear more about the political situation, she cautiously asked, "So, what exactly is the problem on the South Side?"

My father responded, "It's cultural. The problems are predominantly Black-on-Black, Hispanic-on-Hispanic crime. Nobody cooperates with the police, and it's very difficult to make things better."

I left the room and played with my cousin's children, who were prancing around the house with the toys they had opened before the rest of the party.

Thirty minutes later, the family returned to the living room and the pile of gifts assembled under the pine tree. A massive grab-bag game was at play. Each family member drew numbers for the order of picking gifts. Mine was last. Almost every third gift was a bottle of wine, and the rest consisted of cultural gifts and gag presents. When my turn came, each member of the family had gone two drinks deeper and the party was much louder. The only gift left was a single sleeve wrapped in holiday paper, no thicker than a sheet of paper. I opened it delicately. It was a signed photograph of Brian Scalabrine, an obscure basketball player who once played for the Chicago Bulls, and who for some reason my male cousins were always talking about reverently. My cousin Jimmy, standing six foot three and large enough for me to feel his body a step behind me, laughed and apologized from behind me. "Yeah, it was about three bucks on eBay. I'll get you something nicer later on."

My cousin Robbie, with a thick build and a patchy beard, joked from behind him, "It'll give you something to look at while you write Facebook rants."

The party had entered its late stage, and everyone was drunk. A couple of my father's siblings came over for drinks, the fire was still on, and my younger cousins went to the back garage to smoke weed and play drinking games. Some of my other cousins went to a town bar, Potato Creek Johnnies, an establishment I associated with needy divorcees, dad bands, and old faces from the high school football team. I did not want to be in such a place on Christmas, so I stayed and talked with my aunt Vicky, who only became more confident as parties proceeded, and who waved her arms in conversation to own other people's attention. She was telling me about her life and her children and her children's depression. "You know, I call him Eeyore, my son," Vicky said. "He's always moping around, seeing everything as glass-half-empty. Me, I don't exactly look at things the same way. I often think my life is shit. And it is. My life sucks. My kids are a pain in the ass. My husband is a pain in the ass. I've got a million things to do between when I wake up and when I go to bed. But really, I've got a nice home in a nice neighborhood, and my life isn't that bad. That's something to be glad about."

Afterward, I sat by the fire with my mom, who had tipsy eyes and was looking at me adoringly. My Uncle Harry, a short man with long, thinning hair, sat at the piano and played Elton John songs in arpeggios. He sang, too, in a pedestrian tone, "*It's a little bit funny, this feeling inside.*" Miraculously, my cousin's children were still awake and were tapping at the keys beside him. When the child interrupted the song too much, Harry stopped playing, and turned to the child and said, "Hey, do you want to see me play with my butt?" He turned around and sat up and down on the keyboard, clashing it with his ass. The child thought it was hilarious.

For better or worse, I felt at home.

CHAPTER 2

2009

Northern California is not as luxurious as I thought it would be in January. I don't know what I should have expected. I guess when I left the Midwest I thought I'd be in for a climate of relaxation, not weeks of wind and rain. I should blame television for all of those fantasy surfing and beach depictions of California. This weather is nothing like that. It is drab. I feel drab, like a character trapped in an English novel subsisting on posh pleasantries and fake decorum.

I'm still very unsure about my decision to move West, even a year after I committed to attending this university. Dad wanted very badly for me to go to Notre Dame. He talks about Notre Dame so much that sometimes I wonder if he can talk about anything else. All my life I was told that I'd be going to Notre Dame, even though I had never expressed interest in it myself. It always came from him—at the dinner table, at the country club, while being introduced to another couple at a North Shore restaurant. I never spoke up about it. Maybe I tried once or twice, but I was always dismissed as immature. "Of course, she's going to Notre Dame." He did the talking and was so convinced of what my future would be. I gave up eventually and just let it happen.

Sometimes wonder what things would be like today if I had gone. I was admitted, but guilt was the main reason I didn't attend. My grades and test scores were good, but not *Notre Dame good*. I scored a 29 on the ACT, had a B+/A- average with a blend of AP, honors, and average tracked courses on my transcript. Some kids get into Notre Dame with this kind of resume, but they have something else exceptional going on. What made me exceptional was being Tom Harvey's daughter. I'm convinced that his clout was the extra push that got me in. That and the fact that my application wasn't totally my own work.

On a Saturday in the autumn of my senior year, when I was writing college admissions, Dad called me into his office and gave me a handwritten letter. "I know you're writing your essays, and you can write about whatever you want," he said. "But I know the admissions people at the Notre Dame business school very well, and I know what kind of qualities they are looking for in an application." I looked at the letter. He had written the whole essay for me. "You can take this and use some of it, but don't tell your mother I did this." I used it in my application and never told Mom. A couple of months later, he was waiting in the kitchen to shake my hand when I got home from school to let me know that I got in. It didn't feel like shaking my father's hand; it felt like what I imagine shaking a business colleague's hand after making a private equity deal feels like.

I knew there was nothing to distinguish me from the thousands of other kids exactly like me other than my last name, so I never saw it as a clean admission. There's a world of kids who had to struggle to get into college, and here I was waltzing into a program that would pay me $250,000 the moment I graduated from it. I was tempted to go, but I knew it was wrong. Catholic guilt draws me away from it and toward some idea of a "pure" life, one that isn't all about money.

In high school I was a slacker. People called me smart, and still do, but I don't feel it. I did the bare minimum most of the time, and that was good enough. If you grew up where I did, you could do nothing and still get into a good state school like the University of Illinois. And it's true. I got into the University of Illinois, too. Every time I got overstressed in high school, I fell back on that. I never pushed myself too hard and laughed at the students who did. Why on earth would anyone lose their minds to fight between Boston College, Georgetown, Middlebury, or

Dartmouth? They're all the same, anyway. And the sun is shining today, you know?

It made no sense to me. Culture peppers kids like me with so much talk about doing great and being great when it's obvious to anyone that they will turn out alright simply by being born where they were. The same rules don't apply to them. My father and his friends all pride themselves on being self-made men, whatever that is. "We worked this job and that job, didn't have what you have, and then we got rich." They made their own money. The whole notion of success in their world required you to have had nothing at the beginning and everything at the end. Well, what's the point if you start with everything? Do you have to go back to nothing to earn respect?

I never thought about the future in high school, and then the future came. Everyone else who I looked down on for being too serious about college left high school confident and proud, and ready to take on the world. I am jealous of them now. I felt stupid, like I had not given enough thought to questions that would help me mature to an appropriate age. What do I want in friendships? In relationships? For a career? I felt like an underachiever, remorseful over having failed to put my mind to use and for letting kids who I felt were dumber than me do better than me. I was totally unsure about what I was going to school for. Privately, I've always thought I could be an artist of some type, and I think the California world will help turn me into that. A musician, a songstress. A Dylanette. Or a storyteller of some sort. As for the academics or the prestige, I really don't give them much importance. The Doc said the books are the same everywhere, so the student will have to make it their work to make use of them more than the school. He told me to go to college wherever I'd like to live for four years, so I did. I chose California.

I actually did well in my first quarter. I got a 4.0. Mom and Dad were surprised and very impressed. And very pleased. They brought up the possibility of transferring to a more competitive school because I never did that well in high school. I took five classes for the fall quarter: chemistry, calculus, writing and rhetoric, a half-credit introductory course for the engineering program, and a religious course for a university requirement that talked about this mystic named Julian of Norwich. This quarter I'm taking more chemistry, physics, more calculus, and an ancient history course. It's been great.

My roommate and I get along. Her name is Sara. She comes from New York. She has been rushing in a sorority, and spends a lot of her time with the girls she met there. So far, she's more sociable than me, always comes home later, and is gone most of the day. It allows me time to nap when I need to or to do other things I'd only do when people are out. I spend a lot of hours hungry and distracted.

Sara's been seeing the same guy, a lacrosse player, and I told her that I don't mind leaving the room to them. It seems rude to deny them that, even if I haven't received the same favor in return. Truth is, I haven't done anything with anyone. It seemed that in the fall quarter, kids would get so wasted that they'd literally stumble into a hookup with the person next to them. I could get as drunk as them, but I couldn't get as stupid. I'd always end up coy, reserved, untouched. The nerd girl for the nerd guys, which is how I spent most of my social life. When Sarah was hooking up, I'd often be with some of the guys upstairs—BJ, Brendan, Jeremy—while they played Nintendo 64.

Or we have study nights in the dormitory commons on the upper floor, where all of the students taking first-year chemistry can help one another with their problems. Ultimately it devolves into gossip and shit-talk. There's a sweet Southern Californian, Luca—this easygoing boy who lives down the hall—with a gangly but fit build, short, curly black hair and wide, wizened eyes, who can get into a bit of a nasty side. He makes mean-spirited jokes about everyone. And technically he is a cynical loser, but every now and then I see a gentle side to him, and a very spiritual, intelligent side, and I think about him more than I admit to most people and find myself wondering if he should be my first. But he's not the type of person I imagined I'd be with—I've only known preppy, business school types. And though I thought about myself with him, I also wondered if he was "good enough," like I should only be with someone much hotter or of higher status than the rest of them.

I first met Luca on move-in weekend. His dorm is about five rooms down the hall from mine, and I needed a screwdriver to assemble some of my things. I was shy about who to talk to and heard Let Down, the sixth track off *OK Computer*, playing from his room. So, I went to his room and asked him for help. He stood up, about 5 feet 11 inches tall, seeming cool and nonchalant about my request, and had a laidback body language, like he should be holding a skateboard or a guitar. He asked if I liked Radiohead too, and geekily, hunching my neck an inch shorter, I said that I loved Radiohead. Then his mother called for him and he turned away. It was an Irish goodbye, really, like he didn't even think about looking at me. I grabbed the screwdriver from his desk and haven't returned it since. I doubt he's noticed.

We hang out together, but not exclusively. Generally, it is in pre-games or during drifting nights out on the Light Side of campus. Everything that I feel is stifling me—Winnetka's stiff focus on materialism, my yearning for something outside of that enclave, a greater love, greater music, a greater expression of humanity—seems intuitive to him. And I begin to think he is really, really cool. More and more he has preoccupied my mind. Once, after a "girls' night"—that is, some *Sex and the City* styled thing that I don't understand—my girlfriends and I, me especially, all get far too drunk, and I run into Luca's room to tell him what I think. He is sitting at his desk, dead sober. I grab his cheeks and pull his face toward mine. Like a mess, with a smile like a bloodhound in the heat with those dreary, droopy eyes, I tell him, "Luca, you are so cool." He chuckles modestly and shrugs out of my hold and thanks me politely. I grab him again. "No! Luca! You are the coolest person in the dorm!" Then my girls — Katie and Carla — drag me away by the arms, like I'm a screaming loony in the ward. I don't even remember what I did until much later the next day, once the memory clears up.

Our dorm friends had all been invited to a party at my friend Michelle's parents' house in San Jose. They have a lovely backyard with a stone patio and a built-in barbeque. Luca is there, laughing with the other guys, and I approach him tepidly, with almost no confidence, and say, "Hi, Luca."

Was I looking to apologize? For recognition? Absolution? He doesn't make a big deal of it at all, just says, "What's up," and turns back to the guys. *But now morning is clear; it's like I ain't here, he acts like we never met.* From there I try to put him out of mind, and he naturally does the same to me, but for the occasional gesture, or a brief, earnest conversation in the quad, at which point I am again thinking about him regularly, and dreaming, too, sweetly, sensually...

My professors like me. At numerous times in the first quarter, each of them told me I'd do well in their major. I never had a relationship with any of my high school teachers like that. My physics professor in particular has been good to me. For some reason, I'm ahead of the rest of the class. In my senior year of high school, I took AP physics and got a perfect score on almost everything. Same goes for the special physics SATs. I don't know where it came from. Everyone else said this was the most impossible class in high school, and yet it was effortless to me. Is it too abstract? Too much of a puzzle? I don't know. I see a physics problem broken into many parts — how each object breaks into its various elements and the formulas that I need to place those elements in—and my mind reassembles it without trouble. The pieces, while at first dissembled, fall into place for me without any difficulty. Just plug the variables into the formula and know the proper standards: mass here, acceleration there, gravity is 9.8 meters per second. Does everyone not think that way?

My professor, a man named Rogers who had just gotten out of Stanford's Ph.D. program, invited me to his office hours last week. The science labs are on the opposite side of campus from my dorm. I took the long walk through the quiet side of campus, where I wouldn't see anyone. It's a beautiful campus, really stunning. Somebody told me that we have more gardeners per square foot on this campus than in any other school in America. Everything is lush—brick walkways, palm trees, adobe roofs, along with all of the greenery and vegetation at your feet. There are a lot of good places to step out and hide when you need to.

When I got to the lab—an old room full of dated equipment with outworn brown metal and a homely operating sound—I found Rogers working on his laser research. He shut off the equipment when he noticed me enter. "I'm glad you came. Come, my office is right over here," he said. He has a geeky look. His hair is parted near the center of his head, and his shirts hang loosely around his torso. His teeth are large and square. All of the other students complain about him, but I cannot figure out why. He seems like a decent guy. We walked past the offices of the tenured science professors, many of whom look like ex-hippies. I've heard a couple of them left their homes in the South or the Midwest while searching for a freer America and the Grateful Dead in the late 1960s, and then somehow made their way into science professorships in higher education.

Seated in his office, Rogers said, "I couldn't help but notice your codename for the class." He made his test scores available to the class by printing them on a sheet and posting them in the front of the lecture hall. For student anonymity, he had us choose alibis for ourselves. I'd been experimenting with new music in my free time, and have been downloading classic jazz albums and modern classical composers from articles I find on the internet. I made my alibi Billie Holliday, and it was always the highest score posted. The other students started to complain about always seeing Billie Holliday as the top score. "There will actually be a Charlie Parker concert at Stanford in a few weeks," Rogers continued. "One of my friend's students is in their jazz program. I don't know if you are big into Parker, but I also don't have many students who pick their names based on old jazz figures."

"Oh yeah," I laughed shyly. "I've been getting into it a little." We talked about music some more, and he asked me if I played at all. I said that I did a little, but added that I don't have the technical know-how to keep on a whole conversation. Then he changed the topic to school.

"So, I've wanted to talk to you because I think you'd be interested in some supplementary material," he said.

"Oh, professor. I'm doing well because I've had all of this material before. I took it in high school, and so it isn't a big deal."

"Yes, but the rest of the class has seen this before, too, and they still have issues."

He turned to his bookcase beside his desk and pulled down an old maroon book with yellowing pages and the binding that was stretched and worn; the unattractive sort of book that nobody ever checked out of the library.

"These are the Richard Feynman lectures. He was a professor at the California Institute of Technology. I think you'll find a lot of great material here in addition to what we are going through in class."

"Oh, why thank you," I said. After a minute or two of courteous discussion, I left the office and returned to the dorm.

I had similarly kind meetings with my other professors. They all saw potential in me. My English teacher in Fall Quarter also tried to nurture me. For his class, he had assigned us a book on kids growing up in housing projects in Chicago by the United Center. As the only student "from Chicago," I was often called upon for observations, even though I wasn't actually "from Chicago." I was from the North Shore. I hardly spent any time in the city, including the North Side. The furthest I'd ever gone into the city was either to baseball games or smoke shops on Belmont. I'd never been anywhere like the projects, and so I never had anything to say about the book. The professor, Townley, required us to write weekly reflections on the readings, and he invited me to a meeting because he liked one of my writings. I wrote that I imagined two identical spirits in another world before conception into life, and they flipped a coin to see who would end up where. One would go to the North Shore, and the other would go to the Henry Horner housing projects, and the result of that coin flip would be the single most influential factor on how their lives would turn out, even though they would live only twenty miles from one another. He said he was impressed by it, and wanted to push me toward more creative writing.

If I'm being totally honest, though, I don't think much about long-term academic plans. I live day by day. Winter has been harsh. I don't feel drawn to any course of study. My success in the first quarter feels meaningless. I have a lot of dread. It gets me up in the night. It hangs over my day. I have regular dreams of death, full of weeping images of my mother, alone at home on a colorless afternoon. Why is she crying? Did she lose a daughter? Did she lose me? And there are hours when, like a child, I fall onto the beige, perfectly vacuumed carpet in the center of my dorm room, weep, and do not get up.

The morning before I flew back to school after Christmas break, I sat at my parents' kitchen table, hanging my head over a soggy, half-eaten bowl of cereal. Mom, eager to be a part of my life, asked me if I was excited to see my friends back at school. I lifted my face somberly and shook my head. Mom seemed taken aback. She sat upright and didn't say anything. Her expression went from cheerful to worried quickly. Was it expected that I should love college?

She hugged me tightly while dropping me off at the airport, and I got moody on the flight home at peak altitude. I wavered between sad rumination, which made me cry, and bursts of joy, which felt like an epiphany, but also made me cry. I bought the movie *American Beauty* at the airport and watched it on the plane. In the details of the frames of the movie, you can see all of the phone numbers start with 847. That's my home area code. I laughed at that. It also made me want to live without all of the bullshit, and maybe stop caring and get close to a boy for once, like Ricky and Janie.

I hadn't spoken to anyone about experiences like that, or about how that sullen mood has been my normal state for some time. I'd done about two-dozen online tests to check for a disorder, and each one said depression. Only once did I tell my parents, about three weeks after I left home for Winter Quarter. I called home unexpectedly during a sunny afternoon. Mom picked up and was excited.

"Boo! This is a treat! How are you?"

"I'm fine, Mom, I'm fine."

"And how are classes?"

"Classes are fine, Mom."

"Good! So, what's new?"

"It's something . . ."

"Yeah?"

The silence on the end felt anxious, ominous.

"I think I've had some . . ." I felt like I was surrendering. It was really difficult for me to say just one word. "I've had some depression."

"Oh, sweetie, I'm so sorry." Mom poured her sympathy into each syllable. I talked about the specifics for a minute or two, as well as we were able to. An hour after I ended the call with Mom, Dad called. He said he understood that I was having a rough time with things. He sounded very laid back and compassionate. I was really unsure how talking with him was going to go. I'm a bit afraid of being too human with him and usually felt more confident in opening up to Mom. He said that he loved me and was there for me, and if there was anything that he and Mom could do for me, they'd do it.

I privately scheduled an appointment at the school's counseling and psychological resources center for the next morning. On my walk there, the campus was misty quiet except for the sound of sprinklers and the march of ROTC students doing their morning regimen. When I arrived at the counseling center, I was the only person there. I waited in the lobby for a brief time until a professional counselor called me in. He was middle-aged with a teacher's outfit—glasses, shirt, vest, tight khakis. He told me to sit in a chair in a small room, and he sat in his chair right across from me.

"So, what can I help you with?" he asked frankly.

"I don't know, I . . ." I said softly, looking at the floor. I felt pathetic. My shoulders sank in front of my chest, and my arms drooped between my knees. "I've been off lately, and I don't know what it is. Like, sometimes in class I just become this—*ball of anxiety.*"

I was at a loss for speaking after that. The counselor looked back at me blankly. I felt like I was expected to say more, but I interpreted his look as stern and authoritative, and I was afraid to speak again without a prompt.

"Have you felt this way before?" he asked.

"Not like this," I said.

"How long has it been going on?" he asked.

"I don't know. A couple of months, I guess," I said.

He continued to look at me without expression, while I feared I was undergoing a moral examination and did not want to give him the wrong answer.

"Well, I'm sorry," he said, breaking the silence, "There's nothing we can do right now."

He pushed himself up from his knees and walked out of the room. I picked up my bag and left after him. I felt like a child, like all I needed to do was toughen up. *Ball of anxiety*. It sounded like such a bratty, childish phrase. I should have said something else. Something more mature.

I went to Rogers' physics class after meeting with the counselor, still wearing the sweatpants and hoodie I'd slept in. I slouched in my seat near the front of the lecture hall with my hood hanging over my head. I couldn't focus. I felt desperate and obsessed with the dream I'd had in the middle of the night, again about death, the Doc's death, and with the meeting I'd just had and what I had done wrong in it. My insides were brittle, and I basically didn't pay any attention to the lecture. No, not *did not*. I *could not*.

When I got out of class, I took the long route around campus to avoid the traffic of students, traveling instead alongside the soccer stadium and the engineering solar house. I called my parents, and both of them answered almost immediately after the first ring from separate phones on the landline. They asked how my appointment went and through an exchange of their questions and my short, two- or three-word answers, I told them that they didn't have time for me and that it was not helpful. They then asked if I had looked into a private psychiatrist, something I had no interest in doing, as I was too afraid to sneak off of campus and have to tell people why. It was more damning to be known as someone who goes to therapy than to go to therapy privately, and I did not want to risk that for myself. Then they asked, "What about seeing a doctor just to see if medications are a good idea?"

Meds, what a sham. Just another advertising crock. Chisel the abs, blush the cheek, create for me a perfect mind. Show me what I ought to be in heaven so that I may kill myself trying to attain it on earth.

"I can look into a doctor, I guess. But I don't like the idea of being on meds," I said.

My parents paused. "Well, I know he seems crazy, but the Doc is a genius. And if you called him, he would be totally open to talking. It could be very helpful," Mom said.

"I'll keep that in mind," I said.

"How are you doing now?"

"I'm not in the right headspace to answer a question like that," I said.

We made small talk briefly. They asked me what I would be doing with my afternoon, and again told me that they loved me. I then went to my dorm room and back to sleep.

I've only spoken of my weird, indescribable unease to one student. Her name is Maggie, a senior from a social justice group I have spent some time, who spots my doldrums and offers to talk to me about it without any judgment. "I went through the same thing during freshman year," she said. "It's a real shock moving to California at 19. You don't know anyone, but they all seem to know one another. The culture is very different. And most people on the West Coast don't think the Midwest even exists. And if they do, they think everyone loves Fox News. It's hard to adjust to the new reality, but hang in there. You'll find your people." Maggie is finishing a senior English thesis on Steinbeck. Every other Friday she drives a minivan to San Francisco's Tenderloin District, where we volunteer delivering meals to destitute HIV patients and walk over men in the street who are openly shooting heroin. She suggests that this type of work may help show me a new part of the world and put me on a path to figuring out what the purpose of my life should be. She's not wrong, it's certainly eye-opening. And it feels nice to be plugged into reality, even if it's an ugly reality.

Plus, it gives me a chance to spend time with Luca. I didn't know he was into volunteering, but he joined for one of these trips and I was paired with him to deliver sandwiches. With a sack full of food and a map of the neighborhood, we go from section housing unit to section housing unit, up and down dozens of flights of stairs, him always leading the way. He has long legs and rushes up three steps at a time, all the way up to these sad, disordered apartment buildings where frail old women lay in bed and watch Bay Area news on old TVs, alone. When we deliver them their meals, he takes some time to check in on them. Nothing too serious, just, "How are you today? Are the people taking care of you here? What do you wish they could do?" And they're honest with him and tell him exactly how they are and what they wish for. He is remarkably good at getting other people to open up to him. Having never had a conversation with anyone this impoverished, I ask him, "What do you do to get these people to talk to you?" Like there's a trick to it. And he says, clearly, that there is no magic. Just check in on them like you would anyone else.

On a subsequent delivery, I try to follow his advice, but I'm not as normal with it. Do they suspect I come from too much wealth to talk to them? I can't imagine the life of these people, and my awkwardness about that fact comes through my confusing delivery. "So…how did you end up here?" I'm a bad social worker. Invariably, Luca steps in with a pleasant joke or observation when things get too stilted. When we leave these dumpy little rooms, he walks ahead of me with his swift, deliberate strides, and I shuffle behind.

After these escapades together, I think of asking him to study with me more often. The initiative is not there yet. I sort of just wait in quiet anticipation for him to say something or to butt into my life again. There's a little study room on the third floor of the dorm that I go to when I have nothing to do and it's available. It has a small, upright piano I like to play, and a window looking toward the hills in the distance. Mostly I play the same pieces that my childhood teacher Mrs. Wagner taught me in high school: Gershwin's preludes, the opening of a Chopin etude, and that one Beethoven sonata. A Brahms something-or-another. It feels great to get something under your fingers so completely that you can command it as you want. I've lost that.

I've started browsing through online recordings of composers from the 20 Century. "The minimalists" in particular. I'd never developed a proper ear for music and never learned anything through any means other than having someone tell me where to put my finger, detail by detail. I can't even identify a 1-4-5 in all twelve keys, it's that bad. I get a Philip Glass album and try to learn his piano bits by ear. It's a good starting point, and my ear is definitely getting stronger. When I'm done with one, I go to the next. I also discover this guy John Adams and order the sheet music for his piece *Phrygian Gates*. Like the others, I'll never complete it totally, but I take parts that I know and play them over and over. The cluster chords are lovely, and the rhythms are hardly different from playing pop songs on the keyboard.

While charging through a few intense measures, Luca enters. I stop playing.

"Oh, sorry," I say.

"No need to apologize. I really liked it," he says. I look away, eyes to the keyboards. "That's impressive," he adds. "You must have been your teacher's star pupil."

"Not really," I say.

"Really?"

"Well, I kind of was, but my teacher didn't train people for serious study. It was very casual."

"It sounds serious to me."

"It really wasn't. I mean, I can bullshit well enough. My teacher studied under a woman who studied under Nadia Boulanger, and she said that a lot. So, there's some insight there. But that's my only claim to seriousness, and it's a stretch. Actual music students are far more advanced than this."

He gives me a confused, sensitive look. His cheeks have relaxed and his mouth hangs open a bit. He looks concerned for my wellbeing. "You're really hard on yourself, aren't you?"

"I don't think so."

Accepting my answer, his mood lifts again. As he leaves, he says, "Well, keep it up. I'd like to listen more sometime."

I play for another ten minutes and walk to the other side of the floor to my friends Katie Reynolds and Carla McKenna's room. This campus is extremely bubbly. People seem happy all of the time, and by contrast, I make a lot of darker, more sarcastic jokes. I think it makes a lot of people uncomfortable, but Katie and Carla like it. Carla and I really became friends when she heard me mocking sorority girls.

Earlier in the year, a bunch of girls in the dorm were talking about rushing for sororities, and it seemed all too bland and all too normal, talking about the formals, the dances... I made a joke, a Simpsons reference, "And let's forget our troubles with a big bowl of strawberry ice cream!" during a silence in the conversation. Nobody got it but Carla, and she burst out laughing.

I generally think of Carla as a strong, ambitious person. I want to have her confidence, to be honest. She does so much so excellently—work, honors, social life—and seldom shows any vulnerability. And she's an amazing reader, in both English and Spanish, but is very down-to-earth when she talks to people. Katie is more...well, I don't know. I like Katie, but she doesn't seem to have any idea what she's doing a lot of the time. She's very impulsive, and often very self-destructive. There's always a different guy involved, or a blackout, or a couch to go smoke on. And she talks about herself too much. But she's really smart, and she's good to me, and we get along well and hang out a lot. The two of them are like the devil and angel on my shoulder.

I went to their room and slouched on their futon by the window and looked out over the quad. They seemed preoccupied with their computers and gadgets.

An odd noise was coming from across the hall, where Jeremy Carlisle and Brendan Rieland lived. Jeremy came from the same high school class as Carla, from one of the university's biggest feeder schools about an hour away from campus. He was a cad about half of the time, although he was generally decent to me, and I considered him a good friend. I got up and peeked into their room. The noise was coming from Jeremy's computer, a mix of music and human noises. Porn, probably, knowing him.

"Boo boo boo boo boo boo boo!" he shouted when he saw me between the doorways across the hall. I got up and poked into their room.

"Hello, Jeremy. And hi Brendan, too." Brendan was reading in the corner of the room, in a beige shirt and an oversized flannel, with streaky black hair that looked unwashed.

"Hi, Boo," Brendan said. He was a lankier, geekier boy, and probably a mismatched roommate for Jeremy. But it seemed like they got along well.

Jeremy, with a build cut from the lacrosse team and clothing pulled from northeastern prep academies, turned up the volume on his computer. He wasn't actually watching pornography. He was just listening to it while scrolling articles and social media.

"You know they can kick you out for this?" I told him.

"They won't," he said, turning up the volume more. The moaning was fierce and animalistic.

"Suit yourself," I said, and left to return to Carla and Katie's room.

Upon entry, I shouted, "Oh, hiya!" hoping to get their attention this time.

"Oh, hiya," Carla said. There was glitzy pop music playing on her computer. "What've you been up to today, Booboo?"

"Not shit," I said. "Class and piano."

"Yes, Luca stopped by. He said it sounded nice."

"Oh, did he?"

"He did. You should play for us sometime."

"In due time."

A door slammed down the hall. Kelsey, our do-gooder resident administrator, dressed in a university windbreaker, stormed towards Jeremy's room and approached him angrily. "For fuck's sake, Jeremy, this is it!"

"I can't hear you!" Jeremy shouted, looking up at Kelsey as she ordered him, barely audible over the speakers while pointing at his laptop. "I'm listening to pornography!"

Kelsey pulled the chord out of his speakers and slammed his laptop shut.

"No, this joke ends here, okay? This is the last time. This is unacceptable behavior. Whether you give a shit or not, and I know you don't, Susan Nally thought about transferring to another school last quarter. She thought she would be getting a respectable Catholic education, and what she gets instead is a room two doors down from the biggest smut fest in Northern California!"

"She should lighten up," Jeremy said.

"I've had to talk to her parents, Jeremy. I've told them that I'd take care of your issues. It makes her uncomfortable to come back to her own dorm. Do you think about that at all?"

"Yes. I mean, no."

"You think your sex jokes are funny, but they're not. They're invasive."

"They're funny to most people. Right, Brendan?"

"Don't bring me into this," Brendan said, still reading.

"That's it. You're done. You can't be reasoned with. You're not living in this dorm anymore. I'm writing you up, we're bringing in the administration. And yes, I have the power to kick you out," Kelsey said, holding herself taut while looking up at him with demanding certainty.

"That's fine. I'm moving into a house next year anyway. I know the guys who live there now. I can sleep on their couch."

"Great! Fantastic! We're in agreement. You'll get the hell out. Hopefully, I'll never have to deal with you again, and you'll become the problem for whatever sick fucks will live with you."

"Hey, don't call Brendan a sick fuck!" Jeremy objected.

"Brendan, is this right? You're living with this perv again?" Kelsey asked.

"Yeah," Brendan said. "We get along well enough."

"And BJ, John, and Kevin are living with us too, Kels. This is college. Sick fucks are in high supply, as well as high demand," Jeremy said.

"You—stop! You're going to leave, and on your way out I'm going to put up a *fucking* flier with the phrase, *Jeremy Carlisle: Sex Offender* on it. And I'm going to buy pepper spray for Susan Nally and look the other way should she decide to use it on you…"

We listened up until that point and then Carla shut the door. "That's about enough of that. We've seen how that plays out before," she said.

"*Fuuuuck.* I need to go to the library but I really don't want to," Katie cooed.

"Yes, you do," Carla insisted. "We'll all go. Work for three hours. We'll come back, pre-game, go out, and do the same thing tomorrow. Agreed?"

"Yes, agreed," Katie said blithely.

"Booboo, are you coming?"

"Yes, I'm coming."

"Alright, zip up. Let's get this shit done," Carla said.

After work at the library, Carla convinced me to come up to the pre-game for at least a little bit, just to say hi to everyone. I went upstairs to Christian Armstrong and Charlie Peterson's room, where my friends were hanging out. Christian opened the door slightly, peaking through, and let me in when he recognized me. Carla and Katie were already there, and so were Rachel Harrison and BJ Forsyth. I knew BJ a little from the dorm. Rachel lived elsewhere, but I had been seeing her around the dorm more often. I think she had been seeing Charlie. Or Christian. It was hard to tell sometimes which one was with which girl.

Christian offered a round of shots to those in the room and poured cheap vodka from plastic bottles. He served mine in a glass that was wet from previous use. It was disgusting, but I'd gotten used to stomaching terrible liquor. Ten minutes later, we took another shot. Katie took command of the music, and put on Beyoncé's "Single Ladies." Katie and Rachel started dancing clumsily in the middle of the room. "Already?" Carla said to me, "We are nowhere near drunk enough for this yet."

The guys had Bud Light in a miniature fridge under their desk. We helped ourselves to one each, and sat and talked on one of the beds. Someone knocked on the door. The crowd got momentarily quiet and Christian turned the music down. Charlie peaked through the eyehole and said, "It's not an RA." He opened the door and Jeremy, Brendan, and Luca came in. Jeremy was wearing a crisp flannel, Brendan in a looser, grungier flannel, and Luca was wearing a t-shirt for a Berkeley-area musician. They looked very comfortable with one another, like old friends from grade school.

I was disinterested in the scene but knew that would change once the alcohol kicked in. Time passed, things got louder. I wasn't comfortable but faked that I was. Katie, Rachel, and Luca came to sit on the edge of the bed, and we crammed together to make room for everyone. With six of us packed into a tight space, I was slouching on the edge of the bed. For a moment, my attention dozed off. I listened to the sounds of the party, noting how everyone's voices crossed over one another in constant, spastic chatter. I was becoming very involved with this listening exercise when I was interrupted crisply.

"You alright there?" It was Luca.

"Yes," I said, "I just spaced out for a second."

"I do it, too." He took a sip of his beer. "You sounded nice this afternoon."

"Thank you."

"How often do you play?"

"I don't know. Whenever I can."

"Do you listen to any new music?"

"Yes, some. Why?"

"Just for conversation. When I was home over break, my good friend showed me this guy Sufjan Stevens. Have you heard of him?"

"Yes, I think he really knows how to write a song. It's really pretty music."

"He totally does." I looked around and drank my beer. Jeremy and Charlie were joking about "Project Infinity" and "Project Impossible." "Project Infinity" was their code name for getting Brendan laid. "Project Impossible" was to steal a cop car. Carla butted in and told them to "stop giving Brendan shit like that." Brendan didn't seem to care. He also looked a little stoned. Katie and Rachel had gotten up and were talking in the corner by the door, beyond the other conversation. I couldn't hear them. Luca interrupted me again.

"You don't seem very happy," he said, looking at me directly. Had he been looking at anything but me?

"What?" I felt exposed and alarmed.

"Nothing. You look like you'd rather be somewhere else."

"I'm sorry, I'm just tired. I'll perk up once we start walking. I'll be more alert at the party."

Jeremy overheard me and shouted, "Yeah, when the fuck are we going?"

"Calm down, god damn it," Christian said.

"We should go soon," Jeremy whined.

"We will, alright?" Christian addressed the group, "Yo! Everyone get out of my room! We're leaving!"

"Where to?" Katie asked.

"Shit House."

"Will they let us in?"

"Yeah, I don't know. Maybe. Let's just go, we'll figure it out, and if not then we can find another party."

We stumbled outside and assembled on the edge of the quad. The night was shaded and cool, black, off-color. Everything was a tinge darker against the night, the moonlight, and the lamp-posts. I felt boozier after standing up, and the rest of the crowd seemed the same way, though they acted a lot drunker than I did.

We walked towards a stretch of off-campus housing. Other students were walking in their packs. Sometimes Christian or Carla shouted something at people they knew or exchanged information on where to go. A group of guys walked by us, and one of them made a snide remark. I couldn't hear it, but his friends snickered after he said it. Jeremy raised his head like he was going to confront them about something, then Carla cut him off. "No, Jer. Just come." He nudged her to the side and started to shout something, but she stopped him again. The guys jeered at him for being tamed. They left, and Jeremy made a punkish gesture toward their backs.

When the two of them rejoined the group, Charlie commented, "That was impressive."

"What you must understand about Carla," Jeremy said, "is that she does not get fucked. She does the fucking."

After drifting by house parties, along the way losing Luca, Christian, and Jeremy to a hangout at Christian's older brother's house, we turned a corner and found an open garage with couches and a record collection hanging on the wall. Several upperclassmen were hanging out, and there was noise coming from inside of the house. Rachel shouted at them from across the road, and they shouted back. Katie and Rachel crossed the street. Carla followed a step behind and coyly said, "Bye!" to the group. BJ, Charlie, Brendan, and I then approached the house. The guy out front of the house told us bluntly, "She can get in. The rest of you, no."

I turned to my friends. "Honestly, I want to go back."

"Very well. Left behind again, comrades," BJ said. "There are a lot of fun doors that we'll never get into simply because we aren't hot and female. Boo, why don't you go in with them?"

"I'm just having a change of mind about being out. I feel stiff," I said.

The four of us walked back to campus and shared a late-night pizza in the student hall. I appreciated BJ, Charlie, and Brendan; they reminded me of my cousins. They had the same mannerisms and the same taste for dumb jokes and made-up slang. They listened to the same music, like Sublime, Eminem, and jam bands, and did the same things like smoke weed and play Nintendo 64 for hours at a time. It was always relaxing. I didn't feel like I had anyone to impress.

It's Friday and it's raining. It suits me well. I've had a pathetic observation lately while looking at taintless blue skies: "The sun is shining, the world is beautiful, just not for me."

My parents called and asked if it was all right if they visited on an upcoming weekend. Dad said he was in a quiet period at work, so they'd be able to come out for four days or so. Mom wants to do a Saturday in Monterrey and Carmel, and Dad added that we should do lunch at Pebble Beach. My classes end in the morning, and I lazily do schoolwork in the afternoon in the dorm common area where others are often hanging out.

At one point in the afternoon, I walked to my room to retrieve a book and passed Luca in the hall. He was on his way to take a shower, wearing flip flops and a bathing suit, carrying a towel over his shoulders. It was boyishly sweet, like he'd come from the beach at home by Lake Michigan. Our dormitory has co-ed floors, so guys and girls are always passing one another in nothing but towels. It is very healthy, I think. He said hello, but very shyly, and walked by me quickly. As he passed, I called at him, "Did you have fun last night?"

"Yes," he said, "But I don't remember coming home."

"Yeah, it looked that way," I said.

"Oh…" He scratched his head and covered his face while he did it. "I hope I didn't embarrass myself."

"You were fine," I said. "You were funny. Do you plan on going out tonight?"

"We'll see."

"Let me know if you do."

He walked to the bathroom, and I went to my room. I took a nap in the late afternoon, since I was sleeping less at night, and usually woke up feeling unrested. An hour into my nap, Sara returned with her friends. We hung out for a bit and looked at Facebook profiles over Sara's computer. I know I had judged sorority girls to be superficial, but to be honest, none of them were dressed like they cared about appearances, and they were all open to me and pretty down-to-earth. They reminded me of my aunts, actually. We went to the student center for dinner together. I got a peanut butter and jelly sandwich, a banana, a bowl of cocoa pebbles, and cranberry juice. The others got salads and called me weird for my choice.

We pre-gamed in the dorms again and went to a large frat party. Carla and Katie can flip a switch when we go out. It's like their personalities change and they have a different voice, a different physicality when they talk to guys. Chests up, vocal register raised. And I'm just . . . there. Quiet and left out. And still a virgin. Carla's open about hookups. "So, I like to manipulate meatheads into hookups. What's the problem?" She'll stand in the center of three frat boys at a party and run the whole conversation, and they'll follow her no matter what. She gets whatever she wants. Katie frustrates me. She's too confused, always wanting something, then not wanting it, then complaining about it, then going back to it. It comes off as pretty hypocritical. As for me, I can't even talk to anyone in a setting like that. I dip to the side of the party and make smartass observations with the other introverts.

I left the party early. After midnight, BJ and I got into a drunk talk about romance while we sat on the dorm lobby couch, speaking too honestly and loudly. He was wearing a pastel yellow shirt from J-Crew, a backward Seattle Mariners hat, and was slouched so deep on the couch that his knees bent at a point higher than his face.

"I'll admit it," I told him, feeling free enough not to care, "I've never even kissed anyone."

"Really?" he asked. A look of soft surprise came over him.

"Yeah."

"I wouldn't have guessed it. You seem more grown-up than other people. But I don't think it's a problem."

"Honestly?" I said, perplexed that he would describe me that way.

"Not at all."

"I get the idea that if you're this far behind, you're doomed to always be bad at dating and bad at sex," I said.

"Nah, I don't think that's true. I think that's just a scare. It happens when it happens," he said. "Can I share something with you?" he asked, then checked the room to be sure no one else could hear him.

"Sure," I said.

"I have absolutely no idea how to please a girl."

I laughed a little. "I'm sure that's not true."

"My sex is really awkward. It starts, I never see her get into it, I get into my own head, and then it ends before anything happens. Each time I talk to the girl afterward, I feel like I'm being talked to like a child. I know they're being soft with me because they can't take me seriously. I have these fears about girls I've been with comparing notes about me and laughing about it. It's really bad." He seemed limp and defeated as he said this, quiet and helpless in his position.

I actually had heard girls in the dorm do that, a couple of Sara's friends who had hooked up with him after some parties during fall quarter. But I didn't tell him.

"Like you said, BJ, things happen when they happen. Maybe in a couple of years that won't be an issue for you."

"I hope so," he said, disheartened.

"Well, now you know my secret, and I know yours. I'll trust you with it," I said.

"I'm not trying to hook up with you, by the way," he slipped.

"I know, BJ."

The swinging doors of the lobby opened, and Carla and Katie stormed into the lounge with chicken wings and pizza from the student center.

"Heyyyy," they said, loudly.

"How was the rest of the party?" I asked.

"It was alright. Got shut down by the cops," Katie said.

"Same old," Carla said.

We recollected the night's events, and then Brendan walked into the room in his pajama pants, slippers, and a loose t-shirt.

"What's up, B?" Carla asked.

"Jeremy sexiled me," Brendan said.

"No luck for you?" Katie asked while chewing. She chortled a bit as she spoke, almost spitting up her food.

"No," he said dryly. "Not that I was trying."

"Why aren't you trying?" Katie asked while licking sauce off her hand.

"I'm in a cold streak," he said.

Katie laughed again, harder.

"Shut up, you asshole," Carla jabbed at Katie.

"I'm sorry. I'm not laughing at you, Brendan. I'm laughing at something else. I'm very stoned right now. You should understand that," Katie explained.

"She's right. We're both very high. You shouldn't listen to us. She's not laughing at you, I can assure you," Carla said.

Brendan shrugged.

"You'll be fine, Brendan," Carla added. "People learn different things at different times. That's what my mom says. Don't pressure yourself."

"Who did Jeremy come home with, anyway?" Katie asked.

"I don't know, some slut," Brendan said.

"You've got to stop calling girls that," Katie said.

"I'm sorry. I know. I just don't know what else to call someone who goes home with Jeremy," Brendan said.

"Call her drunk," Carla said.

"Hella drunk," Brendan added.

"I actually wonder myself," Carla said. "I'm attracted to assholes. I can't help it. I don't want to be, but I am. I love dudes who don't give a fuck. Not caring is hot. Jeremy isn't. But other guys? Sure."

"My cousin has a line," Brendan added, "Treat women like dirt, and they stick to you like mud."

"That's terrible advice, B," Katie said.

"It works for Jeremy. He's rude as hell and he gets laid all of the time."

"No, don't listen to that. Jeremy is at his peak because he's a college freshman. By next year, he'll be a loser. Your cousin is full of shit. I like guys who are honest and respectful. Assholes are assholes," Katie said. "Besides, so much of sex is about the girl giving herself up to the guy. It's a really vulnerable matter. It requires a lot of trust. Your cousin is just a chauvinist."

"I'm aware of that. He also gets laid a lot more than me," Brendan said.

"Brendan, don't be that guy," Carla said. "It's not you. You're fine."

"But you just admitted that you were attracted to assholes," he said.

"I'm intrigued by asshole qualities in the short-term," she corrected, "but not full-fledged assholes. I wouldn't waste too much of my time with that. It burns out. Every single one of my high school girlfriends has been dead-ended by a dead-ender boyfriend, and they never let it go. I don't need a relationship until guys are more mature."

"So, what kind of guy would you want to date?" Brendan asked.

"Dating? I'm not dating in college. My older sister's in grad school. She says you can't work, do school, and have a relationship at the same time without fucking one of them up. I don't need any complications. I just need to enjoy myself." She took a bite of her food. "And I'll level with you. In college, I'm not looking for some nice-guy poetic shit or a sweet romantic comedy relationship. I'm looking to get *fucked*."

"I don't think you can plan these things," Katie said.

"I'm just saying that's what I want. I'm trying to get into law school and have fun while I can. I don't have time for anything serious," Carla said.

"Why do relationships have to be serious? I don't get that. I'd never want serious," Brendan said.

"And what are you here for, Brendan?" Carla asked.

"I dunno. To get an engineering degree and enjoy college. Not really concerned with much else," Brendan said.

"Why engineering?" Carla asked.

"Because math, science . . ."

"*Math, science*," Katie mimicked in a deep voice.

"Fuck y'all," Brendan said.

"And who would you date?" Katie asked.

"I'm open-minded, provided she's not a psycho killer," Brendan said.

Brendan looked over to me and BJ. We were listening from the couch while the three of them talked over a round table. "You all are keeping quiet over there," Brendan said.

"We had our own talk about all of this before you arrived," I said.

"Do share," Carla said.

"Yeah Boo, when are we going to hear about your shit? You never get with anybody," Katie provoked me.

"We'll talk about it later," I said.

"Hey Boo, why do people call you Boo and not Ellen?" Brendan asked.

"Because I was born on Halloween and my aunts joked about naming me Boo. My father wanted nothing to do with that, and they had decided on Ellen much earlier. Ellen is a family name."

"Does any of your family live in California?"

"No."

"So, why'd you come all of the way out here?"

"To try a new part of the country, mostly."

"Are people in the Midwest super-racist? I've heard they are," he asked.

"People are the same everywhere," Carla said, "Don't let people exaggerate differences. People are the same, and you've got to take them as individuals."

I wanted an escape from the conversation. I was getting tired and worried about judgment. "I have to go back now," I said. "It's late."

"It's college, Boo. Stay up," Katie said.

"I can't. I'm desperately tired," I said and headed to bed.

"*Boooo!*"

The next morning, I woke just before noon and got a late breakfast alone in the mostly vacant dining hall. My throat and head ached, and I consumed extra juice and fruit for my hangover. I people-watched while I ate and tried not to throw up. Afterward, I took a long, hot shower, then went to the library to put my mind to actual work.

While at the library, after doing a bit of schoolwork, I looked at a few online forums about transferring to a different university. They were all written by people who were very dissatisfied with the schools they had chosen, and it made me feel like I'd made the wrong decision. The schools I was looking to transfer to were all on the Midwest or the east coast and all ranked a tier higher than here. Maybe my real problem is that I went to a place where I have no ties at all to the past eighteen years of my life, and nothing to say for myself without them. My friends from home do not have this problem.

When the caffeine started to wear off, a light, tingling buzz ran through me. I sank into my chair, rested my head against my fist, and drifted off into a light sleep. The fabric of my sweater was blissfully nice, and I dreamt about how soothing it would feel to be touched. I could still hear things happening around me, but only through blackness and dreams. In naps, I dream of afternoons at the Doc's pool, and of interpersonal conflicts from high school.

On my way out, back to the dorm, I saw Luca sitting alone at a table on the ground floor of the library. He was reading a thin, old book. I approached him before he saw me. "Hi friend, what are you reading?"

He looked up, a bit startled. "Oh, hi Boo. I'm, uh, reading poetry."

I nodded.

"I hope that doesn't sound pretentious," he said, checking himself.

"It's so pretentious," I said.

"Really?" he asked.

"Oh, totally," I said, provoking him.

"Well, screw me, right? I'm pretentious," he said. His indifference irritated me. He looked back at the book.

I asked, "Who are you reading?"

"ee Cummings," he said.

"I don't know who that is," I said.

He tilted his head, shrugged his shoulders, slouched into his seat, and read again.

"I guess I'll see you back in the dorms. Enjoy your reading," I said and turned away.

"Hold up," Luca said.

"What?" I asked.

"Have you ever been to the rose gardens?" he asked.

"Which ones?" I asked.

"The ones a bit away from campus, into town," he said.

"I haven't," I said.

"I was going to take a walk there kind of soon. Would you like to go?" he asked.

"When, exactly?" I asked.

"I was planning on going in an hour, but now I'm thinking of going sooner. Whenever I'm done here," he said.

I checked my phone as though there was information on it I needed to consult. There was nothing on it. I only checked it to bide time, as manic anticipation flittered in me and I felt less able to keep my dry tone towards him. "I can join you. Could you let me drop my things off at the dorm and then I'll meet you back here in twenty minutes?" I said.

"That sounds good," he said.

As we walked, we talked about people in the dorm and life around campus.

The garden was empty when we arrived, save an older couple walking their dog on the other side of the park. Few flowers were remaining in the garden, and the garden looked like it was at the end of its life.

"This is nice," I said. "How did you know about this?"

"I went for a walk the other week and just happened to come here without meaning to," he said.

I looked around the garden and tried to center my thoughts on peaceful things. Luca must have felt awkward while I gazed around the lawn. He continued, "It was a contemplative walk. I come from a hippie family. I sometimes do things for spiritual reasons that other people find weird. I just walk off without any destination, like you need to be lost to be able to find yourself," he said.

I laughed, "A hippie family?"

"There's no other way of putting it. What do you come from?" he said.

"The opposite of a hippie family."

We strolled alongside the bushes. All of them had thinning branches and leaves. Next, we came upon a bench inside of a cabana overseeing the gardens. "I'm going to sit down," I said while he stood and watched the area. "You're free to sit, too, you know," I said.

He smiled and sat on the other side of the bench. A foot of space was between us.

"So," I asked, "you're a lost hippie?"

He laughed. "You could call it that."

"How so?"

"I have an artsy background. My parents adopted me after a lost weekend in South America. They were doing service down there, and they divorced when I was young. I was raised by just my mother. I like it, but I've always known that it's a little unconventional," he said.

"That's interesting. I feel my upbringing has been pretty by-the-book," I said.

"Really? I wouldn't think that of you," he said.

"No?" I asked.

"Are you kidding? You don't care about the other bullshit that other girls care about. It's very independent. Very cool," he said.

"Both of my parents have MBAs and CPAs, so I feel very normal," I said.

"You're not," he said. I remembered how he looked at me in the piano room, when the façade of joking around wore off and he suddenly appeared as straightforward and sincere as anyone had been with me. I'm not sure if this is a compliment or an insult.

"And what makes you lost?" I asked.

He sighed gently and sank a bit. "I—I don't know. The transition to college has been rough. I've had a lot of anxiety since I got here." This piqued my attention, and I listened more seriously. He stopped talking until I asked him to explain more. He said some things about feeling uncomfortable a lot of the time, about not knowing what he was doing in school, and how his father was pressuring him into law school. Then he said that he'd prefer to study English because that's what he enjoyed, and I smiled at him—a bit patronizingly, actually—and he turned the question back to me. I said that I liked engineering because I'd been into science and there were some advantages to being a female in engineering, then he asked if that was what I *wanted* to do, and I said, "sure," without thinking, but then said, "That question isn't so important, though. That's not what college is for. I like English too, but at the end of the day, an English major is just a library card, you know?" I think I must have offended him. He looked disconcertingly at me and asked, "So, then, why are you here?"

"Well, I'm here because it's what you're supposed to do," I said.

"No, I mean, what do you want? Not in some conventional way, but what do *you* want *to do?*" he asked.

"I . . ." I hit a mental block at this question. Suddenly, dread and surrender fell from the top of my head down the rest of my body. "I don't fucking know." I felt humiliated, and I expected him to say something mean. He didn't. "I really don't fucking know. I've been dealing with…things. I take all of these online tests, and they all tell me the same thing. I may need to get on meds."

"Um," he said, "That's all right."

"Is it, though? It's such a debacle that I cannot manage on my own. Do you know people on meds?"

"Sure. My friends in high school were on them."

"Like what?"

"Prozac."

I could not refrain from crying, and I laughed a big, ugly cough of a laugh, with snot coming down the back of my throat from the tears. "I just, Jesus, I can't even say the word." I covered my face. "Depression. There it is. I want nothing to do with it, but it's there anyway. I have clinical depression, Luca."

"That's fine, Boo. Lots of people do," he said.

"It's not, though," I exclaimed, waving my arm in front of me. "It's horrible! I don't sleep, and when I do, I dream of dying, or of everyone running away from me. My concentration is terrible and I hate myself, and I don't enjoy anything anymore, and I'm such a failure at life."

"How can you possibly be a failure? You're nineteen. Like, Jesus, get some perspective."

"I'm sorry, I know," I cried a bit harder.

"No, I'm sorry. That sounded much meaner than I meant it to be," he said.

"I'm upset with myself, man. I come from all of this privilege and I could have the whole world, but I don't care! I'm a waste. I'm a slacker, and I just landed here, when I could have done so much better. Like, I don't want to be here. I don't want to be anywhere. I want to transfer to a different school each year, get the hell out of here, and go to New Orleans, and then to DC, and then to New York."

"I don't think you can plan things like that," he said.

"I know, and I'm not really serious. I just really do not want to be here, and I don't see myself staying anywhere without wanting to run away eventually," I said.

A bird flapped away from the ground before us.

"Boo, I don't know if you know, but people here think you're great."

I sniffled and gathered myself.

He added, "They think you're really cool. I was talking to Rachel yesterday. She wants to move into the dorm next year and see if you'll be her roommate. I've heard a lot of conversations like that. You're very appreciated."

My tears receded a bit. I made what I assumed was an ugly, contorted smile, and laughed again, more buoyantly than before.

"I don't know what you're going through," he continued. "It sounds awful and I'm not going to pretend I understand it. But if you're open to it, there's a community here that would love to have you."

I calmed down and exhaled. I didn't feel as sad anymore. It was nearing sundown and getting darker and colder outside. Luca was only wearing a t-shirt and rubbing his arms for warmth. "Looks like the weather is pushing us back. Should we start walking back?" he asked.

"Sure," I said. He leaned forward to grab his backpack. "Luca, wait," I continued, and placed my hand on his chest, near his shirt collar. He looked up, turned toward me, and I leaned into him and kissed him. He kissed back, and then more. I was the more assertive one, pinching his top lip while the bottom hung in lifelessness. He clenched my arm and pulled me towards him.

We continued to be dumbstruck on the bench for about twenty minutes before walking back to campus together, huddling to keep warm.

After our tryst in the rose garden, I see him more regularly. I'll sneak into his room to complain about asinine moments of the day, comment on a new piece of music that he should hear, or lay in his bed until he joins me. He always does, suddenly and spontaneously. We never spend the night together, nor do I ever actually sleep there. I lie to him that he's not the best guy I've ever kissed, even though he's the only one I've ever kissed. It sets him off and makes him more assertive to adore me all over my face, my neck, and my shoulders. In our intimacy, we exchange a lot of silly laughter. And I mean bottom-of-the-barrel laughter, such as when the whole of his weight is on me, bare chest to bare chest, and he releases his force from me, and a squishing, flatulent sound occurs. He cannot simply move on from it. He is not mature enough not to laugh, and for that matter, neither am I, no matter how much I'd wish for all of my thoughts and bad characteristics to be sublimated in his caress, his complete attention to me...

But on the weekends, he is often as callous and distant as he was before we met, having fun with everyone but me, talking shit—in the most hilarious way imaginable—about all of the dorm's easy targets. That is, he is distant until we have both had too many shots, and there is a feeling of vomit barely repressed in my gut, and he comes to me with his stupid, drunk Luca swagger. I squeeze him in the middle of the dance floor, with one of those obnoxious Top-40 songs playing—Usher, Rihanna, who knows—with the juniors and their patchy beards and loose shirts, smoking weed on the couch in the corner. Then I feel I have the upper hand on him. As I'd once never admitted what I thought of him, I now understand that he is in the same, vulnerable place.

While I've known him closer, we've never slept in the same bed, and we've never gone beneath the waist. A few times when we've rolled around, he's reached into my beltline, and instinctively I've swatted his hand away. "Boo..." he'll say, and shake his head. "It's okay..." But I'm simply not ready. I'm too inexperienced. But he doesn't suspect that. He thinks it's about someone else. When I retreat from offering him my deepest intimacy, suddenly I become the distant one, and he is questioning my identity. "Do you have somebody back home? I've talked about all of my friends with you, and I know so little about your life before this." Why wouldn't he just assume virginity? Do I give off sexual learnedness? And does he actually—and this is the thought I'd never been ready to accept—does he actually, really care?

I soon learn that he does care, only not as I'd hoped.

He calls me into his room on a Saturday morning. His legs are folded on his bed and his head is bowed, face in his hands. I've never seen him so ashamed before. "Boo..." he sinks further into a down, sorrowful position, "What are we?"

I don't know. I've been waiting for him to define it.

He then explains that he had too much to drink the night before at one of the social justice club's big parties, an annual drag show in support of the LGBT movement. And at the after-party, everything was loose and sexualized and he made out with a sophomore. It didn't mean anything, he insists, it just happened.

While this could have been heartbreaking news, at the moment, it wasn't. "You know, that's alright, Luca, these things happen."

"Really?" he says, surprised.

"Yeah, I mean, we're nineteen. It's alright, don't take it too seriously."

Relieved, he hugs me more sincerely than I've ever felt in another's touch. But in the coming days, as I have time to ruminate on his act, the more inadequate and helpless I feel about it. I cry over it. I feel cheated on. I wouldn't wish that on anyone, feeling that the person they think they love sees them as expendable. I find a spot on campus by the mission, a bit removed from student activity, where there's an arch-shaped window built into the clay walls of a walkway to the church. I curl into the seat of that window, read literature, watch stray cats prance through the grass, and call him to meet me there. In a silhouette in a window in the tallest dorm building across campus, I see a couple having sex. Maybe I should be like them: more intent about presumably meaningless hookups, detached from one another's emotional problems. When Luca arrives, I tell him how weak he made me feel. He bows his head sorrowfully again, sits across from me on the windowsill, reclined with a leg leaning over the side. What we say there I'd rather not repeat. It's far too slow, far too pitiful. But I will say that it ends in tears and a kiss as long and as soft as frail flower lips covering each other in the rain. And when I see him next, he is confident to tell people that he is with me. And we dance in the dormitory halls to dumb music, without any alcohol, and late at night in the common area, when all of our friends are hanging out, I curl into him on the couch.

❊   ❊   ❊

Though I've discovered a new wonder in life, I still can't shake my malcontented side. There's too much free time in college. An open afternoon can turn the body and mind into a swamp if left idle enough. From there I become forgetful, weak, and disordered. This has gone on for too long. I take my mother's advice and I call the Doc. I tell him how things are, and I tell him that I've been trying to keep busy, and he says that's good. And I tell him I am considering medications, and he says that is fine.

It is kind of weird, actually. Usually, he only tells everyone how miserable he is, or he complains about my grandmother, but today he is very cogent. He's had like four strokes and three heart attacks. He always talks about how he should be dead, and he rarely sounds sober. There is none of that when I talk to him. He listens and responds like a normal person. Even as a very compassionate person.

Unconvinced that I'm willing to attach my name to an official "psychiatric patient" label and take pharmaceuticals, I run this prospect by Luca. He assures me that it is no big deal. "We're just people, Boo. Shit happens." He makes it sound so simple.

Without telling anyone, I schedule an appointment at the health center to get medications. And when I go to that appointment, I take a discreet route around campus so nobody will see me and question what I am doing. In the lobby, I again don't see anyone I recognize and am grateful to be called in to see my doctor before anything happens. The doctor, Pam Lewis, is a woman about ten years younger than my mother. She is a thin, gentle Iowan who begins our meeting with a few friendly questions, like "What do you study?" and "Where are you from?"

"I'm from Wilmette." I'm not actually from Wilmette. My parent's home is on the border of Winnetka and Wilmette, and Wilmette is slightly less upper class than Winnetka. It's safer to say Wilmette.

"I have a sister who lives in Wilmette. It's beautiful there," she affirms me.

"Yes, and it's beautiful here, too," I say.

She asks about my mood and how long I've been feeling off. I describe my depression to the best of my ability, how I haven't felt right and that I think I need help.

"These things happen, Ellen," she tells me. *Shit happens*. And yet it feels like purgatory. "We get into blue periods, and our brain ceases to produce a neurotransmitter called serotonin. What

I can do is prescribe a selective serotonin reuptake inhibitor to counter the chemical imbalance in your brain. This will bring you back to a place of stability. And if you like, I can help you find a psychiatrist or a therapist to speak to."

"I was against the idea of drugs at first, but now I don't care. I won't be on them forever, will I?" I say.

"No," she says. "You may not be on them long at all. They take a while to kick in. It may be about three to six weeks before you notice anything. At that time, you can check back with me and we can decide to stay with that or try something else."

"That sounds good," I say.

"Also, would you like me to recommend you to a psycho-therapist?" she asks.

"No, I don't think I'll have the time for it," I say.

As soon as I return to the dorm, I close my door and try to confront my newfound label: clinical depressive.

The next weeks pass mundanely. I ease up on the booze and partying, partly because my parents have scheduled a visit and I want to be in good shape when I see them. I continue to spend my downtime with Luca, fooling around in his bed, making fun of other people behind their backs, being made fun of.

The day of my parents' arrival comes. It is a tranquil, sunny Friday in late February. They check into their hotel and we plan to meet at the university church, a Jesuit mission upon which the school was founded. In the mission, I wander and study the art, and get a narcotic feeling like I had when I was a little girl. Evidently, I still feel something for Jesus. The mission is grand, solemn, and cold, like the churches my parents took me to in France, where the stone architecture makes you feel underground. In my religion class in the fall, I learned that Western faiths aspire for God by aspiring to something beyond life on the ground. That explains building cathedrals to the sky, composing extravagant symphonies, and painting complex, bombastic works of art. Eastern faiths invert this aspiration. God exists in silence, when you remove the noise that people make, not when you try to refine it. There is no yearning for a higher echelon. Sublimity exists in the absence of human obstruction, not through human will. That's what my teacher said, only in more eloquent terms.

I ponder in the part of the mission near the crucifix. Down the hall, across the great space of the church, the doors open and my parents enter. Dad is wearing a cotton, half-zipper sweater with ironed, creased khakis. Every part of his outfit is free of wrinkles, making him appear much more physically fit than he is. Mom stands up to his shoulders, holding a travel bag that's half her size over her shoulder. They look across the space look as sweet and honest as they'd ever been. I don't know why, but for some reason I feel ashamed or apprehensive. I walk across the church and hug them. Mom kisses me on the cheek, Dad squeezes me. I offer to show them around the church, and we walk and comment on the paintings. Dad has become a big patron of the Jesuit order in the last five years or so and is eager to see all of it. When we finish viewing the mission, I show them the campus. Mom is particularly taken. "It's beautiful," she says while kneeling into the flowers to touch them. A few girls from the dorm pass and greet us lightheartedly, and we say hello to them in return. We stop by my dorm room and run into Luca and Christian. As I drop my bags off, Mom nervously rearranges my books and clothes in my room.

We get lunch together in the student hall and talk about the family. Mom tells me about all of the colleges my younger cousins are thinking about attending and then talks about how Kevin is doing in high school. Though he's only a freshman, he's already thinking about Georgetown and Boston College, in addition to Notre Dame.

"He's only fifteen. He's thinking about college already?" I ask.

"There's nothing wrong with that," Mom responds. "Besides, if you called him, you'd have known."

"He was a little shit when I left him. It's no fault that I'm not calling him," I say.

"Oh, by the way," my father interjects, "Do you ever run into Rich Patterson's son out here?"

"I don't know who that is," I say.

"He used to be our Congressman until the Democrats gerry-mandered our district. Now we're represented by crazy, anti-rich Jan Schakowsky. Anyway, I'm pretty sure his son is a Junior or Senior here. He went to New Trier," Dad says.

"I don't think I know him," I say.

"That's too bad. His father's an honest guy. He comes by our office every now and then. He's one of those moderate Republicans who actually gets it," Dad says.

"Uh huh," I say, disinterested. It's like he's trying to control our minds with this stuff. Best to ignore it.

The table is quiet for a beat, save the murmuring of the student body in the background. I speak up. "So, I've been on drugs for about two weeks now."

My parents' attention snaps toward me. They are hanging on each word. I proceed, "And it's hard to tell if they're doing anything."

"The Doc says that they can take a while to kick in," Mom says.

"I know," I say.

"Do you talk to him at all?" she asks.

"I called him a couple of times. Haven't talked to him in a while, though," I say.

"And what does he tell you to do?" she asks.

"To keep busy and put my mind on other things," I say.

"Anything else?" she asks.

"No, our conversations don't last long," I say.

"What about school? Do you want to stay here? Have you given any thought to transferring?" Mom asks.

"I haven't, no," I say.

"I saw the dean of the business school at Notre Dame the other day," Dad says. "He said their doors are always open to you."

"That's nice of him," I say.

"I thought it was a good gesture," he says.

"Have you thought about transferring to the business school here?" Mom asks.

"I haven't," I say.

"Well it's very hard to transfer into, and your chances of getting in are better if you apply for transfer in freshman year than in sophomore year," she says. "And your grades are good enough that you can do it."

"I don't think I'm going to do that," I say.

"Regardless of what you decide, we understand that what you're going through is difficult, and again, we can't stress enough that we love you," Dad says.

"Thanks, I love you too," I say.

Later, for dinner, we got to a French restaurant called *The Left Bank* at a nearby shopping strip. My parents get a nice bottle of chardonnay and lie to the waitress, who doesn't check my ID, that I'm twenty-one. I pour a heavy glass—a "Mary Pour" we call it in my family, in honor of my mother's sister—and share a strip steak with Dad. They take me home afterward and I'm in bed and watching a movie by ten o'clock.

For the weekend, we have a day trip to Monterrey Bay planned. We get there in about two and a half to three hours, first by highway and then by winding roads in forests. We stop at Pebble Beach for lunch, and Dad regales us with famous moments in golf history. Neither Mom nor I give a damn, but Dad likes it a lot. My aunt sometimes jokes, "Your father is a golf whore," and then another corrects her, "No, he's a golf pimp."

After lunch, we go shopping in antique stores in Carmel. Mom identifies a wall piece that my grandmother would like and arranges for it to be shipped to Wilmette. At five o'clock, we have an early dinner at a small, quaint restaurant, this time with a $70 bottle of Sauvignon Blanc. I have two Mary Pours this time, and I quickly forget about everything. At dinner, Mom talks about her favorite movies. She has been taking adult French lessons at the local high school and has developed an affinity for foreign cinema. She is also in a book club with my aunts, and she and I talk about the literature we have been reading.

My parents drop me off at my dorm just before nine, and I fall asleep early. They come by campus one more time on Sunday morning to give me a strong, reassuring farewell and wish me well until I am home for break.

There are only three weeks left in the quarter when they leave, and I am in good standing in all of my classes. I have one written final and three in-person exams to prepare for. The written test is surprisingly small. I'm expected to hand in one seven-page paper, which I finish the week before it's due. The exams I take in person are in introductory-level courses — physics, calculus, and chemistry — and are spread evenly through finals week, with one on each day until the final day, Thursday. I spend little time studying for them, complete them without much stress, and am sure that my grades will be good.

All students are required to be out of the dorms by Friday, and when Thursday night comes, much of the dorm has already left for home. Those of us who remain gather in Luca's room, where we listen to music and drink vodka tonics with cherry grenadine. Katie pours mine with about three ounces of vodka too many into a Big Gulp cup, and goes, "oops," as she does so with a rascally, drunken smile. I don't complain about it. The alcohol stings, even through the tonic and the cherry, and I am quickly buzzed.

We talk shit and get loose with one another. Katie has a late flight to catch and is trying to get drunk before she goes on it. Carla agrees to drive and leaves along with Charlie and BJ. I stay in Luca's room, feeling pleased with the people I've chosen to be my friends.

As Luca cleans up his room, I linger in his bed and shuffle songs on his iPod. He is rubbing off empties and dishes, and, when finished, sits next to me and reclines. I'm now suddenly very close to his face. We roll onto one another and flip positions a couple of times, all in a groping dumb show. This whole exchange is wordless, like I've learned to communicate with him with my body. A new language, a superior language. When he does speak, he simply says, "Boo, have you ever?" I say *I have not.* "Would y—" *Yes.*

We unclothe what is left on one another. We unfurl the elastic as it crumples along my legs, and tug at it while it catches on the edge of my heels. I lay on my back. He kisses me from above, and I exhale and close my eyes.

At home during spring break, I read my grades to my parents: straight As again. They are proud and assume I am working very hard. I feel satisfied with it.

I spend most of my break time on the couch watching premium cable TV series in their entirety. Being on the quarter system, my spring break does not overlap with any high school friends, most of whom are on the semester system. When Mom and Dad's house bores me, I go to visit the Doc. He spends his days drinking watered-down Manhattans in his armchair. He's on the top floor of a condominium overlooking Lake Michigan. In the afternoon, the sun is on the other side of the building and his room is gray, along with the sky over the Lake out the window. The Manhattans sit on a small coffee table next to the chair, and by the time I see him, most of the ice has melted and the drink looks like a ginger ale. The Doc has respiratory issues and I can hear him wheezing. He's wearing a white undershirt and watching *Judge Judy*. He thinks little of women otherwise, but he respects those who can dispense shit on a level equal to or greater than the level he can give shit to them.

Mom insists the Doc has a lot of insight into what I am going through, but I don't have the nerve to bring it up when I'm with him in person. We've only talked briefly, always over the phone. I sit by his armchair in the office in his home. Judge Judy orders someone to pay a large sum for a scam he committed, and I remark, "Enjoy your freedom, chump."

The Doc replies, "Our freedom is in many ways an illusion. Nobody is really free, though we all have our own version of what that means. Or we have our own version of things that limit freedom. Within that, we have to choose our constraints: what is worth pushing against, what is worth giving our time to. Those are things that we can only know ourselves."

Had I asked him to speak to me from the psychiatric couch? What is with this sudden philosophical turn in the man who reared me on jokes about fecal matter?

"Those choices can provoke a lot of fear," he continues, "and that fear has a lot of power to disorient us. We can't always identify the full scale of what's acting around us at any moment, and we get mismatched and make some misguided choices. It's a rigged game. Then we fall into despondent thinking and have to re-learn the terms of that freedom all over again, although in a much more difficult setting. It's important to at least be able to identify this. You can't work something out if you aren't even able to speak to it."

I don't know how to respond. I'm tentative to respond to him forthrightly. Defensively, I laugh at him like a child. "Doc, you're crazy," I say.

"You're right," he says, disappointed, turning to the TV. "I'm crazy." I leave him on his own and talk to my grandmother, who is flipping through design magazines in the living room nearby. She asks me how school is and tells me how beautiful I have gotten.

At my parents' home, I am reading Richard Feynman's popular science writings, and some poetry, *Leaves of Grass*. After dinner, Mom and Dad watch television, and I approach the family room to see what they are doing.

"What are you up to, Boo?" Mom asks.

"Nothing. Just reading some of those Feynman books I was talking about at dinner," I say.

"That's great," Dad says.

"And? Are they interesting?" Mom asks.

"They're…" I start.

"Shhh," Dad says, pointing to the television. His program is about to start. I'm frustrated at this interruption—ignored again for nothing—and go upstairs to browse for new CDs on the internet.

By the weekend I am utterly listless, and back in depression. On the Saturday of my break, I wake in the afternoon after a thirteen-hour sleep and feel that there is absolutely nothing I want to do with my day. I make a small breakfast and eat it around the edges, leaving most of it cold and untouched by the time I am done. During the remaining hours of daylight, I plod around the house, lie on the floor with the lapdogs, and slap their little arms to get them to jump up and play. The dogs had been in trouble, and I want to protect them. Mom ordered a $20,000 rug from Tibetan monks, and it took them two years to create and deliver it. It's about thirty feet long and fifteen feet wide, and Mom rearranged the entire living room around it. When the rearrangement was finished and the carpet was put into place, within one day the dogs pissed on it. It infuriated Mom, but privately I smirked. It was a rebellion that I could only dream of. Mom spent two drudging hours spraying and scrubbing the rug to prevent the stains from sinking in permanently.

Mom's family comes over for dinner, and by the time I'm standing up again and ready to leave the room, they are all having cocktails and chardonnay in the living room. The Doc and Grandma are both there, sitting on my mother's furnishings with their walking accommodations beside them.

My aunts greet me kindly. "Boo! So nice to see you!" I'm wearing jeans and a red sweater. "You look very 'college' right now," my Aunt Vicky says.

"Thank you," I say.

My Aunt Joan walks in with a red cup of white wine. "Boo, my dear! How are you!" She kisses me on the cheek. "So, tell me, what are you studying? Finance?"

"No, physics," I say.

"Uh huh…" Joan replies with a soft eye roll.

"You shouldn't major in anything that doesn't get you a job," the Doc says from his seat. "Look at Harry. He majored in sociology. What the hell can you do with that?"

"They always end up in marketing or economics, anyway," Joan continues as she walks over to join the rest of the party. "Eventually they understand reality."

"With Obama in office, there won't be any jobs when she graduates," my Dad adds. "He's going to tax them all into extinction."

"I'll be fine," I say, though the statement scares me.

My Uncle Harry plays piano, and Kevin jokes with the Doc about sex and other off-color humor. My aunts recap events at the local parish and refill their wine.

Mom calls us into the kitchen to fill our plates. She is serving chili with chips. Grandma and the Doc are at opposite heads of the dining room table. When I sit, Aunt Mary is still talking to Dad about Obama. "He doesn't know what he's doing with the economy. I don't trust him. Boo's whole generation is screwed." The rest of the table agrees. Mary says again, "You need to let things be. They'll take care of themselves."

I reach for the nearby bottle of chardonnay on the table and fill my cup.

"So, Boo, do you have a boyfriend?" Aunt Joan asks, probingly.

"I do not," I say.

"What's wrong with you? Why don't you have a boyfriend?" she says, jokingly.

"I can't deal with you people," I say.

Mom redirects the conversation to my brother. "So, Kevin, how's school?"

"It's okay," Kevin says, shrugging. "My teacher flipped out in class the other day."

"How's that?" Mom asks.

"Well, before, some of the girls in my class were talking about the money they make babysitting, and they were loud about it, and I think it was more than my teacher makes. He went off on this whole tirade about economic privilege and called the girls spoiled brats. I think he's going to have to have a meeting with the school's administration because of it," Kevin says.

"Oh my," Joan says.

"There are not enough manners in this world," my father says. "And so much of success is just treating people with the courtesy they'd like to have in their lives."

Kevin continues, "And then later in the week, he pulled out a knife, put it to his wrist, and threatened to cut himself. And this one girl was like, 'Do it, you coward.' He didn't, but it became this whole thing and I think he will probably end up getting fired."

"Oh, that's uncomfortable," Vicky says.

I try to ignore them. Dad starts complaining about politics and recent administrative changes at Notre Dame. I try to ignore him too by feeding scraps to the dogs underneath the table. Then, from the other end of the table, the Doc asks, "Boo, are you getting laid?"

Half of my aunts laugh. The other half reprimands him.

"Doc, that's incredibly creepy!" Mom says.

"It's important for kids to get laid," the Doc says. "I didn't get laid in college, and I was a nervous wreck."

"Yes, that's right," Mary says.

My Uncle Harry looks at me. "You know, Boo, you're getting pretty hot. You could probably get any guy you wanted."

"Alright, enough!" my father says.

Mary laughs. "You know, when Jimmy toured Europe for the cheese business, the Doc gave him a fanny pack full of condoms."

"And I'll bet he used them," the Doc says.

"Not if he was wearing a fanny pack, he didn't," Vicky says.

Dad grumbles and leaves the room to watch golf on TV.

"Boo," the Doc says, "you date whoever you want to. In the long term, it is best to marry somebody from your own neighborhood. Before that, date anybody you want. Just not any Jewish boys."

"Doc, we don't say things like that!" Mom chides him.

"I heard Boo is dating a black guy," Kevin giggles. "It's a classic good-girl-gone-bad situation."

"Who, the boy we met in the hall of your dorm?" Mom asks.

"Luca?" I say. "He's not black. He's Salvadoran. Adopted into an Italian family."

"And you're not dating him?" Mary asks.

"Well, no," I say.

"'Well, no,' or 'no, no'?" Vicky clarifies.

"No as in no," I say, getting anxious and upset with them.

"That's not what Tina says," Vicky says.

"Tina got her details wrong. I've talked about him in conversation, but not in that way. I'm not dating him," I say.

"Uh huh," Joan laughs.

"Alright," I say. "I'm going to leave, too."

There is no point in sharing any of this with them. I could see a boy for thirty minutes and they'd ask me about him for thirty days. If I told them about the people I met in my life, I'd end up having to write an epilogue to complete nobodies and reciting it for them each time I see them. So, I avoid the conversation completely, except for when my gossiping cousins tell them about my life for me. I empty my plate in the kitchen sink and refill my cup of wine. I go upstairs to call Luca, and we laugh about the ordeal at the dinner table. "Oh, they were talking about my sex life, and my grandpa and brother had these racist comments about who I should date, and my dad spent the whole time complaining about Obama! Luca, I need to get back to campus! It's so much more down to earth there, oh my God!" I say.

He is quiet on the other end.

"Are you there?" I ask, befuddled.

"Yeah, I'm here," he says. I hear some clicking and programming on the other end like he's on his computer or a television is on in the background.

"Oh, I thought you couldn't hear me," I say, my excitement now diminished.

"Yeah, sorry, I'm looking at something else," he says. He sounds clearly disinterested.

"Oh, okay," I say. "Well, I just thought I'd share. How are you doing? How is your break?"

"I'm all right. You know, I'm just hanging out." A long silence from him follows. All I hear is the television laugh track through the phone connection.

"Are you looking forward to getting back to school?" I ask.

"Um, yeah. I think so," he says.

"Yeah, me too," I say.

"Look, I've got to go. Is that all right?" he says.

"Yeah... sure," I say.

"I'll see you," he says.

"Ok."

Then he hangs up.

For spring quarter, the campus has transformed into a paradise. It is far warmer and more luxuriant than when I was here last. Student life is all outdoors, and the lawns are full of people tanning and playing sports. All look as attractive as models. It is like God did not banish Adam and Eve from the Garden of Eden but merely moved Eden to Northern California.

I lighten up in my view toward the world. Life is too good right here to waste it being depressed. Whatever orderliness I have for maintaining a strong academic standing, I relieve to try and be happy. A high school friend calls it the "fuck it" philosophy, and I think any child bred east of the Mississippi should indulge in this while she is young and has the chance in California.

The college experience feels fresh and more radical, full of idle creativity and possibility. I imagine this is how a lot of people in my parents' generation experienced the 1960s and the 1970s. I don't feel depressed anymore, though I cannot discern if this is due to sunshine and a good party or Zoloft.

Luca ignores me when he sees me. I handle this as rationally as I can. It feels a bit like being abandoned each time I walk by him or sit in the same room with him, and he acts like he has no idea who I am. He hasn't given me more than a "hello" since spring break has ended. The more I see him, the more that pain of loss weakens, and the more I view him as a laughable, wrongheaded boy.

After a silent, lonely childhood, I had gotten my first glimpse of realizing myself in another person. I had no longer dreaded my situation. No longer did I harbor and self-recriminations. And that chance at a freer life swiftly foreclosed and turned my image of myself into a nasty smear again. I had come to him with such excitement and he returned to me with nothing. All of this was for what? The petulant mood swings of a do-nothing college boy?

It is a small campus, and I learn that there are not many places I can go to within my friend group in the dorms without running into him or someone who asks about him. I think everyone else has the same issue. You're always next to somebody to who you've exposed yourself to. It's kind of like incest.

I try to get away from the building and develop a social life in other parts of the campus, and fall in with the social justice group, full of many of the campuses' weirdos, bleeding hearts, and dreamers. I turn to Maggie, that silly, approachable senior from the volunteer drives. We had a long, goofy talk about finding community on campus and being involved in student groups, and she encouraged me to check out her organization. She lives on Dark Side in a home named Scum House. I go there in the afternoon when I have nothing to do and want to get away from the crowd and the dorms. Generally, the people there sit on the porch, smoke weed, listen to folk-rock, and play guitar.

I walk to Scum House in the middle of the week and find a bunch of stoned guys watching *2001: A Space Odyssey* in the living room. I come in during the opening scene where the monkeys find the big black stone and start worshipping it. Everyone in the room has their eyes fixated on the film. I walk past them and knock on Maggie's door. She screams and opens her arms for me, and then suggests we go onto the porch for a smoke. She brings a little set of speakers and shuffles through a playlist while she lights a spliff, and in the meantime, I explain some of my issues with my future on campus.

"I wouldn't worry too much about not having your major picked out right now," she tells me as she exhales and passes the spliff. "You're doing fine. If I could offer any advice, I'd say find an awesome group of people and spend your time with them. Don't get too caught up in what other people are thinking or doing, or what they expect you to be studying. And remember, there are only two sides to this campus: Dark Side and Evil Side."

"Evil Side?" I ask as I cough and pass the spliff back to her.
"You know it as Light Side. I call it Evil Side," she explains.
"Why?" I ask.

"The drugs, the partying, the super-rich LA kids, the pettiness of some of the stuff you run into. It's a warp. I've seen many a good person lose their way out there. Better just to find your people, settle into a dope porch to hang out on when it's nice out, and a weird-ass living room to hang in when it's not," she says.

My phone is buzzing in my bag. I reach into it and check. It is Luca. I'm conflicted. He ignores me and I'm smart enough to know I shouldn't care, but I can't deny that I feel some excitement over seeing his name appear. It is an uncertain excitement, and I'm hoping for a warm resolution but expecting disappointment. I don't answer but get a text moments later.

can I talk to you?

sure, where?

Ignatius quad?

K

I explain to Maggie, "I've got to go, but I'll probably be back later."

She has lit another spliff for herself. "Alright, Booboo, Live long and prosper," she says.

Maggie's house is about half a mile beyond campus. I am stoned, the sun glares in my eyes, and I walk dispassionately to the lawn. I enter from a dull side of campus and hear the palm leaves bristling against one another and the wind drifting across my ears as I walk. I am slightly anxious about the meeting, but I am not thinking about it too seriously, nor with much regard for Luca.

He is sitting on a verdant lawn by a statue of St. Ignatius, from which water falls into a round pond. I approach him unenthusiastically with shiftless stoner eyes and sit down in front of him.

"Hey," I say.

"Boo," he exhales, and lowers his head, "I'm sorry. I've been an asshole, and it's wrong. I should be talking to you. I said I didn't want to be serious, but then it kind of was, and then I feared that I got in too far, and that you were more into it than I was, and that I was leading you along when I knew I was noncommittal. I froze up and didn't know what to say, and it's been cowardly. It hasn't been fair. I think it's best if we're just friends."

He seems sincere but also pathetic. I don't want to fight with him but his explanation seems acceptable enough. I'm looking at him and nodding, sitting on the lawn with my legs crossed. "Okay," I say.

"Okay?" he asks.

"Yeah, okay," I say.

He looks perplexed. "Do you feel all right?"

"Yeah."

"I don't really know what else to say…"

I shrug, look away from him, rub my hand through the grass. He looks awkward and scratches the back of his head. Other students shout at the opposite end of the lawn.

"No, I understand. You did the right thing, Luca," I say, "I have to get along now. I have things to do."

"Okay. Maybe I'll see you around?" he says.

"Yeah, maybe," I say.

I leave him to go to the social justice office, where I read on a worn-out couch and do my homework, still stoned and talking freely and somewhat flirtatiously with some of the upperclassmen in the room. I'm not thinking about responsibility, just being young and insouciant.

In the hours in between hanging out, going to class, and doing schoolwork, when I am alone and have nothing to do, the pessimism of the winter comes back in all of its strength. I think years ahead into the future and envision it all collapsing. I'm a fuckup and an outcast, estranged from the mainstream and estranged from respect. It inhibits my ability to sit and write a paper. In this time, when I must work through a dizzying obsession with forthcoming deprivation, I stare at the computer for hours. My work is stagnant. I cannot cope.

This happens for a writing and composition class, with the same professor I had in the fall, Townley, the one who talked about the projects in Chicago. I get stonewalled at a deadline on a film review for the movie *Five Easy Pieces*. At 2:00 A.M. the night before the paper is due, I have written only half of a page, needing seven in total. After that, I give up and go to bed, then skip class. I don't tell the professor, and two days later I drop the course. When I call home, Dad says, "You've had a rough go of it, and you've done very well for yourself so far. I'm all right with you taking a lighter load while you find your bearings."

The next week, I see my peer-editor from that writing course, a brainy boy with a ruffled haircut. "When you stopped coming to class, Townley gave the class a message about the importance of showing up and toughing it out," he tells me. I feel some guilt over this, but readily leave the conversation for less confrontational destinations.

With only three-quarters of a full class schedule, I embrace leisure. I sleep more, and I socialize more. I still cry sometimes, but it is less pitiful and less common than before. I run into Luca, and it irritates me. A couple of times, we had these melodramatic conversations late at night. He slurs his words and says that he's reconsidering things, and then I tell him that he broke my heart. Then he says that he was just never sure what he wanted, and I say that I think he is arrogant. Then we have the same exchange over again, only louder and dumber.

After one of those fights, in the early morning, I walk to his room to talk about it soberly, with some misguided hope of redeeming something with him. I'm in bed with him and resting my hand on his chest. Since being intimate before Spring Break, we haven't had any physical contact at all. He laughs in my face, and I walk out on him immediately, fantasizing, for a moment, of strangling him. I understand that any further consideration of him is a waste of time. I go to see Katie and remove him from my thoughts.

In the afternoons, I read outside and tan, and make my way through a checklist of classic literature. I thought that was what college was for, anyway. I become wonderfully Zen at times, or at least appear so. A friend comments, "I wish I had your life, Boo."

"Don't worry, college is just a racket," I joke.

"Not for you, apparently," she says.

The quarter passes. I do well in the three classes I have and enjoy long nights out in backyards with my friends about four or five nights per week. My friendship with Luca stabilizes a bit. I get on better terms with him. He picks up learning the guitar and starts doing Dylan covers outside on the dormitory quad when he is drunk. As a friendly gesture, I give him a Dylan songbook for beginners that I once had for my own guitar purposes, and offer it to him with the quip, "On the internet, it says that Dylan said that college is a lot like an old folk's home, only he knows more people who have died in college."

"That sounds like something you'd believe," he replies.

He embraces the whole wannabe getup. The harmonica rack, the folk repertoire, the affected stories about picking up songs from bars in Western states. He's halfway decent at it. Kind of good, actually. His fingers move quickly, and he whines and rasps over his picking while perched on the steps outside the dormitory, but only with alcoholic confidence. He is not self-assured enough to use his voice otherwise. Some girls from the dorm sit around him in a quintessential college manner, and he sings,

Go lightly from the ledge, babe. Go lightly on the ground,
You say you're looking for someone to pick you up each time you fall,

To gather flowers constantly, and to come each time you call,
A lover for your life, and nothing mooooooooooore. . .

He holds it for too long.

But it ain't me, babe. NAW, NAW, NAW,
It ain't me, babe, It ain't me you're looking for.

He blows into the harmonica and hoarse, unmusical air comes out the other side. I am not outside but can hear him from the open window of my room as I do schoolwork. I even sing in a whimper, "*No, no, no. . ,*" as he sings. I step outside to watch him play. He shifts his capo along the guitar neck and mutters to himself. "G? No, A? No. . ."

Jeremy shouts from the balcony above, "Play the fucking song, Luca! Stop apologizing, you pussy!"

"Oh, fuck it," Luca says, and starts plucking at his guitar. He pulls the strings so hard that they clap against the woodwork just after the release. Otherwise, the music is both rustic and elegant; just the right amount of unprettiness, just the right amateur touch. He heaves through the harmonica and plays broken, soft arpeggios, then settles into a single chord. He belts in his ordinary, untrained voice,

If you're traveling in the North Country Fair
Where the winds hit heavy on the borderline. . .

I laugh. It is my favorite song.

The remaining days of spring are, for lack of a better phrase, a blur and a shitshow. I awake each morning for 8:00 A.M. classes and sit through lectures on the Carolingian Dynasty in a half-sleep. By noon, my other class is complete. There are only nine lecture hours per week, leaving 159 hours for the rest of the week for whatever I like. Thinking occupies much of that time, which is dangerous. Reading takes a lot, which pulls me toward fantasy and mental sauntering. I nap too much and exercise too little. I go up to Katie's room and together we watch old SNL skits. There is a party every night, usually involving a keg in a backyard on Light Side. We're all becoming more comfortable with ourselves, more confident in our place on campus.

Weed becomes more and more common, too. It's almost like currency, as a social transaction, or an invite to the table. Katie is hanging out a lot with this guy Darren, a sophomore who lives in a dumpy ranch house a few blocks off campus. In our afternoons, we go to his house, where there's always music and somebody is always playing beer pong or beer die on his lawn. We are always offered a smoke when we arrive. I settle into musty armchairs with a light sweat on my body, accept a bowl when it comes to me, press my thumb over the hole and watch the leaves char and glow under my nose. It burns the back of my throat, and I chug two bottles of water to feel comfortable again. Afterward, I am bloated, dazed, queasy, cashed. Life happens around me like a stop-motion scene. I am slow, they are fast, and every word is babble. I go to bed more than once convinced that I am going to die.

When the toxins clear, during last week on campus, I sit in depression after one of these nights and fixate on all of my dumb decisions. I impulsively call in Luca to ask him to talk. He comes. I cry lightly and hiccup over my words.

He shakes his head and puts his hand on my shoulder. "Boo, you're just so lost. You've got to talk to someone who isn't me to talk about these things."

"You once said that I was a beautiful human being, Luca," I sob. "Is that true?"

"You're a beautiful human being, Boo. Now come on. Get up."

On the last night of the year, a group of us goes to Santa

Cruz for a bonfire by the ocean. Luca plays much of *Bringing it all Back Home* on his Taylor guitar. On our way back, we stop at an In-N-Out Burger, and while we wait for our food, I cringe and shake my head. Nobody pays attention except for Luca, who watches from the end of the table. He also cringes. When we walk through the parking lot after dinner, I walk behind the rest of the pack, and he falls back. "I'll level with you," I confide to him, "I get the feeling that there's nothing for me here," and look out towards the highway. "Nothing," I say.

I go home for the summer, and Mom and Dad are glad to have me there. They are very excited about my academic standing. A straight-A student. how remarkable. I get the impression that they think everything is alright, and that I'm fast-tracking toward the life they always dreamt their kids would have. "We were at dinner with a professor from Northwestern's business school last night," Mom said over dinner once. "And he says he loves students who don't come from a business background. Something like physics really appeals to them on an application."

"Nice," I said. They seemed so proud. I felt like telling them that I didn't care would be like telling a child that Santa Claus doesn't exist.

Dad set me up with an internship for the summer. My parents put a lot of money into a Jesuit school in a neighborhood on the southwest side of Chicago. I started as a volunteer teacher's aide, but was soon upgraded to teach a small class of six teenagers. Dad lent me his car for the summer, too. Every morning I drive through Pilsen at 6:00 A.M. in a silver Mercedes. The kids are great, but it's interesting to be on the opposite side of the class. They take the upper hand on me a lot, mostly by switching between Spanish and English when they talk to one another, testing the limits of what they can say in class. I am only three years older than them and we mostly banter as equals. Occasionally, I have to demand more respect from them, but I know they are good kids. They do all of the work that they're supposed to and do well on the tests. I cannot complain about whatever else they choose to do with themselves.

I take an online course through my university to make up for the writing course that I dropped in the spring. The professor coordinates everything through an online message board, and I write a paragraph or two per day for class participation. The hours of depression are still there. They start to stray out of reality altogether. I stay inside and isolate myself in my room. Time is at a standstill. I have no appetite and have to force myself to eat. The food sits on my plate. I space out at the kitchen table for forty minutes at a time and glance at the scattered, inky sections of the newspapers, or Mom's stack of homemaking and interior design books. They are all titled, "The Homes of Paris," or something comparably classy.

In heavier moments, the bleakness covers me like sap on a tree. It's beyond psychological. It's total: physical, spiritual, mental, suggesting a ghost state in human form. I try to avoid it, but it looms all around me. There is no escape, and I cannot confront it without feeling that I am totally lying about it all. I question whether or not the people in my life actually care for me, or if they merely tolerate me for dumb reasons. I am sure they would be better off if I left and never came back. Everything I think about comes back to indict me in some form.

A therapy exercise on the internet challenges me to look in the mirror and say that I am a worthwhile, capable person. I cannot do it. It cuts into me, and I turn away from the mirror in short-tempered fits. I look at my reflection, call it a disgrace, and tell it to go fuck itself.

I go into the family room on the second floor of my parents' house and try to be calm. My mind quakes, the room gets wobbly, and my equilibrium gives out. My face is warm from the power of the dread, I obsess that I have been doing everything about my life awfully, and my sight nearly turns black. I lie on the couch and breathe carefully. The dogs come to the side of the couch and beg, and then turn violent, show their teeth, and leap at me. I recoil in defense, but nothing comes. The dogs are still there, begging and panting. I think I may have hallucinated, but I do not know.

I pour a large glass of water, drink it, and roll into bed. I feel a little more soothed now. The sheets are cooled, tightly folded, and adorned in an asymmetrical mound of pillows. I skip dinner with the family and rest in my room, staring mindlessly into the corners of it until the sun sets. When I get up, I go downstairs to the kitchen and gather a ragtag meal of leftovers and snacks from the pantry. My parents are drinking wine and watching police and medical shows on TV. Kevin is at the beach with his friends, presumably getting stoned.

I make a cup of tea and flip through the entertainment section of the Chicago Tribune. Periodically, Mom or Dad gets up to pour themselves another glass of wine. Mom wraps the bottom of her wine glass in a large square of a paper towel and drops pieces of ice into the gold chardonnay, which crackle and snap when they fall into the liquid. A little tipsy, she rubs me on the back and asks how I am doing. I give her a short answer, "Fine." I'd always wanted to live in a place that feels less isolated, with actual neighbors and people to spend evenings with who acknowledge one another. And yet when I do get that chance, I feel like it's already been closed off. By television. By my own expectations.

A bit later, Mom turns off the news and hands the controller to Dad. She empties the rest of her wine into the sink, pours a large glass of ice water, and from her purse on the counter, takes a fistful of Advil. She tells me, "Good night, Boo. I love you," and walks upstairs.

I say, "I love you" back.

Dad is passed out on the armchair, snoring with his head bent over the top of the chair. A golf program is now on the television, and half of a glass of wine is on the table beside him. The dogs are sleeping on the couch. I go upstairs to fall asleep to music.

In August, my work in summer school ends. My students do well and offer me a bottle of Patrón as a parting gift. I am honored. I've spent a lot of my summer nights drinking with high school friends. My parents have a second garage in their backyard, and we bring thirty-racks and speakers outside and play drinking games and chain smoke.

One afternoon, the Doc invites me to dinner at his country club. He does this with all of his grandchildren. It is how he bides his time. It is his only recreation aside from dinner with my aunts and uncles. If he isn't doing that, he's watching daytime television or burdening Grandma.

I meet him at his place by Lake Michigan. It is a beautiful home with a pool and hanging plants where I spent all of my childhood summers. I cannot step into it without nostalgia. The Doc's pool was my haven. The family band played here every weekend. The Doc and Uncle Harry would sit under the cabana by the pool with their instruments for entire afternoons. Doc played an old, thin, nylon guitar, and Uncle Harry played a banjo. They'd sing Hank Williams and old, three-chord folk songs. They still play, sometimes. The Doc's fingers press frailly on the guitar neck, and he cannot put enough pressure on the guitar to play a complete chord. He tries to strum the guitar, and the music is stubbed by a debilitated finger or flat strings. It sounds clunky and broken.

That doesn't stop him from singing. *Hey, Good Looking* or *Danny Boy*. While he and Harry play, my aunts flip through fashion magazines and drink inexpensive chardonnay, or talk about people around the town, just like they did when I was a kid. The kids would splash in the pool and run around the property, which is closed to the street by a six-foot brick wall with thin vines, alongside a tennis court of dark clay. My cousins and I played games on that court barefoot. My boy cousins, who were often shirtless, outnumbered the girls by about three-to-one, and all had a weird machismo about them. They were all short and scraggly but tried to be tough. It was amusing to watch.

The Doc still practices psychiatry out of an office in his home, with a window that overlooks the shallow-end of his pool, just above the pots of flowers and prickly bushes. I don't know who would still consult him. He's out of his mind himself, and Grandma says that he falls asleep during his sessions. His patients must be really desperate. In his office, he has multiple pictures of Napoleon and a dozen shelves of miniature figurines of French, English, and African soldiers from the eighteenth, nineteenth, and twentieth centuries.

When my cousins and I were younger, we would come to the end of the pool by his window and call for him, and he'd throw candy into the pool. Around two or three in the afternoon, he would take a break from work and come outside to be with the family, wearing clean white pants and clean white shoes and a yellow or pastel shirt. He would tell loose jokes and give his daughters parenting advice, whether they wanted it or not.

Even a decade ago, I remember him swimming laps in the pool with those goggles that fit like suction cups around his eyes. But now he's only a shade of that, physically and mentally. He's sour and insulting toward Grandma. He's angry at God, and always saying things that everyone regrets hearing. He wants to die and lets everyone know.

Though he's been a lifelong psychiatrist, I can't think of any time he said anything about mental illness growing up. If anything, he would make fun of people's insecurities and personal problems behind their backs. Since he saw so many people, he knew about everyone's issues. He'd point out our neighbors in public and tell me that they were batshit crazy. And I realized this summer that this is where I got all of my ideas about "being crazy" from. It was always the butt of a joke or a horror story. Earlier in the summer, I pulled out a journal from grade school that my teacher had me keep. It was from 6 grade, shortly after 9/11, and I wrote a sorry paragraph about why crazy people do things to innocent people. It had a childish doodle of a stick figure with tormented zigzags and a cartoon gun.

I think more about the Doc's patients, too. He had them around the pool from time to time, and gave them simple work. Housekeeping stuff. Custodial work. One of them, Greg, still works for him. The Doc pays him to do yard work around the property. Greg trims the branches, waters the flowers, and rakes the leaves. I always thought Greg was gentle and childlike, like an idiot, though my parents said he wasn't always that way. He came from a family of surgeons, and most of them went to Ivy League schools. They said he was a smart, normal guy before "developing issues." They never said what that meant, really. They said he mishandled them, lost it in the mind, and became what he is today.

He came from a big North Shore family like me, and his nieces and nephews were in my grade. At school, I would tell them that I saw Greg over the weekend, and they went blank-faced when I mentioned him. It's like they didn't even know he was a part of their family, or didn't want to know.

The other ex-patient who came around was named Frank Lato. The Doc never actually hired him for anything, but he stepped into the pool once or twice per summer. He was homeless, I think, and always came onto the property unannounced, with a backpack and a scruffy tan. He looked like he'd been walking along the highway for miles. My parents warned us about him, too. Like Greg, he was at the top of his class before "developing issues" and then losing it as an adult. He went to Yale and dated Brooke Shields, they said, but he "didn't take care of himself." And now he was someone else.

Frank's voice was always hoarse and weathered like he had either been shouting or smoking all night. My aunts welcomed him when he showed up, but they seemed edgy about it. They protectively smiled at him, like you do to a creepy older guy who does not stop giving you attention at the table. Frank did all of the talking, and he talked very fast, jumping from point to point. It was nonsense half of the time, and he could not control his volume. Most of the time he talked normally, but every few sentences he'd shout something. And he had a bunch of wild ideas about starting companies and designing amusement parks. And he complained about police waking him up when he was sleeping in parks, or moving him to another part of town, or arresting him.

I wait outside the Doc's front door; a large, heavy door with a presumptuous bronze handle. That's how Dad describes it, anyway. A lot of the house is like that. Grandma is an interior designer and decorated the house with naked cherub statues, romantic ornamentations, paintings of Roman bathhouses, creaking antiques, and dangling glass chandeliers. Today, for some reason, the Doc is flying an Irish flag instead of a French or American flag.

The door opens and the old man walks out.

"Bonjour, Booboo. Como ca va?" he asks.

"Ca va, bien, mon cheri. And how are you?" I ask.

"Terrible," he says.

He has given me credit for speaking French for years, even though I don't actually speak French. I took it in elementary school and would practice it with him when he came over for dinner. I knew enough to respond to, "ca va," as I was taught. And he always said he was terrible.

The country club is one block away from his home. He walks slowly, with a cane, but with prestige and a distinguished old man smell. I put my forearm out so he can hold it and stay balanced, and we walk together to the country club. The road to our side is built with cherry cobblestone, and it protrudes in the middle, like an arch. Cars pass, and their tires rattle against the edges of the bricks.

We arrive at the club. A doorman—an old black man—walks across the lawn of the club to help the Doc get up the stairs to the outdoor patio. The Doc makes a joke to the doorman that I can't fully hear, and the doorman laughs brightly. When we sit down, the doorman walks away, and the Doc says, "I don't know where your aunts and uncles get the idea that I don't care for black people. I get along great with black people."

The Doc orders a Manhattan. In his skeletal condition, the alcohol must hit him easily. A breeze comes from the lake. The salty air from a freshwater lake runs up my nose and soothes the side of my face.

"So, who have you seen while you've been home?" the Doc asks.

"Just the family and some kids from high school. I saw the Frances boy the other day," I say.

"Daniel?"

"Yes, Timmy and Bobby's friend who was always around the pool growing up."

"Is he doing all right?"

"He's okay. He started off college in Dayton, but now he's transferring to Loyola-Chicago."

"Why is that?"

"It didn't work out for him. He doesn't know what he wants. He's figuring it out."

"You see it all of the time. Party as a kid, problems as an adult. The parents never like to admit it, even as the kid becomes a fuckup right before their eyes. They always think there's something special about him, something exceptional, but ninety-nine percent of the time, there isn't," the Doc says.

The server quietly sets Doc's Manhattan on the table. He nods, she disappears. We talk about my schoolwork. I say I am studying science, and he asks if I am considering medical school. I say no. He nods. I drift off and ask for some of his Manhattan. He grins and passes it across the table to me. My stomach is empty, and the whiskey hits me immediately. I pay more attention to the breeze and the smell of the lake, and while I do so, the Doc goes off on some existential point about a person's purpose in life. I only half-listen and figure this is a good time to ask something that has been occupying my mind.

"Doc, how do you cure depression and anxiety?"

"Die," he says.

"What's the next best option?" I ask.

"Work."

I nod. The Manhattan starts to hit the Doc. I must have brought up a tender point. He cries and turns his head aside and complains about his life. He says, "I've had three heart attacks and four strokes. By all accounts, I should be dead." I sit and listen uncomfortably. He continues, "My mother used to get emotional in her old age, and we would laugh at her and treat her like she was crazy. I feel terrible about it because my kids are doing it to me now. I speak my mind, and they tell me that I'm crazy. I feel terrible. All of my friends are dead, and I should have gone with them. I don't want to be the last one living. The joie de vivre is gone." He cries harder, and I steal more of his Manhattan.

"Your mother," he says, "was the sweetest girl I had. I adored her. And she had cancer as a baby."

I spit his drink. "Cancer?" I ask.

"She had melanoma," he says. "And she had to be operated on. Your grandmother and I were up all night. It devastated us. She wasn't even supposed to have children, and yet here you are."

"What are you talking about?" I ask.

"You didn't know? Oh, never mind. I'm losing it. Don't let

me bother you. They weren't going to have children. They were trying for years. And then in vitro came along, and that's how you were born. You thought you were the favorite because you were the oldest, but it isn't that simple. You were the favorite because they thought you would never happen," he said.

We finish lunch and pay the check. I walk him home and return to my parents' house. Mom is preparing hot water for tea while I get home. She asks if I want any, and I decline.

"How was the Doc?" she asks.

"Good," I say.

"Good."

I look at the mail that Mom has sorted out for me on the kitchen counter. Her tea kettle howls, and she fills the cup she has set aside for herself.

A zap comes into my brain. I abruptly stopped taking my Zoloft a week earlier and learned on the internet that I was having a withdrawal symptom called brain zaps. It comes frequently and feels like an electric hiccup of the spine. I see it as a final episode before I put all of that freshman year moodiness behind me.

After Mom fills her cup of tea, she passes by me on her way to the living room and asks, discreetly, "By the way, how is your mood?"

"It's been good, Mom," I say.

"Good," she says. She leaves. I spend the rest of the afternoon sleeping and then browsing the public library for films. In the evening, we host the Doc, Grandma, and Uncle Harry for dinner. My Mom's siblings had started splitting up the nights to host them for dinner once it got harder for them to make it themselves. When their car arrives, Mom tells me to go outside and help the Doc get in the house. He grabs my arm and wobbles, and I stabilize him until he gets to his seat inside. He is not weeping anymore.

"Boo, do you remember what I said to you this afternoon?" he asks.

"Sure," I say.
"Forget every word of it," he says.
"All right, Doc. I will," I say.

CHAPTER 3

January 2016

I began the new year with a jittery hangover. The seasonal bonhomie of Christmas and being out of work soon gave way to a desolate January characterized by sub-freezing weather, icy pavement, and a colorless sky. To add the appropriate emotion to this setting, Mark left, which sucked every worthwhile feeling out of me. He had his doubts about his work, thought the geographical distance was too great to sustain without forgetting me, et cetera, et cetera. Honestly, I foreshadowed it happening but chose to ignore it. Our relationship was a bit adolescent, but it was the only one I'd ever had. Then it came, and there I was: dumb and born anew in the frozen, uncaring world, slighted and disregarded, and yet somehow younger for it too.

Mark wasn't strong enough for it. The little prick even said that he wouldn't be talking to me again because that was not something he was used to doing. "Well, fuck you then, right?" I laughed at him, thinking he'd see the same humor I did. He didn't. The whole scene of him leaving me unraveled that way. We were in my parents' kitchen while they were in Florida for a few weeks, and he declined a hookup after watching a movie because he had "something to say." I sat on the edge of the marble island, dangling my feet and feeling an old spirit fly out of my back, like I'd taken a Xanax.

"Oh Mark, you know we'll be alright, yes?"

He stood away from me, eyes watery and mouth agape like he'd been cheap-shotted, and said, "I didn't expect it to be like *this*." What is it that compels men to act like they're the ones being dumped when they leave? How can so many of them be both the one who departs and the one who assumes the part of the sad sack?

He said he was going to take a cab home, and I said, "Nonsense, I'll drive you." Very timidly, almost with no voice at all, he said, "Okay," and then pulled his phone out of his jacket, like a stranger trying to avoid chatter in public. I walked upstairs to gather my clothes and holiday gifts, shoved them into a bag, and scurried out of the house with him following behind me. In that brief interim the sun went down and darkness fell on the North Shore. He sat in my passenger seat and didn't say anything while I drove, first over cement roads, and then over the old cobblestone avenues of Wilmette. A thin fog hung in the air all around. In the driveway of his parents' house, I reached over to him, holding his arm and wiping my eyes in his jacket. He quickly peeled away from me, exiting through the passenger door, crossed in front of my car, and walked through a gate beyond the range of my headlights in the fog. I drove away. On the way out, a whiny British singer crooned about his broken heart on the radio, and I wanted to strangle him.

Back to ground zero: alone, serious, depressed, loveless. *Love, what a farce.* That was my mundane American odyssey, from Mark to someone else, to someone else, all the while withstanding the preposterousness of my world with my cloying, sentimental attachment to the phrase *true love waits*. Or, the attachment to the notion that love even exists. Maybe it would arrive at The End. Maybe after I took a blade through a room of suitors to find my one and only; or, more likely, it would come after years of compromising on my ideals, after countless nights of light beer pitchers at dives and making *and* receiving ill-fated passes with cringe-worthy lines, I would find my home in someone else. Nearing age thirty, I hoped to find someone comfortable going to bed with the same television programs I liked, and who shared the same idea of an easy living arrangement. I was sure that could have been Mark Mitchell, that lanky ass. Then I was sure it would never be anybody.

Fare thee well on the West Coast, sir. For the time being, I would try to make myself a bludgeon against Chicago's legacy of racism and create a testament to Mad Pride and justice for the crazies, whatever that may look like. Till he or someone like him returned, I'd spend my nights self-medicating with a glass of red wine, with a little 20-Century music to take the edge off.

I was oddly resilient in the days afterward. Like Effexor, which I still took daily despite its numbing, angst-inducing side effects, my life happenings had a delayed-release impact. The true pummel of the breakup or someone's death did not come until much later, when a new reality had become apparent and the old way could never be retrieved. I knew it would catch up to me soon, leaving a void in my evenings and an apparition in the space next to me in my bed. On one of the nights after the breakup, I turned in my sleep and body-slammed onto the mattress; at that moment on the way down, I thought he was going to be there.

I sent him no recrimination. In a way, I was more confident afterward than I was before, having been relieved from the limbo of a relationship doomed for impermanence and from his ambiguity toward me as a partner. I was never that disciplined in the past. No, not at all. In college, those were my most pathetic moments. I'd get smashed and make things markedly worse, such as in the great blackout after Doc's stroke, my final rite into perdition after that damned bender. Or during any number of events in which I'd drink into the early morning and send a woozy text which I'd regret the second I awoke the next day. Evidently, I'd grown up since then. Now all I wanted to do was clean, exercise, eat nutritiously, and keep busy so as not to think about . . . him.

When the pain did come, there was something genuine about it that was distinct from my usual stupor of psychiatric drugs and 21-Century dysthymia. This was real pain that happened for a real reason, more like my adolescent depression, always drunk and heartbroken, like the disillusioned expatriates of Hemingway. In public, I'd brush up against a man who smelled of the same detergent Mark used, or who had a spray of his Dior cologne, and then I'd remember everything about him. It made me feel alive, pardon the cliché—a feeling I had denied myself for most of my adulthood. When I felt a pang throughout my day, I reverted to old habits — browsing through cell phone pictures, listening to Joni, and, God forbid, praying at night.

Once I conceded to all of that mawkishness, a bigger collapse ensued. I hadn't talked to him in weeks, and the silence overcame me. I wanted to speak to him, and I was negotiating against all of these inconsequential rules I had picked up about when it was and was not appropriate to talk to one's ex; one of many pitiful, contractual neuroses attached to dating in the U.S.A. In a desperate moment, toward the end of my night, I wrote to him. *Mark, I've certainly had a nasty feeling since we last spoke, but if this is necessary for you to flourish in what you want to do, I think I will find comfort in that. Have a safe flight out on Wednesday, and a strong start to your next chapter in Seattle. I will talk to you sometime soon.* I wanted to reveal a lot more than that, but decided it would reflect poorly on me. In nights of pitying self-indulgence, I had gone through old writing I sent to him when I thought that contact was being broken off.

Dear Mark,

I am a fool to do to myself what I do to myself sometimes. A depressive's hangover is a walk of tension and anxiety, with poor memories and lousy ideas about oneself charging toward the front of the mind, taking up far more thought than they deserve, constantly at odds with the details of the day. At most moments, I'm liable to clamp up, grimace, mutter to myself, and exhale, *and then **move on, already** a moment later, since that's what you have to do. "Drink wine and you shall hate the world." I forgot where I learned that from, but I understand this, again. At least hangover passes.*

My teacher was telling me the other day about how she explained drugs to her children. Did I tell you this yesterday? I texted it to somebody. Everything has a spirit, and you must honor its spirit. I dishonored the spirits on Friday. Back to the usual routine of study, solitude, and sobriety.

I don't actually feel that miserable all of the time. Just when I have work, impending obligations, and little time for rest. So, let me rephrase. I do feel miserable all of the time but poetically.

Enough about me. How are you? I was thinking about your Christmas gift, the one I'm getting for you. Nothing is final, but I have big plans. A tour of the Riviera, darling. We can quit for the summer and catch the first ship out from New York harbor. My friend from the exchange can put us out in a villa for a few weeks, and beyond that, we can train to damn near anywhere we want to go. It really would be a nice time, it really would...

I'll leave you to yourself right now. As soon as my birthday finishes, I understand that the year is truly ending. The last sprints are coming up, holidays, and cold, and preparation for life indoors. This season will become apparent very quickly, which you can credit to one of the following phenomena: season-specific emotion, tradition, and mass marketing.

Warmth and affection, my dear.
Ellen

The days after were long and uneventful. I found more time to go to the gym. Every night I jogged alone, set goals for repetitions on the machines, and quit before meeting the numbers. At home, I cooked more, occasionally for hours at a time. It elevated me, reminding me of how my mother would be soothed with gardening at home on Saturday mornings and afternoons in the summertime. I let the steam pile up in the kitchen while I listened to Ana Thorvaldsdottir or some other composer who would unnerve other people's ears if they even knew that composers existed. I ate alone, usually leaving half of my meals uneaten, before falling into motionless, abject contemplation.

I did more schoolwork in public, at restaurants and coffee shops, where I'd drink tea and hope to develop new connections. Those were so difficult to come by in the city. The pop music in these places was bland and soporific. It frustrated my work, distracted me. Invariably my hopes of meeting new people were futile. The closest I ever came to conversation was when others made eye contact with me, vaguely and indirectly, for a second too long. I never actually spoke to anyone.

I started going to Andersonville bars more often. I would go with a book and nurse a pint at a bar. Occasionally, tweedy young men would initiate conversation, pontificate about craft beer, or make a wise comment about the book I was reading, and I'd brush them off and get back to reading. Then I'd go home through the gray of Clark Street, with a paranoiac's suspicion of other pedestrians, pinched in the straightjacket of my winter clothing.

It all came and went, these passing faces and dull hours, time dragging on in a malaise. I'd go to Jude's to do drudge work, which I understood as a pointless, disrespectful grind. Barring any other organization to develop my voice, I was glad simply to take part in her efforts. Jude lived on the Northwest side in Hermosa, and it took me over an hour to get to her apartment by public transit, taking the red line to the Fullerton bus and then the Fullerton bus west. On the commute, I'd read books by psychoanalysts, understanding almost none of it. They heavily referenced Lacan, a thinker I knew nothing about. The text discussed the relationship between infant trauma and adult psychosis. I never understood how anyone could hypothesize so much about the inner lives of infants and promote obtuse theories about Oedipus and toddlers.

I exited the bus several blocks from Jude's small, unclean apartment. My feet crunched softly as faded Velcro against the thin layer of snow on the sidewalk. Jude was a poor woman in economic terms, a rich woman in receiving the admiration of others, and an unfortunate one in health. She shared my condition — stark-raving madness or some form of it — though it held a much stronger grasp on her than it did on me. Be it for lack of environment or supports, she was interminably caught in a much deeper part of the shit than I was ever in.

Seven years before, I'd have never foreseen myself in this setting, obsessed with issues that I'd then had no awareness of. For reasons I was still piecing together, most of my peers from that time landed in big firms and went to New York on the weekends to see college friends. I, on the other hand, landed in the morass of local politics in Chicago, alongside people who were then invisible from the North Shore by the sheer facts of class segregation and psychiatric disability. This was not a complaint — I was glad to have found Jude. Before her, I'd spent years looking for any type of political consciousness and activity about mental illness to engage in, and I found virtually nothing. My madness had never taken me to the part of the mental health system that had a community. I had rich kid's therapy in discreet offices in non-medical buildings with transcranial magnetic stimulation. I never met the other clients, the more authentic psychiatric patients.

I found Jude on a happenstance encounter at a rally in Logan Square for a South Side organization called the Mental Health Movement. She invited me to dinner and told me about her work. "The mental health system is fundamentally flawed," she said in the dimly lit restaurant. "One of the reasons it is so flawed is because the people who have the most at stake are the most removed from the decision-making process. My whole life exists to give those people a seat at the table." The front of her t-shirt read, "I'm One of *Those* People," while the back read, "Nothing About Us, Without Us." Over dinner and drinks, I agreed to be her intern and assistant. I would accompany her to policy and advocacy meetings for service providers and other advocates. Jude was usually the sole person of lived experience in the room. She dominated the conversation at the table and made it all about the point of view of the people who experienced the mental health system as recipients.

Jude had been involved in the earlier psychiatric survivor's movement, a scarcely known social movement of the 1960s and 1970s that never fully entered the narratives of American history in the way feminism, civil rights, or gay liberation did. When Judi Chamberlin, one of the foremost luminaries of that movement, passed away, Jude reinvented the history of her namesake to make it in honor of Chamberlin. Over time, Jude and the psychiatric survivor's movement split ways. She thought it was insular, toxic, and impotent. Eventually, they came for her. She was scorned and excommunicated from their ranks, and condemned as a "capitulator" and a "mentally ill mascot" for choosing to work alongside the people those survivors deemed enemies—providers, psychiatrists, police, and parents. She was told that it is impossible to change the system from within, only in nastier terms. So, she quit and went on her own.

Her work of late consisted of applying for a federal grant to organize a statewide consumer network of people with mental illness. She had once successfully organized a network of 500 consumers throughout Illinois. Afterward, however, she became unwell again, and the whole thing fell apart. That is evidently how a lot of ex-patient groups went: rising with the mania, falling with the depression. When I came into Jude's work, she said she had been getting out of bed for the first time in two years and was trying to create an organization again.

I held on to that observation and was thinking about it as I approached Jude's apartment. The lock in her lobby was broken, so I didn't need a key to open the door into the building. Jude's mail and her copy of the *New York Times* were on the lobby ground. Her physical disability, ankylosing spondylitis, made it impossible for her to retrieve anything from the floor without a grabber, so I gathered her mail for her.

Jude's apartment was dusty. It was a bit before noon, and the place looked the same as I'd left it the evening before: disheveled, roach-infested, and in urgent need of cleaning services. Jude was in the shower, and I sat in her office space at the front of the unit and read research articles on recovery. In her tight living space, she had a desk or a table along every wall. In the desk, her drawers contained file cabinets with papers dated fifteen years back, and underneath the tables, she had boxes of fliers and forms from years of meetings. She had assigned me to organize these files, and that was my work during the days at Jude's organization. It generally went nowhere, as most of these files should have been disposed of. I only stuck around to get Jude's insight and to get access to the meetings she went to and didn't care at all for any of the work that Jude had me do, which frankly existed more to satisfy Jude's compulsions than anything else.

I had to print material for one of my graduate school lectures in the evening. There was a single sheet of paper in the tray of the printer. I knew I shouldn't look at it—Jude was always printing personal statements, and it felt invasive for me to read them—but I did it anyway. At the top of the sheet, Jude wrote "Daily Agenda," with a few small tasks designated between the hours of eight and four. Underneath that she wrote, "I am not going to kill myself today, so I may as well try to make the world a better place."

As I was reading, Jude entered the room, slowly, hunching, and said, "Ah, you're late."

I wasn't, but I didn't object. "How are you today, Jude?"

"Eh, mixed, but thanks for asking. How are you?"

"I'm all right, Jude."

She grimaced as she sat into her desk chair, and put C-Span on the radio. The pundits on the station were talking about Donald Trump, and I instantly put my headphones on and started to organize Jude's boxes of crap. While I was supposed to categorize each paper in the box, most of the material I was sifting through was extraneous, such as action alerts, agendas, notes of meeting minutes, PowerPoint slides, and advertisements. I really didn't know why she didn't throw them away immediately, but then there was a lot about Jude's behavior that I did not understand and would only make sense to me much, much later.

I took a break in her bathroom. It, too, was disgusting. The white tiling on the floor was outlined with yellow stains and what appeared to be feces. Since Jude could not clean herself, again I had to do this work, scrubbing hidden waste out of the crannies of her home. There were prescription bottles aligned alongside the sink for various conditions, which I left unexamined. While I sat for a break, I fell into a lull. Jude's apartment always had that impact on me. The drudgery of organizing those boxes overbore my zest for living, and as always happens when my future is cut off, I retreated into myself. I lost consciousness and drifted into a surreal afternoon fog, dreaming in a collage of images from the past: Lake Michigan in autumn on the North Shore, Northern California in springtime, my parents' manor on a foreboding evening. I awoke when Jude asked me if I would like to go to lunch with her, and I gladly accepted.

We walked slowly toward a local diner two blocks away.

Jude's gait was stiff and slow, and I had to walk at about half of my natural stride to be with her. I spent the walk thinking about the past and said something to myself along the way. Jude heard me and asked, "What?"

"Nothing," I said, and kept walking.

The diner was a wholesome venue in which I could see the grill behind the counter and the food was served on red ridged trays with paper napkins. It was owned by a first-generation family from Greece who Jude liked to banter with about sports and politics. The TV on the corner played basketball highlights, and the talking heads on the sports program were arguing about the career of Derrick Rose and his flawed knees, as fatal as Achilles' heel. I entertained for a second the idea of an athlete having three psychotic breaks, and wondered how he might be spoken about, or if he would even be spoken about at all.

Our order was called to the counter, and Jude and I picked up our trays. The floor was lightly dusted, like the auditorium halls of an elementary school. I slid as I walked. Jude's feet scuffed harder, as if she was barely getting off the ground. All of her years of pain, both mental and physical, made her movement hunched and laborious. Though she was only a year or two older than my parents, she seemed a generation older, and a decade closer to dying.

I still didn't know much about her background. She worked as a lawyer, her spouse left, and everything collapsed from there. She fell into profound manic-depression, stopped seeing her clients, lost her job and then her home. She spent three years in a nursing home—"where every aspect of my life was controlled by someone else," she insisted— and spent two years in a homeless shelter thereafter. While homeless, Jude attended municipal meetings on homelessness policy where she was greeted with statements like, "Homeless people are like wild animals: you have to train them before you let them into your home."

Outraged, Jude demanded a place at the table and was told that homeless people weren't allowed to take part in homelessness policy. "Prove it," Jude demanded. "Show me in the charter where it says homeless people cannot be involved in deciding policy around the homeless." Since there was no such statement in the charter, they let her at the table, where she rebelled and agitated everyone present until they made more seats available for homeless people. That formed the basis of her work from then on: to be at the table where decisions are made.

Years later, she expanded the mission of her work from homelessness to include systems of mental health, substance abuse, and criminal justice. I also got glimpses into a broader life within that: a second marriage and subsequent divorce, broken relationships, and strife within local politics.

Jude—or Judith Adina Friedman—grew up in Lakeview on Chicago's North Side, and then moved to Skokie as a youth in the mid-1960s. Her father was a handyman, her mother was an elementary school teacher and a disciplinarian at home, and her older sister was a budding dissident in an era of ferment. Jude always had depressive episodes as a child. At age eleven she attempted suicide for the first time by taking 500 pills of Aspirin. It left her with a ringing in her ear for weeks, and when her mother took her to the hospital, she received no psych evaluation. Then, on an innocuous day after school, while Jude was biding her time at home, her mother ordered her to come on an errand with her and then dropped young Jude off at a psychiatrist's office. Her mother left immediately, and Jude spent an hour in silence with a doctor who then prescribed her Stelazine.

The drugs did little for her. She remained sleepless and miserable and regularly passed out during school. Her teachers told her she looked so sad that she was about to cry. At home, she fought with her parents. After high school, she followed her sister Amira in a move to Virginia. She enrolled in college but became psychotic before the end of the first semester, again she attempted suicide. Her school kicked her out, and Amira admitted her to Dejarnette State Sanitarium in Staunton. Incidentally, Dejarnette was a site where sterilizations were administered until the late twentieth century.

In the hospital, Jude received a diagnosis of undifferentiated schizophrenia and lived the second-class life of a patient. "Much like the nursing homes, they controlled everything about me, only more so," she said. She was allowed weekend passes, which she says were spent "drinking and fucking" in Charlottesville, and then coming back to the hospital, where the staff again had all of the power.

Jude kept hospital records posted on her apartment wall. The doctor's notes changed from "paranoid, compulsive liar, makes up stories about being bullied by her father," to "Sister Amira visited, confirmed stories about father are true."

When she was released in the 1970s, she came back to Chicago. She stopped identifying as Judith Adina and went simply by Jude. In the hospital, a friend had told her that Jude was the Catholic Saint of lost causes, and in her depression, she took that as a suitable nickname. She dropped "Adina," because it meant "gentle," and there was nothing gentle about her. She also changed the spelling of her last name from "Friedman" to "Freedman" not long after leaving the hospital.

In Chicago, she completed her undergraduate schooling and entered law school at the Illinois Institute of Technology, where she met her future husband and divorcee. The divorce came decades later after another suicide attempt cost the couple $20,000 that they could not pay in medical bills, and he decided he couldn't remain married to a woman like this. The split instigated her period of homelessness, nursing homes, and patient advocacy. After years of antipsychotic use, Jude had put on weight and developed secondary medical problems, which ossified her body and kept her in chronic physical pain. Mentally, she never improved either.

Where others may have found harm in this, I found comfort, as though we were members of the same exiled tribe who found one another after the diaspora. In the diner, we sat, ate, and talked about mental health activism around the city, specifically about a recent proposal to privatize mental healthcare in the city's remaining public clinics. Jude started talking, continuing in the middle of a conversation we had been having at the apartment. There was some debate about the value of private services versus public services, and I tried to improvise my position at the moment. "What we've tried to do is move closer to an idea of mental illness where people who need to use the system are mostly just like anyone else and should live independently and make decisions for themselves. Yet the whole system is premised on other people making decisions for us. Even our supposed allies don't want a system on our terms. When I go to meetings with the Mental Health Movement, a union representative is always there. And since the union is all city employees, of course, they oppose privatization and the Mayor's agenda. In reality, unions have no skin in the game beyond getting jobs for themselves. When there was a consent decree to get people with disabilities out of nursing homes, the unions opposed it, because getting people out of nursing homes meant that they would lose jobs. Barack Obama was a state senator at the time. We met with him and asked him to support the consent decree, and he told us he had to side with the unions for that reason. The unions have no desire to make the system better. If it came between saving their jobs and getting people out of nursing homes, they'd take the jobs every time. It doesn't have anything to do with improving the quality of services. In all of our little policy debates—do we have public services, do we have private services, what do we do about jails and the police? — the important question isn't being asked. And that is, *why aren't people getting better?"*

Both Jude and I wanted to "change the mental health system." Perhaps I wanted revolutionary fervor — it was obscene to me that mental illness continued in a context of silence and neglect, and I couldn't see any way out but through a great social movement. But I didn't have an answer. I lived in a dire landscape for this dream, and Jude was the only person I could talk with about it. Jude probably thought this too, but was more jaundiced. If anything, she wanted an excuse to get up in the morning. Jude continued to talk as I lost attention, stretched my foot into circles under the table, and people-watched in the back corners of the restaurant. When I listened to her again, she was saying, "I want a bigger scope of the problem of the mental health system. Perturbing things are happening at the state level. In the twenty years that I have been at this, the state has cut funding from mental health every year. Between 2009 and 2012, the state cut over $150 million from community mental health services. Because there are other issues with our politics — issues about spending too much and owing too much and taking in too little — we have a businessman for a governor who views it as his duty to control spending and make the state a good business partner. His way of doing this is to slash services even more and let the state bleed out until his opponents start to compromise with him. There are over 500,000 people with serious mental illness in the State of Illinois, and the state only purchases services for 100,000. They have no idea what happens to everyone else. And why is it a good thing that these 100,000 people are using services? Why isn't it a bad thing? Why do people see therapists for twenty years? I don't care if they see a therapist for twenty years, but if they're seeing a therapist that long, it means they're not getting better. Why do my friends who get diagnosed with schizophrenia see a psychiatrist thirty years ago, not take any meds, and get better? While I'm stuck here? And look at you. You got better, and in a year or two you'll have a job and be a part of the middle class."

"What makes you think I've gotten better?" I replied.

"Because you can work and I cannot," Jude said.

"Being able to work does not mean I feel life is worth living or not," I said. "Just yesterday I was talking to a man who said that every day after his job at JP Morgan, he walked by the Chicago River and thought about jumping in. Obviously, he is not well, though anyone who would look at him would think he is doing fantastically. People too often assume I'm well because of my youth or because of the money I come from. And on the other side, if I'm not well, it's because I fail to appreciate something about my blessings. Bullshit. That's not how this works. You think I'm well, but I'm not. I'm healthy only in illusion."

"I'm sorry, Boo," Jude said.

"I had something of a manic episode not too long ago, no, only two nights ago," I said. "My nerves were pulsating out of my skin, begging to be harmed, and my mind was being dragged toward the inferno. At that time, I had the delusion that I'd be in that state forever. I didn't sleep, I haven't been sleeping since, and I've felt incapacitated and agitated ever since. And when I do sleep, the first thing I think about when I wake is wanting to cut myself, very neatly, and very efficiently, in a four-inch line parallel to my veins."

I breathed spastically, jerked my shoulder around in a nervous gesture trying to quell my propensity to prattle, and rapidly tapped my fork against my plate.

"Are you alright? I fear I've triggered something," Jude asked.

"I'm as alright as I'll be. It's fine," I said. "You've done nothing. It's fine. It's not you, it's been like this long before you. Just last night I was eating Ramen noodles for dinner. I didn't want to eat anything, but it was the most I felt up for doing without feeling I would immediately vomit whatever I swallowed. As I was eating, I had a ball of noodles curled around my fork, and I was holding it just above my bowl and staring at it, wondering which is better: to eat it, or to find some means to kill myself."

"I'm sorry again, Boo. I didn't know you were so suicidal," Jude said.

"*Suicidal,* ha," I said. "I don't know what constitutes being suicidal. I used to run cross-country when I was in high school. I'd be so miserable during the races that I would fantasize about stepping in a hole and breaking my ankle so I wouldn't have to do any more running and absolve myself of the pain. The anguish is always there. It's always on the mind but never put in the plan. And I'm always debating it! If suicide is truly the central question of philosophy, then by now I'm Hannah Arendt."

"So, how do you resolve this when this happens to you?" Jude said.

"I ate the noodles, put on Astral Weeks, dimmed the lights, laid down, and looked at my ceiling for the next hour," I said. "Then I decided to live, yet again, but the hope I felt after that was short-lived. An hour later I was raging against myself, against virtually everyone I've ever known, and against those who had ever left me, and that in my isolation I felt I wanted back. It was fierce anger. I need to find a better way to cope. That's how the whole world will come burning down, by acting on what people feel when things get dark."

This was the first time I'd shown that to Jude. After five seconds of silence, I burst out laughing.

"What on earth is so funny?" Jude asked, grimacing.

"I have a morbid sense of humor," I said. "I laugh at the prospect of my suicide far too easily. I laugh at all of my misfortunes; my ineptitude, my misery, my isolation, the emotionally abusive relationships of my past, the utter mediocrity in which I live, and to which I disproportionately contribute. It's prime comedy."

"I didn't know you found our misfortune so funny," Jude said.

"You do, too," I said. "Remember earlier when we were watching Steve Jobs give the commencement speech at Stanford? He was talking about living life to the fullest, or some other platitude for grads, and he said, 'Nobody wants to die,' and we both laughed at him because we knew how untrue it was.'"

"Yes," Jude said. "And then he said that when you wake in the morning, you should look in the mirror and ask yourself if you would be happy with what you are doing if this was the last day of your life."

"That's right," I said.

"So, do you think about that in the morning?" Jude asked.

"I don't."

"Do you think there's something fundamentally different about us and him?"

"In terms of our minds?" I asked.

"Yes," she said.

"I don't know. I was never anything but a sad, melancholic child, yet that's been exacerbated and mitigated by environment. And maybe it always was environment. Misery is the rich child's handicap. Maybe it's not possible to be content in the world with it being what it is and me being who I am."

"Do you think it's more in the body or more in the world?" Jude asked.

"You're very Socratic," I said and Jude laughed. "I don't think it has to be either/or. I don't have a sophisticated understanding of suffering. They tell you it's mainly in the brain, but that's a matter of conjecture. Depression, mania, and schizophrenia do not exist in states of nature, and cannot be physically identified as body pathologies. At least not yet. I'd say it's more about environment. About culture, politics, structures, ideas, and ways of life and how we engage with and against them. How it induces fear, harm, and safety in myriad combinations. Our body enables suffering by predisposing us to it, but the root lies not in the body. It's in the world. Or in the interaction between the two, like how two people could have very bad, ugly sex together, and should not do it again, but do anyway. I could be content in the right setting. It just happens that the right setting does not exist in reality."

"Why you and not everyone else? They're people too, but they do not call themselves mentally ill," Jude said.

"I don't know how they manage. They don't tell me. They would never let on that they're unwell. I, on the other hand, have no choice but to tell. I've gotten in too deep not to call myself crazy and disabled." By now I was poking my straw through a cup of ice, slouching over the table, letting my head drop to the side.

"You don't talk about it with them?" Jude asked.

"Why would I? It's the damnedest thing. I confided to some-one close to me about my suffering, and she asked me if there was a drug for it. I'm already in the crosshairs of drugs, I don't want to complicate it further! Seroquel at night, Effexor in the morning, withdrawals if I miss a dose. I loathe having to start and finish each day on these drugs. They make me feel incomplete, dependent, and controlled. And when I said that to her, she didn't even acknowledge me. She treated me like I wasn't there. Just as it was when I was down and out. No, I don't talk to others, because it makes me irate. I'm afraid of what they'll do to me, especially when I'm mad. All I really need is acknowledgment and understanding, and it just doesn't come to you when you're mad. I swear, people remain insane for years just because they never get even a basic level of recognition."

"There's no place where you're content?" Jude asked. She seemed unmoved, unemotive, lacking in any body language or gesture aside from her inflexible misery.

"I was content with Mark, I suppose."

"You suppose?"

"Well, I liked him."

"What did you like about him?"

"I liked that he was kind and modest. And he listened and was caring, and I'd never had that before. He grew up where I grew up, in the same high school class and everything. Only we didn't know one another then. It made our worlds very similar, and I was comfortable with him for that. But there were things he didn't understand that are very important to understand. His emotional range doesn't go to places that mine does, lucky him. He's not enough of a hell-raiser to live with someone like me. Had he not left, I think it would have ended in a different way eventually."

We sat in silence. "I said I loved him quite a bit, but I don't know if that's the truth or if I was just starved for connection." I crumpled my napkin, threw it on my plate, then rubbed my hand up and down the side of my head, generating a lot of friction. I was breathing heavier and suggested to Jude that we go for a walk to clear our minds. She agreed.

Outside it was bleak. The exhaust from cars along Fullerton Avenue drifted toward the sidewalk and the open air smelled of exhaust. I, tall, thin, limbs clenched for warmth, and Jude, short, robust, pressing her wide arms into my side as she wobbled.

"What makes you uneasy with the world?" Jude asked.

"Is that a serious question?" I said.

"It is."

"I don't know, Jude. These questions are very difficult because it's so aggravating to come up with a coherent response, but I'll try. I was never well to begin with, but now when I despair, it's deeper. I get apocalyptically scared. It's been true for a long time that most of the dollars made in our world go to a very small amount of people, and that most of the dollars controlled by the state go either to paying for past wars or preparing for future ones. A great amount of what's left of that goes to locking people away or punishing them by other means. I don't see this carrying on without some dreadful, dystopian uprising, either internally from the far right, or externally from a terrorist faction born out of our mistakes. I'm scared of the bomb. I'm scared of environmental destruction. I'm scared of epidemics. I'm scared simply to meet new people. I don't like looking into the future, Jude. I can't see anything there. I think we're headed for something terrible. That's what makes me uneasy. As a result, I'm pushed inside myself and live with all of my errors and disappointments instead."

"It's not the end of the world, Boo," Jude said.

"I know. Oh, what am I saying? No, I don't. It might be the end of the world. It's in the realm of possibility, in many different ways."

"Focus on more concrete things."

"You've confused me, Jude," I said. "You've asked big questions and I don't have concrete answers. I think too much and read too much. I've lost my sense of wonder. When I was younger, I didn't know how deeply everything went, how people felt and how individuals fit into the world, and how they couldn't seem to communicate it. There was something very exciting about being on the surface of a discovery, wondering what it was all about. But now that sense of wonder is lost. I've learned too much. I don't see it as poetic. It's just sad, hard, and painful."

"Why do you do it? What do you want the mental health system to look like?" Jude asked.

"I don't know," I improvised. "I can't disentangle it from everything else. Environment, poverty, social roles. The system is in the business of treating symptoms. What we need is a revolution. Replace the stigma of handcuffs and the peril of the emergency room with a place to be quiet and accepted. Nowadays what happens is you'll get admitted to a wing, the x-y-z of all of those things happens to you, the doctor will come by for five minutes and check on you, and give you a diagnosis based on his observation, and the questions are worthless. The most important question asked is when the person who has been there before comes to you and asks, '*Why are you here?*' How do we get more of that? Historically, we understand the need for liberty in mental health care. For us to be free, we would also need positive conditions of respect, support, consideration, and, dare I say, love. A lot of that isn't even about a publicly or privately funded mental health system. It's a matter of culture and of seeing one another as human beings. Or it has to do with a broader mental health system that concerns housing, health care, and having an income that can meet a pleasant standard of living. That part of the broader mental health system has been left not only unresolved but openly under attack for decades. The end goal of integrating us into a public, open, social whole is still very much a matter of a dormant social movement, and that's what I aspire for. I want to expand the, '*Why are you here?*' question from the peer on the psych ward to the entirety of the world. I want a cultural, social, and political revolution to unfold, with the question of suicide and human flourishing at the center of it. Which, incidentally, is something that often the crazy people feel most acutely."

"You say you want a revolution?" Jude asked.

"I don't mean it literally. More so rhetorically—as a tactic and a rallying point. I'm probably not that radical at heart," I said. "Revolution is a watered-down term. I read this phrase from my peers all of the time: *revolutionary act.* They trivialize the concept to the point where I have no idea what a revolution even is. People sometimes say that disclosing personal details that others don't want to hear—such as about suicide, or sleeping with another woman—is a revolutionary act. They're correct, in a way, and I'm being callous when I dismiss it. But I have a hard time seeing the revolution in sexual moaning when bombs are dropping and banks are foreclosing homes. My queer orgasm was a breakthrough the first time, but after that, it's just an orgasm, full stop. *The personal is political, bah.* The personal is masturbation. We are constantly dividing things into distinctions of cultural nonsense at the expense of realizing a unified cause. Granted, class distinctions matter a great deal when the Titanic is sailing normally, but in the era of the iceberg, they mean nothing at all. It's an all-of-us or none-of-us scenario. As for that little word, "revolution," I don't want to associate too heavily with it. Only fools take it seriously. And serious people who take it too literally will eventually become fools. The few people I see in this world are thoughtful, and treat me without judgment, and that's nurturing. When I step outside of that, I often feel asphyxiated, and it makes my pain worse. I don't get through that life without alcohol."

"You're not making any sense to me, Boo. I don't understand. What are you getting at?"

It was true—I wasn't. But this is what happened when we talked. We'd set a mission of *fundamentally changing the mental health system,* setting goals for ourselves at nothing short of *revolution,* yet what were we able to accomplish as two miserable, disturbed people complaining about the system? Our work did not amount to much. We didn't produce anything and were barely able to sustain a not-for-profit advocacy organization. We would go to political meetings, call ourselves the mentally ill representatives in the room, and give voice to everything we complained about. But that's all we had the power to do: hold the conversation in gridlock before the managers of the system took it any further. Outside of that time, all we did was rant and hypothesize amongst ourselves. Jude would pressure me to come up with solutions, I'd struggle to do so, then I'd get agitated and a bit manic and we'd end far from the point we started at. This time, she provoked me into a rant on capitalism and socialism, on the narcissism of millennials, the callousness of boomers, and the "great lovelessness of it all." A strong breeze came onto us and Jude coughed. I leaned into her and rubbed her back, and hugged her, laying my head on her shoulder for warmth.

"I'm sorry, Boo, I've agitated you. You're too jaded. You need to hang out with smarter people," Jude said.

"It's the reality of the matter, Jude. It's loveless, and it's hard. I'll try to resist and build a community around madness, but there's a chance that it won't work. So far, you're the only person I know who identifies with it openly. There's a chance it will end up alone and painful, just as it started. If I'm being realistic, that will be the case. And then what? Ground zero. Suicidal depression all over again."

"No, you cannot kill yourself," Jude said.

"Hypocrite, Jude," I said.

"I have a reason for wanting to die. My life is horrible," she said.

"And I repeat—for years, people have thought that being young and well-off is some sort of palliative for madness. For years, people have thought I have been well," I said.

"But you're functioning. I, on the other hand, can't do anything when I'm unwell, and I'm unwell all of the time. My sole reason to live is to create something that will change the mental health system. Without that, I have no reason to continue. Since you're my legacy, you're not allowed to go," she said. We blathered on like that, rolling the ball up the hill, then tumbling back into nonsense and despair.

When we arrived back at Jude's apartment, we planned our schedule for the remaining meetings of the week, and I left shortly after to have some quiet before my class that evening.

The lecture, unlike Jude's apartment, was at least somewhat stimulating. We had talked about mental illness as a social construct, hypothesizing it as a concept pieced together through observations rather than through testing. Another student was outraged and said that mental illness was real because that's how she experienced it. We devolved into a tense discussion about the topics.

"Of course, the experiences we call delusions, hallucinations, and depression are real," the professor explained. "We don't challenge their existence. We challenge how we understand them. That's where the concept of mental illness comes under fire."

The student was reluctant to concede to this, however. "I've been there," she said, "and there's got to be something chemically wrong for me to be that way. There is a strong biological component to all of this. I need my drugs." I was sitting in the seat next to her and tried to console her, but her body was much too tense, her face too trembling, like something wretched was claiming the best of her and she was on the cusp of a breakdown. I told her it was as though she was pulling the words from my journal from three years ago. I didn't have the nerve to tell her that I later rejected that line of thinking for myself entirely.

After the lecture, while walking to the train on State Street, I saw a distraught adolescent complaining to her friends. "I just can't do it. I don't give a shit about white people. I'm over it," she said. Her friends leaned against the rails, and everyone on the sidewalk walked by her, even as she wildly threw her limbs and her body all over the middle of the pavement. I'd encountered these expressions in literature, and very often in media, but rarely in person. The fact of segregation meant that I had little to no contact with this exasperation, and I quickly began ruminating on the multidimensional nature of the structure — how it manifested itself in the mind and the heart, as well as in the home, the neighborhood, and the wallet.

I recalled a night in high school when my cousin Tina was dating a graduate student at Northwestern named Kamil, the only black man anyone in my family had ever dated. They took me to see a play in Edgewater. It was about love in the time of miscegenation laws, and I had coincidentally been reading *Romeo and Juliet* for my British Literature course. They let me hang out and smoke with them afterward, and I had asked them what they thought of the play. The weed made them relaxed and open, and Kamil left out a stream-of-consciousness unlike and anything I'd heard before and wouldn't hear again for a long time.

He leaned onto the edge of the couch, with a beer to compliment himself. "You know, honestly, I wouldn't want to be white. When you're white, nobody tells you when you're wrong, at least not in the ways that I'm told to check myself. You can go years being laughably incorrect and nobody tells you anything. Nobody tells you what's in your blind spot. They teach you that you don't have blind spots. It's an identity of self-deception. If you want to go through life thinking people get what they deserve and the world is fair, you can do that. If you want to go through life thinking that you're capable of extraordinary talent even as all signs point to your ordinariness, you can do that. If you want news and history that suits your biases, it's all over the place. You can hold it up, call it the arrogant truth, and elect leaders around it. I don't see that as a fulfilling life, and that's why I don't want it. It's complacent and insecure at best. I can't imagine how it would feel to be so distant from your fellow humans and have this vague fear surrounding your view of their existence. I wouldn't want to be on the other side of the line, no matter how big the house or how enormous the fortune.

"But then, the terror film of American history almost always goes the other way around, does it not? I don't know what you grew up learning, but I know that my grandparents said they couldn't own a home beyond Cottage Grove Avenue unless they wanted to see it and their children burned down. And their grandparents told stories about people they knew on plantations. Two degrees of historical separation.

"The fear on the other side is indulgent, navel-gazing, and insular. They also have the leisure not address it and can go years without doing so. Each year we get further in time away from slavery and Jim Crow, and each year white people think they've reached a standard of racial fairness that their ancestors didn't have, as though rising above proud slave-owners and segregationists were the benchmarks for reaching a state of full humanity.

"White Supremacy is how this house was built, and that's how its structure remains. I love you and you love me, and we don't let any of that have power over us. What they ought to be asking is what they are doing for racial justice now? But their home is too comfortable for asking.

"And please, don't tell your family that I say this. Between us and them, there's no upside to it. It won't accomplish anything, and it will only make it difficult for me to be around them. They've been very sweet to me, in their way, and I don't want to become the crank in their conversations when I come for family dinners. I don't want that tension when I walk into the family party. Yet at the same time, it amazes me that such sweet people can go to sleep thinking such wrong things about the world."

After thinking about all of this over and over, I laughed to myself, remembering the last Thanksgiving with Kamil when he was still Tina's boyfriend and the family thought he was straight. When the aunts got drunk, he'd give them dance lessons. It exhilarated them. Meanwhile, my uncles would sit and watch football and see the dancing from a distance, and say to one another, "I really wouldn't get Tina's hopes up about marrying Kamil."

It was less than five degrees Fahrenheit outside and close to 10:00 P.M. when I boarded the train for home. The car of the train was almost at full capacity and the floor was spotted with muddy Rorschach blots from the boot prints of other passengers, which had marked and melted throughout the day, all brown and black and gray along the floor. Looking over the anemic buildings, where the smoke from the chimney pipes was indistinguishable from the sky and the gentle frost, I felt eerie and intrigued.

I leaned against the glass pane behind the doors, which were long and metallic and striped with the fluorescent lighting from the floor. Across from me, a woman was speaking to herself in intensely pornographic language, while the rest of the passengers pretended not to notice her.

The woman shouted, "Cock suck, girl. You need money, slut. Do it. Do it, you butt slut. Little boy, you don't know me. I'm fifty-six years old, you don't know me. You think you can make a thousand dollars around here? Cock suck, girl. Cock suck. And find a job. My oriental girlfriends and I are trying to help you. Girl, you can make a thousand dollars tonight. Let him pee on your butt. You can do it, girl. Butt slut."

A man in a business suit shook his head and muttered, "Jesus fucking Christ." The woman continued with conspiratorial ranting.

"Floyd 'Money' Mayweather is innocent. I suspected him of going around and selling crack to trannies. He's pretending to be Shaquille O'Neal's cousin. I don't trust women, these black women don't like me. I'm not a racist. I'm not even white. I'm Syrian, and as soon as I told people that, I stopped being racist. I come from Syrian royalty. My grandmother used to be a queen. I was raped within the last 48 hours, I have the rape kit to prove it. I could be getting killed by the Zodiac Killer and nobody gives a fuck. . ."

When I arrived home, I was drained. Between the tedium of working at Jude's, and the garrulous three-hour lecture I sat through thereafter, I had little stamina left.

Back at the apartment, I rubbed my hand over my forehead, stretched out my shoulders, and tried to keep alert. The prejudice of my strained relationships during my sickness came at me in these quiet moments, in all its criticisms and hostile gestures. I fell onto my couch and laid against my head, felt momentarily consoled by the thought of Mark, but refused to gratify in the sentiment further. I went on my computer, and found an email from a younger woman, a student at Loyola or UIC or someplace, distraught over the shooting of a young man in a mental health crisis. The email read:

I am so devastated at the police killing of another person living with mental illness. I just wanted to reach out to my few connections in any sort of mental health community to share my grief with others who must also be mourning.

Even though I am now introduced to a mental health community of support, love, and compassion around mental illness that I did not previously know existed, I still don't know how to disclose my mental illness with those close to me, which I have never done before, and it pains me to see so many die without proper remembrance for who they were, how they lived, or why they died.

I have been so depleted by this shooting. He needed help, not a bullet. And yet what did he get? How much time did they give him? I wanted to share with you my response that I shared with friends and family, below. Please let me know of any response by your organization or any community response.

Today, as I celebrate the holidays with my family, so many of them (including myself) having recovered from mental illness and addiction, Chicago families are mourning the murder of their son—yet another state-sanctioned murder of a black person experiencing a mental health emergency. Jerome Aldridge, 21, was murdered when his father called for assistance and hospital transport. His neighbor Jennifer Carter, 53, who was supporting the family during this emergency was reported "accidentally" shot and murdered during the altercation as well.

This follows after the killing of John Williams, tased to death in police custody after they jailed instead of hospitalized him during a mental health emergency. His father, who was also a south suburban police officer, Marcus Williams, called the police for hospital transport, but upon arrival, the officers countered, "We don't do hospitals, we do jail."

The police murder of black people and people living with mental health conditions is egregious genocide. My family members, or I, could have easily been the victims if my skin color were different.

I mourn the loss of my brothers, sisters, and siblings of color and living with mental illness.

I responded:

Thank you, Amanda. That was beautiful. Mental health is absolutely a missing link in all of these conversations. Incarceration, police violence, poverty, racial inequality. Our silence only acquiesces to it. I have emulated others by trying to draw attention to confrontations between police and law enforcement, and have found my community to be quiet and unresponsive. There's a lot of information that's needed to have these conversations, which most people have no awareness of. The result is that the conversation never happens. It was a breath of fresh air to read this email. It is always encouraging to find someone who has the nerve to care about people with mental illnesses and to give their time and effort to justice.

How rarely those voices of affirmation came to me, those who were not quiet about being Mad. Outside of Jude, this was one of the only ones; a comforting distraction.

On the next turn online, I watched political interviews and read articles on President Obama's executive order on gun control. About half of a billion dollars had been distributed toward early mental health screening for children. How that related to an executive gun order, I was personally not sure. Though I understood that a connection between violence and a psychiatric diagnosis held sway almost everywhere else, I had combatted this for reasons of self-actualization. I was reminded of this sanist imagination's more lurid forms moments later.

On the next article in my feed, Congressman Culhane, the self-proclaimed "savior of the mental health system," was giving an interview, with much gusto, about mass shootings and public violence. A sensationalized video image showed camera footage of an Arab man sprinting toward a police vehicle and firing a bullet into the officer; an assault I wish on no one. A conversation on the dangers of Islamic terrorism ensued—hawkish, bellicose, vacuous sharp-talk on curbing this threat militarily—followed by a critique of the President's executive order. "I think the President is too concerned with what is in people's hands," Culhane said, "and not with what is in their minds."

I had done a lot to ignore that point and build identity in spite of it, but after watching that, I was reminded that my world was to a substantial extent built by people who believed that I was capable of one day running toward a car and shooting someone in the head and that the people who said they wished to "help" me were no exception in believing this. To assuage my vexation, I had to occasionally look away from these bait-and-blame tactics, such as when the head of the NRA called for a federal registry of mentally ill people. What were the implications when a reactionary organization like the NRA blamed a social minority for violence and advocated for government surveillance of that minority group? At worst, it built a case for future, state-sanctioned security crackdowns, or there is a young Dylan Roof in his audience being radicalized into an ideology of hate. At best, we remained silent and non-confrontational, the scapegoating gets ignored a day later, and we return to our normal problems. But the suspicion of latent reaction did not leave. As bed bugs infiltrated one's head, I ended up believing that something I could not see was an omnipresent threat.

I shut the computer there, stunted by the excessive intake of media, thought, and politics, and went into my bedroom. Outside I could hear the wind split against my window. It was the end of a twelve-hour day and I thought, *the thickness of it all is coming over me again.* I put on a CD by a composer I hadn't heard of before. I let it play for about ninety seconds, though it quickly became intolerable. It felt as though I was within a stale sheet of metal, cold and incapable of intuitive thought and feeling. I lied in my bed, looking into the corner of the wall while the string chamber achieved intolerable sonic anhedonia.

I got out of my bed, turned off the music, went into the kitchen, and poured myself a whiskey. I brought it into my room and sipped it in quiet while planted in my woolen blanket. It warmed my empty stomach, which curved a couple of inches below my ribcage. My dinner plate was beside me on the floor: balls of meatloaf beside a grimy fork.

The weight of my mind intensified. I put my head against my pillow, and then, after forty sleepless minutes, opened a document of screeds written through previous bleakness.

I don't write, I ramble. This is the best communication that explains what the world feels like to one who lives at least halfway in depression. And perhaps there is more to reveal about this world in disconcerted rambling than there is in rational argument.

I am not happy. I am in fact quite awful. I have always been melancholic. Rather than grow out of it, this melancholy, as I grew older, I only grew more intense in it. I allowed it to consume me.

With technology and the financial auspices of my parents, I maintain stability. Without it, I might be dead.

I'm trapped in a cage, and on the inside, I have been denied everything that makes life worth living. On the outside, when I express even an honest moment of this reality, at best I get pity. Pity, like an animal at a zoo. Otherwise, I am ignored, or silenced.

How sad it is that any living thing should be there. No one asks how I got here, or what exactly this cage consists of. It is, after all, invisible. People pass and get on with themselves. I may see them as condescending; they think nothing of it.

"A sad person is just a sad person. Don't give her the attention she wants." Sometimes when I speak, if I can get even five honest words across, I am treated as though I have committed a crime. You are not allowed to be unwell.

I am so alone that to have someone tolerate my thoughts for even a minute feels like a revelation. I have been given seconds of air. I am allowed to speak my mind. I have overcome sanism.

A minute ago, I could foresee a life that extended fifteen minutes into the future. Now that number is maybe four or five minutes. If I am not alive when that time passes, I won't care.

Since others often don't think Depression is real enough to impact someone's life, I look at the decline in my life under depression, and I sometimes lie to myself. I don't say that I became unwell.

I say that I failed. Just to be impartial. Just to open to the other side of the story. Because there is always another side to the story, even the story of my life.

They don't understand how a person can be beaten by Depression. They think my suffering is a fabrication. I am excusing myself for quitting. But they don't know what they're looking for. They don't see anything. They don't know the signs. They don't respect the warnings. They aren't attuned to the far side of the mind.

They don't see that when a person's life deteriorates, there's always something deeper acting on the individual than her own will. Because this is America, and there must be a bootstrap solution for everything.

I don't want to be living. Living is miserable. I also don't want to be dead. Life and death are both horrible absolutes. I want a limbo state, as though attempting to die would send me into some state more desirable than either being alive or being dead. I want a brief passing ground. I want the bliss and the remorse of the last moments before death, but I don't want to check out entirely. I want to put a wrench in the process. It's an active protest of both life and death. Like a drug escape, but with fiercer intention.

This makes little sense, but that is madness.

If I attempt suicide, I believe it will be said that I did it to be noticed. Maybe there is some attention that I want. I want to be in a bed in a cool room, with homely, caring angels monitoring my life. I want to know I am safe amongst the living, and that love and understanding will be made available to me.

This is my tortured logic, but it must be said. You should not expect caged beings to want to live, for what exists in a cage cannot be seriously called living.

Can a warm person know what it is like to be freezing? I am Depressed now, but when I am not, I forget what this is all about. I need to document my words and thoughts, even if I am doomed to reject it as "tortured logic." Then I can remember the deadness, and how liberated I should feel when I am out of it.

A day later I think about this: life is an absolute, and death is an absolute. Does this make any sense? I was wrong. There is no binary. There is no separation. We die as we live.

Life and death are not points of beginning and conclusion. They happen simultaneously. They are a part of the same process. If I am not thinking about the other, then I am not thinking about either of them.

To the world, a Depressed life is an allegory of death. You lose the decencies of thought and emotion. You are less like the living and more like the dead. When I am unwell, I am the living allegory of death. That is why they evade me. That is why they fear me. That is why they leave me alone.

Other human qualities may remain: a semblance of rationality, physicality, little exchanges like hellos and goodbyes. But the soul is lost. And what is death if not the departure of the soul? Who would want to be without the good that the soul provides?

Last night I contemplated an ambiguous phase. Neither living nor dead. There is no such thing. You are part of the living and the dead forever.

Depression illuminates this somehow.

One does not become "unliving." They are still here. The Christs, the segregationists, the war volunteers, the radicals, the tillers, the midwives, the historians, the suffragettes, the fascists, the musicians, and so forth. The history and future of humanity are all around us, blended into one story, in which every act extends into the future, and hope of futures influences the past. Our existence is a medium in which these tensions conflict, and that shapes our being.

My feeling of deadness is only an illusion. It is a trick of the mind, like being in a living hell. It is fluid. Sometimes I am dragged miles toward Hades, and sometimes only a few yards. But as this happens, I never become anything other than myself. Nor do I become less of a part of everything else. My participation in the story is removed only by delusion, not actuality.

It may be nonsense, but this nonsense is better for me than anything else.

I give my other time to prosaic, real-world readings. These do little to make me happy, and I've determined that they are mere weapons to fend off the ignorance of the world. If not for them, the ignorance would consume me if it got the chance. And it always has the chance.

But these interests don't matter to the soul, not to mine. The soul is beholden to something else.

I didn't want to be a fighter, and I didn't set out to be political. These are worldly sins and moral flaws. And the world is painful. But I must be this way. It hurts me. It limits my spirit. But it is a duty of mine, something I cannot avoid. I have to understand that there is a need to fight. And once I recognized this, you no longer had the choice to be passive.

And if I didn't hurt, I would be passive.

I capitalized the "D" in Depression to distinguish minor sadness—like the feeling a child has when her ice cream falls onto the sidewalk and her brother laughs at her—from mortal sadness—something far closer to the feeling of death. We're in a place and time when we've made the concept of feeling erroneous by applying catch-alls over broad swaths of the real estate of life.

Depression is a million things at once. It is garden variety misery and lack of satisfaction at work, and it is the period after a mother going through it gives birth, a perpetual day-after-Christmas feeling, only with more body image issues and a screaming little thing who she'd like to love and it kills her all the more that she cannot.

My cousin said she had that while staying home all day with her newborn son alone. At times, she said the dimming of the light in the early evening sank into her eyes in a way that made them feel that they did not belong to her. They were merely two space-like pits within a numb fuzz.

She said she couldn't put words to it but it felt like she didn't have eyes at all, and couldn't feel like sleeping or eating or doing anything but stare until her son screamed loud enough to remind her that she had some higher purpose to serve. "The hours are long, Boo, and you have nobody to spend them with," she told me once after a sigh, with her little one farting and squealing with a bottle in his mouth, alongside her moppy old dog, after which point I got the impression that she didn't have many people to *talk about this with. "The suburbs were designed that way, you know," I told her. "We designed the dream around the private, not the public, and privacy is what we get, of the home as well as the soul."*

But I digress, as Mad minds do, never knowing what is and is not appropriate, replaying one moment from out of time as life persists in the present. It's like a cinematic filter in which the apparitions of the past cast over your life, perhaps even of the past well before your life.

Depression is also the high school student who doesn't get into their favorite college, but gets into a good one anyway. It's the widow who is left hollowed out into an ineffable place, while her children make chores out of tending to her in her elderly madness and joke about it behind her back. The plight is spiritual, but it is also context-specific.

It's like how at one time a man was sent to war and we knew the exact process that made him rattled when he came home. Shell shocked. Event and response packed into a clear phrase. Then it became diffuse. Post-Traumatic Stress Disorder. There are questions left unanswered. What is the trauma? The shell? And what's the stress? The shock? And what constitutes it as a "disorder"?

It seems to me that the order of events makes perfect sense, given what happens to people. It's only "disordered" insofar as we fail to re-integrate it into an "ordered" whole. And that's half of the problem: once one is dis-ordered, they are perpetually dis-ordered, because the "order" of the world is designed to keep them that way.

The asylums were a segregationist model. Drugs are only the façade of integration, two-thirds of the time. We can never talk about them or why they are there, and when we do, people cower and leave, or worse. It's integration, but with a mask. The lesser of two options, and you're never really validated within it. The mental impact is to have people think it's all their fault. That it's an individual problem. Just look at how I speak myself: I became "unwell." "I fail." I'm still learning not to do that. I'm still learning how to find self-actualization in the horizon of mental illness.

I'd call it a whole new system of oppression to be identified and pulled above the surface—sanism—but I come from too much privilege for the people of my time to like to hear that from me. This is also a part of the problem, of making me think I am the source of the problem rather than a symptom of it, one who should not be identifying myself within structures of oppression.

I'm many years into understanding myself as a problem, and it has gotten me nowhere. So, I've started to ask: what of the world?

This inchoate, desperate writing put me to sleep. What it may mean to me in more stable moments, I do not know. Winter air came in through a crack in the corner of my window and I rested.

CHAPTER 4

2010

In my days, I need more coffee at the beginning, more noise and effort to get out of bed, and at the end, more beer. It is normal for my age. Everyone else says they have it, the anxiety, the sadness. They deal with it, they say. It's no disease. You've got to tough it out. But it's more than sadness. It's a vacuum of creativity that keeps me locked into an inert presence, within which there is no reason and no standards. There's no escape, only distractions.

I wake up with seething anger. Throughout my day I become lightheaded, weak, and have unexplained pains in my legs and my back. This is most maddening in sedentary positions, such as in class, where it builds to fury and I want to shout and run away. My mood dampens regularly. I don't even have the will to smile a lot of the time, nor to care what people think of me if I do not. Peppier people rub me on the back and say, "Smile, eh?" I sneer in return.

I've got that "special gene," I have learned. The one the family jokes about, the one that makes us drink all of the time, where we just keep going and don't talk about it.

Other people drink, and they dance and get laid, and laugh about it the next day. I drink and I want to get hurt. Or fucked, though not in a pleasant way.

A few times, I have wandered off in the night on the edge of a blackout. I want to vanish into a strange, reckless oblivion, like that one Elliott Smith song. I wake up many blocks away — always safe, miraculously — and then walk back.

The booze is frequent and excessive. I drown in it. At parties, I sulk, cross my arms, and withdraw myself from everyone else. The muscles of my face tense up. I stand like a freak and nobody speaks to me.

It is a cold, moderate-chance-of-rain Friday evening in January, and Katie and I are going to a house party. We went out the night before, too, and it took me an extra drink in the dorm during the pregame to feel ready. As we walk, I am distracted. I'm fixated on an old moment in my life and talking to nobody. When I am back in reality, Katie is talking about her dating life. Apparently, she thought I was listening.

"I was hooking up with him for a while, but I always got the sense that he thought I wasn't good enough for him," she says. I am not sure who she is talking about, but he sounds a lot like the other guy she was talking about.

"Yeah," I say. "And what is his name, again? Blaine? Brad? Brian?"

"Brad."

"Sorry."

"Yeah, he's cool. I met him at a party after one of the improv shows. I think he plays in a band. I don't really remember," she says.

We arrive at the party. It's calm, at least in comparison to a party we were at in the dorm, where Carla had gotten a stomach issue and started vomiting. Katie and I are probably too lit, too early for the scene. The crowd is about twenty people large and spread across an open, messy room with wooden floors and music playing from a playlist on a big-screen television. Katie's friends from theater greet us and make a few unfunny quips. We laugh cordially.

Her friends lead us to a white countertop, which divides the kitchen from the living room. It is a plastic countertop outlined with little squares, and the little crevices in between the squares are overflowing with spilled alcohol from the night, the smell of which makes me queasy. There are handles of Smirnoff Vodka and a brand of rum that I don't recognize, but it looks unwholesome. We all take a shot of vodka, and then Katie grabs plastic cups.

As we walk to the keg, Brad enters from the backyard, hugs Katie, and then introduces himself to me. He is smiley, likely stoned-smiley. He pumps the keg and pours our cups. We stand and make a little small talk around the keg.

"So this is Boo from the dorms?" he asks.

"Yep!" Katie goes.

"Awesome!" he says.

This conversation is already doomed. I cover my mouth with my cup and survey the party. Across the room, people are sitting in pods of fours and fives. Occasionally one of the guys from the pods looks at me and maintains eye contact for several seconds. I look away.

I don't want to be here, but I feel it is something I must do — a social obligation, a courtesy to a world that allows me the opportunity to be here while others struggle. Yet if this is fun, why does it feel like suffering? More suffering than work and school. Why am I drained, self-conscious, and anxious that one of these people will look less charmingly upon me than they do with one another? What have they ever given me that has me feeling that I want anything that these people want?

If this is the dream, why do I need to drink myself to nothing to pretend that I enjoy it?

The kitchen is crowded with guests — guys and girls in equal numbers, huddled closely together, almost interchangeable from how they look and interact with one another. I am at the edge of the room, crossing my arms by the corner and peering in. There is moody music playing — cool, reverberated synthetic music with melancholic vocal harmonizations that clutch at your emptiness and lure you to it with sonic sugar. There's an ironically detached and deadpan female singer crooning about her Saturday afternoon. The room smells like secondhand backyard weed and the indoor smells like the residue of a chronic, alcoholic stomachache.

"Dude, Tahoe is sick, but you've got to get to Park City, the powder is just so much cleaner there," explains one of the guys, Tim, to another guy, seconds before another suave inhale of a spliff. Jason, the guy receiving the spliff, cocks his head back and opens his mouth widely, showing broad, whitened teeth and cackling a possibly contrived but generally agreeable laugh. When Jason is finished smoking, he passes the spliff to Katie, forgoing me in the process. I am just enough outside of the circle that he could have easily looked past me and meant nothing of it, and yet I am here, just a foot away, and he did not even consider me before turning to Katie, coughing with his cheeks perked into his eyes, with that same careless panache I noticed a moment earlier, and asking her if she was smoking tonight.

Katie and Brad disappear without telling me. My friends always leave me alone like this. I lean against the wall and scroll through my phone. Nothing there but texts and notes I have already read. I finish my beer, refill my cup, and move to an awkward position on the edge of one of the groups. The students in this portion of the party are more mature. There are those of us who came to college to entertain as many indulgences as we possibly could, then get passing marks on Adderall and the friendly opinions of others, and there are those of us who look like the honest prepsters I once went to high school with — goodhearted, relatively sheltered kids who take care of their minds and their bodies and treat others kindly before going off to engineering and pre-law work. They've played drinking card games through the night, now half of them are slipping out of their seats after taking their fifth shot of vodka in under two hours.

They don't acknowledge me until eventually one of the girls notices me and invites me to sit down. They introduce themselves, say it is nice to meet me, and then talk amongst themselves again.

I sit quietly and try to pick up on the conversation. Two or three times I try to contribute, but nobody notices.

Michael Daniels is there, tippling on a red cup in the middle of the crew. He is one of BJ's friends from high school. On a few occasions, all three of us did cardio boxing classes together at a gym just off of campus and then went to a Mexican restaurant nearby afterward. He made the joke in between rounds, "What grade boy do you think you could beat up today?" and I replied, "I don't know, a second-grader, a third-grader." "You're getting stronger!" he smiled, then returned to his side of the gym. I think that was his way of flirting.

I sit next to him and he invites me to play a card drinking game. *No thank you,* I tell him, *I'm already close to over-served.* "Really? You don't seem drunk." He is prematurely balding and has shaved his head to look better, though there is some grown hair on the sides. He's also put on too much cologne and is wearing one of those "I'm getting blacked out tonight" American Eagle shirts that I see too much of. He asks me how I am doing otherwise, where I have come from tonight, et cetera, and I ask the same thing in reply. "I got off of a phone call with a girl I'm seeing…she's in LA but honestly it has been shaky for a while. I always do that, get into things too easily, and it's almost always with people who probably aren't good for me." I chortle, sip my drink, and eye the other side of the house. "How about you?" he says, like a public announcement directly into my ear, "Are you seeing anyone? Taking anyone home? Who gets more guys, you or Katie?"

This time I take my phone out and laugh, limply, "No, no I am not. Um, I've actually been looking for Katie. She was here a minute ago, I think I should go find her."

I excuse myself to use the bathroom and to look outside to see if Katie is still here. I had texted to see if she left, but I've gotten no reply. Then I see she and Brad arguing on the back porch. She seems distraught and he seems exasperated. "Look!" he says, "I don't know why I'm getting all of these texts at 2 AM! We haven't even seen one another that long!" And she says, "Brad, I just really need you to be more present for me…" Has she been harassing him? I don't know. I could fairly easily picture her doing so, and it doesn't bother me. I go back inside and see Michael again.

"I'm sorry if that was weird. That was weird, wasn't it?" Michael says.

Nothing is weird anymore, I have no standards, but I am exhausted in his presence as I am with everyone else's. The social situation is another arena where everyone but me has a claim to my time and my health. It's survival of the fittest, the wittiest, the sexiest. I know I will lose, yet here I am, again and always, allowing someone else to play for me, leasing my mind to the culture. I don't respond to him directly, but he is talking anyways, this time more contemplatively, with his elbows over his knees and his shoulders hunched forward. "I know I'm straight, but every now and then…well, these things are a spectrum, you know? I'm not saying someone has to be one thing or another, or you have to insist on being totally straight…"

"But you just did, didn't you?" I say.

"No, I have a girlfriend in LA, but—"

"But it's an open relationship?" I ask.

"No, well, it kind of is. I don't think any of this means anything anymore. It's confusing."

If I stay any longer, I won't be able to sleep through the night, so I tell him and the party that I have to get up early for volunteer work, even though I don't have it, and start to go. He says he looks forward to seeing me at boxing and adds that he doesn't think he has my number. Without resistance, I give it to him in full, without a wrong digit at the end.

Before leaving, I go to the bathroom, lock the door, and look at the mirror. I'm disappointed and find the image distasteful. I run the faucet, drink what is left of my beer in about thirty seconds, run my hands under the water, and throw it onto my face. I help myself to a hand towel to dry off. Katie and Brad are gone now. I exit the house without interacting with anyone on my way out.

When I walk to the dorm I am in a disoriented temper. A couple of times I laugh to myself insanely, and students on the other end of the campus walkway stop and watch me. When I arrive in the dorm, I play choral music and go immediately to bed with bitterness grating across my forehead.

In the A.M., I walk off campus for twenty minutes to a coffee shop, body as limp and hollow as a sad lo-fi recording, convinced that physical activity will bring me to equilibrium – a stable center for living that I doubt I'll ever find. In the coffee shop, stimuli overbear me the gentle inquiries of strangers, the classic rock music, the tasks of the exchange – I have a life to organize and work to schedule, yet here I am stranded. As rapidly as possible, I hand my payment to the barista and leave with a small coffee.

A run might help. I get into my athletic clothes at home and then bolt from the dormitory almost immediately after returning to it. Listening to leaves scraping on the protrusion of the sidewalk against the road, I heard a constant, rewinding scattering that no amount of running could outpace. The decaying foliage on the periphery of my view pitter-patters as softly and cruelly as a drip of old blood. This ought to stabilize my anxiety into enough focus to complete my schoolwork for the early half of the week, and when that is completed, most of this will seem like nonsense.

My appearance is getting lazy. I wear old, oversized denim shirts, and pants that haven't been washed in weeks. When I'm done, I toss them into a dank pile of clothes in my closet. As it grows, it makes the room feel sleepy and discouraging, with that smell of fabric that has compiled too much lint and linen. I leave everything unorganized and walk to Jeremy's house to hang out. The guys are always there, usually playing drinking games. They've invented a game for themselves called "Man Ball." It consists of high-contact, one-on-one basketball on a lowered hoop, and the loser of each point has to chug half of a beer. While they play, their house is open, and I bring some reading material and listen to records. Carla and Rachel and I play a Fleet Foxes vinyl and talk. Charlie is seeing a girl, Jess, a chain-smoking hippie type who asks us to step outside for a cigarette regularly. I lazily read a couple of chapters for class, underlining key phrases for discussion as I skim and socialize. The guys come inside after their game and pass a joint around. I decline. The living room fills with mist and feels like sloth. BJ and Jeremy are talking about one of BJ's cousins who left school. "He had to drop out because of depression, which is just fucking sad," BJ says. There is a big screen television in the corner of their room, and when they are finished smoking, they put a basketball game on. Carla, Rachel, and I return to the dorms.

There, I am damaged. I shiver. I gaze emptily into the wall. Grotesque images are running through the mind, but I am afraid of revealing them to people. Without awareness of doing so, I pull a shaky arm to my head, form my hand into a pistol, and press it into my temple. When alone, I curse. I do not eat and don't desire to. My eyes feel drained and burned, like a child who has been inside watching TV all day. I stay in bed for hours at a time, never leaving, never reaching out to the world. I masturbate occasionally, it is grungy and unsatisfying, and I feel emptier after the act than I did before.

Ever since that one party, Michael Daniels, the nice boy who thinks that he might be gay, had texted me infrequently. The texts were about nothing too significant, just little, friendly messages to see what I was doing or to invite me to one of his friend's events. Many of these invitations I'd neglected to respond to, out of disinterest to his proposal or of merely not feeling like getting out of the dormitory. This does not stop him from reaching out. I thought I'd just leave him alone, but in a black period when I'd felt ugly about myself, I thought that becoming more open about sex would help me be comfortable with myself, I reach out to him to see what he is doing. He invites me to his friend's party, which I attend with him, and quickly tell him I'm bored. We go back to his house. He puts on television and asks if I want to smoke a bowl. I decline but tell him that he is free to smoke if he wants. He does, and when he is at case, I lean against him. Soon we hook up. The television goes off and we play indie music instead. The weed pacifies him, and I wrap myself around his side, kiss him on the cheek, rub his erection over the pants, and them blow him to finish. Eventually we have sex. I don't really feel anything in it—it's a bit awkward and stilted—and either unsatisfyingly brief or unsatisfyingly long. The only time I'm relaxed is afterward, once the embarrassment is over, and we are naked and talking shit with one another. The ugliness, the abjection of those moments – while our intimacy has been duly anti-climactic, and I am alone and vulnerable with a daft, stoned 20-year-old – behooves me.

I invite him to my dormitory a few times. Sara rarely comes to the room, so I can sit here like this for as long as I wish. Although, sometimes she and her sorority sisters come by to grab something and quickly leave. They say hello, fearfully, and stand awkwardly in the room while looking away from me. "How have you been, Boo?" Sara asks. Her friends all offer soft-spoken pleasantries. Then they leave, and while I get used to having my own space again, I hear them whisper to Sara, "Why are you still living with this girl?" She stays with them much of the time, leaving time to entertain Michael and be disappointed with it. Surely he can sense how miserable I am, but he hasn't really probed the question, nor have I said anything outright. In our little dialogues together, he says things like, "They say if you sleep on your back, you're open to the world, and if you lie on your stomach, you're closed off to it." He doesn't touch me or caress me in any particularly intimate way, but he lets his head fall on the bed beside me and looks up to me for an answer.

"I sleep like I've been tranquilized," I say. "And the effects of the tranquilizer don't wear off when I get up."

"It probably doesn't mean anything," he says.

When I shared thoughts like that, I could tell these morbid statements made him uncomfortable. I was cautious about letting him know too much about what things were really like. It wouldn't be fair to him. It was unwise. I had to get out. And I texted him, sweetly, that I'd enjoyed getting to know him, but school had gotten busy and I would not be able to commit more time to him and that I wished him well but I would not be able to see him any further.

By the middle of the quarter, the academic stress becomes overbearing. I don't think that I had any more responsibility than anyone else — I had less, probably — but it's all distressing. When asked, I can remember little of my course materials. But I was there in class, I sat through the lectures, I read the works, and I did the homework. And somehow I know none of it. Upon contemplating that fact, I realized, far too pitifully, that there is no use in showing up.

To think of a time when I went to a full day of school and then ran for three hours for cross country, every day. I'd become a truant, sleeping through critical lectures and brushing off half of my assignments. I'd thought that this might be liberating — to refuse my participation in *the absurd* and spend my time how I wanted to — but by neglecting my duties as a student, I only felt more worthless. Then that worthlessness becomes a rationale for why I should not enjoy myself in the evening. And if I did need to enjoy myself, I'd cut through all of the vacuity and death of my insides with substances, drift into parties full of fit, anonymous California students. I'd wander off back home, with the cherry brown campus roads blacked out from memory, or wake in other people's beds.

I feel like a resident of a plague-stricken town. I'm nauseous, disoriented, disheveled, caught in an emotional morass. I cry for no reason. My head tics. The other students snicker and leer at me, and I've stopped walking through the crowded parts of campus. Everywhere I go, I take the long way. The quiet way, where I won't be seen.

I've stopped eating at the student center. I go to lunch off campus instead. There is a sandwich shop almost a mile down the road, and I order the same thing every day: ham and cheese, no garnishing whatsoever, and an orange drink. After I swallow, I want to vomit. It comes from a deep place in me. My stomach does not accept food anymore, and I end up sitting at the table feeling ill, like I want to pass out, picking at the edges of the bread. I roll the remains of my sandwich into the wrapping and go to the bathroom to force it out of me, kneeling over the toilet with my arm stretched over the rim, and my head resting on the softness of my sweater. I hack against the back of my throat and force my finger down until drops of blood and soggy crumbles of my meal drop into and ripple the toilet water. Once I have relaxed, I cup faucet water in my hands and clean off my mouth.

Outside, I take long, slow walks back to campus. It feels like the middle of nowhere, with the lazy sounds of traffic fleeing to and from me alongside the bland lots of one-story businesses and advertisements—the sort of architecture you could drop into any commercial strip in the suburbs. Closer to campus, I stop at 7-11 and buy a bottle of water and a pack of cigarettes. I wasn't a smoker before, but now tobacco levels me. It focuses my mind, makes me feel confident and relaxed. The taste is harsh, and my saliva is thicker and undoubtedly dirtier for it, but I get clarity from it. Then, half an hour later, I crave another. It is a jittery, scratching sensation at the center of my chest. I cannot even pretend to sit still, and it makes me want to run down the center of the street. I smoke and watch pedestrians and flick the last ashes onto the pavement outside of the dorm before walking back inside. Sara is there, folding her laundry with an open book on the desk. She gives me a strange look as I enter, smells the residue of nicotine on my shirt, and rolls her eyes. She is only in the room for another five minutes – likely to avoid me – and as soon as the door closes when she leaves, I fall onto my side, pull my duvet over my shoulder, sink into a groggy place, and stay there for the next hour and a half.

My father is in town for a business trip and I have plans to meet him for dinner. I roll out of bed around five and walk to the Caltrain station, arriving there about ten minutes before departure. The sky has opened up, and there is more color in the world than I I've become used to. Orange over blue over the grey of the mountain. The train arrives, and I take a chair on the upper tier of seating. I rest my book on my lap and watch the train pass by gravel lots by the tracks, cement walls of graffiti, and bright California homes.

The Palo Alto stop is about twenty minutes away, and I walk to the restaurant from the station. It has an air of business prestige, with a staff of strikingly fit, attractive women, entrees costing at least $25 per plate, and a casual, professional crowd. Dad is at a table drinking a Manhattan. He said he chose the spot from a list of suggestions from his colleague, presumably a very rich Bay Area man.

A waitress comes, and we order seafood, steak, and white wine. Dad tells a story about his afternoon. He went to a golf club with his colleague, and a billionaire CEO, Jim Davis, was also in the clubhouse.

"I'd met him before. He's a really down-to-earth guy, humble guy," Dad says. "He's developing a vineyard in Napa for about one hundred million dollars."

"Uh huh." I nod.

"It's an amazing property, and everyone in the club knows it, and they know the price tag, too. So we're having a drink after our round, and Jim finishes his round and enters the clubhouse. Everyone is murmuring and whispering to themselves, and Jim goes to the bartender and orders a drink. Doesn't say anything. When he gets his beer, he clanks silverware against the glass and addresses the room. 'Alright, alright,' he says, 'I know what you're all thinking, so I'm going to come out and say it. Yes, you have the number correct. It's one hundred million. I'll bet many of you have spent three percent of your net worth on a home before, so it's no different for me. Now, can we please go back to enjoying ourselves?'"

"That's nice," I say.

"Yes, well he's a nice guy. You'd never guess how much money he had based on how he carries himself," he says. "And it is going to be a beautiful property, too. His other home is stunning," he adds.

"Right," I say.

"He gives away staggering numbers as well. The local public education system where he lives is really struggling, and he and his wife are stepping up to almost singlehandedly keep it running." Dad clears his throat and takes a sip of his wine. "So... what have you been up to?" he asks.

"I don't know. I go to class and do homework. Yesterday Carla and I hung out and watched an episode of *The Bachelor*."

He laughs. The waitress brings our plates, which are hot and full. We clink our glasses together and eat.

"Look," he tells me, plainly, "I know that this whole college thing isn't really off to a clear start. That is fine. For me, it was always clear that I was going to do something in business, but circumstances change. It isn't the same for you and Kevin. You don't have the same things influencing your education, and maybe it will take some more time to mature into a track that you'll be on for the rest of your life. But that's alright. Frankly, the world is your oyster. Personally, I'd be happy to see you take some finance courses. You and your brother stand to manage a foundation with a lot of wealth in it, and it's important to me that you are literate in your finances. I may be biased, but I think it would be great if you considered business. I think you'd excel at it. But all that foundation stuff is a long way off, and right now it is more important to your mother and I that you find your passion and do what you feel is right for you."

I twist my fingers around the neck of my glass of wine, swirl the liquid around the bowl of the glass, and observe the flashes of light shift through the alcohol. Then I rest my gaze on the middle of the table, halfway between myself and my father.

"Thank you, Dad," I say. "That means a lot."

"Relax a bit," he adds. "You're in a beautiful part of the world. You're doing great in school, taking classes that would have kicked my ass had I taken them. Remember, you've got a mind. Your SAT and subject test scores were scary good. Like, frighteningly high. As good or better than most of the kids who end up working in my office, who then go off to Harvard and Stanford MBA. You're doing fine. Your grades are good, you'll be okay. What's important is that you find something to put your mind towards. And if that takes a little wandering, so be it. Take a year and go abroad. Who cares. If it takes you five years to graduate, so be it. You shouldn't feel restricted by artificial social deadlines. That isn't what education is about," he says.

I'm listening more closely.

He continues, "It's also important to understand that the mind atrophies. I've always been a little ADD. I always find myself looking a dozen different ways in the office, and I always have to remember how to zero myself in and bring myself back into the moment to do whatever I need to do. Sometimes that's an asset for my work, sometimes a hindrance. Whatever the case, you have to take yours for what it is and work with it realistically. The mind is a muscle. You have to exercise it like anything else or it goes away."

We spend the rest of the dinner talking about class and business. I tell him again that I am doing well with everything—a little white lie. Dad talks about how he plans to retire in a few years, but he has been saying that for a while now. He then muses about his career some more, and lightly boasts about how he is the only person in his industry to work for four decades and never receive a lawsuit.

"Once there was a billionaire who was threatening litigation over some ticky-tack stuff on a deal we had. We had our lawyer address it though. We had the guy look at all of the boards we sat on and look at all of the mutual connections we had. He realized how dumb he'd look if he tried to pursue it, and we dropped the case."

"That sounds incredibly stupid," I say. "It's like he was willing to say, 'fuck you,' just to bully you into a few million dollars more."

Dad responds straightforwardly, "And that's exactly how my business is."

"Is that how you treat people in your business?"

"Not so much. My partners have joked that they'll buy me a tombstone that says, 'He was too Midwestern for his job,' or, 'He always left money on the table.'"

"That's reassuring."

When dinner ends, Dad puts his card down for the bill and sends me home with sixty dollars cash. On the train, I flip through

Truman Capote short stories and ponder how much of Dad's money might be "bad money," and why. It is dark when I arrive on campus, and as soon as I am back, I am disinterested in life again. I am not tired, and I go for a walk to the library barista for tea. The night feels stilted and removed. A guy from class is having a cigarette during a study break and offers me a Camel Blue. I joke around with him, make ironic remarks, and then he goes back to his studies and I go to my bed. The nicotine gives me a rush, and I am compelled to get ahead on reading when I am at the dorm. Fifteen minutes later, the crash comes back, as does the dread, the fear. Time stops, I cannot think. Slowly, I close my book, rest it beside me, and roll onto my side. I may as well be paralyzed.

All of the classes that I have missed begin to impact my academic standing, unsurprisingly. I have gotten low marks on multiple papers and outright failed a midterm. I promise myself that I'll go to my professor's office hours to discuss my performance in class. His room is on the top floor of a social sciences building, and after walking several exhaustive flights of stairs, I arrive in a vacant hall. From the opposite end of the floor, a student and teacher enter from a classroom. As I approach them, I recognize the teacher as Townley, the rhetoric professor whose class I dropped during the spring quarter of my freshman year. He sees me and swiftly turns his head towards the floor after we make eye contact.

The door to my other professor's office is cracked open. I approach it with dread—I have suspected that I am failing the class and feel obliged to speak to him about it, though we have never said anything before. I glance through the opening and watch him at his computer. His back is turned, so he cannot see me. I hesitate towards the door, almost tap it open, but retreat, and hurry away from the office. Minutes later, I log on to a computer in the library, access my student profile with the university, and withdraw from the class.

There is a long walkway in front of the campus mission. It is a one-way lane for vehicles—mainly gardeners and custodians who drive through on golf cars—that runs for nearly one-quarter of a mile, right to the foot of the mission. I walk on it sometimes just to move. Nobody comes here, so it is sort of like a vacation. And the more restless I get, the more danger there is in sitting still, so I have to come out to walk.

My conscience is nagging at me. I know things are coming apart, but I don't have anyone to talk with or any sense of direction. It's all a big haze and I cannot think straight. I need to get out, quickly. I might drop out of school, even if that's the most shameful thing I can do. My family is encouraging me to study abroad in Rome. I do not think it is a good idea, but I am also tempted to go. When else will I be able to live in Europe? They want me to apply for the John Felice Rome Center at Loyola University in Chicago, and they want to visit me while I'm there.

Before I call home, I'm eager to talk to my parents. During the talks, I feel no connection. I get the standard, "*Good!*" responses to everything I say, leaving little space to elaborate on what is actually happening in my life. Then they tell me about their next vacation plans and what Kevin is doing and quickly hang up. I spend the hours after that in debilitating self-loathing. It's not about me at all. It's about them. It's always been about them.

I pretend to be indifferent to my family, but that's a front. The feigned apathy is there because I feel too intensely about them in other ways. For one, I have a desire to pass their standards—to be the golden girl, advance to a prestigious life, and have them smile and glow when they talk about what job I've gotten (this is only possible through finance). Or I feel anger. In that mood, I want to take an impractical route with my life so I can get retribution for what they did to me: they tied my life to money and trapped all of my choices within it. I want to make a mockery of their narcissism.

I impulsively call home, believing that I need to confess everything to a higher authority—a very Catholic feeling. Mom answers. "*Honey! So good of you to call!*" When asked how I'm doing, I say that everything is shit. "*If I could look at any point into the future and identify hopelessness, that would at least take me a step closer toward hope.*" How melodramatic. Confused, Mom asks if I've been on top of my classes. I say that I dropped one and didn't tell her about it. "*Do you want to continue with the sciences, dear? Have you thought about transferring to the business school? Or Notre Dame? Northwestern?*" It doesn't entice me. Nothing does.

I finish the quarter respectably enough, just as I told Mom. I expect to get an A, a B, and maybe a C. The C doesn't bother me, nor does the A and B feel special. The last night of finals, also the night before I go home is St. Patrick's Day. It is a rainy evening, and most of the campus has left. Elise's friends were all seniors. All of them are mentally checked out of school and are spending their last days getting hammered and going insane. Tonight, many of them are tripping acid and dancing. I am drinking mixed Jameson drinks and hot toddies while observing them—they warm some humor into me. Enough to laugh, talk to people, enjoy myself.

On the first day of spring break, going to the airport, my head bursts and I am hardly able to speak. It is cold back in Illinois. Arriving in my hometown, I feel passive and restrained, like how friends from less affluent backgrounds would behave less like themselves when I had them over to my parents' house. I do little with my days.

On Thursday night, we go to a restaurant in Wilmette for dinner with Grandma and the Doc. My cousin Rico serves us and comps us Kendall Jackson Chardonnay. Dad and Kevin arrive late. They went golfing at Bobolink, a male-only club with a big price tag that's full of lawyers, retired football players, and guys who used to be in a Bush Administration. While we waited for them, Mom and I drank wine and worked through conversation with Grandma and the Doc. After some political talk regarding our military involvement in the Middle East, Dad shares a story from his old teacher, Art Laffer. "He worked very closely with Ronald Reagan," Dad says, "and he once told me that when Reagan was wondering whether or not to invade Grenada, he secluded himself in his room, poured a Seagram's and Seven, drank it, and asked himself, 'What would the Duke do?'"

"Who is the Duke?" Grandma asks.

"John Wayne," Dad says.

"That seems pretty stupid," I say. "What is Grenada anyway? Is it important enough to invade?"

"Well, there's more information going into the decision than that anecdote. And the guys in the office know it best. I just thought it was a funny story," Dad says.

"I'm not sure there's all that much information behind it," the Doc says. "I think a lot of the guys who send our boys off to war think like children with toy guns and cowboy hats. It's always been that way. We should never make it our business to police other people the way we do."

Dad coughs, the conversation stalls. The band Chicago is playing over the restaurant speakers, and Mom tries to make small talk. Grandma says, "What?" a lot. Her hearing is not great. The Doc seems lost, almost as out of consciousness as I am. Kevin is looking at his phone. Mom looks at me and smiles when I notice her doing so.

In the center of the table, there is a wine cooler with an empty bottle of Kendall Jackson. Dad flips the wine bottle upside down in the cooler. "The universal symbol for, 'we need more wine,'" he remarks. Rico brings us another bottle and pours everyone's glass, and Dad makes a toast to us all. The mood lightens a bit, and Mom and Grandma talk about the family. Dad's presence weighs most heavily on me. He seems stiff, stubborn, closed-minded.

I never know when he will and will not be like this, or when I will stop seeing him this way.

I turn towards the Doc and tell him a joke that BJ told me earlier in the quarter.

"Do you like Freud, Doc?"

"Sometimes."

"Did you hear the one about Freud's grandson meeting him in heaven?"

"No."

"So his grandson dies, and Freud greets him." I put on a Germanic accent. "Grandson, it is so good to see you! Tell me, how are my theories holding up on earth?' 'Not good, grandpa. A lot of people have discredited what you said.' 'Even ze Oedipus Complex?' 'Yes, even the Oedipus complex.' 'Zose motherfuckers . . .'"

The Doc doesn't laugh, and I feel I have flopped. "Sorry," I say, regretfully.

"Don't apologize," the Doc says sternly. "Never apologize to people."

Food arrives, we eat, and Mom probes Kevin about life in school. He says he is trying to get at least a 32 on his ACT. Dad says that he is going to arrange a meeting with the administration at Notre Dame for them later in the spring. Kevin agrees to it. "Good!" Mom and Dad say. Afterward, there is a pause at the table. We finish our meal and wait for the check. All we have left are our glasses of wine.

"Can we go?" I ask.

"Not yet," Mom says. "I have a bit of wine left."

"But we haven't said anything for minutes," I say.

"Boo, stop whining," Kevin responds.

"Easy, Kevin," Dad says.

"Yes, you two haven't talked to one another the whole time you've been home," Mom says. "Why don't you hang out more?"

"We talk as much as we need to," I say. "We're different people."

"No, Boo, you just try too hard and are too judgmental," Kevin says. "That's why I make friends easier than you."

"Kevin, I think you should excuse yourself to the restroom right now," Dad says.

The Doc says to me, "For once it's fortunate that your brother's an asshole. It'll give us something to talk about."

"Can we go when he returns?" I ask.

Mom says, "Boo, I'm going to finish my drink, and in the meanwhile, we'll talk. Tell me, are you dating anyone?"

"No, I'm not," I say.

"All of the other cousins talk about their dating lives. You never did. Not in grade school. Not in high school. Not now. Why not?"

"Because I didn't have anyone," I say.

"Not anyone?" she asks.

"No, Mom. I was a loser. You didn't notice?"

The Doc interjects, "You weren't a loser, Boo. You were precociously decent. Kids don't appreciate that in their peers. I was the same way."

"Whatever the case, I wasn't getting any," I say.

"Sex is overrated," the Doc says. "There's nothing I got from a woman that I didn't get better from my own hand."

Grandma didn't hear this, I don't think, or she's too generous for her own good. Mom cusps her mouth, trying to keep wine from spilling out. Dad's face is red. He pinches his hands over his eyes and says, "Alright, let's go. Honey, finish your drink."

We drive off in different cars. Dad takes Kevin in his Porsche, and Mom takes me and my grandparents in her Lexus. Mom plays 1960s radio as we drop Grandma and the Doc off at their home. We drive to my parents' home via Sheridan Road, perhaps the most illustrious strip of real estate in the Midwest. When we arrive, Dad is pulling in at the same time.

Once inside the home, we disperse. Dad has a swift, assertive gait, and walks directly to his Blackberry at the kitchen counter to check for emails. Kevin and I are shortly behind. Mom pulls her car into the garage and enters last.

"Oh, great," Dad groans.

"What's up?" Kevin asks.

"Oh, nothing. I'm reading this email about these regulatory guidelines we're being subjected to under Obama," he says.

Kevin scoffs indignantly, as though he understands.

"I've never felt more attacked in my profession than I have under this administration," Dad adds. I feel he is about to give Kevin one of his "I've never been hired by a man who wasn't rich," lessons, and I stop paying attention to them. I saunter to the far edge of the kitchen and kneel to the floor to scratch the lapdogs behind their ears. Mom speaks to the room, "All right, I'm going to get my night clothes on, open a bottle of wine, and watch some shows. Who wants to join?" Kevin is still asking Dad about business and politics.

My family goes into the TV room for their show. The dogs follow. I grab a Stella Artois from the refrigerator, go up to my room, and flip through a book of modern art that I checked out of the Wilmette Library. I put Aimee Mann on my computer and recline across my bed. When I finish my beer, I walk downstairs for another—a forty-five-second walk in total in this vast home. After I top the cap off another beer, I walk into the TV room to see my parents. Dad is in his armchair, half asleep. He yawns, scratches the top of his head, and takes a sip of wine. Mom is on the couch and pauses the television when she sees me at the end of the room. I sit against the arm of the couch, two large cushions away from Mom.

"So are you doing alright with school?" she asks. She seems happier now—tipsier.

"Yes," I lie.

"Good!" Dad says, as though immediately waking up. He coughs again and takes another sip of his drink.

Mom asks, "Do you have a living situation for next year?"

"Me, Katie, Carla, and my friend Alexis are looking at a house. We are looking for a fourth roommate, too," I say.

"And which one is Katie?" Mom asks.

"The girl from Southern California," I say.

"Oh, right. I remember her," Mom says.

Mom is smiling at me again. There is a formal pause in the room, and the older, more deranged lapdog starts rolling on the floor and moaning. Mom tilts her head back and laughs at the dog. Dad wakes up and orders her to put the show back on. Together, we sit and watch the cop drama on basic cable, with attractive yet dull actors.

I wake to the noise of landscaping in my parents' backyard, where five or six men have been working since 7:30 AM. Accounting for the cleaning maid in the home, the number of Mexicans working on the property on a typical Friday outnumbers the number of Harvey's by a ratio of at least two-to-one. I spend the day watching television and texting my friends to pass the time. Mom is either out running errands or reading at home. Kevin is in school and goes out with friends afterward. Dad is in New York.

Around 4:15 in the afternoon, I pour a glass of Chardonnay and watch *Law and Order*. Mom is in the room, documenting the family's finances. She comments, "It isn't five o'clock yet, dear. Pace yourself is all I'm saying. Or go call one of your friends."

"I don't have friends."

"Don't be so down, dear. You have friends. Anyways, I'm not going to be here for dinner. I'm going to be out with Mrs. Clark and Mrs. Purcell. Would you like me to leave money for pizza?"

"Yes, please."

At 5:45, I order a thin crust pizza from my favorite place while Mom is getting ready upstairs. I tip the delivery guy modestly and pocket the leftover cash. I set the pizza on the kitchen counter, put a few slices on a plate, pour myself a glass of Chardonnay, and watch two more episodes of *Law and Order*, both featuring a pedophile plotline. The dogs are begging on the floor, and I toss them bits of cheese and pepperoni.

By 8:30, I have drunk all but one glass of Chardonnay from the bottle. Bemused, I wander the house and flip through my parents' collection of books and photo albums, as a drunk might do when left alone in a museum or a library. I put on a collection of Beatles and Fleetwood Mac singles that my family listened to on a European road trip in my middle school years, and gloss over old photos. The child in the pictures feels like someone I don't recognize, be it the chubby toddler in the Doc's pool, or the elementary school girl who is hanging out with girls I no longer see or speak to, or the gawky teenager. There are pages of photos from a summer trip to Montreal we took during my junior high years. Dad was out of town for a long business deal, and Mom took Kevin and me for a weeklong trip. The three of us are huddled together in the first picture. Kevin, no older than 8 or 9, is bursting out of the photograph with messy hair and a joyous smile. He is tucked under Mom's arm, though she cannot keep a hold on him. I am standing in the embrace of Mom's other arm with a limp smile and a pouty expression. Mom is perfectly postured and photogenic as she bends into us in the center of the picture, her teeth and her glowing eyes hovering around the vanishing point of the picture, as though in a portrait of the Madonna.

Then there was a ski trip in Park City, where I am packaged into jackets and winter pants on top of frail little skis. Hard boots locked me onto the skis and made my feet blister, and my face was beaten by the frustration of falling into the snow over and over and having a mountain wind howl into my face.

And there is a picture at the airport before a trip to France in high school. Kevin was 11 at the time, and I remember the

Doc telling him about the birds and the bees after pointing to a prostitute at O'Hare and asking Kevin what he thought of her.

Next, there are pictures from family holidays. My cousins are all dressed up. The boys are roughhousing and laughing. I think they were secretly getting high by that time. I sit more demurely at the Christmas table, amongst the adults and younger children.

Sometime between 9 and 10 o'clock, Mom and her friends come home. They enter the house halfway through a retelling of a story from the Doc's pool in the 1970s. I hear the familiar beep of the open refrigerator. Then, the mechanical workings of the electronic wine opener, the pop of the cork, and the miniature cascade of liquid into the wine glass, one after the other, three in a row. Mom puts music on. It takes me a few seconds to recognize it as Chopin, then Mrs. Clark says, "Oh, this is lovely. Who are we listening to?"

"Chopin," Mom says, with a delicate European inflection that leaves the 'n' inaudible.

Mom and her friends continue their conversation around the kitchen isle. Mrs. Purcell and Mrs. Clark exchange glances of astonishment after spotting a piece of Mom's jewelry on the counter and recognizing it as the work of a merchant in Highland Park. When not with my family, I spent childhood summer weekends with the Clarks and Purcells at their second homes in Lake Geneva, Wisconsin and New Buffalo, Michigan. The Kelly family was also in the mix, though my parents were never as close with them as they were with the Clarks or the Purcells. They spent a lot of time on the East Coast, after their children went to Fordham, Boston College, and Georgetown, respectively. The Clarks had five children: three daughters and two sons. The smart ones went to Notre Dame, while the fun ones went to Marquette. One of them was in my class in high school. The Purcell's had two kids: a quieter, older son, the "weird one" growing up, who I hadn't heard about in a while, and a younger, more sociable daughter who was currently in a sorority at the University of Wisconsin, Madison.

"Did you hear that Catherine Hoffman is going to Wharton?" Mrs. Clark asks.

"I did not!" Mom says.

"Well, she did very well on both the LSAT and the GMAT and was debating between Harvard Law and Wharton for business. Ultimately, she decided that business was a lot more fun. And she's correct—nobody likes a lawyer," Mrs. Clark says.

"It's a fantastic opportunity either way," Mrs. Purcell says.

"Yes, but don't be mistaken about Catherine. She's totally fun, and very far from being a bookworm," Mrs. Clark says.

Mom invites the ladies into the living room, where we sit on antiques that I've never thought were comfortable. Mrs. Purcell asks how my father was doing. I groan.

"What?" Mrs. Purcell asks.

"He's been getting on Boo's nerves," Mom explains.

"Over what?" Mrs. Purcell asks.

"Nothing," Mom says. "He and Boo snapped at one another at dinner the other night."

"Kevin was talking about some story in the news," I say. "I don't remember what. It wasn't a big story, but it was a rude story about rude behavior. And Dad said in response, 'Every citizen ought to be required to spend two years on Wall Street. Then people would learn how to respect one another.'"

"What does he mean by that?" Mrs. Clark asks.

"He means that Wall Street is where people go to learn good manners. And apparently where people are capable of going. And he seriously believes it," I say.

"He means it is a professional environment where people have a lot of discipline," Mom says.

"There are a lot of hard workers on Wall Street," Mrs. Clark adds.

"There are a lot of other things, too," I say.

"Oh, he means nothing by it. Your dad is a good guy, you know that," Mrs. Clark says.

"I know that," I say. Mom is holding back laughter. "Mom, why don't you confront him on these things?"

"You can't change people, sweetie. I'm sorry, but you can't. It's funny to me that you think you can, but you'll learn. I was your age once," Mom says.

"He's a very generous man, too," Mr. Purcell says.

"Yes, he does a lot for the poor," adds Mrs. Clark.

"So Boo," Mrs. Purcell asks, "what are you studying?"

I speak quietly. "Physics, but I don't think I'll stay with it."

Mrs. Clark leans back and forth in her seat, tilting her head as she moves. "And what do you think you'll do instead?" she asks.

"Economics, I think," I say.

Mom pretends not to listen, but I see her eye me from the periphery of her vision. She seems relieved.

"That's a fine major. At least kids with economics degrees get jobs," Mrs. Purcell reassures me.

"I hope so," I say.

"Wasn't Brian an Econ major?" Mrs. Clark asks Mrs. Purcell.

"Yes, but he's trying to do this whole band thing. Richard keeps trying to get him a job at the bank, but Brian just isn't interested," Mrs. Purcell says.

"Oh, Boo, did I ask you? Do you ever run into the Fowler girl in California?" Mrs. Clark asks.

"I've never heard of her," I say.

"She's out there near you. She's a Lake Forest girl," Mrs. Clark explains.

"John and Barbara's daughter?" Mrs. Purcell asks.

"Yes, John and Barbara," Mrs. Clark answers.

"I don't think I know them," Mrs. Purcell says.

"Yes, you do," Mrs. Clark tells her. "She's Julie Wilson's sister."

"Oh, yes!" My mom exclaims.

"That household . . ." Mrs. Purcell sighs regretfully.

"Who, the Wilsons?" I ask, trying to keep myself in the discussion.

"Yes, Julie and Jim Wilson. You'd like Julie a lot, Boo. She's on the opera board at Ravinia and does a lot with musical education for the poor kids," Mrs. Clark says.

"And yet Jim is so unmusical," Mrs. Purcell responds.

"Oh my god, he never even smiles. He never asks her opinion on anything," Mrs. Clark says.

"He's out of the house a lot. We think he has a secret role with the Pentagon or the CIA. He never tells Julie a thing. She has no idea what he does with his time," Mrs. Purcell says. I think there is some acting in the way that Mrs. Purcell mourns over this.

"So anyway, she makes the music students her kids," Mr. Clark tells me.

"She doesn't have kids of her own?" I ask.

"There's Jimmy Jr., but . . ." Mrs. Purcell hesitates.

"But what?" I wonder.

"Nothing important," Mrs. Clark interjects.

"I don't understand."

"Jimmy hit a rough patch when he was about your age, and he's been sorting some things out since then," Mrs. Clark says soberly.

"Yes. It's not our business to talk about," Mrs. Purcell sighs, shaking her head. "It must be hard growing up in an environment like that. Jim is such an invalidating man. He doesn't take either of them seriously."

"I don't think they love one another," Mrs. Clark says matter-of-factly. "Rest assured, a child growing up in that family is going to have adjustment issues."

"This conversation is too severe," Mrs. Purcell states. "I

really don't want to talk about it. Boo, please tell me, where are you going to study abroad next year?"

"I don't think I'm going to. My academic future is too uncertain," I respond.

"Oh, but Boo, this is your chance! Go to Europe on your parents' dollar! You've got to do it!" Mrs. Clark urges me enthusiastically.

"We'll see," I say.

"Go to Rome, Boo," Mrs. Purcell says.

"Everybody goes to Rome," Mrs. Clark agrees.

"Oh, yes! Annie went to Rome, and she had the cutest apartment in Trastevere. It was the time of her life! Richard and I brought the kids over during Thanksgiving and rented an apartment in Piazza Navona," Mrs. Purcell says.

Mrs. Clark and Mrs. Purcell trail off with one another about the cute little places visited in Europe. I sip my wine and throw cashews at the dogs. After some time of dallying like this and listening to the music from the kitchen—the Chopin measures getting wilder and wilder—Mrs. Clark asks me, "Now Boo, do you and Kevin talk much?"

"We talk a little," I say.

"And what do you make of him," Mrs. Clark asks.

"I don't know," I say.

"Carol, what do you think of Kevin? What's he going to be like?"

"Kevin is just fine. He's Tom's heir," Mom says.

"Kevin? Not Boo?" Mrs. Purcell asks.

"Boo is her own person," Mom says.

"So what is Kevin doing nowadays?" Mrs. Clark asks.

"He's a busy teenager. We just got him a tutor for the SAT and ACT," Mom says.

"So what colleges is he thinking about?" Mrs. Clark asks.

"Stanford is his dream, but we know he won't get in. We're

encouraging him to apply, but we expect him to end up in South Bend," Mom says.

"Where is young Kevin tonight?" Mrs. Purcell asks.

"He's out at the Lynch's," Mom says.

"Oh, Liz was at the Lynch's house the other week. Gregory was having people over," Mrs. Clark says.

"Boo, who do you see from home?" Mrs. Purcell asks.

"Jenny and Kellyn, mostly," I say.

"Kellyn?" Mrs. Purcell asks.

"Kellyn Schmidt. She's from Park Ridge," I say.

"Okay. I don't know her. And Jenny? She's from Winnetka?" Mrs. Purcell asks.

"She's from West Glenview, but she goes to Purdue now. In the engineering program," I say.

"Now Boo, are there many Chicago kids out in California?" Mrs. Clark asks.

"There are a few. I know a girl from Hinsdale," I say.

"Are you friends?" Mrs. Clark asks.

"Yeah, she's cool. I just don't know how I feel about Hinsdale," I say.

"How's that?" Mrs. Clark asks.

"I don't know. Something about the way they handle money. They make it known that they have money," I say.

"Ah, yes. It's a new money thing," Mrs. Clark says. "People here have been socialized into wealth. They know how to carry themselves with it."

"I can see some of that, but I don't want to go too far with that thought. I don't want to suggest that we are better here than people are elsewhere," I say.

Mrs. Purcell leans forward and says, "But Boo, we are better."

Mrs. Clark points to me and Mom and says, "You two are so civil around one another when you drink. My daughter is such a mess. It always ends in a fight." She laughs.

"We have neither the courage nor the honesty for fighting, drunk or otherwise," I say sarcastically.

"Nonsense! Don't be funny like that. It's a matter of civility. Your parents have raised you very well," Mrs. Clark says.

"I suppose they have," I say dryly.

"Boo, dear, you don't have to be like this," Mom says.

"Be like what?" I say.

"It's so hard to get things out of you. You never tell me anything, and then you make comments like this…" Mom says.

"I don't have anything to tell," I say.

"Well you're so far away all of the time, and you have this whole life that I never hear anything about. What do you want in life? What makes you happy?" Mom says.

From my gut I wanted to proclaim, "Nothing," but I pushed it aside and let it fester and disappear. I improvised. "I don't know what I want with my life, okay?" I say. "There are a lot of things to study, and I don't know what is right for me. And there's a lot wrong with the world, too, and I don't know where my skills lie. There's so much that's messed up and so many things to confront, and I don't think I'm in the right place for it. College is kind of full of shit, anyway. It's a bunch of hiding your head in the sand, and I don't think I'm necessarily turning into a better person because of it. Nor do I think anyone will be better off because I'm there."

Mrs. Clark and Mrs. Purcell are now uncomfortable. Mom isn't paying any attention to them. She says, "It isn't healthy to be this upset, dear. You can't hold yourself responsible for everything in the world. There's too much that will get you down, you know? Reality is harsh, dear. It is. I had a hard time looking into the future when I was your age too. I know we don't see it from here, but it's a cold world. We can only handle parts of it. We have to pick what we are going to give our lives to, and just kind of…make space for the good things with the rest of our time and enjoy our time with our family. And please, Boo, don't turn bitter on us. You have too much to offer."

I bite my tongue before saying, 'But you don't actually give yourself to anything.' The Chopin recording ends. Mrs. Clark tells me, "Boo, just relax for me, dear. You're a wonderful girl. You have time. You'll figure it out."

"I'm sorry for this. I really am," I blurt. "I've had too much. I should be going to bed." I pick up my glass and sweep the crumbs I'd left on the table into my hand. In the kitchen, I throw away the bits and the box of pizza and put my dishes in the washer. The three of them in the other room are talking again, though much softer than before. My glass is half full, and I take it upstairs to my room, and finish it while I listen to music—newer composers I'd just discovered, Nico Muhly and Anna Clyne, and then old vocal jazz, the tender kind that makes me both weepy and lovey-dovey at the same time. I lay in my bed and look at the tops of the trees on my parents' acre of land, half-lit and half-silhouetted by the sky and the outdoor lights, crooked, still, and elegant creations in the night.

Downstairs, I hear Mrs. Clark and Mrs. Purcell say goodbye and leave. Moments later, I hear the clink of Mom's glass against the marble countertop, and the running of the faucet as Mom cleans the last dishes of the night.

My door is about six inches ajar, and the dogs scratch at it and butt it open with the sides of their bodies, and then paw at the side of my bed for me to pick them up and let them sleep with me. Mom passes by the hall and shuts off the lights.

"Good night, dear," she says from the outside of my room.

"Good night," I say from my sleeping pose. I then hear the door of the master bedroom shut.

On Saturday, I sleep in until after ten. I feel like I am still asleep and upset until I finish two cups of coffee. Mom isn't around in the morning; I think she is assisting Grandma with some rearranging in her apartment. Jenny, my high school friend, has a box of my things at her parents' home. It's full of clothes, books, and other trinkets I have left around over the years, and I've promised for a while that I'd come to her parents' house to pick them up. Today I intend to do it.

I shower and drive to her parents' house in Glenview. I park in the cul-de-sac in front of their house and walk to the front door. It is open, and I push through the screen door and announce myself.

"Hello?" I say.

Mrs. Allen comes to the front hall from the back of the house. "Boo! Sooo good to see you!" She hugs me.

"Hi, Mrs. Allen. How are you?"

"That Boo?" Mr. Allen asks from a lazy boy in the other room, which is where I always see him. Mrs. Allen is the bread-winner of the family. Mr. Allen has a room with a computer in the basement where he spends much of his day, and I'm not sure what he does with his time. I think there's a weed or painkiller issue in his life. He was in Dad's class in high school and is kind of a punching bag for my uncles when they get together. I don't care. He's always been sweet to me.

"Yes, Mr. Allen. It's Boo." I walk into his room, he's watching WGN daytime news.

"How's the family? Your old man still a Republican?" he asks.

"Yes," I say.

"How is school? Do you want some tea?" Mrs. Allen asks.

"School is fine, and thanks for the tea, but I'll pass. I've got to be on my way," I say.

"It's such a great school you're at, and such a great part of the country! I'm jealous every day!" Mrs. Allen says.

"Oh."

"You know, Bill's sister has a place just East of Oakland. They're the nicest people on earth. If you ever need anything, they'd love to have you. Their son goes to the University of San Francisco," she adds.

"I really appreciate that. Oakland is pretty far from me, though. I don't get there often. Actually, I don't go there ever," I tell her.

"Jenny says she sees pictures of you, and everything is so pretty. And there she is in an engineering program in West Lafayette, where there's nothing to do, and she's up all night solving these complicated engineering problems. But you're a physics student, so you understand that," Mrs. Allen says.

"You're a physics student?" Mr. Allen asks.

"For now."

"Is it social, or just sad and demented?"

"I beg your pardon?"

"Are you familiar with the Breakfast Club?"

"I've seen it before."

"Well, you should see it again."

"You and Jenny are really going after that STEM route," Mrs. Allen says. "I love it."

"I think STEM is kicking our asses," I joke.

"Well if it's kicking your ass, then it's kicking everyone else's too," she responds. "Anyways, Jenny says that of all of her friends, you were the one that made the best choice in college."

"Ha," I laugh it off. "Well, let's hope so. Anyhow, I came for some things. Jenny said she left a box for me in her bedroom. Is it okay if I go grab that?"

"Oh please, go right ahead," she says.

On my last day home, Mom drives me to O'Hare to go back to school. As she drops me off at my terminal, she says, "Come here, Boo," and hugs me from the driver's seat. "Give me a text when you land, ok?"

"Okay, Mom. I will."

In Spring Quarter, I am enrolled in a full class load, but I have decided to drop out of the physics track. I have not changed my major, but I know that I cannot justify my existence with physics. My course load is a hybrid of economics, electives, and leftover physics classes that I enrolled in through sheer inertia. Economics is not too difficult. We are taught concepts like the gross domestic product and comparative advantage, and neither requires complex calculation at this level.

My friends are more type-A than me. With each year we advance in academia, I notice that my classmates are more attuned than I am to changing social queues and to how kids are expected to mature and carry themselves. I do not have the same peacoat jackets as they do, no Ray-Ban sunglasses, and I do not know what campus gossip is. I have not started smoking all of the time.

Katie, Carla, and I walk nonchalantly around the dormitory one day, conversing in free form, biding our time.

"Did you see them on Facebook?" Carla asks, referring to a couple I don't know, people they see at Light Side parties that I don't go to.

"Yeah, I think they've been a thing for a while," Katie says.

"Who?" I ask.

"Johnny Tyler and Alex Wallace," Carla says.

"Don't know them," I say.

"How come you aren't on Facebook, Boo? This is where you learn things," Katie asks.

Weeks earlier I'd had a fit of rage in my room and fixated on a girl from high school. We were friends on Facebook, and she'd put a lot of energy into aggression toward me at the start of high school, always manipulating, always cutting into me where she knew I was vulnerable. She became more decent with time, and we ended on good terms, but I couldn't get that anger out of me, that sense of inadequacy, that image I'd always kept of her. I rushed to her account to unfriend her and then, fearing that she'd notice this and spot it as a "crazy" move and repeat all of the aggression, I sent her another friend request. The day after, I thought this was insane, and deleted my account completely.

"I got off of social media. People sit on the other end judging you. I don't need that in my life," I say.

Katie stops walking and exhaustedly says, "Boo, nobody does that!"

"Yes, they do," I say.

"They really don't," Carla adds.

"Whatever then. I don't like it. I don't like thinking about it. And I don't care much for Light Side ever. It does not seem like these people care for one another," I say.

"Boo!" Katie yells. "Oh my god."

"To each her own," Carla shrugs. "I'm going to go to Hugo's house later to hang out. Are you interested in coming?"

"I think Hugo is artsy and pretentious," I say. Carla looks concerned.

"What on earth do you have against everyone?" Katie begs. "You're so judgmental."

I pout and look away. "Nobody says anything substantive. I don't know how to be friends with them. Thanks for the invite, but I don't think I'll join you, Carla," I say.

"Whatever," she says.

In the evening, I went off campus to a senior's house. It was a guy, Kyle, who I met at a party at the end of Winter Quarter at Elise's house. We have been hanging out and casually hooking up, but not doing much else. His roommates are out, and we watch half of a Will Ferrell movie together in his living room. I think the movie is slow and boring. Frankly, I think the same of him. I am with him more for convenience than anything else. He leans over to initiate a hookup. I accept, more or less passively. It doesn't last long, nor do I feel any real joy. He has a heavy build and a clumsy hold on my body, and I never get outside of myself and into being with him. But I kiss anyway, and say, "sure," when he tries to go deeper. Upon finishing, he extends himself across his couch, and I sit with my legs crossed on his floor and flip through his books. He is disinterested, and I tell him I have to go.

When I return to the dorm, I feel unfulfilled and regretful, just as I had over previous encounters. I fret that I've ruined my chances at enjoying sex — another Eden spoiled. While low, I slip outside for a cigarette. There is someone else smoking — Tori, a slim, cerebral girl with a punk haircut, tattoos in Arabic, and one of the most mordant senses of humor I've ever met. The cigarette is temporarily sobering, and Tori is easy to commiserate with. Many of the guys from the dorm come boisterously out of the door with their skateboards. They go every night to an empty parking garage across the street, get stoned, and skate. Tori says she has to go off to the art studio, and I become neurotic again, alone with the bad thoughts, and I go back to my room and take four Advil to calm the cigarette rush. Invariably, this doesn't calm me, and I put on religious choral music for distraction. I fantasize about old European cities, Catholic nunneries, and monasteries, and the high culture of European art as the choir sings. All these images melt in my mind's eye, come to me as a salve for my disturbances. Around half an hour after midnight, Sara returns from studying and doesn't say anything. She drops her bag and goes to the bathroom to clean up. I turn off the music and look in my drawer to see if any of the Valiums I had bought off of Katie were still there. There were none, and I fell asleep after ninety minutes of flipping in bed with hectic nerves and a rapid head.

There is little comfort in the social world, save one outlier, who I don't speak of. Her name is Charlotte, one of the only other women in my physics classes. I do not speak of her partly because I do not know how to say what I feel for her and partly because

I am ashamed to. She is attractive to me, but not in the way that I can tell women are attractive. Her features are transgressive. A bit masculine, though the body is clearly not that of a man. There's an *otherness* about her that I can't define, and yet I feel drawn to look at it from across the classroom and contemplate the person behind it. I feel drawn to her confidence as well. She is easy with her humor, and when she asks me something, I am certain that she means what she is saying to me. I want her to ask me more than a trivial question about studies.

Our physics lectures are filled with chatty, geeky young men who crack jokes with the professor about old researchers and obscure films. I don't get the jokes half of the time. She doesn't either. And after these jokes, she looks over and winks a knowing gesture to me. About one of the geeks, perhaps? Or frustration over the course itself? We have been doing homework together, painfully. Our professor had warned us that modern physics is the course that weeds out the true physicists from those who thought it was cute to talk about ramps and balls. Given my grades, I think I'm the second type of student. This is the first time in college that I am not getting As and Bs easily, but that's acceptable for a class like this one. The professor spends an hour deriving concepts like the speed of light through long explanations demonstrated on a two-tiered chalkboard. When he is finished, he says "Eureka!" in a purposefully (I hope) corny impression of a scientist. To him, this is poetry. That a number like the speed of like could be found in the natural infrastructure of the universe is to him evidence of intelligent design, as part of God's artwork in the world. Science, he says, is God's how. To understand God's why, he advises us to consult the Jesuits.

The dimensions introduced in this course make no sense to me, unsurprisingly. After class, I emerge from the lecture hall into broad daylight. It rips into my eyes, and I find shade while my vision adjusts. The sudden visual stimulation disables my cognition as well, and I almost pass out. I sit on a concrete bench and watch students mingling. Some kids I know from the dorm in freshman year are in a huddle with others I don't recognize. They must have branched out. From my side, someone says, "Hey, Ellie."

I turn. It is Charlotte. "Oh, hey," I say, and use my hands as a visor to see her more clearly. Charlotte is dressed plainly, in a strong yet unpretty way. Again, I feel there is something handsome about her. It's more of a feeling of charisma than a physical observation. Charlotte cracks a couple of jokes about class, then invites me to go with her friends to a hiking trail on Saturday. I say that of course I would, thinking I've come off either tepid or eager to her.

When Saturday comes, I meet Charlotte and her friends at a house on Dark Side. I have a small headache from the night before, along with a tight stomach. Charlotte greets me, offers me coffee, and introduces me to her friends. There are five of them in total, all are juniors or seniors, and they are all friendly. Over coffee, Charlotte explains to me that she went to high school in the area and kept a tight crowd of people from home with her.

We drive to the hiking range in two cars. It's about thirty minutes north on the highway, and Charlotte and her friends smoke weed along the way. There is a broad, open field of cattle, water, and uncontrolled grass at the entry to climb. The hill runs quickly upward at a steep far more strenuous than what I am used to. When we've gone hiking in the past—myself, Carla, BJ, Brendan, Jeremy—we go to lazy, relatively flat trails in the Santa Cruz mountains, or along the oceanfront. The guys take hallucinogens while the rest of us wander and drink water. It's a spiritual cure for the excesses of the party. Mission Peak, being the highest climb in the area, demands much more exercise. We can't waste our time and waddle and watch our friends talk about seeing fake people in the hills. Charlotte's friends are smart. They talk about politics and the environment while I keep quiet and lag a step behind.

We get to the top of the hill and stop to look around. The peak sits above the clouds, an impenetrable mist covers most of the vantage point. The parts of the sprawl on the ground that are visible to me look like towns underneath a plane — a mirage of lights over buildings and miniature cars. When we return to the ground level of the hike, after passing through pockets of wildlife and other quiescent scenes, Charlotte's friends decide to go to a burger place about twenty minutes away. Charlotte tells them that she isn't feeling well and takes one of the cars back to campus. I go with her.

In the car, I sit in the passenger seat and browse through Charlotte's iPod. She has one classical recording, a Tchaikovsky piece, and I listen to it to be calm. I rest my hands on my thighs and look at the hills through the window. Charlotte chuckles. "You're a deep thinker, huh?"

"No," I say. "I'm just happier when it's quiet. I'm more comfortable with myself in these settings."

"I understand," she says. "Social life can take a lot of energy. It's nice to be chill sometimes."

"I agree," I say.

I am tired. Looking at the hills underneath a damp winter sky, I am ready to fall asleep. While I am not watching, Charlotte moves her hand onto mine. At first, I am frozen, unsure of what to do. I place mine over hers and continue to watch the farmland. I forget why I had any inhibition, and it soothes me. I glance at her, and she glances back and smiles. Then I squeeze her hand tighter. We don't talk, and I continue to choose music as she drives us home — St. Vincent, The Tallest Man on Earth. Charlotte pulls near campus and asks if she should drop me off at the parking lot by my dorm.

"Um. . ." I procrastinate.

"Or we can hang out at my place," she suggests.

"That sounds nice," I say.

We go to Charlotte's and I am too nervous to speak. There are wrappers and other bits of trash lying around her house.

"I'm sorry for the mess," she says. "We had some people over last night. They didn't leave until about three, and we didn't have time in the morning to clean up."

"That's okay," I say. "It's really not that bad, and am I a neat person myself."

I wait on a couch in their living room as she brings me a glass of water, my body's tucked on the edge of the cushion. Charlotte arrives with water in a cheap plastic cup. I drink it quickly, taking long sips to delay talking.

I try for conversation, but it is rigid, insincere. If only I had a more experienced person's composure.

"So," I say, pointing to a collection of books against the wall, "those are yours?"

"Yeah, some," she says and clears her throat. "Look, I invited you over because. . ." she says.

"Yes?" I nod.

"I just—" and then, stopping and lowering her head, she moves into me and kisses me, and I return it. It lasts for about five to ten seconds, and then I push her off. I open my eyes, cough, and sit upright.

"I have to go," I say.

"Oh," she says. "Sorry, if. . ." Charlotte says as I walk off.

"No, don't be." I have my sweater in my arms and am stumbling towards her door. "I will see you in class. Everything is fine, really."

When I kissed her, I was suddenly aware of what I was doing, like "giving it away." I felt I needed to put good thought into it before just letting it happen, and so I left, rudely and curtly, and did not talk to her about it. And in that time, I hardened into more misery and crass anti-lesbianism, denying myself both what had happened and what I actually felt within myself. I can admit it only later, that I felt more tolerance for myself and my world when she held my hand on that drive than I did with any of these drug-addled man-boys and academic try-hards that I'd been loafing around with. But I also felt more disgust for myself. And I could never permit that feeling I had with Charlotte coming into clear view.

From there, I become insane again, only this time more frighteningly. Maybe even psychotically. To reassess my sexuality, I jump into squalid hookups where the both of us are so drunk that I hesitate to say we even had sex. And sometimes there is no hookup at all. One man I see has a cocaine habit, and though I go home with him, nothing happens. He is up all night talking and snorting, and I am there, hanging out in his apartment. Something about being around a junkie is appropriate for my position. There's nothing for either of us to hide. I can tell him what I've felt, and he passes no judgment. At 3 AM, when I tell him that I have no intention of hooking up with him, he looks put off but accepts what I've said and passes out. I sleep on his floor. There's nothing unnatural about it.

I spend more of my free time with my senior friends, Elise's friends more specifically, who are rampaging out of college by trying drugs they'll never get a chance to try again, and having long, obscure talks about life, work, and love. My friends in my own academic class go to Jeremy's house on the weekends, an equally drug-infested pit on the fringe of campus, next to motels inhabited by transient meth-heads. I go there sometimes, too, often reluctantly. On a Saturday midway through the quarter, Katie, Carla, and I walk to Jeremy's house, and Katie and Carla are bickering about something. The two of them still live together and still argue about things regularly.

I hear the club-banging music coming from Jeremy's house

from a block away. His front door is open when I arrive, and I already feel the sickness in myself that I'll feel a day later. We enter the home to find, as expected, a room of guys lounging on damaged furniture.

"We did molly last night, so we don't have the energy to do anything today," Jeremy explains.

"So you're just going to sit, get baked off your ass, and play video games?" Carla responds.

"Yeah, pretty much," Jeremy says.

The three of us grab light beers and talk to the guys who are more alert and engaging. Charlie and Christian are in the backyard arguing about a girl that Christian has been hooking up with. "Tim used to hook up with her," Charlie tells him, "and he says she's crazy."

"So?" Christian shrugs, "People say everyone is crazy."

"No," Charlie cautions, "I mean actually crazy."

I am still figuring out what that means to other people.

Jeremy's house shows no signs of becoming more active, and we catch word of a few gatherings on Light Side. We leave to find kids hanging around a backyard bonfire, drinking, and listening to EDM, where the timbre of the synthesizers is as easy and tacky as glow-in-the-dark neon. Carla's friends offer us shots and weed. I take a bit of both. As I exhale, my vision gets blurry and I start to stumble. People ask me if I am okay, and to the best of my ability, I say that I am. Katie and Carla stay close by to be sure that I am all right, and eventually I stand upright and manage myself. Luca comes to the party with his new girlfriend. I am happy to see them, and they seem entertained by me. She is a girl from the social justice program, and I don't think she goes to parties much. Both of them laugh as I make an ass of myself and slur my words, but it is all in good fun. That's what I tell myself.

We go home around 2:00 A.M. and drink as much water as we can before passing out. On Sunday, Carla wakes at 9:00

A.M., takes an Adderall, and plans to study until 5:00 P.M. I, on the other hand, feel like hell. I wake with the gentle tingle of a mind wandering elsewhere, the palpable coat of depression and anxiety around me. I get breakfast by myself in the student center, and as I sit and eat, tremendous fear blooms inside me, and I begin to think that I will be caught in it forever. It nauseates me, I can't eat, so I throw out half of my plate and go to the dorm.

As I walk, my vision blacks out again, and I sit on the ground to catch my breath. Nobody stops me to ask if I am all right, even though I am cowering with my head in my hands.

When I feel clear enough to do so, I stand upright and walk to my room. I look into the mirror. My eyes have deep bags under them. The panic escalates into a state of incoherence and I almost faint again, so I wet a rag, lie down, and put it over my forehead. Suddenly I am in the world of nonsense, unable to put words to anything. With no one else to contact, I call Luca. Our conversation devolves into me mumbling before he hangs up.

A minute later, he sends a text.

Boo, what's going on? You don't sound alright.

I slowly make out a text in reply.

It's ok. If you want to be with that girl, that's cool. Just, please don't come around me much. It wouldn't do any good.

There is no immediate response, but I get one about ten minutes later. It is long, and I think he has put thought into it.

Boo, don't be weird. You can't be saying things like this. If things are getting bad again, please just —

He has written much more, but I don't want to read it and close my phone.

I am still frightened. My sheets are wrapped tightly around me, and images of the mind's eye are again evaporating in front of me, only this time they are more grotesque: wastelands, gravediggers, muddy trees.

It is Sunday, so I make an obligatory call to my parents. Hello, hi, how are you, miserable, it's the same thing. Dad informs me of Notre Dame's latest pickup, I remind him that I didn't go to Notre Dame. I confess that I'm not doing too well in my classes. When they press me why, I say that I don't know and, after a series of confessions that I cannot even remember, I begin to cry and tell them how much I love them. They simply say, "Toughen up, honey," and hang up.

I cry myself into a more relaxed state and call Katie. She does not answer, but texts to remind me that she planned to spend the day in San Francisco with Bryce, an effete, dry toned boy that she occasionally brings to hang out. He is sometimes nastily mean, and only speaks if he is going to rip into other people with biting commentary. I despise him for it. He treats me like a prudent, Midwestern bore, and I interpret nothing but condescension from his statements. But really, it hurts most because people like him say what everyone else thinks.

Around two in the afternoon, I get out of bed, put on sunglasses and a peacoat, and take a walk. There are too many vices on campus not to go insane. I need to get away, and I do, walking through the neighborhoods for about forty minutes. Very quickly I learn that the fear follows me everywhere. There is no comfort in this walk. My saunter lasts for about forty minutes, after which I sit on a park bench and ruminate and reminisce. But this too is no haven.

I return to campus and reflect on a bench in front of the statue of St. Ignatius. By now I am fragile and wholly unaware of my surroundings. I rest my elbow on the arm of the bench, cover my eyes in my hands, and cry. How long I do this, I don't know. By coincidence, Katie and Bryce return from San Francisco and walk by me on their way to the dorm. I duck away, but they notice me regardless.

"It's fine, it's nothing. Really. It's fine, it's nothing," I tell them, urging them to leave me alone.

"Jesus, Boo, I don't mind you crying, but not in public," Katie says. "You can't get away with doing this shit."

I dry my face against my coat sleeve and walk back with them. In my dorm, I sigh, weep more, and go to sleep early.

Assignments are due in the coming week, and I am many hours behind on my workload. Too many to overcome, probably, especially if I spend all of my "work" hours twitching, worrying, and imagining the various ways my relationships may end. I do not look at any of my phone messages or emails. Before reading anything, I assume that the content of each message is going to denounce me or force me to acknowledge an unnamed crime I have committed. I have given up on one class entirely, the one on scripture and the environment. I'm convinced that it doesn't matter whether or not I pass or fail this course.

Noticing my decline, my other professors request meetings with me once they have seen my strong opening of A-papers and perfect attendance disappear. The meetings are loathsome, and I can barely make eye contact with the professors. There's no chance I can hold a conversation about my work. Bowing my head before my Greek literature professor, I shout, "I didn't do it, okay!" The professor, an elderly, pedantic woman from Chicago, wants to help me with my writing anyway. She has my first draft in her hand.

"Obviously, it is very incomplete," she says, looking at three hastily developed paragraphs underneath my name. "I want to know if there is anything I can do to help you grasp the concepts."

"It's not the class," I tell her. "It's not. I love the plays we read, and I think I read them well enough. It's something else. I've been… I've been a bit emotional lately."

She looks from me to the paper and slowly nods. "Okay," she says, in a drawn-out, avoidant way. "Well, the Greeks have a saying: he who has begun, has half finished," and then she encourages me to finish the paper and submit what I can. I have almost the same encounter with one of my other professors, and he tells me that my emotions aren't an excuse.

There is a period over the next two weeks in which I miss at least half of my classes. I'm up after midnight, often in a frenzy for four hours, running my legs underneath my sheets to calm down, and when I do sleep, I sleep through my alarm in the morning. When walking, there are steps of incredible lightness that feel as weightless as a child's balloon. These are outnumbered, however, by longer, more consistent hours of heaviness. Other nights are quieter, yet nonetheless irritating. My mind reverts to a very small and juvenile place, full of humiliation over neglected crushes and friendships that have since moved on. The sleep I do get is brief and bleary, and when I wake, I feel thick. At times I feel too feeble to leave the house, or too afraid. How is one supposed to maintain responsibilities if everything is to be feared and avoided?

Sara asks me one day, out of nothing, "Boo, who are you talking to?"

"What do you mean?" I say.

"I asked you who you were talking to, and you said you were talking to BJ. You said you were going to kill yourself," she says.

"No, I didn't," I say.

"I was sitting here right now," Sara insists. "I saw you look at your computer and talk to it like you were having a conversation. You said it was BJ. You said you were going to kill yourself."

I genuinely have no recollection of it happening, but then I have no recollection of the past five minutes at all either. I fear that she is correct, and it terrifies me. My vision blacks out and I fall to the floor. When I regain consciousness, Sara helps me up to my bed and prepares a glass of water for me. I have to miss my class.

Everything grows stranger from here. By the afternoons, I am without a mind. I forget where I am going or what I am supposed to do. Time is chopped up. Either I have no concept of it at all and I lose it without realizing where it has gone, or it proceeds very, very slowly, and very, very difficultly. My thoughts are more volatile. I engage in fantasy and conspiracy theories. Sara asks me in the dorm, perhaps jokingly, perhaps derisively, "Having any more imaginary conversations with yourself?" I never respond to this.

At parties, I am weird and unwanted. Students look at me with sympathetic concern, "Are you . . . all right?" they say. Others keep a secure distance from me, eyeing me as though in preparation for me to explode.

One weekend the social justice program puts on a drag show in honor of LGBTQ rights. I dress up in men's clothes and put on a fake beard for the occasion. Apparently, there's some side of me that can't be expressed through the body and gender I have, for whatever silly reasons the world puts upon me. The event itself is an electronic dance party, all underneath a banner with a RuPaul quote: "Ego loves identity. Drag mocks identity. Ego hates drag." The after-party is slovenly. Charlotte is there, and without provocation I mock her for being a homosexual, saying vicious slurs to her face. She says nothing in response and leaves me to crawl home alone. The next time I call home, I recall the drag show to my parents, without the sordid details of the after-party. Dad rebukes me in a seething red tone, "This shit doesn't happen at Notre Dame."

My dreams are lucid and ungodly, full of unwanted sex acts and famous figures. I set several alarms and sleep through all of them. On the times I do wake, a grave heaviness comes onto me, and I collapse onto the floor. Only coffee gets me up, but it does not heal me. It merely changes my mood. Instead of death and stupor, hysteria: a great excitement propelling me into twirling lunacy.

I realize that I need a haircut, so I do it myself. The outcome is uneven and patchy, and I buy a skullcap to cover it up. One of my teachers is filling my inbox with statements of encouragement, writing *Hang in there* and other messages.

School means less and less. I want to get away again. Far away. In a drunken state I spend $700 on a plane ticket home for Memorial Day weekend to surprise the family, then cancel it the next day. I start having unprompted conversations with students around campus, telling them how smart I am and how unnecessary college is. I'm going to change my name and move to Paris to join a bohemian expatriate of some sort and become a great artist. No, the best artist! Which kind? I don't know. A musician, a writer. The environment will choose it, as will my hunger and my separation from you all. I am convinced I should get up and leave.

I toil through some of my schoolwork, accomplish almost nothing, but get Cs anyway. My papers are longwinded and full of personal asides and sidebars. The formal exams are no better, but who cares? After a particularly hopeless exam period, one where I am certain that I failed, I return to the dorm, babbling and howling and shouting obscenities from the scorched back of my throat. Thankfully, most of the building is gone. Sara is the only one who hears it, and she stands in the corner of our room with her jaw dropped and her eyes widened. Again she asks me what I just said, and why. I deny that I said anything. She looks scared.

In summertime, the turmoil settles. I feel defeated, sort of like being on land after a hurricane: muddy, contaminated, embittered by the storm. But I am safe. And quiet. My final grades are poor. I failed one class and got Bs and Cs in the others. I decide it is best not to think about it. I go back to Illinois for the summer. I hope this is what is best for me.

CHAPTER 5

February 2016

The Doc's ashes sat in a small white box in the center of the table. For three years they had been in that box, and my mother's family hadn't yet decided what to do with them. Toss them in an urn, perhaps. Or wait for Grandma to pass before resting them somewhere with her ashes. Bury them in the backyard of the old house by the lake, or put them in the lake itself. Or send it up with illegal fireworks from Wisconsin or Indiana on Bastille Day. They'd reach an answer sometime. For now, however, the Doc was condensed in a plastic bag in a white box on the center of the table in my parents' magnificent dining room, with Victorian ceilings approaching the base of the firmament and six-feet-tall paintings on the walls.

My parents were hosting my extended family for the Doc's birthday, and also for a remembrance of his life.

"Boo, what advice do you have for Gaby before she goes off to college?" my Aunt Mary said. I looked at my little cousin, who was seventeen, and soon to hear about her college acceptances and rejections. I told her, implicating my older relatives, "If you listen to any of them, you'll end up miserable."

My aunts laughed, "Hey!"

Over a meal, we were listening to the pianist Brad Mehldau playing long, hypnotic covers of alternative rock songs and jazz standards. "My Favorite Things" was playing.

"Raindrops on roses and whiskers on kittens . . ." my mother sang through the conversation of the guests and the musical speakers.

"He loved *The Sound of Music*," added my Aunt Joan. "Remember when we did *The Sound of Music* trip in high school?"

My mother and her siblings raised me and my cousins on Rodgers and Hammerstein growing up, that musical in particular. In the upstairs hall of my parents' home, there was a picture of my mother and her sisters from the late 1960s or early 1970s on that trip. In it, my grandmother, who was so young that I did not recognize her, spread her arms across eight children in lederhosen and dirndls, whose expressions ranged from euphoria to total anomie. It had the tint of old film, and for most of my life, I was embarrassed to show it to other people.

"Yeah, and he took that stupid van on the Autobahn," said my Uncle Harry. "With that cane?"

I'd heard the story before. On that same trip, the Doc drove all of the children in a Volkswagen van and assailed speeding cars on his left with a walking cane while he drove.

My cousin Hannah asked, "What cane?"

"Oh Lord," Aunt Vicky said. "We took that van across Europe one summer. The Doc would drive it on the highway, and cars would pass him going 80, 90 miles an hour. He'd keep that cane up at the driver's window, and reach out the window and smack cars as they'd go by."

"Wild geese that fly with the moon on their wings," sang my mother.

My cousin Michael hit a butter knife against his beer. His wife Meghan was next to him. "Before we continue reminiscing about the Doc, I've got news. Meghan and I are having a child," Michael said.

My family applauded.

"It's time for a girl. This family has too many boys," Hannah said.

"What difference does it make? Our girls like poop jokes and our boys are comfortable with Broadway and cheap chardonnay," my Aunt Joan said.

"Yes, they're fucked either way. Let's not make the difference too important," I said.

"Even so, we need more girls," Hannah said.

"I don't mind having grown up with so many guy cousins," my cousin Gaby said. "It's made me tougher. I've never taken anyone's shit."

"It'll be a boy. It's always a boy," my Aunt Joan said.

"Because the child always takes the gender of the weaker parent," Mary said.

"Bullshit," I said.

"It's true, according to the Doc at least," my mother said.

"So in that case, Michael is having a girl," my father said.

My cousin Michael took a sip of his beer and raised a middle finger towards his mother.

My aunts laughed. "He only said that to get a rise out of us," my mother said.

"I still don't get the reference here," I said.

"When we were growing up, the Doc would push all of these bullcrap theories about the world onto us, probably just to screw with us. One of them was that kids took the sex of the weaker parent. He only said this because he had five girls and two boys, and he wanted to piss off both his wife and his daughters," my mother said. "Then one day, Mary called him on it. She called it chauvinist crap, and the girls at the table stood up and applauded her. She was our hero for the week. Then Mary had five kids of her own, and three of them were boys. The Doc asked her, 'What do you think of my theory now?' And Mary said, 'Dad, you were totally correct.'"

Everyone laughed. Mary interjected, "Enough—a toast! To the new baby and to the Doc."

"All right, well who else has memories of the Doc?" said my Aunt Mary.

"I'll go," Michael said. "So the Doc brings me to the race track around age fourteen or fifteen, and we're sitting in the grandstand before the races. There's this old woman looking at a horse, and the horse is just . . ." he stalled for words, and held his hands parallel to one another with a foot of space in between them.

"Hung?" my mother interrupted.

"Yes," Michael continued. "The horse is absolutely hung. Like, full-blown. And this old lady is just standing there looking at it, for way too long, really, and the Doc is sitting next to me, looking right at her, and I'm young and awkward and trying to ignore everything. Then he says something about how all of these old women get caught up in size, and I don't really know what he's getting at. Then he looked me in the eye and said, 'Don't worry about the size. The size is just right, every single time.'"

My family laughed again. "The Doc never held off when it came to sex, even about the things that you're never supposed to talk about," my Uncle Harry said. "He used to treat sexually repressed priests in the Chicago Archdiocese. He'd listen to them negotiate between God and their urges until he'd eventually cut them off and say, 'Father, just beat it to death if you want to. There's no crime.' They loved him for it. They loved that someone in a position of authority gave them permission to do that."

"That's gross," Gaby said.

"That's your grandfather, who incidentally was kind of a pig, but we loved him," Aunt Joan said.

"Can we talk about something else for a change?" Hannah pleaded.

My grandmother blushed. "Did you know that in the more than fifty years that we were married, we never once fought?" My Uncle Harry reached over and rubbed her shoulder. My grandmother was wearing a fur coat. A little white dog sat anxiously at her side. My Aunt Mary leaned over to me and, underneath her breath, said, "Yes, let's keep her thinking that."

"All right, I've got one," said Uncle Harry. "This was back in the '70s when we had Lucci the dog. I was out in the yard while the Doc was putting up a wooden fence. Out of nowhere, a hawk swoops down, grabs Lucci, and starts flying away with her. The Doc picks up this large piece of the fence, like six feet long, and throws it like a Frisbee. It nails the hawk right in the middle of its body, and it drops Lucci and flies away."

"Holy shit," my cousin Jimmy said.

"But that's not it," Harry continued. "The Doc walks over, looks at the dog lying on the lawn, turns to me, and says, 'Go get a garbage bag.' So I do it and toss Lucci in. Then she starts moving around like, what the fuck are you doing with me? I'm not dead!"

Mary spoke. "On that note, that reminds me."

"What, the cats?" my mother said.

"Yes," Mary said, her face flushed red. "The Doc got these cats for the kids—you all know the story—and he goes to the veterinarian to ask about getting them spayed. The vet says that it would cost something like $500, and the Doc decides, eh, fuck it, I'll do it myself. He takes the cats down to the basement of the house on Michigan Avenue, assembles all of the kids to watch, and knocks the cats up on something. I don't know what—pain killers, tranquilizers. He has his children around for a demonstration and then he goes through the whole procedure. The kids get to see their little science experiment, and it all goes fine. A day or two later, the cats are still knocked out. So Mom goes to check on them to see if there's still a pulse. She thinks, 'Oh, God, the Doc has killed the cats.' She gives them a little nudge, and things wake up, spaz out, and croak. The Doc says, 'ah, well,' puts them into a plastic bag, and dumps them in the Wilmette harbor by the Bahai Temple."

"I'm not sure this is the best way to remember the Doc," Michael said.

"It's the only way to remember the Doc," Aunt Joan said.

"How about a nice story?" Michael said.

"Did I ever tell you what he told me about marriage?" Hannah asked.

"No, what?" Michael asked.

"I was sitting with him at some family function, and he says, 'Ask me why I got married.' So I say, 'Doc, why did you get married?' And he roars back, 'Because I'm a masochist!'" Hannah said.

My grandmother's cheeks were puffed up over the bottom of her eyes. "I told you! The Doc and I never fought!" she said.

"I'm going to take this in a more serious direction," Jimmy said. "I feel like there was a special connection we had with the Doc for being his grandchildren. Granted, you got all of the good stuff. You were the first generation. But there was something different about the way he taught us."

"The Doc said that grandparents and grandchildren get along well because they share a common enemy," my mother said.

"Exactly!" Jimmy laughed. "But I'll never forget what he told me about the fifth commandment, about what it means to honor your mother and father. It means you do things that honor the family name. You keep it strong. You keep it respectful. You keep it decent. And you don't do things that bring shame upon the family."

We all sat quietly. The piano played over the speakers. I was next to speak, and my aunts looked towards me. "Well, Boo, what do you have to say?"

I started. "This is all one side of the Doc that we always talk about, but there's another side. You know how in Mozart's letters they found him writing poop and sex jokes? Well, the poop jokes are great and all, but we've got to remember that the Doc was also a genius at what he did."

"That's right," Aunt Joan said.

"I didn't appreciate it 'til I was starting college. As you all know, since I talk about it all of the time, I had my bouts with depression. It was what it was. I came out of it eventually. But about the time that I was getting unwell, around nineteen or twenty, was the same time that the Doc was really miserable. You know, when he said everything was terrible. We shared a common nihilism during those years, and we knew one another in that way then. And before that, I didn't know just how good he was at his craft. I didn't realize it then and I didn't appreciate it. Really, we just hung out and both felt close to death, even though I actually wasn't. He was. I simply had the delusion of being near death. I had glimpses of it then, but didn't realize it fully until I started talking to Diane Kennedy and the Mulvahils, because he treated Maggie and Tommy O'Connor and Mrs. Mulhavil."

"That's right," Joan said again.

"I didn't get it growing up, but to a lot of people, he was the spiritual guru of the North Shore. People had these problems, and they didn't know what to do with them. They couldn't even put words to them. He was the one who could navigate that whole part of the world that people didn't talk about. He helped get people through to the other side," I said.

"Yes. He was very compassionate," my Aunt Vicky said.

"He really knew what it was to be human," my Aunt Mary said.

"Absolutely," my mother said. "Just look at Greg. He still comes to the house to take care of things, and the Doc hasn't seen him as a patient in thirty years."

"Remember how he used to take the patients from the Evanston psych ward and bring them to the pool?" Uncle Harry said.

"And he knew that there were limits, too. Maggie O'Connor killed herself on the Metra line. When she did that, it was like the third or fourth time that she tried. And when Mr. and Mrs. O'Connor called him beforehand for advice, he had to tell them that it was beyond their control," my mother said.

"He said some people are going to be determined to do it, and there's nothing you can do about it. It devastated the O'Connors," Mary said.

"Yes," my mother said.

"And then Tommy killed himself later on. That poor family," Aunt Joan said.

I looked at my father, who had been silent through all of this. Something was coming out of the corner of his eye. I noticed that it started when I mentioned *a common nihilism.*

My Uncle Joe spoke. "You know, after Tommy O'Connor killed himself, I was really hurt. And angry. But I knew everyone was grieving and that it was only natural, so I decided to give it some time. Time passed, and I was still upset with him. Deeply upset. I hated him. So I called Diane O'Connor and told her about it. She told me this in response, and I'll never forget it. She said, 'You aren't allowed to be mad at Tommy. You don't know what kind of pain he was in.' And then she read me Tommy's suicide note. It was lovely. And remember, Tommy's last years had been really rough, and really uncomfortable for a lot of us. He got into those hate groups, this neo-Nazi stuff, and was going door-to-door with it. He was scaring the neighbors, and we really didn't know what to do about it. Then after doing that for half of a year, he came back to earth again, and he was like the Tommy we used to know. And it was so nice to have him back. And then . . . then he killed himself. But in the note he left, it was like none of that weird stuff had happened. It was like Tommy was talking to everyone as a brother, as a friend, as a son who was leaving. And he talked about how much everyone meant to him and how he would miss them. And his final words were this, which Diane still keeps on her workstation: *Only love and understanding can conquer this disease.*"

My Uncle Harry's face was red and drenched with tears. He backed out of his seat and rushed out of the table. Everyone else nodded, and the table became somber for several moments. On the speakers, Mehldau was now playing "On the street where you live." The eleven-interval jump during the phrase "all at once am I . . ." pierced through them as they sat in the aftermath of that conversation, with the Doc's low moaning of the line coasting through memory.

I drove home to the North Side after the commemoration for my grandfather. I poured an extra glass or two while I was with the family, though I thought against doing so. My coworker had gotten me to drink at the restaurant earlier in the day; shots of Jameson during our Sunday rush, which, in addition to the caffeine I took on account of waking up hours before the sun rose, put me in a precarious and somewhat stupefied mental position. Not that I couldn't think straight or reason, I just felt like sluggish dirt about it. I enjoyed being with my family that evening, and I poured the extra pour, drank the extra drink. It was a mawkish, self-indulgent drunk, just to feel sweet and at ease. On the drive back to the city, Sheridan Road glowed with the wonder of a childhood fairy tale. I was listening to some CD I had gotten at a concert before by an up-and-coming composer. It sounded like it came from the West Coast composers of the 1970s, and went on for about an hour with some skittish electric voicings alongside the piano. This is what I meant by mawkish: driving through my hometown while the alcoholic buzz lightly coated my thoughts and vision, as Keats did with his nightingale. What exactly was waking and what exactly was sleeping, that was the question. For most of my time, the states closer to sleep — and therefore furthest from consciousness — were where life was finest. It was a clear night, the streetlights were beautiful, the Bahai Temple harbored over the trees like a small moon. I was in love with my home again.

I then passed Mark's parents' home and got a harsh pang in my chest. I had a decent amount of wine, so I couldn't help but be a sap. I remembered that when I picked him up for the last time, before he called the whole thing off, I was listening to Mozart's Requiem, and I pulled into his driveway about a minute into the Dies Irae. I used to take things as omens, back when I was blacking out and spending the next day feeling haunted and damned. Three or four times, when I really was at my worst, I walked across a dead animal, and every time I took it as a sign of impending doom. In a different mental state, I would have taken the Dies Irae as an omen. And I would have been correct.

Driving by that house was hurtful. I still remember my dizziness and the fragility of that night when he left. I remember how vicious my suicidal ideation was that night, how dark the winter was as I drove through it into the city. It had been a while since I'd actively thought about him, but I suppose this was why people say and do the most regrettable things to their exes while it is late, and after they've had something to drink.

Mark and I spent that last day together getting coffee and watching a movie. I was sleeping on him the whole time, and at the end, he told me he had something to say. In so many words, he left me, and now when I think of him I think of things like how the last time we slept together during Christmas time, he positioned himself apart from me in my bed in a way that now seems calculated and withholding, with his body angled away from me at the hip, so unlike the touch we usually had with one another. It was close to meaningless at the time, but later, that gesture seemed like it had years of unresolved staleness behind it. I understood that he knew he was going to get out of it, and he was going to wait to tell me while being with me through the holidays, even while being inside of me. And now I am pondering: if I could handle the distance, why couldn't he? He was not strong enough to love. For once, I was not to blame for things being screwed up. I loved, or tried to, and I had no misgivings about the matter.

But why bother with the details. The details didn't do me any good—that was where the devil was, after all. By the time I was in bed that night, I was still obsessing over that memory from the day he left, passing involuntarily between states of sleep and wakefulness in a despondent frenzy. The descent into depression happened almost immediately as I got home from my parents' house. And it went far deeper than normal. I wrestled between the sides of my bed, at times flipping from my back to my chest and feeling that Mark would be there when my chest landed, but only passing through an apparition.

I was vulnerable. In those hours after midnight, I was filled with a longing, a sentimental whimpering. It was the cry of the depression of one who lives poorly; a hollow, self-induced sadness. I turned empty and romantic, deluding myself about the people who used to be with me but aren't anymore.

I never had to get over somebody before because I had never actually had an intimate relationship. Most hours I didn't think about it, but when the arrangements I'd built my day on disappeared—work, social associations, study, food, exercise—and I was left with only myself and the space we used to share, he reappeared. It was truly pitiful. The hour passed midnight, and I remained restless. I needed some distraction, something to move forward with. I went to my email folders and retrieved the eulogy my cousin gave at the Doc's funeral, which ended with a line about the right to determine one's constitution in the world, and I felt emboldened. It kept the inner beast away, and for a moment, I was in command.

The night continued, I became unnerved. I hardly slept and had to be up in mere hours. I had done myself a disservice with all of this booze and coffee. Why did I do this to myself, knowing how destructive it could be? Because the alternative was more unpleasant, I suppose. My mind would have its comeuppance for me, I understood. Live one day, die the next three. Or, live never and die every day. That was how it was in clinical depression. What proceeded was difficult to articulate in the moment, as it was too feverish of a madness. The next morning, I hastily documented it in my laptop:

There is nothing about lying in your bed next to a half-eaten peanut butter and jelly sandwich that merits saying — nay, shouting — "Oh, fuck me" a dozen times over a thirty-minute span, and yet here I am doing so. It is not clear to me whether I will be leaving the house today, or if I will be staying in and watching a slothful amount of television, and cramming a work-filled day in later in the week to compensate for it. I need a place of respite, and I think today that place is my bed, which is where I am now writing this, the day after a vicious night.

Because I didn't eat enough yesterday, I can feel myself withering twenty pounds thinner. I also felt it last night while I was lying in bed, when my stomach was tight with undernourishment. I didn't take proper care of myself. I needed water, but was arguing against rolling over to my dresser, where a full glass of water was only an arm's length away on my backside. I was convinced that it was poisonous. My intuition told me it was better to starve and parch than to make the basic effort of drinking water. I felt, clearly against my own interests, that I needed to remain passive and endure the mental torment being put upon me (or which I had brought on myself), which occurred so late that as I drifted between being asleep and being awake, I thought I was passing into psychosis, hearing and seeing things that clearly weren't there, the things of a nightmare. Eventually, I did roll over to get water, and then I stood up and went to my kitchen to get a bite to eat. As I stood in the dark, I felt as close to possession as I ever have in my apartment in the city. The intensity of my emotion was so thorough that it felt to be viscerally throbbing and pulsating around me.

This fervor lasted from about two to five o'clock. Rarely has the impulse for self-harm been as insistent and dominating as it was then. I don't know where it comes from, but I get the idea that cutting myself at the side of the arm will mellow things out. I've heard from people who have had histories of self-harm that it feels like taking cocaine, a drug I am wholly unfamiliar with. The thinking in cutting isn't that anyone wants to die — although they do, that just isn't the immediately intended outcome. The thinking is that they want to get lightheaded, feel high, fall asleep, and make the bad thoughts go away. It also allows them to play out all of the things they've been repressing and denying: that they hate themselves and desperately need to learn how to love themselves.

I can dimly trace the veins on my arm as they curl from the side of my wrist, down through my forearm, and disappear into the crease of my elbow. I see it as a wire to be snapped with clippers; a bad system to be shut off. I see them and the thought comes to mind, and there's a mental force drawing me to the kitchen knife in the drawer. But I don't do anything destructive in that way, and I never will. I have and always have had a remarkable discipline against self-harm.

Laying out suicidal ideation as bluntly as I do probably terrifies people, and has almost certainly pushed people away before. If they leave at the first glance of madness, who needs them? As for being scared, I don't believe a little anxiety about the matter makes anyone necessarily hostile towards people like me, though the potential for it to become hostile certainly exists. Suicidal ideation is an undeniably unsettling concept, especially when made explicit. But then so is war, rape, murder, environmental destruction, and yet I know plenty of strong, decent people who can engage in an honest examination of those horrors without running away from anyone who mentions them. What is it about "mental illness" that does not merit that standard?

I have an exhaustively revealing approach to madness that doesn't fit into any preexisting voice I've encountered, and because of that, I have found that I might be particularly well-suited to push the idea that a person can have a largely aberrant psychological landscape and still have all of the same human qualities as anyone else. So I do, without apology. Besides, the notion of a mental constant or "sane" standard of humanity is an under-scrutinized yet remarkably dangerous assumption, for it implies that humanity fits into a relatively narrow, content mental landscape. And yet every person on earth either knows fully well that this isn't true and has firsthand contact with the consequences of that repression, yet regulates this knowledge carefully. They don't talk about it. And that's amazingly counterproductive, and I oppose it. I want to help reframe our understanding of humanity to account for the range of experiences of the mind as we would for any other diversity issue, and dissolve any personal or social constraints born of sanist proclivities to uphold distinctions between "crazy" and "not crazy." But for today I am just an invalid, trying to clean myself of the madness around me.

I don't know what I would do if I didn't get out of it. This. This thing that comes to me. This thing I drink myself into. There was a time when I wouldn't get out of it. When I would never be anything but insane and useless, when it was all that there was. But then I did. Because of technology and because I was able to move to a different environment, I did. But what if I didn't? Would I be still able to grasp this state so rationally? With one straight sentence after the next? It was plausible that I could have deteriorated indefinitely for the rest of my life if circumstances were even mildly different. But now, madness feels like a country that I have visited before and has gone from alien to familiar. It's a perverse homecoming. I can speak about it even as it holds a different language and a different physical and mental constitution. I can move in and out of the condition as a fluid state, not a fixed point of consciousness or identity. But the fact that I can do that is only because I have crossed lines so many times before, never truly inhabiting a sane life or an insane one, and have seen it through many different psychological lenses. If I didn't get out, if I don't know this would wear off in several days, what would I be saying? Too much time in the extremes of Depression equates to death and unspeakable irrationality. I think it might be like Sarah Kane and 4.48 Psychosis, which I have somewhere in this ostentatious stack of books of mine. It would be like her utter contempt for herself, rendered in lyrical disgust and incoherence. She hates the product with all of hell, but somewhere through that, she knows it is true. She knows where she is, where she has been, and that she could not escape. I envy her for it, for being able to express what I feel but could not express, at the sacrifice of her own life. I envy her for deciding to get out. "I sing without hope on the boundary." How I cherish those words, which I can say over and over as though a lullaby to my child. "I sing without hope on the boundary, I sing without hope on the boundary, I sing without hope on the boundary . . ."

I had a dream that night during the few hours that I slept. It was a lucid dream. I was aware that I was sleeping; I could feel my sheets against my body. I wanted to wake up, and as I tried to rattle myself awake, something pushed me back to sleep. It was an unseen force, and it felt a lot like that repressive thought cycle I was in during my bad acid trip. I was in a dreamlike version of my bed, an almost exact replica. During the dream, I was sure that I was about to wake up to reality, but never did. Instead, there was someone in bed beside me, and I was kissing the person's chest. It started as a male's chest, flat but firm, and then blossomed into a woman's breasts. The stomach thinned out and arched at the back, and I rested my face on the body, allowing myself to be naked next to it. I turned toward the face, but it remained out of my focus, hidden in the cloth or the shadows, always eluding me as I turned towards it. The sheets blew over me, as though the dream was stolen from a Hollywood montage. I woke up deeply tired and anxious, but also aroused

A day later, I remained detached from the rest of the world, recovering from the part of truant and shut-in that I had been playing from the bad night. Which was a pity, because there were life-and-death happenings that I should have attended to. I woke with several notifications and voicemails, all from old friends from high school. Without reading a message, I understood. Molly O'Brien, my friend from high school, died. I'd heard that sometimes the phone rings, and in a superstitious way you understand the content of a message before you have heard it. Your awareness of the news precedes any real delivery of it. This morning, I knew by premonition alone. Molly had cystic fibrosis and was consigned to dying young. Though I had seen her go into the hospital and come back on countless occasions, I had taken for granted that there would eventually be a final encounter. But what was I to do, view her as though she was interminably in hospice and be prepared to let her rest? That would have been a humiliating way to treat a friend. And she never wanted to live that way, to have anyone understand her as a kind of limited human. And we never did. Everyone else knew it would happen, too, and yet we never really spoke about what it would be like when she died. Over the summer, she had been direly ill. She was in intensive care multiple times and had to walk with an oxygen tank, which she carried like luggage everywhere she went. Even then, it never occurred to me that she could pass away within two weeks. Her returns from the hospital were always sprightly, and it tricked me into complacency. Some people with disabilities are so gifted at dispelling the dependency and debility within their lives that you neglect to understand the medical and mortal implications of living with a disability. Molly's disposition never let off the reality of the disease.

I didn't have an immediate emotional reaction. I usually don't with death, not until the ritual begins. I was in an enfeebled place from the madness and the sleeplessness, with damaged nerves and muscular atrophy. Mark messaged me about Molly's passing, and that was the first text I read in the morning. It was also the first time I'd talked to him in weeks. He was desperate. He was friends with her long before he got to know me, and I think he hooked up with her twice and may have privately cared more for her than he ever did for me. I realized I'd be seeing him at the services at the end of the week.

Aside from class, I had no obligations that day, and ultimately did not even go to class. I spent it mostly in bed, in a state of near-catatonia resembling my senior year in college, taking extra pills of Effexor to restore stability. It did not work. To activate myself, I decided to get up and do errands. Doing groceries was a trying, paranoid task. With each fraught step I made in the market, I believed that people were looking at me distrustfully. It took all of the fragile mental focus I had just to get the little things right, and by "little things," I mean sticking to the most basic, unnoticeable principles of going out in public: "walk on the right side," "put one foot before the next," "don't stop in your tracks," "don't go too fast or too slow," "don't stand too close to others," "pick up the grocery and put it in your bag," "don't speak to yourself," and so forth.

When I got home, I tried in vain to read. Nothing registered, not a single phrase. I finished each page and realized as soon as it was over that I processed nothing of what I had read. Again, it was like being a student at age twenty-two. Thankfully, I was in a position where I could afford to have useless hours like these, and I'd know that my full mind would return to me soon.

The sun set, and I wrote to occupy myself. The sky outside

the window held sundown's flame behind winter's solemn freeze. I was in bed, mostly unclothed, and mostly dissociated from existence. It felt like purgatory. I had no sense of how long I'd been lying where I was, stiff and thoughtless. The birds chirped beyond my walls. The sounds resonated from all directions: above, below, across, left, right. In my room, the air was chilled as a freezer, and I was consummately listless. Only through writing did I feel that I was making any sense or was a conscientious part of the world. It was my only gateway to a rational life in an otherwise anarchic condition. Without it, I had no feeling that I was taking part in anything, other than fitting into this picturesque evening as merely another object, with as much animation as a stone or a crumpled leaf. My eyes felt the same closed as they did open; which is to say, alien and absent, more like a bar on the window rather than a tool of perception belonging to me. There was a polluted current around my body; an anxious, depressive current that kept me from thinking and moving too liberally.

Whenever I would return to the world, I would be a shade. I'd move, I'd speak, and I'd interact, but it would be lifeless and hollow. The only reason I would seem functional would be because I could find a way to look at people in the eye and use proper grammar. If I could reach that baseline minimum, I'd seem as capable as anyone else, even if I'd have no real feelings or thoughts on anything.

I writhed in my bed. A sharp, antsy feeling sprouted from my chest. It grew and grew. Then it receded, and then it grew again. Every few moments I rose towards an inspiring thought, then it faded, and I couldn't recall what I was trying to think about. I couldn't even recall what I was glancing at just a moment earlier, whether it was the book on my floor or the cup of water on my dresser.

I didn't know how to define my physical ambiance in these times. It was a vague tactile sensation swooning around my body.

It lurked behind my eyes and made everything disorganized like a sporadic film sequence cutting from one image to another without concern for linearity. Every so often I felt a twinge of self-loathing. I cringed with my shoulders and shouted as a madwoman might in an open field. Or in my case, in a neighborhood in the city for all to hear. Otherwise, this was not a painful feeling, or at least "painful" was not the best way to describe it. It was a nullified feeling. It was the feeling of "nothing," which was possibly more cruel than pain. I would almost always rather be sad than not feel anything at all. Sad was poetry compared to nothing. Sad could become laughter. Sad could become music. Sad could make an evening walk an act of contemplative wonder. Sad could spark an epiphany. "Nothing" was exactly what it promised to be.

I did not feel that any of those beautiful things that sadness may bring were available to me. Time moved slowly, I repeated myself often, things were done without any sense of importance, and my life felt to have no relation to anything else. It was times like these when I used to stare at the television for hours, just to disappear. There were ways I could get out of this feeling for the evening—namely by drugs and substances. Alcohol would have helped, but prolonged this inhumanness into the future. Tobacco could have stimulated me for the short term. Coffee would only have transformed it into a spastic panic, where I would be likeliest to attempt harm. Rather than any of those devils, I took two pills of ibuprofen. Whether those would do anything, I didn't know. It would give me a negligible placebo effect at best. All I could hope otherwise was to make it to a reasonable hour, having left myself in a comfortable position in the morning, where I might feel zest again, and where, hopefully, my spirit would be waiting for me.

When night came, I went on my computer. I tried again for thoughts, but they were impeded. The anxious orgy in my chest moved around my body and up the top of my spine toward the back of my head. My arms felt like they need to be incessantly itched or rubbed off. There was cramping pressure on the back of my head and neck, different than the anxiety. My jaw was clenched tight, and I struggled to undo it. The anxiety culminated into intense hilarity, like that of a hyena, which I restrained to myself, laying on my own, looking like an ass.

The next day I was almost normal. I did a lot of work during the day to distract myself, in addition to going to class at night. My sleep was mostly disturbed, and my dreams were again clear and hellish. I took more Effexor to become stable, and it helped significantly. I started to think about more real-life things. Molly's death took on a larger place in my consciousness, and it felt religious, tragic, and cathartic. The spiritual rituals of marriage and burial were the only times I felt that I shared a communal soul with others.

During these weird days, I didn't talk to Jude. When I did eventually get in contact with her, she said she had also learned about the death of a friend. When I asked her who, she said, "Nobody you would know," and changed the topic. She wrote something on Facebook about it, though. She was so blunt about telling people how miserable she was, and by the number of responses that she received, I understood that she knew a lot of people that are comfortable knowing that someone can be manageably suicidal, whereas I didn't think I had that with anyone.

I've saved her Facebook post, as I save many of her posts:

Trigger alert. If you find reading about thoughts of suicide triggering then you should not read this. Move on to a pic of a cat or a story about Trump or almost anything else.

I am working on a big, complicated project, the biggest I have worked on in many years and perhaps the most complicated I have ever worked on.

I have spent most of the last three months on this project.

While I was working on this project someone died. Many of the people who will read this know who that person is. I did not find out about his death until now — no time to process.

Many tributes to him have shown up on my feed.

He deserves them. And for those who love him and those who will miss him. I am very sorry for your loss.

As many of you know, I have a strange relationship with death. When others die, either famous people or people I know in real life, my first reaction is: How come they get to die and I am still alive?

As most of you know, I am poorer and in more physical pain than most people in the United States. Certainly poorer than most of the people who have had the gifts that I have had. Except for an occasional bad moment, I am not jealous of those people. I am immensely jealous of people who die. It seems wrong that people who want to live die and I still live. If I had more gumption, I would kill myself. I am ashamed that I lack the gumption to kill myself.

Even this project does not change that. If I had the gumption to kill myself, I would gladly not do this project. Most of the time I work on the project, I think about how I wish I was dead so I would not be working on this project.

There have been moments when working on this project, I have found myself in "flow" working at something I think is important, and that I can do, and time passes without my noticing it. I love those moments of flow.

I have been given tremendous support on this project, people have made and kept commitments to me that are nothing short of amazing.

Someone is working on this project when I know that she would rather be with her husband and kids.

Only a handful of people in this country could do this project. It is the result of the best part of my work over the last fifteen years of my life.

And yet . . .

If I was dead, I would not be working on this project. I wish I was dead.

I hadn't seen her in a week or two. She also wasn't getting out of bed, nor was she talking to anyone. There were days when I arrived at her office, let myself in, and found her lying in an unmade bed, next to stacks of books, boxes, and half-drunk glasses of water. When I'd prod her awake, she'd scream—not in anger, but terror. "My god, I was having the worst nightmare," she'd say, and then I'd give her an hour to gather herself and see her in the office. Often I was afraid I'd give her a heart attack like this, or that I'd find her dead.

Jude and I arranged to see the Governor of Illinois address the state legislature on the State of the State. After years of neglect from the people who ran Illinois, the dominance of the Democratic machine cracked and an unalloyed businessman won the governor's office. Businessmen, being the most formidable of America's residents, have always been endowed with the qualities of a captain or a general in the public, even in situations that have nothing to do with making money, such as in public service and public finance. The Governor was sketched directly out of the playbook of robber barons and corporate reaction to the New Deal, with a corresponding corporate libertarian ideology, based on right-to-work laws and re-regulation in favor of corporate growth. The goal of the Republican Party in the Midwest was to turn the region into a southern red state.

Based in a conservative philosophy of property rights, individual liberty, limited government, and supposed free enterprise, the logical consequence of a further rightward shift in political economy would maximize the influence of a handful of private property owners, while in the long-term limiting actually existing democratic power and the quality of life of most people. By then, the Republicans had perfected this cycle over decades through clear manipulation: when in power, run the government on debt and deficit, lessen revenue by reducing taxes and expanding spending on corporate subsidies, military, and punishment; when out of power, blame the fiscal shortcoming on the soft hand of the state, such as on human services, and oppose any increase in spending that does not come from their authority. Whereas old conservatism was ostensibly a governing philosophy of prudent inheritance of the past and incremental change regarding the future, new conservatism was a radical ideology of non-governance, holding government office for its own ideological ends with no concern for balance, accuracy, or consequence. And whereas prior generations of conservatives viewed communists as anti-Americans, newer conservatives viewed anything to their political left as communism, regardless of what the facts said, thus normalizing incoherence and paranoia as the default setting of American politics and media. Yesterday's capitalism was today's socialism. The new conservatives demonized fractional public benefits while regenerating garish figures of wealth amongst board tables, year after year, and browbeat even anodyne dissent as a step towards hell and the death of America. Ideology and centrism followed a rightward shadow, beginning with Reagan's revolution and moving from Bush to Bush to the Tea Party, fated to end in a corporate feudal system, if not fascism outright. The Governor fully endorsed this radicalization to the Right, though in smoother, hidden language, and the prior rule of Illinois Democrats, led by a tyrannical, Machiavellian Speaker of the House, had provided him with generations of failure and corruption to exploit, making his agenda a very alluring sell to a desperate populace. If successful, however, it would eventually leave most people living either in frustrated, overworked mediocrity or in a contemptible state of poverty, transferring more public goods and wealth into private board rooms, leaving a small number of people fantastically wealthy by comparison.

My father knew the Governor somewhat well. They'd been on golf trips together, and my father had visited one of his nine homes before. He described the Governor as he does most other rich men: "a decent individual who does a lot more for the poor than people would give him credit for." Even though as soon as he took office, the Governor neglected nearly every poor, minority, and disability leader who tried to correspond with his administration, essentially discounting their existence in the state. This modern Republican insurgency operated in exclusivity, with small, anti-democratic, heavily funded think tanks assigned to produce policy. Rarely if ever did they give their opposition consideration in public. It was suspect, then, that my father would speak of him as someone who was foremost concerned with the interests of the needy, and that he did so without irony. It took me a long time to speak honestly to this point, but I noticed that the richest among us displayed solidarity to one another by ceaselessly upholding these facile accolades of goodwill, as my father did to the Governor, regardless of the honesty of his positions regarding towards society's less esteemed ranks. They front-loaded the conversation so tightly with their supposed merits—for example, prestigious higher educational degrees and large charity donations—that there was hardly any space to open up a critical conversation about them or of the basis of how wealth and poverty are generated and distributed. In so doing, it asserted both the triumph of the will of rich men and the social and moral correctness of their pre-eminence, while simultaneously erasing any interrogation of the conditions that produced wealth in the first place—barring, of course, the individual merit of the rich.

Noble as my father saw the Governor's work to be, whatever sacrifice these rich men were actually making on behalf of the whole was difficult to identify, for sacrifice implied a loss of status which then risked an individual's security. At no point did anyone of my father's or the Governor's class standing live outside of a position of surplus, while a majority of the rest of the state lived in precarity, particularly people with disabilities. Given that he was entering into power in a government long controlled by cynical, corrupt agents within the Democratic Party, the only way to advance his platform was to obstruct the most basic procedures of government by refusing to sign a budget, therefore pitting labor and social services against one another via fiscal starvation until somebody conceded both to his demands of austerity and his rearrangement of the structure of policy in Illinois. For an entire year, this stalled the functions of government, regardless of whether those functions were good or bad, and threatened the existence of any entity that received state funding. As for the burden of the rich in this deal, sure, they gave away some of their money to philanthropic causes, and in some instances, they gave away more in one day than what others have ever held in a lifetime. Though, if the starting point for this act consisted of one person having everything, and another having nothing, then this wasn't an exceptional feat, at least not any more exceptional than an elephant bragging about taking a bigger shit than a mouse. Nor did it at all prevent the elephant's propensity to crush the mouse under its foot without noticing.

Within my lifetime, whenever the system came closest to catastrophe, I'd never seen the rich put their own bodies on the frontline in the name of the common good. No, that responsibility was always placed on the multitudes who lived elsewhere, who were so often said to be lacking in responsibility and concern for their welfare. One asked for the other to compromise on a basic standard of dignity to spare the surplus. The other asked in return to compromise on a surplus to spare dignity. Most vulnerable amongst the have-nots were people with psychiatric disabilities, who had long been amongst America's most marginal sociopolitical constituencies, if not the most marginal one. I had been reading about the asylum reformer of the 19th Century, Dorothea Dix. Through an astounding life in civic performance, she galvanized support for the US federal government to allocate millions of acres of federally owned land to the development of asylums for the care of "the indigent insane" (we've never been at a loss for awful terms for the people we believe to be crazy). Disregard, for a moment, that the asylums were eventually a doomed model: the humanitarian rationale in the era was to save people from greater decrepitude of life in jail. What was remarkable of her life was that Dix was successful in passing such a bill through Congress through political conviction and relentless campaigning, only to be vetoed by the sitting President on the grounds that aid to the poor constituted socialism, and was counterintuitive to the American ethic. The President subsequently sold that land to railroad developers for a stunning profit.

Two centuries removed from this smash-and-grab, that core thrust of the American id did not change. If anything, it had only been amplified. When the market crashed in 2008, the state legislature—namely Democrats, those cheap, manipulative bastards—cut nine figures of funding from community mental health services in Illinois, putting the brunt of the axing into rural southern parts of the state. Many of those counties would then face the trifold scourges of political and economic isolation, unemployment, and drug addiction. All of this was done in the name of necessary austerity to save the state while we staved off complete disaster, only to result in complete disaster for the people it promised to save. I wonder if a single person in the legislature had asked, "what did people with psychiatric disabilities have to do with the crash?" But then, it was about saving the economy as its leaders understood it, which never actually viewed the welfare of people with psychiatric disabilities as an essential part of its operation to begin with, as businessmen were always organizing to discredit and disinvest from social services. When the Governor took office, he cut seven figures more for community mental health, again to recalibrate the state for the success of business. What we were left with was, in Jude's words, "a mental health system so dysfunctional and so full of holes that one cannot speak of it rationally." With tenuous integration into public and economic life, and with a massive incarcerated population of people with psychiatric disabilities, nursing homes and psychiatric institutions appeared too many to be a humanitarian cause, and those lobbies organized themselves within the state to win the battle for mental health policy. Barring a political collective to counter these interests, decisions would be made for them on behalf of elites, rather than on the conclusions of people who used the system about what constituted social good in mental health care.

This locked them into a stratum of political and economic irrelevance, for it ensured that they would always be amongst the first to be dismissed when times are bad, and the last to see a penny from the gains when times are good. In economic periods outside of crisis, even fair-minded employers had a rationale for discrimination. Why hire someone who would be unable to work several weeks or months per year? Some of us might have been able to advance into successful material lives. In a system in which a basic standard of welfare and material protection is dependent on a private contract, a majority would be diminished to lower tiers of economic power and transient work solely by psychiatric disability, made second-class both by the social stigma of madness and the poverty of unemployment. When caught in the cycle of stockpile and austerity American capitalist political economy—the simultaneous removal of funding, benefits, and supports at the least powerful levels, combined with repetitive accrual of wealth and execution of public disinvestment at the highest—the end for them in the American dream was a path of destitution amounting to social invisibility and death.

My father had gotten us tickets to sit inside the legislature during the address, which meant that Jude and I would be cozying up with the Governor's appointees in a time of major class antagonism and assault. This was nothing new to me. Coming as the child of an investor, I'd always been somewhat of a bourgeoisie imposter any time I engaged in poor people's movements. As a fat person got thin and remained mentally fat, I would never be able to undo the mentality of being a rich man's child when I interacted with others. Whether Jude was comfortable with that or not, I didn't know.

When the day to travel came, and I had gotten well enough to get out of the house, I drove southwest from my apartment to pick up Jude. It was February, and the roads in Chicago were disgusting. I arrived at Jude's, and we routed our trip to Springfield. She had to pack, and I helped her throw her belongings into a travel bag. All she had was a couple of t-shirts and pants, along with some fliers for her organization. I asked her how things were going with her grant proposal. Jude brushed me off and said that she had gotten into a fight with Kristin about it—Kristin being a nonprofit manager who was helping Jude out with her work.

"We had some extra money in the proposed budget," Jude said, "and I was thinking about working more and paying myself more. Only if I made that much, then I would be ineligible for my welfare and benefits. Kristin said it would be suicidal to do that, only I didn't listen to her. As you know, when I think I'm right, I don't easily change my mind." I didn't ask her anymore, though I suspected that if Jude did want to kill herself, it would be done under the guise of something sophisticated like that.

We left her apartment and drove down Cicero Avenue through various Westside neighborhoods before getting onto the interstate highway. The drive was smooth, and for the first thirty minutes, we didn't speak.

"What are we doing tomorrow at the capital?" I asked.

"There's a rally at 10:00 A.M.," Jude said.

"By who?"

"One of those groups that wants more revenue," Jude said.

"Which one?"

"I don't remember. I knew earlier this morning. You know, one of those Republican caricatures of liberal groups that want money," Jude said.

"Are we for them?" I asked.

"Yes and no."

"What do you mean?"

"Well, I may be old and crotchety. Actually, that's not a point of debate. I am old and crotchety. Mainly I have a philosophical difference with them. Their agenda is to pressure the state to find revenue to pay for services, which includes nursing homes. I don't want them to give any money to nursing homes. I want them to give less money to nursing homes, yet they see nursing homes as a benign force and don't understand why I object," Jude said.

"My teacher calls nursing homes the NRA of state politics," I said.

"Ha! Bastards," Jude said.

"So you agree?" I asked.

"Oh God, yes. They send representatives to get in favor with every part of the system. Legislators, social workers, you name it. They're always trying to redirect people toward their institutions. There's a lot of clout in Springfield, too. A number of representatives come from families who are very invested in nursing homes. The Governor too has made some money off of investing in private nursing. And, though I'm pretty sure this is illegal, there are state legislators currently on the boards of nursing homes, and people who used to work for state legislators now run them," Jude said.

"And what does that mean for us?" I asked.

"For people like you, probably not much. For people like me, everything. I think with inequality being what it is, we have this system where poor, disabled folk have diminishing means to take part in the mainstream. They have very few streams of income and very high costs of living. And as they struggle to maintain a livelihood, there are going to be people who will point to their plight and say something needs to be done to care for them. Rather than community supports, they'll say the solution should be in nursing homes and institutes of mental disease. I'm very cautious about the long con here. There is a lot of money to be made in warehousing people, and pieces are quietly aligning to make that a reality. You may see a push for snake pits to come back, only people will say they are going to be more benevolent this time around," Jude said.

Jude paused and winced her eyes. Her body was tilted against the side of the door. She continued, "Almost every time I've been in the capitol to testify or partake in some policy discussion, the nursing home representatives outnumber me five to one. I'm always the only one there who has ever been in a nursing home. And while I try to educate them and badger them toward something more decent, they have every incentive not to listen to me. Yes, it's a very one-sided fight. The lobbyists have almost all of the power. To change policy, you've got to be able to convince people that money can be made, and nursing homes and pharmaceutical companies can make that sell in a way that we cannot. On the welfare side of the game, this country has an obsession with worthiness and frugality. Speaking bluntly, people with mental illness are not seen as deserving enough to get resources on their own."

We drove south and the wind tore against my care. I worried a part of the car frame might tear off and roll onto the highway. The surrounding environment became sparser and flatter. The signs we passed by the countryside endorsed Bible verses, rest stops with fast food locations, and pornography superstores, while the landscape was otherwise tranquil, save the billboards and planes with banners. Advertising executives claimed even the open sky as their territory. We turned on AM radio—a personal fascination of mine while on the road in America—on which an old man was talking about the dangers of socialism and godlessness. He was angry at almost everyone, and in his sermon, evangelicalism and anticommunism blurred together into a paranoid, hysterical genre of Americanism. He was bent on converting, on drawing lines between right and wrong, saint and sinner. Capitalism equated to God, which equated to the Bible and goodness. Socialism equated to Satan, which equated to "hell in a handbasket." These rhetorical ploys loaded every viewpoint with the weight of salvation and damnation, and these ideologies interbred into a mindset that was unlike anything I encountered in person: homosexuality would erode civilization, men needed to find the right women to enter heaven, feminism was a conspiracy, and you needed guns to protect yourself from the thugs who do not mean well to God's country. Providing healthcare to all was feared as a pathway to mass impoverishment, while direct impoverishment through austerity and disinvestment was said to liberate individuals from the corruption of poverty. All roads were doomed, except one promised route.

"So religion was big to you?" I asked.

"To my family, yes. To me, not really. Were you religious?" Jude said.

"I was up until a point, but I gave it up around 14 or 15," I said.

"Crisis of faith?"

"A crisis of fundamentalism. As I look back at it, fervor for Jesus was my earliest madness."

"Tell me more about it."

"I'd rather not. Tell me about your religion."

"How do you explain Judaism to goyim...for starters, we have a lot of holidays. A lot of events, but the basic concept behind all of them is the same: someone tried to kill us, we survived, let's eat," Jude said.

"What about the orthodox part?"

"That's a fundamentalist issue, too. In Orthodox Judaism, God essentially micromanages the world, and everything that occurs in the world does so because of his will. When I was younger and became crazy, the faith would have me believe that I was crazy because God wanted me to be that way. I had a hard time believing in a God that willed me to be crazy. The God of the Old Testament was always doing petty, vindictive things to Jews when he got upset. He was kind of an old, bipolar asshole."

"And Jesus was a schizophrenic for thinking he was a Christ," I said.

Jude laughed. "Exactly."

"Did your religion shape how you understood insanity?"

"Not exactly. But it shaped how some of my more committed orthodox relatives saw it, although in time they would grow to understand me on very human terms. I remember my uncle talked to me when I was older, and he expressed to me that it didn't matter to him whether or not I believed in the faith literally. So long as I maintained decency and respect for myself and others, that was good enough."

"I think that's where a lot of people end up at."

It got dark, and we discussed our respective upbringings further as we approached Springfield. I asked Jude, "Do you ever think that your mental health problems are mostly social or economic in nature?"

"Well, I was a lawyer, and I had the chance to make a good living but didn't. So socially, no. And economically, no."

"That doesn't preclude problems," I said. "Lawyers are drunks, and lots of people who have good lives are unwell. The Governor's son used to shoot heroin with my neighbor, who was also the son of a rich man. People would say it's because he's spoiled and has the means to screw around, but couldn't that also be used to fill something inside of you? What happens to a kid when your upbringing neglects everything that isn't about business?"

"I don't think I follow," Jude said.

"I don't think privilege is the flower you think it is. More of a Venus flytrap. Look at my brother—he's one of the most poorly adjusted people I know. And it comes directly from being the son of a rich man. He couldn't go anywhere without my father telling him how to dress, how to comb his hair, or trying to set him up with a finance job or a position on a Republican campaign. My brother used to struggle against it. When they'd go to skybox baseball games, Kevin would want to wear jerseys and basketball shorts, and my father would not take him unless he wore a collared shirt and khakis. You know, he's not his own person. He's a presentation for my father's business friends. So he stopped resisting, he stopped trying to be himself, and he accepted being a young facsimile of an older man with money with the hope that he'll grow into the role if he plays along with their game. He's cocky now, but the moment he has real problems, he'll have no idea how to get out of them," I said.

"So you're saying white men aren't happy?" Jude said.

"No, that's not it. My father gave my brother the 47% rant but he did not give him the sex talk. How is that possibly good for the soul? I'm saying that you can be a lawyer and have a nice life and still identify the source of your misery in your environment. Is that how you've ever thought about yourself?" I asked.

Jude didn't offer a defense of that observation. "I was having this conversation with my cousin who just turned 70. She's in a mental health crisis and has been in a deep depression for longer than she knows. We were polar opposites when we started our adult lives. I had a career, and she never even thought about having work. It didn't occur to her to pursue that. She was looking back at the choices she made as the source of her present mental health crisis. Her kids are out of the house, her husband is sick. And when he isn't sick, he carries himself like he owns everything around him. She feels that something is lacking because of all of this, and she's right. But at the time all of those decades ago when she decided to have a family rather than a career, she felt there was nothing else she would do with her life. She never considered the alternative. Even with a cousin like me, who took a torch to every obstruction put on me, she never considered it. As she was saying this, she told me she was jealous that I wanted to have my own life, not my husband's life. She said I'd made the right call. But what could I tell her? I'm not well. I'm even worse off than she is. I lost my job, my spouse, and my home. I'm unable to work for months at a time. At any given moment, I cannot think without getting exhausted. It's a persistent struggle just to exist. My life choices have done nothing to make me well."

"I don't think that particular choice of yours is to blame," I said.

"Well, it didn't work out! So what do you make of that? Am I to blame?" Jude asked.

"Nobody is to blame, Jude. It just is. And it would have been different for your cousin, I can guarantee it," I said. "Look at me. I was born into money and it has only messed with my head. You think I don't have a freer life cutting ties with it?"

"I think you'd still feel obligated to the money, but in a different and probably more restricted way," Jude said.

"I understand that. It doesn't stop the self-hatred, nor the feeling of never being worthy enough," I said.

"I wouldn't beat yourself up for it, Boo. You're choosing to do good," I said.

"You think? I haven't actually accomplished anything, and who's to say that I will be able to do anything? I'm not even that deeply into the movement you're involved in. Sure, I seem like a do-gooder now, but there's probably some corporate Democrat down the line thinking about buying me off if I ever become remotely appealing as a political actor. Think about the young Hillary Clinton, or the young Barrack Obama, or any other person who is close enough to the money."

"They're different. All three of you are brilliant, but they're different," Jude said. "The young Clinton wrote her thesis on Alinsky. Alinsky then offered her a job, and she turned it down for law school. She said that organizing was too simplistic and idealistic to make any change. Then she became a corporate lawyer and married her husband, they took over the Democratic Party, and then the world, and by the end of this year, she'll get to be president a second time. And I worked with the young Obama. We were on a campaign together around asbestos in low-income housing. He was awkward in the position, from what I remember. I remember him as an over-achiever who was uncomfortable in his own skin. Over time he became more relaxed around people. Then he started to act like them. With white people, he talked white. With black people, he talked black. I don't think many people can imagine what that sounds like, Obama talking outside of the context of politics, like a black man at ease from white pressures. He has the remarkable ability to act like the people he is surrounded by. That's what I thought about Obama then, and I certainly think it of him now. Whether it is with bankers in Winnetka or poor folks in Roseland. But he wasn't meant to be an organizer either. An organizer famously asked him, 'What are you angry about?' To which he responded, 'Nothing.' So the organizer told him he had no business organizing. And then, of course, he also went to law school and became president. And it's true: he was angry about nothing, and he didn't want anything to change. He made that very apparent from the start, though nobody wanted to see him that way. At your age, you're far more sophisticated as an actor for justice than either of them were, and far less of a capitulator to the people who control the wealth in this country."

"The comparison is overblown, of course," I corrected her. "He's president, she's going to be president, and I'm never going to be anywhere near any office."

"But what does that matter? I respect him more than I respect her because he organized for three years and she organized for none. And I respect people who have organized for twenty years more than I respect both of them combined," Jude said.

"I still don't know if I have anger like others have anger. I more have resentment. I'm a rich kid who resents her upbringing while remaining dependent on it. It's not the same. I don't know how I fit into this," I said.

"What's the source of your anger?" Jude asked.

I replied, "The question of money and privilege. Money, money, money. It makes the people I want to work with view me as a perfidious actor, like I'm a latent racist or a latent Republican. I spend a lot of effort trying to prove otherwise, and I don't know if that is possible. No amount of political correctness and virtue signaling can stop a Winnetka child from being taken as a Winnetka child. And on another point, the money is on the table for me in a way that most other people don't deal with. For some, organized people plus organized money is a hypothetical scenario. The fact of my inheritance means I have the responsibility to take the power of organized money seriously and develop an exhaustive plan of action for it. That's the power of money, and I'm still in its grips. My father pays for everything. I'm a dependent, dammit. I'm not my own person. I'm my parents' person. And I know that if I divorce myself from that, I could very feasibly be Mad on the streets the second I have another breakdown," I said.

"Doctor King's father paid for his rent while he worked. Everything he got came from daddy's church. I don't think it matters that you've got a bed secured for you. I think your security should be used as the basis for a great life," Jude said.

We turned towards the exit onto a state highway leading into Springfield. On the road, I said, "Everything about party politics is shallow and insipid. Nor does anything ever move. It is all performance and extravaganza. Remind me, why are we coming to Springfield to see these people?"

"Because the table is set by people who show up," Jude said. "If we aren't there, someone else will be."

"But at no point did we talk to anyone who had our issues in mind," I said.

"So we have to put it in their minds."

"And how do you intend to do that?"

Jude did not respond.

The next morning in Springfield was near freezing. We spent the night in a one-story hotel several blocks from the capitol building, the dome of which stretched magnificently over the road before us as we walked towards our work. In the night, I wrote and fell asleep to a talk show on television. I had to wake Jude in the morning and check us both out of the hotel and pack the car. As I did so, Jude had walked ahead to the State Capitol building. I ran to catch up to her.

"How does it feel to be heading into chaos?" Jude winked at me as I arrived next to her and slowed my jog to match her walk. Alongside us were mounds of snow and local businesses that had not opened yet.

"I'm not moved one way or the other, to be honest." Outside of the capitol building, there was a statue of Lincoln. "It's hard to imagine a Springfield that produced anyone like him," I said.

"You know he was one of us, right?" Jude said.

"I do."

"He was one of the finest corporate lawyers of his time, and yet he spent months if not years in severe depression. I don't think he thought he would live beyond the age of thirty. I marvel that a man him that could rise in an era like that. I cringe at what they'd do to him if he were around today."

"He'd have probably never seen the light of day in politics."

"That's true, but things change back and forth."

"In a way it's ironic. The president who issued the Emancipation Proclamation might not be electable in the era of the first black president."

We entered the capitol building and had to move through a metal detector as we entered. When we entered the lobby, I could see that we were underdressed compared to the staffers and members of the press who circulated throughout the building. I was wearing a modest dress and jacket. Jude was in her standard t-shirt and old jeans.

There were several rows of chairs prepared in the center of the room for a demonstration, and we grabbed two of them in the middle of the row. Since we were meeting my father's friend, the State Comptroller, I tempered my behavior for the sake of decorum and respectability, betraying the anger of the moment, turning it inward, and silencing it. I noticed that I was doing this and felt powerless to prevent myself. As the lobby became denser with the irritable citizens of Illinois, I felt the ominous spite of those who had been slighted by the state fill the room. My anxiety heightened, my breath rising into the upper chambers of my chest.

I turned to Jude and frantically, punctually, ordered to her, "We are going to have to go to the Comptroller's office around 11:15 to pick up our tickets. My father reminded us that we are technically going as guests of the Governor, and he has asked us to be respectful."

"Would we be disrespectful if we weren't?" Jude said with a discerning and offended brow raised. Truthfully, Jude might not have been, but I didn't tell her that.

"No, my father just enjoys telling us how to behave."

Jude was about to make another affronted gesture when a woman approached us from behind. It was an older woman in a motorized wheelchair, and said, "Is that Jude?" Jude shifted her body around her chair to see the woman.

"Mary!" Jude said ecstatically, "How are you?" I watched the two of them engage while I fidgeted in my seat and smiled unnaturally. Jude introduced the woman to me, "Boo, Mary is a lobbyist, which, if I may bore you with etiological details, means that she quite literally creeps around the lobby and bugs people, as she's doing to us now."

Mary laughed and said to Jude, "Well, I try to save my sharpest points for those who deserve it. You're lucky enough to be on my good side sometimes."

"What do you expect the Governor to say today?" Jude asked.

"Oh, it won't be anything honest or motivating. And I don't think he'll take any responsibility for the lives that are being ruined. I've met him a few times, and I've felt a great disconnect with him. It's like I'm talking to an automaton. Sometimes you get this feeling when you look in someone's eyes and feel that something's missing in them. That's the feeling I get from him. He either cannot see what's going on right in front of him or refuses to see it. Whichever way, you're not there," Mary said.

The lobby started to fill with demonstrators and became more hectic and more animated. As the numbers grew, there was an incipient sense of insurgency and purpose underneath the dome of the capitol. When Mary was feeling cramped in the fray, she said, "I've got to get going."

She then looked at me and said, indicating toward Jude, "Stay close to her. You could learn a lot."

The clamor of the people converged into a mass rumbling. Mary left, and we were quickly surrounded. The crowd that coalesced around us consisted of various community groups, trade organizations, and faith-based organizations. Generally, I would not think of this collection of people as particularly radical, though their temperament seared with burnout and latent revolt. While in its midst, I eavesdropped on various factions of the room. Each pocket of individuals was talking about a home that had been foreclosed, dwindling welfare, healthcare debt, or a service agency that had been shut down.

A preacher took the podium in the center of the lobby and told a Biblical story about a wealthy man holding a town in his hands, and not allowing it to eat until he can assert full control over it. At the periphery, two women outside of the demonstration snickered about why the protestors were not talking about the Democratic machine of Illinois.

The pastor proceeded with a litany of arrested lives and people left out to die, then concluded with an open list of demands for the state, all sung with a performer's panache. The crowd grew louder, and the preacher's cynicism turned into a loud call for unity. Jude leaned into me and explained, "Rallies are an act of misdirection. You are led to believe you are going to change something, but you are only there to change yourself and to build strength and identification in a cause with others. Truth is, nobody in power right now is going to change their minds because of what is happening here."

A young man from a college on the South Side of Chicago spoke next, dressed in plainclothes. He talked about how his school was going to be closed just weeks before his graduation, and at that moment I ushered Jude away. "We have to go now, we are expected to be present in fifteen minutes," I said.

We bludgeoned ourselves towards the edge of the building. As we walked, I asked Jude if she thought that the Governor was the problem with Illinois. "The Governor isn't the story," Jude said. "He's the conclusion. There's no problem here that we haven't lived through before. He's just making it naked and worse."

We arrived at the Comptroller's office after taking an elevator to the floor above. At the end of a long hall, adorned with portraits of past politicians, the Comptroller's husband met us outside of a grand chestnut door. He was tall, broad, greying, and a little red in his face. "You must be Tom Harvey's daughter," he said, offering his hand to me.

"That's right. And this is my associate Jude Freedman." They shook hands, but immediately he talked to me again. "Your father's been a very generous man to a lot of good causes. He's helped us out many times over."

"Oh, why thank you. He tries," I said demurely, scared to offend the man.

The noise from the demonstration rose towards a crescendo, and he ushered us along and said, "Let's go inside where we can escape the mess."

When the door closed, the screaming of the crowd was muffled. The Comptroller's husband looked at me and said, "Those people are being a little discourteous. I think they just want to get on TV." Jude stood next to us quietly.

The office was neat, delicate, and empty except for a receptionist. There was antique furniture in the lobby and political portraits on the walls. Two staffers emerged from the hallway beyond the office lobby. One in a prim yet unattractive dress came with our passes to the speech in hand. The second asked the first, "What are they out there for?" referring to the demonstrators.

"I don't know, housing or homelessness or something," said the other.

I felt uneasy in the office. It was stilted in a way that made me keep my viewpoints tight as a wire. To break the tension, I made small talk about the state. "Yeah, interesting times for Illinois. We haven't even passed a budget, there's no funding for anything, nobody wants to raise taxes, and nobody knows when it will end. I can't thank you enough for getting us into this speech. It could be historic," I said to the Comptroller's husband.

"Jesus, I hope so," he said. "The problem is pretty clear: outdated pension standards, unfunded liabilities, anti-growth tax laws. It's all bloated out of control, and people are leaving the state in waves of tens of thousands. Thankfully we have a Governor in office who gets it. Finally, someone who has the nerve to say, 'actually, you cannot have an unlimited credit card.'" He looked very directly at me as he said this, some six inches taller than me. I felt intimidated and only nodded back at him.

He momentarily left Jude and me in the lobby to get his wife, and we sat on an antique couch across from the receptionist's desk. I'd never seen Jude as pacified and awkward as she was then, hushed amidst the gentility of the Republican space. Minutes later, the Comptroller entered the lobby from a room in the back of the office. She looked unnatural to me, all tall and packed into a business jacket, like a model walking a forced runway. As she introduced herself to me, she smiled through her teeth. "Hello,

Ellen. So glad to have you," she said and cupped my hand with her left hand as the right one shook it.

I thanked her effusively and then introduced her to Jude. "This is Jude Freedman. Jude is my mentor," I said. "We're with the same organization."

"Ah, and what is that?" the Comptroller asked. Jude explained her work about mental illness and homelessness, and the comptroller smiled and nodded with great attention and focus. Meanwhile, Jude talked and talked. "We work on four different systems of care: mental illness, substance abuse, criminal justice, and homelessness, all of which produce results that nobody would ever want, despite a great number of good people working on them."

A courteous exchange ensued, almost nice to the point of fraudulence. The Comptroller acknowledged the importance of Jude's work, and in return, Jude acknowledged how difficult it must be for the Comptroller to work in this climate.

The comptroller's husband returned to the lobby and asked what we were talking about, and Jude explained her advocacy work again.

"We work on advocacy for people with mental illness," Jude said.

"Ah!" he said. "Did you know that Meg used to be on the board for a home of people with mental illness up in Deerfield?"

"I didn't," Jude said. "Which one was it?"

"Riverside. They had people with all kinds of mental illnesses and developmental disabilities, people of varying degrees of ability. Meg served on their board for several years."

Jude nodded tepidly, looked at the Comptroller, and said, "Ah. Why thank you." Then she added, "By the way, I'm confused. Was this a home for people with mental illness or people with developmental disabilities?"

The Comptroller replied sheepishly. "It was a home for people with developmental disabilities."

"Oh," Jude said.

"Yes," the Comptroller tried to elaborate. "Yes, you know, we have Christmas parties and holiday dances. We go over and play board games. It's a nice little time. It really makes the residents happy."

I could feel Jude losing her breath in the back of her throat, and the four of us stood wordlessly before one another. The Comptroller's staff members emerged from the back of the office and urged the Comptroller to start moving to the floor of the legislature. They got in position to escort her, as rugby players assemble in formation for a drive, and as they opened the doors to the rest of the Capitol, the uproar was calamitous. The protest had grown exponentially, and all floors of the building were occupied with demonstrators, all of whom were jeering at any politician they saw. The Comptroller's husband bustled ahead with other state workers, huddling through the crowd and eluding the abuse. Jude and I followed several steps behind. There was a procession of attendees walking through the upper floors of the capitol, all many steps away from confrontation. I felt like a phony as I passed the protestors.

I tried to avoid thinking about it too deeply, and whispered to Jude, "For the record, I don't think these people know a god-damned thing about our issues."

Jude replied, "It always irritates me when people conflate mental illness and developmental disability." Then, after looking by her side, added, "It's also funny how people can think they're being nice while actually being quite condescending."

The building was lit with fervor, and we walked obediently amongst prominent Illinois Republicans, most of who came from suburbs outside of Chicago. We took our chairs on the balcony of the state legislature floor, where seating was arranged for special guests and spectators. To our left, we were seated by honorees from state police departments, and to our right, individuals from conservative political action groups. Jude and I made introductions, not as Jude Freedman and Boo Harvey, but as somebodies from somewhere, so as to signal our political allegiances and agenda.

After hearing about our work, the woman to our right said that her adopted daughter, an old foster child, had multiple hospitalizations for depression, and had once attempted suicide. Jude and the woman empathized over this point, both relating to the angst centered in the conversation, albeit on different fences. Moments later, when the woman was done talking to us about psychiatry, I heard her ask the man next to her if he was going to attend the pro-life rally in Mundelein. She then chastised the hypocrisy of liberals, "who shame gun owners but have nothing to say about aborted life. Why should anyone even listen to what they have to say?"

The time hit noon, and the Governor entered the floor below with other members of the state government. He stood tall, and the entirety of the floor stood and applauded. The Governor spent ten minutes executing the salutary political gestures towards his colleagues on the aisle, and whatever protest outside of the room was made unnoticeable by the pageantry inside of it. Once he reached the podium, a loud, elongated ovation continued. At that moment, the crowds in the lobby had gotten more raucous. The doors behind me were shaking, and I could begin to hear them vocalizing in unison.

When the ovation settled, the Governor addressed the attendees in a direct, colloquial style of Midwestern American English. His delivery had a cheek-pinching "aw, shucks" color that dropped g's at the end of verbs, as though he was as a common man of the country rather than a Chicago investor who owned nine homes. In his introduction, he alluded to obstinate public unions, the state's hostility to business, and the contempt that Chicago holds for the forgotten, hard-working taxpayers who were stranded within it. "All of our neighbors — Indiana, Wisconsin, Missouri — have gone conservative, all have opened themselves to business, and all have grown. What is this race to the bottom that this is supposed to lead to? We are on the bottom. We can make Illinois a great place to live in again," he said. I could see the Comptroller on the floor applauding gallantly, as though commemorating a war hero.

The walls continued to shake from the demonstration outside, thumping again and again. The Republican legislature stood in applause after each statement the Governor concluded, most of which highlighted the piecemeal advancements made during his rule, as though they were landmark achievements — a program for heroin addicts, a program for ex-prisoners — while the Democrats, who constituted about two-thirds of the floor, offered at most half-hearted recognition of his address, or none at all. The woman beside Jude and I was uproarious, standing in adoration every time he spoke. She would grow more aggressive in her agreement as the speech went on, as a true believer escalates in love of the Lord.

The Governor concluded with an invocation of hope and compromise. I never heard him mention that the state had not been releasing any money, nor did I hear any mention of Illinois's lower economic classes, nor of the many people with disabilities I knew who were now isolated from contact with the most basic of support and recognition, left to be alone in the country or policed in the city. As soon as he finished, the legislators in the room dispersed to their typical, clerical activities, while in the lobby, the outrage reached its apex. We departed the legislature, and the attendees inside bustled towards the elevators and exits. The noise was total. There was little room to pass through the crowd while Jude and I left, and I often turned around to be sure she wasn't caught behind me.

We had to return to the Comptroller's office to return our

access badges. On the outskirts of the crowd nearest her office, a security guard told us we needed identification to get through. I showed him my guest badge, and he let me pass. Jude followed immediately behind, and the guard put his arm out in front of her and said, "You can't get through."

"No, sir, she's got a badge," I corrected.

"My apologies," said the guard.

We returned our badges and left the Comptroller's office. I said to Jude, "Let's find our way out of here. We need food or air."

We walked towards the exit and saw activists from Chicago's disability community overlooking the action below. There was a vigil being put on by nurses, teachers, and medical students. We stood for a moment with them, and Jude asked, "Where do you feel more comfortable: out here, or back there?"

"Out here," I said. "And you?"

"I don't feel comfortable anywhere," she said. "But I feel relatively less uncomfortable here because of the strategy I've chosen to endorse. That's the paradox of what I do. I try to be both at the table and a part of the people. I try to be inside and outside at the same time, and I don't truly fit in anywhere."

I suggested that we go, and urged Jude toward the exit. We drove back to Chicago in the mid-afternoon. Jude spent the rest of the drive sleeping or reading the newspaper. I left her at her apartment and did not see her for the following week, as she did not return any of my calls. In the meanwhile, I attended class, worked at the restaurant, and spent most of my nights sleepless and predictably angry and suicidal.

The following weekend I attended Molly O'Brian's wake and funeral in Northwest Chicago. The line before her displayed body was hundreds of people long, as Molly was one who made a concerted effort to enjoy her life while she had it. I spent nearly an hour in that line, mostly by myself. Through a slim opening in the doorway, I could see her casket, her father, a firefighter, her brother, a police officer, and her mother. Her mother had always been sweet to me and the rest of Molly's friends. She would message us about Molly's health while she was hospitalized, letting us know when we could visit. At a glance, I could also see Mark intermingling with the mourners by the casket.

While waiting, about half of a dozen people from mine and Molly's high school met me in line. "Well, this sucks," my old friend Sam moaned. I'd hosted a group at my apartment the night before. We got quite drunk, played music, and stayed up until about 4:00 A.M. I knew that this impacted their misery as they waited in that line, as we had avoided processing a single sad thought while we remembered her. Being in the funeral home, near Molly's death, made me feel light and insignificant. It was a liberating state of being, in a morbid way, though I kept that to myself.

Another guy from high school, Will, a former hookup and unrequited lover of Molly's, arrived late and cut in line behind me. He was patently devastated, and his eyes were lubricated, though he pretended to be stable and optimistic. He greeted me and said, "I see Mark's here. That's good news."

"Actually, we split up," I corrected him.

"Oh no, what happened?" he asked.

"Distance, in a word," I said.

"I see. That's rough," he said.

"Thank you, but I'm getting along just fine." Though the truth was I felt his presence in the other room, like how an emotional manipulator or a dramatic schism nags you towards its direction. I checked my phone for distraction and saw a note of cut-rate cell phone poetry that I had drunkenly written to myself at the end of the night. I'd forgotten that I had done so, and forgotten that I'd even been thinking about Mark in that text. It read, "What does it say of me that I'd fake a life-threatening illness to get a person to see me just once? I've stolen half of the world's music, and I'd rather listen to you." I put the phone away and talked to Will. "Yes, it's been fine. I've been getting out into the neighborhood, meeting others who seem to be thoughtful and have initiative."

"How's that going?"

"In all honesty, all of the men I meet are gay, and unfortunately none of them are named Mark Mitchell. But this is dumb. That is not at all why we are here," I said. "Tell me, when was the last time you saw her?"

"Last Saturday we all went out to Ricky's bar," he said. "She had gotten out of the hospital earlier that week and was sitting at the bar ready to take a shot. Joe asked her what she thought of being in a bed on Monday and out with all of us by Saturday. She shrugged it off and held the shot glass up and said, 'Joe, life is for living,' And then took the drink like it was no big thing."

"That's a good Molly story. It tells you much more about her than mine," I said.

"Yeah? What's yours?" he asked.

The truth was that we had gotten in an argument over the Internet a few weeks earlier about police brutality, as she came from a police family and I did not. It was contentious at the time, and we never met in person to discuss it and never resolved it. But now it felt irrelevant, nothing to take beyond the grave. "It's nothing, actually, and it doesn't matter now. Not one bit," I said.

As I entered the room of the casket, I examined the montage of Molly's life arranged for her remembrance. I was in a few pictures: two taken from high school and one from very recently. The girls in line ahead of me were crying once they saw the body. When I finally made it to her, I stood entranced above Molly. There was something on her skin, a light plaster, and she was laid in a white dress with a necklace. I kneeled before her and devoted my private thoughts to her, and then embraced the O'Brien family and thanked them for her life. Mark was in the back, looking stoic. I didn't approach him directly, nor did I intend to, until we stumbled into the same immediate circle.

"You look nice," I told him.

"Thank you," he said.

The funeral was held in a church in Park Ridge the next day. There was a scattered attendance throughout the church, and bagpiper in a kilt held a single note and led a march down the center aisle while playing the famous melody from Dvorak's New World Symphony. Young men were struggling to stop themselves from crying, and young women dabbed their eyes. During the homily, the priest commended Molly for her joyous approach to life.

"She was dealt an unfair disease," the priest said, "but understood who she was and what she was constrained by, and played it as a blessing. Because she wasn't just given a disease, she was also given community, compassion—in sickness as in health—and inherent zest for living. And with that, she was able to live more fully in twenty-six years than most do in many years more."

At Communion, a choir sang an old Irish hymn, "Take me home." Mark was sitting in the front row with his mother by the Eucharistic minister. I received the Eucharist and walked by them without looking away from my path of walking, and kneeled at my pew several rows behind them to meditate.

CHAPTER 6

2011

A law student leaped from the university library's top-story balcony and died during week one of Winter Quarter in my junior year. To prevent further deaths, the university installed glass barriers alongside the balcony's railings, tinting the scenic outlook. Before, if anyone wanted to jump, they'd look at the mountains and the palm trees and do it. Or, maybe not. Maybe for some, the scene was too beautiful to jump away from. Now, if anyone wanted to jump, they'd have to look at a glossy, light reflection of themselves against the glass—a classic last image—and make some contrivance to get over it, such as by pulling a chair up and climbing over the glass. The balcony is a bit less free as a result— the glass blocks the high winds and the sunlight, and dilutes the scenery—but to the administration, this is a necessary restriction to prevent students from exercising the ultimate freedom.

"Why do people kill themselves in public? It's such a plea for attention," Katie asks from our living room couch after exhaling a hit and passing a joint to Brendan, who has hijacked the speaker system with electronic music. The girls and I live in a duplex, two to a room. It looks like any other home around campus—dumpy, one story, with couches around a brown center table, and boys who are always coming over to smoke weed.

"It is," Jeremy agrees. "My cousin was like that. He attempted suicide once. It was very manipulative."

"Yes! It is manipulative," Katie says. "You can't reward that behavior by acknowledging it. That's what they want."

"Yup," Jeremy nods, slouched on the couch with his legs spread, flipping through his phone.

I don't understand the reasoning behind this and never have.

It contradicts itself on an obvious level: the surest way that you will never get a moment of attention on this earth is to leave it. But perhaps their experience is different from mine. Anyway, I stay out of the conversation. I prepare for a jog—a self-preservation habit I've picked up, part of adopting a healthier life and work regimen—and make no mention of my mental illness. As far as I know, they are a little aware of it, but only superficially. As much as one can know about someone from the outside, which is probably close to nothing.

The joint ends with one of Jeremy's friends, whose name I have already forgotten. He has thin scruff and a flat-billed hat and doesn't do much beyond smile and say, "Yeah," "Right," and Nice," in a deep, agreeable voice. He only comes to get high, like everyone else the guys hang out with. Sometimes they bring an XBOX and play soccer video games for what feels like six consecutive hours. He puts the roach out in an ashtray on our coffee table, next to a little weed grinder.

Jeremy, Brendan, and the other guys have their own home about half of a mile past ours. Ours is that much closer to campus, so they make it their daily hangout just because it's easier. I can't blame them for preferring ours. Their own home is in decrepit condition. What I don't understand however is how the response to one messy house is simply to spend all of your time in someone else's house. What you ought to do is clean your own damn house.

"Booboo, how come you don't smoke more?" Jeremy says, still looking at his phone and not at me.

"It's not for me, Jer," I say, tying my running laces with my foot against the edge of the wall. Though the real answer is that it might make me psychotic.

"I forgot. You like the sauce," he says.

I walk in front of him and put my hand over his phone. "Are you still talking to me?" I say.

"I don't know. Yes. I'm sorry. I love you, Boo."

"That's better," I say. "I'm going to go. I'll be back in an hour."

I run out the door and the fresh rubber of my new shoes bounces me over the pavement. For the first time, I am an athletic person. More than that, I am desirable, young, sexy, and getting attention. The first phase of the jog comes with resistance from my anxious self-doubt. *I should stop and lie down,* the compulsion of my conscience says. I am usually a little worried and absentminded by the time I leave, either from the night before, the comedown from the coffee in the morning, or the general course of school. My muscles tauten, I overthink, and I become far too self-critical. A mile or two in, I reach a confident pace, jumping up and down when I have to stop at the crossways to keep motivated, sprinting when the walk signal allows me to run again.

There is a remarkable feeling I get once I have returned home. Something in my chest releases and a wave of relaxation and satisfaction runs through my body, like a doctor putting me under on wonderful drugs.

At home, I do twenty minutes of core workouts and stretching in my room: sit-ups, planks, bicycle kicks, and all their variations. Maybe some push-ups, but my chest and arms are not yet strong enough for many of those. Everyone who was home when I left is still on the couch. Katie is doing homework and singing lightly to herself as she looks over her English texts, and the guys are squatting in the room and watching prank shows on TV.

In the bathroom, I look at myself in the mirror before I shower, tucking in my stomach, twisting my torso to see how my lower back looks, taking a look at my ass. After I dress and pack my backpack, I relax in the living room with my friends. The guys laugh uproariously at a gag of a man putting a firecracker up his ass. Katie looks up from her laptop, shakes her head at me, and then returns to work.

I leave for the library and read for personal leisure for half an hour—Brooke Shields's memoir on postpartum depression. Once I am more activated and comfortable, I do two hours of homework. Monica Garza and Brianna Braun, two girls who hang around the social justice group, join me at my table. They invite me to the city over the weekend for a poetry reading, and I tell them I'll think about joining.

At night's end, a crowd of people smoke in our backyard around a plastic table—an insubstantial table with a hole for an umbrella to go through the middle. Brendan has music playing from handheld speakers—James Blake's first LP. Rachel jokes about setting him up with one of her friends who is visiting, and he gets disgruntled and tells her to fuck off—in a friendly way, I hope. I grab a light beer from inside and join them. Katie is reading short stories and coyly reclining on her chair. Carla and Brendan are arguing about Barack Obama. Carla says that he's working pragmatically, while Brendan says that he thinks he's same-old, same-old. I close my eyes and practice a breathing technique I read about in a health journal, focusing my breath low and into my abdomen. Then I talk to BJ's girlfriend, who I am only now meeting for the first time. I miss her name while meditating, and am too embarrassed to ask for it a second time. She says she comes from the South, and we talk about being in California from a different part of the country.

It's 11:00 P.M., and Jeremy lights another joint and passes it around. I accept it and do exactly as my cousins taught me in high school: take a hit, inhale a breath of fresh air, hold it in my lungs, slowly exhale. It hits me immediately. I am untroubled, but also tired. The crowd appears to be in for a couple of hours more. I tell them goodnight and rub Brendan on his head, kiss Katie on the top of hers. Inside, I brush my teeth, then tuck myself into the corner of my bed against the wall. My window is cracked, my room is chilly. There is a sliver of light from the moon that enters my closet. Through the window, I can hear my friends laughing, along with the music I am falling asleep to: the adagio in Mahler's Fifth Symphony. I am carried into a dream, and I fall asleep giggling about how such a nerve-wracked man could come up with music like this.

I vowed to take care of myself and manage my life better, to find a balance between work and play. I've done a good job of it. While my roommates were in Europe during fall quarter — drinking every night, taking low-class flights across different cities, and experimenting with mushrooms and sex shows in Amsterdam — I lived quietly in the house with two subletters. I spent more time in the library, drank less, managed my caffeine intake; I practiced positive thinking, gratitude, new experiences, fitting in socially, caring for my appearance, and studying economics for the last two years. Life requires fitness, strength, and a reasonable plan. This is a daily practice, and slouches will fall off. Before wellness, I must first be worthy of wellness. This, unfortunately, includes dating, too. I should not try to be in a relationship until I get my affairs in order. This will only result in somebody getting misused and hurt, and I should not strain others by involving them in my trash. That would be a mistake.

The crazy girl muttering doesn't get anyone anywhere, and so I've been conscientious to talk in ways that are direct, communicable, and relatable to others. Never too obtuse or unhappy. That's how relationships start, right? And how is one supposed to not be crazy if they cannot keep themselves from acting crazy? My physicality is changing, too. My figure has never been tighter or more arousing. The exercise shows — firm stomach and thin, tight arms. People notice, too. I notice them noticing. I'm thinking of addressing my clunky, imperfect teeth. Nobody likes those. I'm considering braces. The crazy girl hair, like I wasn't even trying, is gone. So is the sloppy wardrobe. I dress like anyone else does, normal and fun.

And I downplay my reading and my interest in classical

music. Nobody else does that. It's too heavy. It serves no social purpose but to reveal one's pretensions.

The whole college thing needed a rethinking, so I changed myself. It is a blessed opportunity. Why choose misery? I am in California, the envy of all the world. Not only do I get to live here, but I have the privilege of getting an education, a degree, and a job along with it. It is my duty to be happy for it — anyone else would be grateful to trade spaces. I need to be well for them. Anything less is an insult.

I changed my major to economics, though it's through the College of Arts and Sciences rather than in the business school. It is the quickest, simplest major in the university. Most students take it as a second major to bolster their resume. I've got nothing else to go to. Physics is done. I need to take fourteen more classes in the major over the next two years and I can leave with a degree. If not for myself, at least for Mom and Dad. They've done so much for me. They've laid the road, all I need to do is follow their advice and get it over with. Any minor depressions will be over with.

For a time at the end of last year, during all that erratic pessimism, I thought about dropping out of college, at least temporarily. Part of this was a sheer delusion. I was becoming unwell, and reading the wrong books — the books of inconsolable, libertine prophets and poets. I wanted to go underground, ruin myself with alcohol, and come out of it with scathing, profound visions of society. Eventually, I came down to earth, on my parents' couch in Illinois, shaking and gaping at the television for days on end, like an addict in withdrawal treatment. It took a while to get rid of my persecution complex, trying to dismiss the thought that others were planning to harm me. I spent hours reading articles about serious psychopathological disorders and saw much of myself in sociopaths and psychopaths. I felt certain I met the criteria. The disgrace of being in this population immobilized me, and I accepted that I had to do serious work on myself to avoid becoming a horror story.

Then I became afraid to be seen with the books. The poetry, the classics — I picked them up and threw them into a hole in the back of my closet in Illinois where they'd never be seen. They now rest in the walls of my parents' house, and I will never be linked with them again. No one will ever know what my head was getting at. As I rested, the coup within me settled, and I decided that it was best to stay in college and complete it within four years, as everyone should.

It was harebrained in retrospect, the "oh, woe is me" and the pipe dreams of an untenable life. Thankfully nobody at school witnessed much of it, except for Sara and some of the seniors around Elise's house. I have a carte blanche. I've accepted responsibility for going astray, and I've been given a chance to come back. Only in America could this happen, God bless it. I need to be more centered and more competent as a person and a student. Whether or not the course of study is right for me is beside the point. It would be insane to reject higher education or to suspend it. The whole world is arranged so I can be here, and it would take a brat to turn it away. It would be an insult to everyone who has toiled to make me happy.

No, I couldn't do that. I had to change everything: the moping, the lack of exertion, all of it had to be reorganized if I wished to be taken seriously, if I wished to be worthy of happiness. It could be done.

Fall Quarter was quiet and allowed me time to nurture these habits. While my roommates were abroad for the quarter in Rome and London, I lived with Marcella, a friend of mine who had difficulty finding housing by the end of sophomore year, and Anna, a graduate of last year's class who had neither found employment nor was prepared to leave. Marcella made for good company and often had interesting friends over from either her yoga studio or her environmental studies program. Anna was a bohemian layabout but was interesting too, despite living her life almost entirely within an altered state. She went out every night, returned at 4:00 A.M., woke the next day sometime past noon, and then got high and pondered art and fashion.

There was a lot of indirect time-wasting in the house, which I guess is acceptable in college. I had classes in the morning, a couple of hours of homework thereafter, and then found time for the jog and core workout routine. But even that left most of the day unaccounted for, and I was still coming to terms with the ennui, which was always at risk of turning into prolonged depressions and placed difficulty onto hypothetically effortless acts. Toward the late afternoon, it would come back in its most heavy, surreal, and enervating form. I'd drift five years into the past and be absent in the present, and I'd have to snap at myself to remember to look attentive. An insouciant beer with the friends helped to center me, and while going through these days of languor, I began to appreciate why the Doc spends all of his days watching courtroom dramas and drinking watery Manhattans.

When not at my house, I went to hang out with the guys. They loved living out of the dorms and spent their time getting stoned in exponentially more bizarre ways, using varying kinds of paraphernalia and different household objects. Jeremy declared Jeremy's Law, which stated that if something exists, there also exists a way to get high off it. And they were dead-set to prove that true. Love them as I do, it also became apparent that they started to lose their ability to conduct themselves outside of marijuana havens. Take them anywhere else and they'd be timorous if they had to be halfway cogent. Thankfully for all of us, these scenarios did not often occur. Besides, that's one of the perks of being in a place like that, where everyone is out of their minds. There is no "normal," and therefore no standards to follow. In that way, my stoner buddies make for some of the best friends I could have. Their down-to-earth quality makes me feel saner than anyone else.

When everyone came back to the states for Winter Quarter, the town changed. I saw people outside of our immediate social circle—where friends had slept together too often and still saw one another as friends, and where we lived on lewd inside jokes and had too much knowledge of everyone's foibles, vices, and dalliances—and started going to parties with the rest of campus. More of us were turning twenty-one, and we took advantage of bars and clubs in San Francisco and Palo Alto. The partying became more potent and more expensive. My orderliness has slipped, but I think it is worth it.

Once, Katie, Rachel, myself, and Katie's friend Victoria went to a club in San Francisco. I've never been into the lifestyle, and still don't understand what others see in it. But I go anyway. As my older cousin said, "Try everything once." We pregame in a cocktail bar beforehand, and all of the drinks have exotic, prestigious names and cost at least $15. "It's just booze, not art," I laugh, but the others share in my observation. We go to a club near midnight, and I act sober. Maybe I am still undoing my Catholic upbringing. The Puritan strain remains, as does the discomfort with open sexuality of the type you see here: MDMA, DJ music, groping on the dance floor (invited or otherwise), courting with expensive bar tabs. All under the cover of a dark, anonymous club. It's prostitution by another name if you ask me. Or, as Brendan once observed, "Free sex is the most expensive sex." "You aren't having any sex," Carla quickly thereafter reminded him. Oddly, I think they're both correct.

The other three enjoy it far more than I do, and I feel somewhat like a babysitter. Trepidatious, protective, looking out while the others play. It's an unnecessary and self-ordained part, mostly due to my anxiety about the bodies around me. Nobody asked me to be anyone's older sister. You should see the way some guys line the outer rims of these places, however, how they jump on and off the dance floor while Katie and Rachel dance. I don't know why my friends are so easy with sexuality, and I feel so fraught. Two older men with shirts unbuttoned halfway down their chests approach them, hovering over them, and Katie and Rachel pull themselves aside and start making out. The guys first look at them astonished, then laugh, and thereafter leave. I cannot hear anything, not even my own shout. Another guy approaches Victoria, and before he does anything I can tell he is a scumbag. He has that kind of look, as though he'd spent the whole day getting high and now he's at a club staring at people. His eyes are glazed and his mouth is hanging open, and he walks behind Victoria and strokes her arm. She brushes it off and keeps dancing. The same guy steps a bit closer, and leans in and kisses her on the neck, and one of his friends, a girl, steps between them and pushes him away.

Next, we go to a larger arena with laser lights and a pit of people batting their thighs against one another, feeling other people and being felt under the shirt—basically an orgy without climax. We stay in the mob until closing time, at which point the lights blow up, the music halts mid-song, and bodyguards in suits come into the area with broomsticks to usher everyone away, as though shooing rats into the night.

Rachel has a sister who allows us to stay at her apartment, and we smoke a bowl and huddle together on the couches and floor mattresses she has left out for us. In the morning, we wake early, maybe five hours after we went to bed. I feel alert and impulsive, but also uneasy. The other girls look lousy, and Rachel gripes that we should skip public transport and take a cab home. She'll pay, she says. Apparently, someone is giving her the money for it. At our duplex, I pour a massive glass of water and nap to music. It is a bit euphoric. Though I should feel exhausted, I feel in the moment, more eager and curious than sleepy and despondent. The guys have a bonfire at their house in the evening, and I join them to hang out, have a few more beers for myself. Little ashes catch the corner of my eye and burn me, and the guys kick soccer balls around and trip on mushrooms.

On Sunday, I am warped with regret. I reinterpret little things I said over the last thirty-six hours with overblown meaning, as though a casual joke or a choice of words I made while partying cut into someone else's soul, turning me into some sort of a terrible person. There is a spineless side of me that wants to write to everyone I know and apologize to them for everything, but I got this reprimanded out of me last year. Now to let it pass and not belittle myself like this. How vain of me to think I am that important to anyone else. Katie has asked me if I want any Adderall to help with Sunday work. "I'd be stronger in the long-term getting Cs without steroids than I would be getting As with them," I say. "Suit yourself," she says and takes a pill. My roommates are in the library early, and when I am energized to do so, I give the duplex a thorough clean. It is cleansing: it helps wash out the muck I've accrued during the party. By night, my attention span has somewhat returned and I can do some schoolwork, though much less efficiently than I would otherwise. At half after 1:00 A.M., I fall asleep to NyQuil and Debussy.

The middle of the week brings many of the same frights and diversions. Wednesday night is an established party night, either at someone's house or local dive bars with specials on Long Island Iced Teas. Being out doesn't make me easy. I get slapped on the back, ironically, "Hey, don't be so high-strung! Loosen up!" Obviously, this only makes things worse. Carla offers me sweet mixed drinks throughout the night. The dancing is tawdry, the guys act like they are embarrassingly out of place, unable to talk to anyone but themselves. We leave at closing and return around two o'clock in the morning, and in lecture the next day, I may as well be back at home, sleeping in bed.

The "work week," if you can call it that, ends at about three o'clock in the afternoon on Friday, when I have decided I will not think about or look at academic work and enjoy my weekends with my friends. Generally, I will unwind with them and prepare for an evening out, but this week, I hold off. My family is visiting for Presidents' Day weekend, and I have organized friends to go out for dinner with them. I come home to an empty unit and wonder where everyone is. The guys, I am told, have started cooking weed butter to sell edibles. Invariably this means a couple of them will be too baked to meet my family.

Kevin is visiting for the first time. He's been odd over the last year. Dad got him a volunteer job on a Republican congressional campaign, and he has been obnoxious ever since—quick to be offended, quick to give offense, and often making broad, unprovoked statements about politics and economy. "Boo, I know you have a good heart," he says, "but the policies you endorse end up hurting the people you want to help. I think you'd do well to open yourself up to some more conservative points of view," he texted me a month ago. Dad did the same thing over a winter break once. I was reading in the living room when he came downstairs to say something about job creators and increased government revenue through deregulation. I have no idea what he means by things like this, or with other statements about business and the role of government in people's lives. We have never talked politics before, and I think he has an ill-defined notion of me turning into an obstinate, bleeding-heart stereotype in California. "Stop, Kevin. I do not know what you're saying. You're seventeen. Please stop," I tell him. He also has started dressing like he is always headed to a job interview, and I call him a "total stroke" for it. I hope with some exposure to campus he'll mellow out.

My family spends their afternoon at the hotel. It is a monotonous, rainy Northern California winter day, and they decide it is too ugly to come to campus. Reservations are at a French restaurant, and Katie, Brendan, BJ, Carla, and I take a cab from our house after a couple of vodka-tonics. Jeremy got uninvited because he was too drunk already.

My parents are at the bar with a Manhattan and a chardonnay when we arrive and greet us openly. The party orders several bottles of red and finishes them easily. Kevin steals a few glasses for himself while Dad is looking away, and Mom guides the conversation with my friends rather smoothly. That is my parents' natural element, after all: wine and dinner. In a moment of wistful honesty at the end of our meal, Dad tells me that while he wishes I had gone to Notre Dame, he likes the friends I've made here.

Well-served and ready for a night out, we take a cab back to campus and bring Kevin with us. Brendan and BJ ask him in a deliberately creepy tone of voice, "So, do you smoke weed?" Carla then skewers them for being weird. Jeremy and his friends are at our house when we get back. The friends are new company, while Jeremy is exactly where we had left him.

"Do you all have a key? Seriously, what is this shit?" says Carla in disbelief as we get into the house. They are holding drinks and listening to strange, avant-garde hip-hop. Carla rips the auxiliary cord out of Jeremy's phone and announces, "We're going to put on some normal music." Chris Brown plays and Carla organizes a round of shots. Brendan and BJ roll a personal spliff for my brother and make overly-polite efforts to bring him into their circle. Kevin is happy simply to be there.

We stay in for an hour more before going to a larger party hosted by some of our friends from the dorms — Charlie, Christian, and some of the friends they'd made in campus groups. The crowd at the party looks more diverse and decent than us. From what I can tell, we are already the sloppiest people in the room at the moment of arrival, the ones most acquainted with saying, "Fuck it," and throwing one back.

Katie and I get beers at the keg and talk to ourselves against the wall. The guys have taken Kevin away to do something depraved, probably, and Carla is entertaining a pod of individuals with her ability to play drinking games. Katie nods her head across the room and points me towards a guy from one of my math classes that I used to hang out with, Vinnie. I'm annoyed by this. I harbor the suspicion that Katie looks at me as hopeless and inept when it comes to the opposite sex, kind of like Brendan, and I think her efforts to intervene are contrived and condescending. Nonetheless, Vinnie sees us and walks over. He asks how we are doing, wonders if we are enjoying ourselves, all of that. We ask him the same, and he goes off about his math classes with a gauche rhythm and delivery. Then he apologizes for talking too long about his classes, recognizing that math is a miserable topic of conversation.

"Nonsense!" Katie corrects him. "Boo used to study physics!"

"Used to," I correct her. Katie then proposes a round of shots, which we all take. By now I feel funny and talkative, and genuinely interested in enjoying the company of others. Vinnie excuses himself to go to his room for a moment, and I linger in the party. Katie has left me, and I am also not sure where the others are. The party has grown, and the clamor is making me dizzy. When I realize I have nobody to speak to, I walk into Vinnie's room. He doesn't notice me. He is checking his phone in the charger over his desk, wobbling slightly, like a tree in heavy wind. I pick up an upper-level math text on my floor while his back is turned before he notices me.

"Is this interesting?" I say.

He is startled. "Oh shit, I didn't realize you were there."

"Don't mind me, I'm just helping myself to your space.

Sometimes the parties are too loud for me. I need a quiet space to gather myself for about ten minutes."

"I understand," he replies.

I ask him about his math courses as if I could follow along with the conversation. He explains a bunch of meaningless technical concepts, and when he completes his thoughts I ask, "And do you know what you want to do with that?" I soon realize this is a poor question for a party, but let him answer anyway.

"I'm thinking about tacking on an Econ minor and then looking at business school, but I don't know. I'm sort of figuring it out, but if I could get into Stanford MBA, I'd have to strongly consider going," he says.

"I think you'd probably be leagues ahead of the finance crowd," I tell him. "They don't really push you that hard in business school."

We keep talking, and I sit down next to him on his bed. "Do you have my new number?" I ask.

"I don't think so," he replies. I give it to him, we talk for a minute or two longer, and I stretch out and yawn. "Well, thanks for letting me hang out for a bit," I say. "I think I'm going to go check up on my brother."

"No problem," he says. As I walk out, Vinnie stands up behind me, and, as though entranced by impulse, closes the door halfway, leans me against the wall, and asks, "Do you want to make out or something?" His face is intoxicated, looking down into mine.

Taken aback, I say, "I think that's a poor idea, Vinnie." He mumbles something and puts his head down shamefully, and I squeeze around him and return to the crowd.

There is a dance party in the middle of the floor. I see Kevin on Jeremy's shoulders. I'm glad that collaboration is going along well. Carla finds me and screams, "Your brother's the life of the party!"

"Yeah, apparently," I say dryly, and grab a cup of water and take a spot on a couch with kids who aren't drinking as heavily, and spend the rest of the party with them. Vinnie comes back to the party, noticeably disconsolate, far, far away from me.

We all leave sometime after midnight and go back to the house. The guys roll another joint and put music on. Kevin sits beside them with red, woozy eyes and a shit-eating grin. There is a Lil Wayne song on the speakers, and when Kevin recognizes it, he stands up and raps every verse, much to the guys' amusement. He then starts talking about all of the "bitches" he's gotten in his cheap "black person voice." The guys eat it up, howling with laughter. I ignore it and go into my room, drink water, set my belongings down, and bring a pillow and sheets to Kevin for him to lie on the couch whenever he is ready. I also leave him Advil, take a handful for myself, and go to bed listening to Ravel's string quartet. The music stops before I have fallen asleep, and I feel sick. My midnight thoughts get abusive, and I am pulled inward into a very distorted space of mind before passing out.

My phone has numerous unread texts in the morning — mostly from Vinnie, in which he apologizes profusely for his behavior. I do not respond, and quickly block him as a contact. Mom and Dad want to meet for hiking, and we drive together to a path along the Pacific Ocean at Santa Cruz. On the drive, Dad sits in the front seat and points out directions every step of the way, as though he actually knows the roads in Northern California. We arrive at a pristine field on the coast, with grass as tall as our knees and the torrents of the waves in our ears. Kevin and I are dazed from the night before, and during our walk, I drift towards the edge of the cliff by the ocean. This makes Dad extremely worried, and he pleads for me to step back, almost like a whimpering dog. Mom smirks in the background at Dad's insecurity. Kevin lags about thirty yards behind us and vomits several times onto the rocks beside the ocean.

Over the quarter, my affect stupefies. I become the deranged Boo again, unable to show zeal. I believe it is a normal stress reaction more than anything else, or a symptom of my setting or lifestyle. Every day I panic, and every night I return home to stoned people. I have no place to be myself. No place to think or relate to others. It wears me down. Is this honestly where we send our children to achieve a higher life of the mind?

I do well in my classes until a point toward the end of the quarter when all of this becomes stronger than me. Then I break again. I don't eat. I take long walks alone by the local cemetery to try and get my head straight. It never succeeds. I postpone schoolwork to the next day, as though something will be different tomorrow. It never is.

Katie is also getting stressed out, and we have long, therapeutic talks in our bedroom together. She lights incense and plays moody acoustic music. We talk about our families, and she shares odd anecdotes about her brother accidentally sending sex pictures of his girlfriend to her, how her father left her mom when she was young, and how she and her mom were drinking wine together at age 16. But writing is her therapy and her passion, and she wants to go to the Iowa Writer's Workshop after college. The conversation dwindles toward personal grudges and unresolved phases of adolescence. I confess that I never felt heard or valued in my life before college, and accepting that silence, allowed others to tell me how to think of myself too easily. In another environment, I might actually be a normal, happy person, I say. Katie pulls up old emails from her high school boyfriend, Jeff, re-reads them, and says, "Oh, Jeff, so lost, so very, very lost…"

I do poorly when I take my finals. Mostly my exams are half-pages of non-answers and speculative writing. In complete honesty, I know nothing. I wonder if my friends endure the same phenomenon, but I get pushback whenever I try to broach the experience in conversation — snappy tempers, disgruntled looks, a diversion to a painless topic. If they do have these problems, they probably just take drugs for it.

I fail to turn in a final paper for an upper-division Philosophy class called the Philosophy of Science. The class fulfills an elective requirement, one that I've already satisfied, without impacting my expected graduation date. I took the class for amusement, just as I would browse the library shelves for hours of a Saturday for curiosity. It gave me something interesting to look at, but when the quarter becomes bleak, and I'm uncreative and unthoughtful, the project wilts. It beats me, the apathy, the torpor. I fail, and I own that failure. I own that I am useless. But it doesn't matter — I'm not here for grades in anything but the courses I need for graduation. I'm not here for achievement, I'm resigned to that.

During Spring Break, I fly to southwest Florida to meet my parents at a luxury hotel. My entire upbringing, Dad was taking us to resorts in Mexico, the South of France, and the islands off the Carolinas, and then telling us, "I never had it as nice growing up as you guys did." I meet my parents in the lobby of the hotel, and the first thing I tell my parents is that finals hadn't gone great. Except for an A in Game Theory — a delightful class, mind you — everything else is a disappointment. I tell them that I might be expecting bad grades. Mom examines me closely as I say this. She has concerns and observes me watchfully. But she does not interject or ask anything of me. Dad quickly says, "It's done now, you've done the best you could do." I feel helpless, as though everything I do has to be reported to them. Everything is doomed to be overlooked, there is nothing in it for me but stigma, and I do not know how to be myself in their company. We spend five days together in Florida, reading on the beach and eating at premier restaurants. I have multiple sleepless nights overlooking the gulf from my balcony, where the oversized moon shines an opening into the waves. Kevin and I share a room, and he steals beers from the mini fridge and watches movies while I muse above the water.

In Winnetka, when the trip has ended and I have nothing to do, I am stunned. At dinners, my parents look at me approvingly, as though my docility is a sign of success. During the days at home, I walk the dogs in the yard, play card games, talk to myself, and huddle in my room. When I do see Mom, she checks in on my mood and gives me menial orders about housekeeping and chores.

"Oh, Boo, we're getting a new carpet and a new bed in your bedroom. We're going to need you to clean everything out," she says.

"Okay," I say.

"And if you want to give anything away, call Mary. I think Claire is looking for some things for college."

"Fine, I'll do that too."

"Oh, and don't put anything out for trash tonight. The village is picking up trash a day late this week, save it for tomorrow."

"I'll keep that in mind."

"How's the summer job search going? You should be sending out applications right now. Employers fill up positions pretty quickly with kids coming home for college."

"I sent in an application to Joan's clothing store."

"Oh, perfect," she says. "And if you are going to go visit the Doc and Grandma, try to do it early. He is going to bed earlier and earlier and he tends to lose it by the late afternoon."

"Okay. Thanks, Mom."

On the evening my grades are released, I overhear my parents talking in the kitchen as I lie in the adjacent room, fretting and rubbing my forehead for comfort. We had the Doc, Grandma, and uncle Harry over for dinner. Toward the end of the discussion, my uncle asked, "So, what are you doing musically these days?"

I snapped at him. "Nothing, and I'd prefer not to talk about it."

Mom looked nonplussed and I left the table early and went to the television room. Dad was at a business dinner and came home late.

I remember once when I was twelve, my cousins and I jumped off the rocks of the blown-up pier at Gillson Beach. You aren't supposed to do that by law, but I did anyway, and jumped into shallow water, breaking my ankle. A week later, in the Doc's kitchen, my aunts, uncles, and parents were talking about it. "Harry's kids made Boo go," my Mom said.

Uncle Harry correctly responded, "I don't think that's true. They're kids. They go into these things together. They like to do dumb things like that."

"No, they made Boo go," my parents said in unison.

Dad says to me tonight, "Boo, your mother and I are concerned about you."

"Why?" I say.

"Mom says you snapped at Uncle Harry at dinner tonight," Dad says.

"Not really," I say.

"Well, it was very unlike you, that's what she said, and she's worried something is off," he says.

"It was honestly nothing. He asked me if I was playing music and I haven't been. He asks me that every time he sees me and I did not want to talk about it again," I say.

"But you're usually very nice and patient with people," Dad says.

"So? I have one moment that's perceived as a 'snap' and everything has gone wrong?" I say.

"We saw your grades, too," he says.

"I'm sure you did."

"You failed a class on Microsoft Excel?" Dad asks.

"Yes."

"How?"

"I didn't care. It was about Microsoft Excel."

"But you still have to do it."

"Sure. But have you ever been in a business class like that? There's literally no critical thinking. It's a waste of time."

"Yes, but that's not the point. The point is doing it. Did you even go to class?"

"I didn't. I went to the library and read whatever I wanted to."

"Ok, so you're well-read. Great," Dad says.

"But you need Excel to get a job," Mom says.

"Then I won't get a job that requires Microsoft Excel," I say.

"So, what kind of job are you going to have? Nothing else is out there," she says.

"I don't know. I'm in economics to get a degree and leave. I'm not there because I want to be."

"But why not?" Dad asks.

"I've told you before," I say, "There's no reason for me to be there. I do what I like with my time. I have my own curiosities and I follow those."

"I know," Dad says formally, "but doing that and doing school are not mutually exclusive."

"Sure," I say.

"Okay, so grades are just a score in the system," Dad says. "Fine, so you don't want to go to graduate school. There's a theory in business that says that people rise to their level of competence, and your level of competence is high enough to do very well in an organizational setting."

"Dad, come on," I say.

"I'm just saying, we are concerned for you and want you to do well, and we believe you could still be a great success one day," Dad says.

"What are you basing this off of? Level of competence? Do you actually believe that? I've never been at the top of the class. I've always been good but not great, and I've never been driven in school."

"I don't understand," Dad says. "You were so good at math. Your skills would transfer so well to finance. I've never understood why you didn't go to business school, we've been saying this since you were sixteen. It would have been so sensible."

"That's the only thing you've ever told me, Dad. I don't care for it. How more plainly to I have to state it?" I say.

"But it's so easy. It's so perfect for you. I don't understand," Dad says.

"Dad, are you not listening? I don't give a damn."

"Well, what do you care for?"

"I don't know... Dad, I'm not well. I shouldn't be there, but I also can't step out of school. That would be worse. This has been obvious. I just need finish and get out in four years so I'm not the shame of the North Shore, then I can go and try to be a writer or a musician or something"

"No, Boo . . ." Dad's face goes red and he vigorously scratches the side of his head. Mom smiles.

"Do you care that other people care? Do you care what they think of it?" Dad asks.

"No, I don't," I say

"Will you stay for us anyway?" Dad says.

"That's exactly what I'm doing," I say.

"Well, will you let us know if you are feeling unwell?" he asks.

"Yes," I say.

"Good," Dad says.

"Good," Mom says.

"Do you want to watch TV with us?" Dad asks.

"Sure," I say.

Dad turns on a reboot of *Hawaii Five-0* on the TV. I watch half of an episode with them and go upstairs.

"It's a spiritual experience. When it's done, you feel totally at peace with yourself. And it stays that way for a few months," says Jeremy on Highway 1. We are on our way to Big Sur for an acid trip. It's worked for people like John Lennon and Steve Jobs. And all of that talk about resetting your brain, showing you how your mind works, and seeing the beauty behind the horror is too alluring to ignore.

I've always been prejudiced against drugs like this, and the last thing I wanted to be when I moved west was some pantomiming fool in a park in San Francisco, attaining free enlightenment with free venereal disease. But I'm more open-minded now.

Big Sur is a pocket of natural reverie by the Pacific Ocean. A landscape composed of ocean, mountain, and forest that could only be imagined through the mind of a master artist. I've heard that it was a temporary home to artists of the beatnik and phased-out persuasions, and later to folk-rock artists and other countercultural figures. And, later on, of college kids experimenting with hallucinogens.

Our road trip takes us through the back channels of the abutting mountains, first through an inactive military base in their valleys, and then through stumbling roads in snowy hills, which look as icy and white as a manipulated Christmas advertisement. We arrive in Big Sur with a campground reservation and spend the night talking around a campfire, and sleeping in frigid, grimy tents with our backs pressed against one another for body warmth. I don't sleep. You can hear everything that happens in the rest of the campgrounds, when the others talk, when they cough, when they rustle and have sex.

I wake in the early morning with a dry mouth and the taste of old crackers and granola and dawdle to find a water source to brush my teeth. There is none, and when I come back to the campgrounds, my friends are awake and eating a breakfast of fruit and plastic-wrapped bars. BJ is rolling joints for the day, and Carla is doing stretches. Jeremy is hyping up the experience to me, as he sees I'm becoming disinclined. When we are ready, we walk a quarter of a mile to the ocean, across two lanes of the road, and through 100 meters of tall grass. BJ and Jeremy survey the rocky beach below us, find a nook concealed by a wall of mountain steep and declare it our post for the day.

We take a brief walk back up to the main road and tread into the tall grass. It itches against my legs and the wind blows my hair into my face. BJ removes a sheet of tablets from a plastic bag, softly rips them apart, and hands two to everyone present. "Just let it dissolve on your tongue," he tells us.

Jeremy takes his first and announces, "I came into this world innocent, and I don't intend to leave it without getting a little fucked up." I am the only one present who hasn't dropped before and swallow my tabs after they disintegrate into wet paper balls. BJ puts his hand on my shoulder and tells me, "Boo, you're going to be just fine."

I am one minute in, and nothing happens. We take a walk back to our recess by the water. Jeremy and Brendan quickly say they are hallucinating. Brendan sees a dragon in the hills, BJ and Jeremy walk into the water and stare at it. Carla and I sit next to one another on the beach, laughing heavily. I pick up a rock and rest it in the palm of my hands. My senses are flourishing. It feels like nothing I have touched before, and yet I know it is familiar to me. I don't know how to hold both of these thoughts at once — there is a breakdown in meaning materializing. The colors of the rock glint and twirl with galactic vividness. I follow a spectrum of color in the details of the rock, from green to turquoise to gray, with myriad variations in between, none of which I have the vocabulary for. I have less of a vocabulary for anything and am enraptured by the primacy. The sun glistens ecstatically against its pointed edges. Carla is idiotic, too, grinning underneath her sunglasses. I look at the ocean, and it is a transformed natural body. I used to see it as one monolith of water. Now, it is a collection of billions of infinitesimal shifting, twitching pieces, each square inch of which is constantly altering its shape and direction, and reflecting the sun across its boundless surface points.

I put my headphones on and lay on the ground. Beethoven's "Eroica" plays, and the clouds arrange themselves into horses and chariots that charge into one another and disperse into new forms. I look at Carla, who has suddenly turned bleak after noticing something in me. "Who are you talking to?" she asks.

"What?" I reply.

"Nobody is there," she replies.

I feel accused and become pallid. It is strange to feel emotion as though it is temperature, and have it consume me like the air of a tundra. Acid dissolves all perception, and releases thought and sensation from their containment, turning sight into sound, sound into taste, and thought into all five senses. I fall into a moribund place and worry that I will never get out. I've gone mad, and Carla has noticed. A walk is in order. Something to straighten me out. There are large, crystalline rocks toward the ocean, and as I walk over them, I slip. My leg falls in between the rocks and gets caught. Then I black out.

I awake on my back on the beach. My socks are soaked. I assume it is in water, but when I turn my head to my side, I see it is not water. They are drenched in red. My wrists are pulsating—this is where I feel my heartbeat most, in place of my chest—and there is a pile of blood beneath me. I do not know what happened. Did I fall? Did I cut myself? My friends are looking over me with care and discussing a course of action.

"Am I all right?" I ask.

"You'll be just fine," Carla says.

"This will help," BJ says. "Do you remember how to do this?" He hands me a joint and assists me as I move it to my mouth. I breathe heavily and ask for medications.

"Make sure they get me the right drugs," I plead. "Promise me you'll do that for me."

"Yeah, we'll do that," Carla says mordantly.

The paramedics arrive at the road above us, and Brendan is talking to police officers. He seems very composed for someone who has dropped acid. I am still on the ground at beach level, and

I can see them pointing toward me while they talk. Then I pass out again. When I awake, it is in a hospital bed, hooked up to a machine, and dressed in white. My mother is there now, and so is my aunt. They're talking to me like someone who is about to go under, trying to get their last words in, all saying comforting, nice things about me. My pulse accelerates, as does the beeping on the machine beside me. The people at my bedside become mournful, and then the beeping flat lines. I close my eyes into darkness. "Goodbye, Boo . . ." I hear.

I envision a montage of cinematic imagery from my youth in rapid succession: my grandparents' pool on an early September day, my Catholic grade school classroom in the afternoon with plaid jumpers and brown desks, the willow tree in my parents' backyard with the sun fading behind its dropping leaves, and lastly, the Pacific Ocean at Big Sur. My vision goes purely white, and I am serene.

The heat scorches the earth and the rocks. I feel burnt, hungry, dehydrated, and unclean. My vision is lucid. I am still at the ocean, though with a fiery glow. Carla, Brendan, and Jeremy are around me, speaking in disoriented tongues. I back away and try to ascertain my surroundings. There are snakes on the beach with black and orange striped scales moving in and out of the rocks. In the mountain, I see wide, contorted faces trying to break out of the surface. They are protruding from inside of the stone, somehow, and long, ghoulish indents of shadow emerge where their eyes and mouths are.

I walk through the godforsaken beach and am felled onto the earth by an unseen attack. Something powerful has infiltrated my brain, shocked me, cut off my equilibrium, and erased my memory. I can recall nothing. I do not even have language. Dumb and afraid, I put all my attention into trying to think of something communicable, something in a dictionary. Any word will suffice, but they all come to me as meaningless abstractions.

I mutter and mush unintelligible syllables together, and clasp the air with my hands. Every few minutes I have an epiphany, and approach the meaning of a word, and forget it entirely a moment later. Steadily, this state wears off, and I can think in sentences again, though with minimal intelligence. Where am I? What happened? What am I trying to do?

I think very carefully and remember the last images of my life before entering this lurid underworld: the fall, the paramedics, the blood. That is it: I died and went to hell. Then that attack hits me again, and I have to learn this all over again: how to speak, how to think, who I am, what I am doing, only to arrive at the same conclusion: I dropped acid, died, and went to hell. Then I forget again and return to total illiteracy.

This circular, futile incomprehension continues for days. I am released, and I can recall my actual life, now. My life before death. I have enough recollection of it to think about it in moral terms, good decisions and bad decisions, and reasons I may or may not be in hell. In the hills beyond the road, I see a feast at a large table, with dozens of people laughing and drinking. There is a reason they are up there and I am down here. That is heaven, for the worthy.

I find my friends again and caution them not to make my mistakes. I urge them to live rightly and pound them with the importance of finding hope in situations where they feel dead. "Don't make my errors," I say. They nod silently and courteously, and then shun me completely, push me to the ground, and leave me alone.

I am taken to a padded room on the beach with no ceiling. Someone comes to visit me and gives me a tray with nothing on it. There is odd music playing in the air—whistling, bending frequencies making childish, unintelligent harmonies. How long have I been here? How many lifetimes? Syd Barrett comes to mind, that crazy diamond. This must have been his fate.

Then, as if passing into a different body, I am at the beach
again in Big Sur. Everything looks typical for a beach at sunset.
I'm wearing the clothes I was wearing earlier, listening to Liz
Phair's "Exile in Guyville" on my iPod. The sun is golden, and I
feel safe, like coming home after a long exodus. BJ asks me how
I am, and I say, "Okay." We walk up to the road together to get
water. There is an old man with a white beard and a fisherman's
hat carrying a carton of water.

"Are you St. Peter?" I ask him.

"I most certainly am not," he says, and offers me a cup of
water.

BJ and I walk back to the beach to find Jeremy, Brendan,
and Carla. On our way down, I check my phone. The time is
4:50 P.M.

"Is it still Saturday?" I ask.

"Yes, it is Saturday," BJ tells me.

"Do we have class on Monday?" I ask.

"Yes, we have class on Monday," he says.

"All right, then," I say.

Carla and I start a weeknight exercise routine: half of an
hour of jogging, three or four machine exercises, followed by a
cool-down run and stretching. She heard about a new nutrition
and workout regimen called "The Six Week Bust: Summer
Shape in Less Than Two Months." "It's a crap title," Carla says,
"but it works." Whenever we exercise, I want to stop and relax.
Without Carla, I would. She gets in my ear and pushes me to
the completion of each set. When we are finished, my focus and
strength are impeccable, and I can work for the rest of the night.
I also join a recreational soccer team on the nights when we do
not work out. We lose every game by about six or seven goals
to none. I tell myself that I have to do something productive,
and exercise is a good rationale.

The house is overtaken by more and more weed, and it's

destructive to be around it. The guys have gotten a weed hookup from Christian's cousin, and that has made them very popular. New faces are coming over to smoke, mostly from Light Side. There's a circuit of people who go from house to house to chill. They all know one another and are incredibly happy to be there and to meet new people. I'm offered a smoke, and decline. "Suit yourself," they shrug and then settle into watching television or listening to music. Jeremy has put a ladder up to our roof despite our landlord's warning that it is unsafe for people to be on. He has set up chairs for "roof joints." We go up there at the end of the night with a small set of speakers, stargaze, and find peace. One night on the roof, Jeremy says his older brother is going back to school for an English degree.

"That's a little late for that, isn't it?" Carla says.

"I don't know," Jeremy says. "He wasn't happy. He wants to go back and do something else."

"Well, to each their own," Carla says. "Reality is, you're set with what you choose for yourself now. You can try to go back, but it doesn't work. You just pick something and go with it."

"I relate to your brother, I was kind of like that," I say to Jeremy. "I could have gone to Notre Dame for business school, graduated, and made $200,000 at age twenty-three. I understand."

"Why the hell wouldn't you do that?" Carla asks.

"It didn't feel right, mostly," I say.

"You should have gone there," Carla says.

"But I didn't want to," I say.

"But people don't get what they want. So many of us would kill for that," Carla says.

"Whatever, I'll figure it out," I say. It gets cold on the roof. I go back into the house to get a hoodie and then return. Rachel, BJ, and Katie are smoking at our kitchen table with this girl Stephanie who I have not met before. She looks like she is from a well-to-do background, with her attractiveness, fitness, and social elegance.

"I visited my friend in New York last weekend," she says. "It was insane."

"Woah, no way," Katie says.

"Yeah, like, California needs to get its shit together," Stephanie says.

"Yeah, that's so cool," Rachel says.

Most of their conversations seem this way to me, full of easy acceptance and empty gestures. I grab my sweater and return to the roof, and read articles on my phone while Jeremy puts the Red Hot Chili Peppers on his speakers and rolls himself a cigarette.

On Friday, we go to a house party with dozens of people hanging around the lawn and backyard. A month ago, we were never invited to these events. Now they are a weekly occurrence. As we arrive, carefree, euphoric frat bros greet the guys and say, "Dude, so good to see you! Yo, we've got to hang out more often." Often, the first house we go to is a dud. Either nothing is happening, or there are too many dudes. We text around for more activity and eventually find someplace more happening, a house more packed and belligerent. Katie and Carla have started doing cocaine on weekends. They don't tell anyone; they just disappear to a bathroom for a bit and return very activated. I'm getting better at faking it. So often when I talk to people, I introduce myself unenthusiastically, and they get awkward and sag their heads. Now, our introductions are more normal.

"So, what do you study?" someone shouts over music and calamity.

"I study economics!" I shout.

"How do you like it?" they shout.

"I love it!" I yell. "I'd like to go back to Chicago and do business school at Northwestern or University of Chicago!"

"That's awesome!" they say.

Someone who has been around our house observes, "I like

how you're, like, always doing your own thing at your house! There's always, like, a party going on and you just do whatever you want. It's so cool!"

A couple of guys surround me, asking me question after question. Sometimes they are rude or make fun of me, but they're giving me all of the attention in the world, so I go along with it. Carla is right—it is quite easy to go along with it and use it to your advantage. I end up making out with one of them, mostly out of drunken impulse, and go no further, though he invites me to another party. We go home around 2:00 or 3:00 A.M., and there is a group smoking a bong at our table, which by now is exclusively for weed and weed-related products.

On Saturday, it is seventy-five degrees, and the trees are in full bloom. I wake up at ten and everyone else is still asleep. I walk to the grocery store and buy a fruit salad, coffee, and juice, and return to my home and have a long breakfast at my table in the backyard, listening to The National and Arcade Fire and reading poetry. I am riding a high from the night before, eager for pleasure and an aesthetic experience. At one o'clock, the guys skate over with beers, a soccer ball, and an Xbox. We hang out for a couple of hours and then go to a backyard party at one of the frat houses. This involves potent vodka drinks and going home early with intoxicated people. I do not go home to anything but my own vomit. By evening, we are all back in my living room watching a Liam Nelson movie. I retreat to my room and put on an art-house film I got from the library. On Sunday, we are on the couch until after dinner, when our attention span is competent enough for schoolwork.

In class, my excitement is uncontainable and I titter. The class stops and looks at me, and the teacher pauses the lecture, shakes his head, and moves on. After class, I pace through campus in pants and a sweatshirt. It is eighty degrees, the wind is tranquilizing. I close my eyes and dream, and without realizing it, I pull my sweater up to feel more of the air, just to the base of my ribcage. Some students laugh at me. I realize what I am doing, and put it down again.

At home, Christian, Katie, and BJ are smoking and recollecting a party they were at the night before. I sit away from them at the kitchen table, eating a leftover salad.

"So, like, you know how around ten or so it got super crowded, and you were running into everybody? That's when I saw him. Only he had a haircut, like a crew cut, so I didn't recognize him, since he usually has Samurai hair. Anyways, he starts joking around with me, and he's like, 'You got some Rufalin in that cup?' And I was like, 'Nah, man, but I can get some if you want,'" Christian says.

"You get Rufalin? Dude, gross," BJ says.

"Obviously, I don't know where to get Rufalin, but I thought it was a joke, so I kept going with him, and he's like, 'Yo, so you've ever done recreational Rufalin before?' And I'm like, 'Nah, man, but you know the rule: try everything once.' And then we arranged a hypothetical time to go do Rufalin in his apartment," Christian says.

"That's a breathtaking story, BJ," Katie says.

"He'd probably like it," Christian added, "taking Rufalin with a stranger."

"That's fucked up," Katie says.

"Well, anyway, that's the story of running into Mark Reyes at the Poplar house," BJ says.

"Ah, that reminds me He was there when Pat Belinsky was losing his shit," Christian says.

"What do you mean?" BJ says.

"He was on the back porch having a crisis. It was pathetic. He was crying and wondering why his old roommate didn't like him," Christian says.

"Yeah, that kid's pretty edgy," BJ says.

"He's more than edgy. He's off the deep end," Christian says.

"I was trying to explain that to Rachel the other day. She thought he was sweet, and I was like, no, he's moody. She's like, 'well, people have their issues,' and I'm like, no, he's far gone. I used to respect him, too, until I found out he was just a depressed loser," Katie said.

"None of you have any idea what crazy is," I interrupt from behind them, "nor do you know what depressed is. You just say shit, but it's all noise."

They look at me like they'd forgotten that I was there. I continue, "You say these words, but you have absolutely no idea what they mean. Each time you say them, it means something different. You have no idea what you're talking about or who you're talking about."

"You doing okay, Boo? Would you like some weed?" BJ asks.

I ignore them and eat my salad. They eye one another, laugh, and continue to chat. I fear I'm losing it again—when I get depressed, it compresses me for hours, and more of my lectures contain odd spurts like the one I have just completed, full of agitation and disquietude. I excuse myself to my room and read a bit of Toni Morrison's *Song of Solomon*, which I'm told is Obama's favorite book. The text doesn't resonate—I'm losing my powers of comprehension, and I go through whole paragraphs with no remembrance of what I read. The illness has an iron grip on me. Everyone leaves for the evening, and I take the opportunity to clean the house and stay in. It's best for me to be by myself, and get a recovery period from seeing others all of the time. I still collect books and CDs from the county library and often retreat to them in my bedroom when there are too many people over.

Around 9:30 P.M., Christian and a man I do not know come into my home. The man is carrying a bloated, black garbage bag over his shoulder, like drunk uncles playing Santa on Christmas.

"Um, hello?" I ask.

"Yo, this is my cousin Jason from Humboldt County," Christian says.

"Sup," Jason says. He has long, unkempt hair and an easy demeanor.

"Oh, hi Jason," I say. "What do you have in the bag there?"

"About thirty-five pounds of Sour Diesel," he says.

"About thirty-five pounds of what?"

"Sour Diesel. Comparable to '91 Chemdawg."

"Christian, what the hell is he talking about?"

"It's weed," Christian answers.

"Christian! What the fuck! That whole thing is full of weed? Don't bring that here!"

Jason has already walked to the back of the house, looking for a place to store it. "Hey Christian, do you, like, not live here," he shouts from one of the bedrooms with teenaged air-headedness.

"Nah, I do!" Christian shouts back.

"Why isn't this at your place?" I say.

"Because my roommates will smoke it," Christian says.

"Okay, true, but that doesn't mean you can bring contraband into my house! Why the hell do you even have that much weed?" I ask.

"We're going to supply the campus," Christian says.

"Christian, this is really weird. I'm not comfortable with this. That's a massive amount of weed," I say.

"It's just one night, one night is all. Carla said it was alright," he says.

"Did she? She didn't mention that to me," I say.

"Yes, she did. Besides, I think the place next to you is a meth lab, and they've never been caught," he says.

"Jesus," I say.

"It'll be safe, trust me," he says.

"Why the hell would I do that," I say under my breath as I go back to my work.

"Can I put music on?" Christian asks.

"Sure, why not?" I say.

"Sweet," he says.

Jason has no concept that he is in someone else's home. He is telling stories about his night in San Francisco. "I was at the Four Seasons," Jason says.

"Excuse me, the Four Seasons?" I interrupt.

"That's right," he continues and then regales us with a story about how he walked to the Tenderloin District to find heroin and bought a ball of black tar heroin from a homeless man on the pavement, who was also receiving a blowjob at the time. "I ate the whole thing because I had nothing else to do with it. It didn't do anything, though," he says.

"Riveting," I say.

"Christian, who are we selling this to?" Jason asks.

"Jonathon Mariano," Christian says, though I know him as Jonathon "Marijuano." "From one of the Cal Phi houses, JP Molina from Lafayette Apartments, Kyle Ross at Ice House, and Nate Fegley, who's just kind of on his own."

Christian is rolling another spliff, and I decide to go to bed, resigned to having an illicit drug ring in my living room. "Whatever happens here, I don't know about it, I don't want to hear about it. I don't want to be implicated," I whisper to Christian before going to my room.

"Yeah, sure," he says.

The following afternoon, all four dealers that Christian referenced are sitting in my living room, with a scale and numerous plastic bags on my coffee table. Jason measures the product for them and hands them each a bag in exchange for a wad of cash. Carla comes home with an LSAT study book and looks at the coterie of stoners occupying our living room. I see her begin a statement and then retreat. "Fuck it, I can't fight it anymore," she says to me in the kitchen. The boys in the room are talking about their favorite strains of weed, and "the game" of selling on campus. It reminds me a bit of how pimps talk when they meet in films. Only ten minutes later, the people in my room have gotten too high to continue a serious dialogue, and spend the next two hours on my couch watching one of the *Blade* movies on cable.

Carla and I move to the coffee table in the backyard of our house and get some clear air from the cannabis tavern that our home has become. "It's weird," I tell her, "I don't think you can find braindead slobs outside of higher education as easily as we find them here."

"Yeah," she agrees. "Sometimes I forget that people consider this, like, a good school, you know?" She takes a drag. "For what it's worth, I love them for who they are. Life is sweeter and more unexpected with them around, like having drunk puppies."

She has a cigarette and twiddles through her phone. I kick back on my chair and scratch my head, crack my neck to face the sky, and thinly trace my pencil over one of my economics textbooks. Jeremy rolls through our alley on his longboard, kicks himself off, and leans his board against the wall.

"They got the bud in there?" he pants. We nod and he rushes inside. A half an hour later, we hear yelling from inside the house. It is Katie, outraged over the condition of her home. Her voice is muted through the walls. "I don't know who any of you are! What the fuck is this?! Get the fuck out?!" she yells.

We laugh and then go inside. The boys are slowly packing their bags and telling her to chill out. She does not receive this as good humor. When she sees us, she reacts, "You were here? You allowed this?"

"I don't know, Katie, it's college. Things get weird," Carla says.

"Go, get out!" Katie ushers the last of them away. Jason still has half of his garbage bag full and closes it by the grip of his fist as he walks into daylight with his sunglasses on. "Jesus," she sighs.

We sit on the couch and put music on. Carla organizes some

of her books and does leftover dishes. A vexed Katie scoops trash into a corner bin. Brendan walks through the front door and says, "It smells like bud in here, but more than usual."

"A bunch of dudes settled into our space and got blazed without us being here. Sounds like a day in the life, no?" Carla tells him.

"A day in the life," I agree.

"Enough of the weed, for once," Katie objects. "Let's talk about something else."

"Very well, Katie," Jeremy says, rolling a spliff. "If you're so above the weed, do tell us what is interesting in your life?"

"Eh. Nothing really," she shrugs.

"No dudes?" Jeremy asks.

"I've been hanging out with this guy Scott," she says.

"What's his story?" Jeremy asks.

"Don't really know yet," she says.

"Good guy?" Jeremy asks.

"Sure," Katie says.

"Funny?" Jeremy asks.

"I think so. My professor is this old literary fag, kind of like Gore Vidal, and he does a spot-on impression of him. Makes me laugh," she says.

Brendan scoffs at her. "Jesus, I didn't expect that kind of language out of you," he says, seeming genuinely put-off.

"So be it. I can't bear being correct all of the time, we all need to lighten up," she replies.

"Who the hell is Gore Vidal?" Jeremy asks after exhaling and coughing.

"What does it matter?" Brendan says. "It doesn't make her any less of a hypocrite."

"What is that supposed to mean?" Katie confronts him.

"It means you're the one responsible for people not lightening up," he says.

"Excuse me?" she says.

"It means I have my doubts about girls who on one day are livid about oppression, and then spin around and let themselves off the hook for the type of behavior they'd excoriate," Brendan says.

Jeremy hits and coughs again. "Excoriate?"

"Oh, quit being weak and bitter," Katie tells Brendan.

"I'm right to be bitter, and it's not weak," he says. "I'm just pointing out the obvious. I'd be chewed apart if I called anyone a fag. You and your type don't actually do anything. You just want to get away with whatever you want and criticize others at the same time."

"Nope, don't do this!" Carla yells. "I've seen this conversation before! We are going to relax and enjoy one another!"

Katie does not listen. "Oh, give me a break, Brendan. Firstly, I'm getting an education. That is caring. Secondly, nothing is so hard on you that you have to launch off and get all pissy like this over nothing."

"I'm sorry, I just can't take it anymore. Everyone here is getting an education, but only some of us are stuck-up about it! I'm always being corrected, examined for sexism, talked down to like I can't think for myself. And people hold themselves like they're the tolerant ones, Jesus." Then he adds, "And you're the queen of it!"

"That's not true and it also isn't hypocrisy. And that's the last time you'll single me out and generalize me here before I actually do go for your jugular," Katie says.

"Oh, give me a break! You're constantly laughing at people for being racist or sexist, over really dumb shit. And then you walk into a party and treat people like they're nobody! Because they're, like, boring or ugly. They don't do anything, and you treat them like they're untouchable, whisper rumors about them, and then go dumb yourself down for some pretty boy, who actually is kind of a creep. People do nothing to harm anyone, and then people like you are just...terrible," Brendan says.

"Woah, woah, woah," Jeremy cautions him. "Brendan, man, you haven't had your dose today. Be good, man, relax. We didn't need to be this way."

Katie tilts her head back and laughs. "Okay, okay, I see what this is. It's a getting laid problem. You know what, man? If you haven't figured it out yet, don't take it out on me. It'll happen."

"No, that's not what it is," Brendan says. "You say you're feminist, you say you're against the oppression of people, but what you actually want is to be part of the in-crowd without dealing with any of the male crap that comes with it, nor any of the people who come below it. Like me."

"Alright, fuck this," Carla says, getting up and going outside.

"You all are weird," Jeremy says, "I'm going to have a beer outside."

"I'll join you, Jer," I say. There are two craft beers left in our fridge, and we take folding chairs out to our front lawn and watch our neighbors across the street. Girls are tanning on beach towels and guys in tank tops and sunglasses are playing beer die, this new dice game where people toss die about fifteen feet up and hope to land it in a red cup of beer.

"Man, Brendan's being a fucking cock stroke," he laughs. "He's always got this uptightness about being himself, and he just has to come into parties being sour and negative. Then he flips out over nothing. Katie was right, he just needs to get laid."

"Eh, he'll get over it," I say. Katie comes outside with a beer of her own, grabs her hair, shakes her head, and then laughs. We joke around for the rest of the afternoon. Brendan leaves angrily on his skateboard, and Jeremy shouts, "Bye, Brendan!" as he goes. Brendan gives him the finger in return. As the sun sets, we have another beer and sprawl across the lawn, talking shit about the last three years of parties and people's mistakes. Suddenly, life is not so frantic or bad again. Jeremy regales us with his drinking and sex stories, and while we tell him to shut up, he talks anyway. He mentions that people are going to the dive bars later, and compels us to join him.

"I can't go alone," he says.

"We're going out tomorrow night," we tell him.

"Who cares? Go out both nights. They'll have specials on Long Island iced teas," he argues.

Three hours later we are blacked out and dancing. I wake up the morning after not recognizing my own room, not knowing how I got home, wearing the same clothes I went out in. My head pierces and a dormant terror lurks inside of me. I check my bag for my wallet and my phone—everything is in order, thankfully. Vaguely, I remember some of the night. After leaving for the bar, we quickly get two rounds of iced teas, and are thereafter smashed, and likely drink some more. Jeremy may have taken hard drugs in the bathroom with people because he was acting particularly aggressively. We are on the dance floor with him, and then we go outside on the terrace. I remember Katie being woozy at one point, and then serious at another. Did I puke? Something like that. She takes me home with her hand on my arm, guiding me as I stumble. I have some images of that on the sidewalk.

She's not in the room now, so I can't ask her anything. Sara, my old roommate, is there and asks how I'm doing. I haven't seen her in a while. Her sorority friends are there too, though in an unpleasant way. Something vicious is said. *You're a freak. You really shouldn't be here.* She runs away with their face in their hands. I don't totally trust the memory, but the image is there, and the words are too, and then it consumes me. The only time they knew me was during those episodes of insanity. What else would this refer to?

I check the time. It is fifty minutes past the start of my class, and I am definitely not trying to be in attendance for the second half. There is a morning-after rush that comes with a binge, a strange confidence that propels me into activity. I am becoming more acquainted with it, and ride it into the afternoon to clean the house, do schoolwork, do laundry, fix meals for the week, and ignore the night before. The productivity burst is prolific, all factors considered, and when it ends, I fall onto the couch with a glass of ice water and put my head against an arm pillow. The nasty thoughts are vying for control of me, and I practice yogic breathing techniques to disarm them. I get up and take an Advil, slowing to a tremulous crawl. It is back again. *Freak, freak, freak.* The rendition of that moment becomes more bellicose each time I think of it. With a woozier hangover and a head riddled with intimidation, I put on music and do more cleaning, repositioning little items around the room, reversing directions, picking up the little items again and shortly forgetting what I wanted to do with them.

I collapse onto the floor in my room with my knees tucked just under my eyes. I mildly touch my cheek with my fingers and let my mouth hang open, almost like an Alzheimer's patient or a shell-shocked soldier. The sound of the door scraping open comes from the front of the house.

"Hello?" Katie shouts. She shuffles around the kitchen and hums to herself, then walks closer to our room. She enters and sees me.

"Oh, come on," she says.

"I'm fine," I reply, my face still covered under my limbs.

"Come on, get up. We aren't doing this anymore," she says.

"Leave me be. I'll get up soon," I say.

Katie sighs heavily and tries to lift me from my arm. "Come on, you aren't allowed to do this."

I flip my arm out of her grip, "No, get off of me."

"Boo!" she says.

I cry a little.

"Boo!" she says.

She grabs my arm again, only with a tighter grip, and jerks me off the ground. The pull tears at the muscle between my arm and my shoulder, and I shout.

"You can't do this! I'm taking you to counseling and psychological resources," Katie says.

"Katie, please . . ." I whimper.

"No, we're going," she says

She finally manages to pull me up and escort me through the hall. I'm rubbing my eyes and trying to stay composed, and she hands me my hooded sweater and orders me to put it on. "I'll drive, we're getting you an appointment," she says peremptorily.

"Okay, I'll go," I say obediently.

Katie takes me to the health center and holds my arm the entire way. Even as I present myself to the receptionist to ask for an appointment, Katie speaks on my behalf.

"She's come in many times before, and she's always been turned down. We need help," she says.

The receptionist, after some prodding, finds a counselor for me to see and schedules a time for my meeting the next week — a tight, forty-minute time slot in the late afternoon on the following Thursday.

I abstain from substances throughout the weekend and hide in the library for schoolwork and collecting CDs. On Sunday night going into Monday morning, I go halfway manic around two o'clock in the morning. I cannot stop moving beneath my sheets, and I have to go outside. It is cold. I'm wearing only a t-shirt but I stay out for forty minutes. I do not leave the bed that day. On Tuesday and Wednesday, I do two weeks of reading and homework without getting tired, then run for nine miles. Despite my productivity, I am easily upset by bad news and eager for sex at all times.

On my counseling engagement on Thursday, I am both prompt and utterly unenthusiastic and flip through health magazines in a cubicle-sized office while I await the counselor. She enters cordially five minutes after our appointment time.

"I have to let you know that I can only take you for a couple of sessions," she tells me, "but maybe even that time can be of some help to you."

"Very well," I say. For the next half an hour, she asks me what I am studying and why, and what I would like to do after school. I mostly do not disclose to her. A couple of things she says sting me. For instance, I talk about wanting something better for myself and getting into a life where I could thrive, such as a life in writing.

"Perhaps you should get into an MFA program and find like-minded people," she says.

"No, I do not think I would enjoy those people very much," I say.

"Have your experiences been bad before?" she asks.

"I've never had any," I say.

"So, what do you do exactly about this interest of yours?" she says.

"I don't think I need to do anything about it now. I think I'll just go off and make it one day," I say.

She tenses and says, "It seems like you have high aspirations for yourself, but do not know how those may be addressed with where you are at in your life. Can I ask, do you need to be the star of your setting? Would you be alright being just, I don't know, normal?"

I pause and think about it. "Yes," I say, "Yes, I think I would." Looking at the clock, I say, "I think I have to go now."

Life will get better, one way or another. Either in the future or a few moments, when an attractive California kid offers it to me. The real world is coming close, and my friends are preparing for it. Carla is set to take the LSAT in the summer and studies at least three hours per day for it. She will start her law school applications shortly thereafter. Brendan is going to Uganda to engineer a water delivery system for a village. Jeremy has an internship with an entrepreneur in San Diego. Katie wants to complete a book of poetry and pursue publication. And I will be working retail at my aunt's clothing store in Skokie, Illinois. Whenever people ask how I like California, I will say, "I love it!" But I tell myself I will enjoy myself while I can, just to salvage my time. The lifestyle is expensive, and I go below zero in my bank account. Dad secretly puts $3,000 back into my account to make up the difference.

Enjoy your freedom while you have it, and put the hard part off until later. In a frat house, speakers drill into my earbuds, and though I can see Katie's mouth moving, I cannot hear a word of what she is saying. Aside from the laser lights, it is dark, and the volume of the music creates sonic darkness, rendering the noise of others obsolete. The euphoria comes through me in waves, amplifying my sense of touch more than any other sense. I am never this comfortable in a crowd this large, but that's why we have drugs like MDMA. Katie pulls me by the wrist and we dance next to one another. Now I get it, finally. How to unlock, how to be wild in the present. I close my eyes and run my arms through my hair while I thrust all of my energy into my contortions. The music is the sort that I'd usually crap on — stupid simple, not soulful simple — Vegas synths mixed with pounding baselines. Tonight, however, it is the best thing I've ever heard. It's a supernatural experience: the sound is circling above me like a flock of birds does, because this is how it feels on the drug. While entranced in the moment, I feel a body come from behind it. I lean into it — the torso of its muscle is hard, clothed in a soft designer shirt, and smells of irritable cologne. Its hands reach over me, caressing my sides and moving toward my center. I bend further into it, pressing the side of my face against it, inhaling the fragrance, wanting more. Then I am grabbing it, groping it. This charade ensues, and I am engrossed in it. And then, somehow, I don't know how long later, I am in bed with it, unclothed, under it, on top of it.

In sobriety the next day, my body has the weight of a mountain, and I have little to no recollection of what happened. It's two o'clock in the afternoon and I am in someone else's room, so I leave as quickly as possible. It is Saturday, I think. That will become clearer later. On the walk back, I examine myself in a car's side-view mirror. My hair is disheveled. I look like I haven't slept. Kids joke that this is the "walk of shame," but I've lost the ability to care. I stop by the grocery store for Gatorade and a bottle of Advil, guzzling most of the cool liquid in the parking lot, haggard in the sober light of day.

In my room, Katie is lying on the ground in an incoherent state. "Katie?" I prod, and she mumbles back. An empty bottle of wine rests on the nightstand, along with a mirror with white residue. I roll her body around and try to wake her up. Her phone is resting on the cusp of her outstretched arms. I pick it up and glance at it:

Ok dude, wtf was that? She had sent earlier in the day.

No reply.

Twenty-five minutes later: *So, you're not going to talk to me?*

No reply.

Seventeen minutes later: *Seriously, that was fucked up.*

No reply.

Twelve minutes later: *Say something.*

No reply.

Seven minutes later: *Please…*

I pull her up and lay her into a safer position on her bed, ask her if she's going to be fine. She nods. I leave a trash bin under her bed. I laugh to myself at the thought of bullying her into psychological counseling services.

The house is empty and I pour myself a glass of water. A clawing shame comes to the forefront of my mind. I'm told the hangover of ecstasy is particularly brutal, and now here it is. As my body starts to shake, I mutter to myself, "Now, Boo, remember what the Doc says: don't believe everything you think, don't believe everything you think, don't believe everything you think." I open the freezer and take a pull from a bottle of Grey Goose, and let my mind settle.

It is warm and bright out. I pour myself more vodka and feel better about things. Sometimes, I have hangovers so deep that I'd pay any amount of money to be relieved with them. Other times, I have moments of inspiration, with more confidence in what I say and think than I have in any other state of mind. No self-consciousness, all impulse, believing it to be brilliant even when it is not.

This is the rule of hangover: go as slowly as your environment allows. I write into an empty Microsoft Word page.

I am, I believe, an utter drunk, one who knows the essence of words like "dirt" and "hell," which is what I feed myself, and where I live. Technically I am in school, though I am not learning. I refill my vodka, biting the hair of the sordid dog that bit me. I fuck, here and there, though I cannot remember if I am doing the fucking or receiving it. Nor can I attest to the quality of either. The rest of my life is babbling stream-of-consciousness — sometimes elegant babbling, but most of the time, not.

I'm a long way from home, 21st Century Dorothy whines, but what was home, anyway? Father Speiss was all fire-and-brimstone — good riddance to him. My youngest cousins spent all day running around shirtless, throwing balls at one another and accruing the sun on their tan, bony hides. Samuel Clement Stone had the largest home on earth, and we stood at its gates, a Xanadu on Sheridan Road, and gaped at its grandeur. Northwestern University seemed like a place for a noble future. Grandpa bribed the security guards to sneak us in to see losing teams. The CTA took us to Wrigley Field for a dollar each way. There was no threat of going it alone. My cousins' feet, black with the tar of months on the summer ground, shoulders burnt into a new complexion of red and brown.

The school days were regrettable. Ten 'Our Fathers' for penance, and five 'Hail Marys' to sleep well. I was "the weird one," one fit for puerile shaming and whisper networks, the one who talked to herself, and should have been institutionalized, who other parents would caution their children not to hang around. I took in the shame and felt humiliation over everything, every joy, every touch of another person. I was made expendable that early on. That's the start of it all, when I'd become An Other. But that was a particularly nasty grade school, with its mean girls and upper-class prettiness.

With adolescence, I cocooned myself in the world of fiction, a safe haven made of teen novels and Jeff Buckley songs. My brother learned how to be vicious as a child, particularly to girls. I don't think he's escaped, nor have I ever left my own little fantasies about reality.

To call it a morbid phase was to overstate the meaning of the word "phase." It is and has been a morbid life, always unhappy despite the peppiest, cheeriest, and most opportune of environments in this world, with parents prodding me along as good parents do, ushering me to sports programs and always asking about my friends—how kind of them to assume I had any. And through all of this being unaware of the cultural Achilles heel—the utter willingness to believe the phrase, "It's all right."

Now all of this innocence comes back to me in vodka-soaked visions in the middle of the afternoon in California, and I drift through them with a tear in my eye, as they carry all of the wonder of a life a child dreams turned rotten through improper care. There was supposed to be a breakthrough on the horizon, a leap out of this sordid condition. But it never came, and it never will.

How sweet that girl was, I remember her as a mother remembers a child. How sweet those spring evenings were, with dinner out-doors and crickets ringing through the air. My father boasting, my brother giggling, my mother sitting in tranquility. And I, losing my gaze in the swaying willow that drooped its arms like lines of poetry swinging down from the sky, while my dog yawned and rolled onto her side in the grass.

Today is one for a lost cause. Today is one of a second life.

CHAPTER 7

February – March 2016

I had a curious yet all too common dinner in the suburbs during the early months of 2016. Kevin was in his last semester at Notre Dame and had come home for a long weekend. Often the discussion at our table was very political, but also very narrow and predictable. Dad flipped between varying degrees of right-wing sensibility. At his most tolerable he was open and validating, and at his worst he was morally indignant, one-sided, and thin-skinned, assuming the part of the victim despite being the most powerful person in the room. Mom was also peculiar. Sometimes she was my most compassionate parent, other times she was perhaps more obstinate than my father, such as when I talked about the Palestinians. Kevin had yet to learn how to think for himself and was in it more for crass shits and giggles than for any real principle. He appeared assured of everything he said, but that assurance broke the second he was made even minutely vulnerable to the sort of attacks he instigated. I was left as the righteous outlier, just as prone to outrage and stubbornness, but from a different angle. It was a testament to our generosity as a family that I had not yet been disowned.

It was a quiet night. All four of us w°ere at the table. The dog begged for food next to my chair. Dad had commented that one of his banker friends was donating body armor to Chicago Police Officers. "When you become a cop," he explained, "the city only gives you one vest for chest protection. It lasts about three years, and after that police are responsible for buying their own equipment. Charles bought new equipment for officers who had been on the job five, seven, ten years."

"Imagine how hard it must be," Mom said, "When the bad guys have assault rifles and all you have is old equipment."

"Not to downplay the reality of crime," I said, "but we've had this conversation fifty times before and it never changes. And it's always from the distance of the suburbs. We never actually go to the neighborhoods we're talking about, and on the instances when I do, I sometimes hear things about cops that terrify me."

"Yeah, what kind of things?" Kevin asked.

"Extortion, intimidation, torture, murder," I said.

"We're talking about criminals, Boo," Kevin responded. "Who cares? I'd oppress the hell out of them if I got the chance."

"Criminals, thugs, n-words . . ." I said derisively.

"Don't blow it out of proportion," Kevin said.

"Guys, settle down," Dad said.

"All I'm saying is that it's easy to moralize and punish, and maybe that's overgeneralized and maybe it doesn't actually work. We have real power here, maybe we should start talking about how we could use that to change something, no?" I said.

"Power?" Mom said, incredulously. "What power do we have?"

"I mean here, broadly. Winnetka, Glencoe, Wilmette. Money. That's what we have. There's a three hundred trillion dollar transfer of wealth from the boomer generation to the millennial generation, and whatever part of that wealth that exists in Chicago is going to be in the North Shore. Obviously, the boomers aren't going to do anything about it, so I want to know what can be done if and when that money is passed down," I said.

"You think that could change anything?" Mom said, still upset.

"Yes, I do," I said.

"And do what, just give it to politicians and see them waste it all?" Mom said.

"No, I mean if we're going to talk about what's wrong with these neighborhoods then we've got to form relationships with the people who—"

"Then go out and do it! We'll support it!" Mom said.

"Oh please, all we ever talk about is, 'Oh, they kill so many of their own kind! What's to be done?' And anytime we go down a different route, the conversation gets cut off. Well, let's be real! Let's talk about what's to be done. We can organize money. That's power. Where are the organized people? What are we going to do? Huh?" I said.

"Your mother and I give a staggering amount of money to scholarships," Dad calmly interjected. "We currently have six students from Englewood going to college through the family foundation."

"That's great! That's fine! That's still just six kids! The city shut down about fifty schools just a few years ago! The problem goes way beyond that!" I said.

"And you think that's our choice?" Mom said.

"I think our time would be better spent talking about how to attain full resources in communities that need them, and that's a hard thing to do when you never actually go there and only talk about it from Winnetka," I said.

"You'd be surprised who put the most money into trying to keep those schools open," Dad said. "It's the Governor, out of his own pocket. Everyone wants to demonize him, but the public system stayed afloat because he poured so much money into it."

"Am I supposed to like a public system that's dependent on a single rich man?" I ask.

"Honestly, Boo, let them close down!" Mom said. "Those schools were failures. They weren't working. Yes, it's tragic, but at least let the kids who could go to college get a chance! Don't you think they deserve something?"

"Of course I do," I said.

"So give it a shot," Mom said.

"Look, there are blocks in Austin where we spend a million dollars on incarcerating people. If someone tells me we don't have the money to do that but don't have the money for education, I call bullshit," I said.

"Well, what would you do if that kind of crime was in your neighborhoods?" Dad asked.

"Honestly, I think people are locked up far more than what's healthy, and I don't think it stabilizes anything. It does the exact opposite, actually," I said.

"Oh, Boo, please! Yes, it's a terrible situation. But the families who are down there and are trying to do right have their right to peace and opportunity. Don't they deserve a chance?" Mom said.

"Yes, they do, but do you think the answer is to incarcerate people?" I said.

"If gang bangers are terrorizing their neighborhoods, then yeah, lock 'em up!" Mom said.

"You don't even know what people get into gangs for," I said.

"For drug money," Mom said.

"No. That was in the '90s. The kids in gangs today are hanging out on their blocks because they've got nothing else to do, or they've picked up a case already and they can't get any work. And when someone is shot, it's usually over some stupid fight," I said.

"So it's even dumber than drug money," Dad said.

"It's because there is no hope, Dad. There's a whole generation of youth who act like they have war trauma by the time they're sixteen years old. This Mayor and the last Mayor both demolished housing, schools, and resources, and put nothing back in their place," I said.

"I don't think you're giving the Mayor enough credit," Dad said. "Most people only see what happens in the newspaper. They don't see what happens behind closed doors. I've been with the Cardinal when he's had to close Catholic schools in predominantly minority communities. It pains him. It absolutely breaks his heart. But when you break down the numbers, and it's the schools in African-American communities that cost the most to keep running, then you've got to make that decision to save the larger operation."

"The Mayor is a psychopathic Napoleonic bastard, and I don't believe he has a heart to be broken," I said.

"The city is broke, Boo. It has a soaring pension obligation that it will never be able to pay off, and money will have to be cut from somewhere," Dad said.

"The city is trying to spend ninety million dollars training new police officers, and therefore it is not strapped for money. There are large stocks of wealth that have been diverted from various authorities and tax districts and set aside for private developers. Chicago has the money. It's only broke when it needs to allot one million to keep mental health clinics running. It's racist, frankly."

"There it is," Kevin jeered. "Not everything is about race," he added.

"Kevin, you do appreciate the irony at play when a boy who casually uses the n-word considers himself an impartial judge on the matter?" I said.

"You're taking things out of context," he said.

"Look, we operate on a double standard that says the rich do good through profit and reward, and the poor do good by being disciplined. A drastic reconsideration of values and resource allocation is needed if—" I said.

"And what?" my mother said. "Have government waste it?"

The conversation continued this way until we shouted into a hysterical, dumb show. Nobody was changed, nothing was accomplished. Mom said, "Why does it always have to be like this? Why can't we just have a nice time together?"

That's how these conversations occurred. Or rather, did not occur. My friend Cathleen referred to these exchanges as "don't disturb dinner racism"—the tendency for your nice relatives to shut down most earnest attempts at dialogue. Though I did not quite think of it that way, that is, as "racism," cut and dried. It was a fair term, if one wanted to use it that way, but it was not predicated on strict racial ideology. That implied a "one's boot on another's neck" standard that did not reflect the reality of how my hometown operates. The North Shore was not exactly a haven of race reaction. Some of that existed, but it was also true that the most peaceful moment of the Chicago Freedom tour of the Civil Rights Movement was during its visit to the Village Lawn in Winnetka. John Lewis later said that some of the most generous funding his organizations received was from Winnetka and Kenilworth. To dismiss my home outright as cold and unsympathetic was not accurate. And yet, the stain was not washed entirely. No, this was a degree more subtle. This dinner table scene was a manifestation of a specifically American psychopathology, a Freudian projection of sorts. There were blunt, horrific truths about American history—even very recent history, even the present day—that had been dismissed from our upbringing. The psychic implications of these omissions were wide-reaching. In failing to address them in their full breadth, we made ourselves susceptible to endless psychic permutations of the design of racism, each one an extension of root disease, each one capable of complicating and limiting the existence of black and brown people, but very few of which were ever a manifestation of the illness in its purest form. No, this dinner scene deserved a different title, though I did not know what that may be. Perhaps "politics as usual" was a part of it. Or it was the logical consequence of the world we had inherited. Or I could call it White Schizoaffective Disorder, a makeshift DSM label along a continuum of neurotic to psychotic definitions of racial psychopathology, all born of reckoning with the reality of the United States of America from the context of an Anglo or European heritage. Hence this dinner scene, in which nobody is primarily impacted by any of the issues discussed, yet everyone is irate about it anyway.

Somehow, at conversations like this, everybody participates in the discussion rhetorically purporting to mean well, either in terms of public safety, opportunity, or social justice, yet no common ground is met, and everyone remains implicated in the mess. There is a lot left unspoken—history, guilt, the prospect of complicity, the stigma of being racist, the suspicion that someone is concealing racial resentment, truly racially charged sentiment—which makes the conversation fraught and intolerant. Each time discussion emerges, it constricts itself immediately. We all end up angry and consternated, and perversely, at least one rational option is not to talk about it at all. That would spare the individual an absurd ritual of venting everything and achieving nothing. Yet since nothing is done, inequality persists, the status quo wins, and the venom directed at "thugs, gang-bangers," and, in extreme, rare, very private moments, "n-words," maintains its place of respectability in households. Then it is clear that there is more to the anti-crime rhetoric than superficial concern for the safety of the "good, deserving families," and "having a nice dinner" is dependent on niceties that come at the exclusion of disturbances.

This process was replicated all over our world, on the internet, in our group text threads, our cabs, our schools, our bars, and our media. When college students missed finals after the verdict on Eric Garner's killer, citing grief as a disabling factor, the response was, "Grief? Get over it." Then those who were temperamentally similar to me scolded them as heartless or racist. When we saw the video of LaQuan MacDonald's killing, the reasoning was that the police had poor information, and could not be faulted for shooting that boy, even though anyone who had seen the video of how that boy died knew that it was a stone-cold killing. We fought again, and then someone asked, hardly even a beat later, "Did you see who the Bears signed?" Then we forgot about it altogether.

It was all at once tragic, bewildering, and strangely self-serving. Everyone here was fleeing from a deeper weight within themselves. It was a moral confrontation delayed from generation to generation, which somebody eventually had to own up to. Until that happened, race sat in our consciences as though we were American Raskalnikovs, forever dodging the full implications of the crime, extending punishment into the future, forever seeking impunity, though at the direct expense of one's sanity and humanity. Whiteness became a psychosocial debility, albeit one with a comfortable living room. In perpetually turning away from this simple reality — that the foundational arrangements of the American dream discredited the concept of the dream itself, and projected this asymmetry and brutality indefinitely into posterity — what exactly did we achieve for ourselves? What did we achieve by preaching liberty and equality while sustaining such senseless restrictions and injustices? To invert the question, what happens to a dream deferred? Does it dry up like a raisin in the sun? Or fester like a sore and then run? Does it stink like rotten meat? Or crust and sugar over, like a syrupy sweet? Maybe it just sags, like a heavy load. Or does it explode?

I had recently finished *The Reader*, in which a character in the immediate generational aftermath of Nazi Germany confronted the collective guilt of his inheritance. How could the children of the Third Reich, or the children of the children of the Third Reich, take their inheritance seriously? And how could they look away from it without falling into delusion? The protagonist warned the reader: the past and the present come together in a single reality. It was not difficult to see this in my backyard, nor my country, unless you were adept in the art of denial, which, admittedly, many of us were. The shadow of race — the phantom extending from the pure form, that great monolith standing between us and the light of a history without corruption—loomed over our country, with different shades in different parts and countless dialects. It may not have been legally codified or publicly expressed as it once was, and yet it remained a nonetheless insidious, invidious, and lethal devil.

The Nazis, as the protagonist acknowledged, lived on. Many of them returned to normal lives, holding positions of state and civic authority. Their influence continued in less conspicuous ways, and in its subtlety demanded a different, more finely tuned analysis and confrontation than those who openly wore swastikas. Similar statements were often made about Chicago. The Devil of a Chicago politician like Bill Daley was more sophisticated than a Devil of Alabama in that he would refrain the attack dogs and eschew derogatory language when the lights were on. But when resources were prescribed, and the fine print of public policy was designed, he nonetheless architected a chronically racialized, ghettoized, divided city, setting in place a pattern of intense segregation, disinvestment, and inhumanity that continued far beyond the era of publicly sanctioned white supremacy.

All that said, the Nazis lost the war. Germany was brought to trial, and Germany had to pay. When would America have its trial? When would America pay?

On the North Side of the city, where I lived, I did not see much. And on the North Shore, I saw even less. At moments I sensed a soul-transforming uprising on the horizon, a modern-day civil-rights awakening led by burgeoning black feminist work around prison abolition, police brutality, and community safety, yet in my daily life, I felt that almost everyone I met was detached from it. Segregation created alternate centers of gravity, formed by race, place, work, and class, which demarcated the amount of interaction one could have with life on the opposite side, thereby making it an apportioned universe. Anyone who attempted to bridge it would be met with challenge and resistance, both internally and externally, though this looked different depending on which direction one is heading.

Once I read one of those old leftist books, *The Pedagogy of the Oppressed*, and was comforted by the sentences that suggested that members of the privileged classes, should they wish to achieve solidarity with those outside of their gated communities, had a path of their own to follow that was distinct from anything that could be articulated from a position of oppression. An over-whelming amount of the philosophy of liberation that I previously engaged with, be it in high text or Millennial conversation, was rooted in a bottom-up framework; that is, led by black and brown people acting against a white society, or women acting against male-centrism and domination. Not that others were not justified in harboring critical confrontation with, or even intense rage against, the conditions that restricted them, but the prevalence of this rhetoric, which was often highly inimical towards a broadly understood concept of privilege—whiteness, masculinity, class prestige—risked erasing the question of whether it was even possible for one to engage in a personal quest of solidarity when coming from a place of privilege. Many would laugh at it with dangerous and often thoughtless certainty, but for me, the question was not so trivial. It may have even been the most important question of my life.

The paradox was much like that of Coetzee and Disgrace: faced with the rape of his daughter in a context of hyper-segregation, the narrator was simultaneously bound to address what was an immediate instance of trauma and injustice, but from a heterosexual, white, and male position. Conscientiousness forced attention to the former, but the gendered, racialized social formations of the latter prohibited him from any authentic claim to the reparation of the violence of rape and apartheid, even if it directly entailed his home, his daughter, his blood, and his suicide. And he had been a perpetrator in his past, defining what it meant to be heterosexual, white, and male in the oppressive definitions of each term. Which was his resolution in this paradox: exile from the land, or restoration within it?

To find release and engage with the matter at hand, he would have to somehow transgress gender or racial boundaries. But that was not possible, at least not without humiliation and disgrace. The result would be conflicted and ugly, even if it was personally and ethically necessary to somehow move beyond these boundaries, and quell the abuses of history in totality. And thus, trying to formulate a plan of action about the horrors of Chicago from Winnetka created a setting in which action was demanded, though within the cultural constraints of whiteness and obscene privilege and with sparse recognition of what it meant to pursue such a path from this background. This complicated impasse was where I spent most of my time. The result was well-meaning and possibly even noble, yet also tepid, neurotic, isolated, and often helplessly ridden with mortification and feelings of being an imposter within someone else's struggle for freedom. Which should I have chosen: short-term exile, or long-term restoration?

What did one see on this hypothetical road from the peak of the bourgeoisie to the most impoverished ghetto? For me, it was many things: how propaganda had shaped the culture of my home, how my home shaped my psyche, and how there was much that I had once said, thought, felt, believed, and acted upon that I would later reject as outright wrong, but which I could neither forgive myself for nor admit to it without being shamed or shunned. Against the backdrop of a depressive mind, the moral power of race and inequality exacerbated my condemnatory tendencies, just as a stern Roman Catholic was always interpreting herself in terms of saintliness and sin. In Depression, I was constantly reminded that I too was one of the oppressors, one of the "people who believe they are white"—more an obstruction to someone else's livelihood rather than one who was seeking livelihood herself. Within myself, I was never allowed forgiveness for the smallest transgressions against justice. At its worst, it precluded any real action against this dreadful setting and made me ashamed to have a voice of my own.

In trying to move towards something nobler, I was often corralled back into the position I was trying to disown, which only confounded my neurosis. When I discussed it, I was met with myriad reminders of which side of the line I belong on. This included, but was not limited to, accusations of race-baiting, race-betrayal, racial voyeurism, white bias, white fragility, self-righteousness, white liberalism, hapless utopianism, hypocrisy, white saviorism, cultural appropriation, white supremacy, or something similarly condemnatory. On any given day, at least one of these things was said about or insinuated toward me. If invective and dismissiveness were the predictable responses, why speak? Why act? These put-downs had no particular theoretical connection to one another—the abuse was equally left-wing, right-wing, racist, and anti-racist—aside from some association with whiteness and its relationship to racism, and how one chose to interpret my actions and statements in accordance with that. The subtext of race could not be escaped.

Despite the world's many problems and many ways to ghettoize and stratify humanity by arbitrary characteristics, I grew to accept that this power to categorize was uniquely powerful to race. While I had access to spaces where men behaved like women and women behaved like men, or where the realm of sexual and romantic possibility broke out of a small menu of heterosexual sex and courtship, I could not at all see race reaching the point of irrelevance that I had occasionally seen the universe of gender and sexuality collapse into a new utopia of possibility. Something about the race line behaved like a self-perpetuating firewall. Race—though it was a made-up idea from the get-go, existing not as a natural fact of human difference but as a byproduct of racism—remained as entrenched culturally and mentally as segregation was entrenched physically, economically, and geographically. While I had my reminders of this, I knew that they were more urgent on the other side, and the total impact on the individual was far more life-threatening. Similar derision was launched at those who crossed lines: Uncle Tom, sell-out, thug, criminal, prisoner, welfare cheat, "not like other black people," class climber, bourgeoisie, "too urban," "too ghetto," "articulate and educated," "not authentically black," deadbeat, drug dealer, and so forth. No, unlike the queer world, I did not see any bohemian unraveling of reality, where race dissolved and prior designations of racial identity or categorization bore no significance at all. Anyone who ventured out of their preordained box was doing so at their own risk, and there would ultimately be more force that pushed back than force that welcomed constructive transgression.

For the white person, guilt was the clear inheritance of a history such as ours, which, when looked at soberly, had great cause to inspire guilt, terror, and a crippling sense of futility. It was loosely in the family of survivor's guilt, or the easy, pseudo-innocent guilt of "the good Germans who did not know what was happening"—those who evaded both victimhood and full-on persecutor status, yet who were nonetheless acquiescent participants in the process. In this more ambiguous state of privilege and oppression, the guilty conscience was malleable to both compassion and evasive posturing. Those in this situation both recognized the crime in certain forms, yet denied aspects of intervention in which they could take part. "It was not I who held the whip, it was not I who carried the fire hose," they said. And soon it would be, "It was not I who polluted the earth, nor I who incarcerated East Garfield Park, nor I who voted for the fascist."

Baldwin suggested that guilt was the thing that drove many whites to say they had nothing to do with the crime. He was probably right in many, if not most, cases. I really did not know; I had given up on trying to be anyone's mind reader, and the nature of historical guilt was too complex and gargantuan to look at without feeling asphyxiated myself. For all I knew, many people may have not wanted to be bothered with looking at the crime. The issue was not contempt so much as indifference and the avoidance of stress. They may have been happier not having to care, callous as it may have seemed. The question I had begun to ask about guilt was whether or not it served a deeper moral function. I was reading an article urging whites who accept the persistence of racial injustice to abandon their guilt, the logic being that they held no responsibility for the American past and that they had nothing to be guilty for. Time spent on guilt, the author argued, was time that ought to have been spent on more active tasks. My response to the article was that it only addressed one type of crime: crimes of commission. While I saw the author's point, it also allowed one the space to say, as always, "It was not I." From Catholic school, I knew that there was a second type of crime: the crime of omission, the failure to do what someone ought to do, passivity in the face of injustice. And by one of its dictionary definitions, guilt was "a feeling of having done wrong or failed in an obligation." And the German word for guilt was the same as the word for debt.

I was not one of the slaveholders, nor did I come from them. I was not a perfidious Jim Crow belle, nor did I come from one either. My parents were not racists. Like me, they were not perfect on the question of race, but they were not racists. My grandparents, on the other hand, were racists. Or I should say at least two out of the four of them were. The Doc certainly was, and at least one of my grandmothers was, though this was far from the defining point of any of their lives. My father's father was a radical who had his kids read Eldridge Cleaver and other Black Panther literature. When Fred Hampton was assassinated by the Chicago Police, his home was opened for public viewing, similar to the open casket of Emmitt Till in Chicago, and then, later, to the public footage of the killing of Laquan MacDonald. Hampton's body was not there, but the home was still destroyed with bullet holes from the invasion. There was a photograph of this day in the Chicago Tribune in which a sole white face stood out in a black crowd, and that was my father's father. That man died when I was young, and we never met on an adult level. Despite this upbringing, my father and his siblings fell for the tenants of Reaganism without ever questioning its implications: demonize the public, sanctify the private, replace shared responsibility with moral scolding toward the individual, ignore the impact this cultural and political revolution would have on those who were not already comfortably situated.

The anti-revolution advocated "personal responsibility," meaning someone else's responsibility. It amplified the presence and power of police and prisons, and allowed them more reasons to exert pressure and more reasons to imprison. It replaced financial assistance with a lecture about being a negligent father or a public leech of a mother. And if my relatives did question it, I had not once heard a critical remark or a reconsideration of values. I often wondered: how were my parents, aunts, uncles, and their peers able to transition from a youth of racial awakening—in which civil rights and insurgent black power movements, along with other social movements, were clear influences on American life, particularly on its youth—to an adulthood of severe segregation and inequality without ever saying a word about it to their children? The crude yet accurate answer was: they never actually cared in the first place, or they got into business, wanted to establish themselves in the upper-middle class, with all of the luxuries and expenses that involved, and the tax breaks were too appealing.

My father sometimes spoke about his father's admiration for the Black Panthers. When drunk, my father also referred to the

Black Panthers as a terrorist gang. Perhaps the radicalization of their upbringing should have been more of a total obstruction of the culture that allowed them to take this materially advantageous turn, and less of a reading club exercise and a matter of personal etiquette. For as adults, they were repulsed by the idea of a distasteful stereotype, but if you indicted the history and conduct of either of America's major political parties or America's economic and social priorities, they become infantile, as if they were never schooled on the matter beyond what existed in a seventh-grade textbook.

It was a process like this that convinced me of how firm, multidimensional, and reproducible segregation was, and how tenuous and fleeting exposure to the other side could be. Despite a set of transformative experiences in their youth, a whole generation of simpatico liberals cashed out at the expense of the very people whose cause once defined an era of their personal development. That was the danger of being a liberal. The heart of the liberal could be won by either the left-socialist or the right-business-conservative capitalist, and the business conservatives won the heart of the liberal handily. Clinton and Obama Democrats were to the ideological right of Nixon Republicans, and their Republican contemporaries were an extremist insurgency; "The most dangerous organization in world history," as Chomsky correctly observed. In this transition, the monolith of racial inequality retreated from public ferment and into the fine print of the carceral capitalist political system, where accountability became more diffuse. Dominant narratives of race that supported these transitions generally did not address restrictions and pitfalls of segregation beyond codified civil rights legislation and primary discrimination. Economic differences widened, the suburbs boomed, and the ghettos, in numerous ways, hardened, all within a moral universe that granted the rich with the qualities of virtue, and the poor with negligence, deviance, and irresponsibility.

No, I was not guilty because of things that my ancestors had been caught doing in the history books, nor because of blood they had drawn by their own hands. I was guilty because I was born into great wealth in a nation that was never brought to trial, in a time and place of brutal separation, in a nation that nurtured its kids on narratives of exceptionalism while obscuring the part of its conduct that mimicked apartheid. The hypocrisy was bewildering, just as it was to an awakened sixteen-year-old. As an adult, however, one became more resigned, though that did not change the fact that adolescent outrage was often the most authentic response to this situation. Nor did the outrage ever become resolved in the mind of the adult. Guilt and awareness persisted, but anger became ossified. The child turned into the next generation of the old white parent—ossified, pacified, accepting of absurdity, concerned foremost with surviving day by day; dried up, festering, and sagging.

Because I had not reached a level of moral action to justify the gift of my wealth, I was failing in my debt and probably would be for decades, if not my whole life. Everyone of privilege had it if they were honest. And when this guilt was provoked, I saw it turn into something frantic and useless, in others as well as myself. I had known well-meaning whites who were so unnatural when they met someone poor and black that their rattled psyche and their fecklessness in the face of urban poverty looked like a bizarre form of racism itself. They revealed their good intentions and their ineptitude over and over. It could be painful to watch and see them cringe and lose their words in the presence of a sad story, apologize for their whiteness, compliment the individual as smart and sophisticated for displaying basic intelligence, never quite realizing how to look at the person as just another person. This too came from the same root as the outright, unapologetic bigot, although in a different and slightly more benign direction.

At other times, I felt morally pinned between contradictions.

I heard from radicals, "How will you be John Brown?"—a militant demand to be a militant leader. I heard from another, "Step back and allow others to lead"—a militant demand to take a back seat. "Center black voices and listen," despite the fact political and cultural centers of such voices were far away from me, and that many of the "race ambassadors" were false prophets willing to manipulate racial anguish for their own gain. One person said, "Only we will liberate ourselves," while the next said, "Whites created this problem, and it is their problem to amend." While there was some truth in each of these imperatives, there was also great paradox. The prospect of betraying racial justice was always hidden behind dissent, and therefore, the prospect of being racist was implied in every possible act in which race was mentioned. At that point, there was no place to go but stand still or move backward. The space between these imperatives became one of fearful, stifled silence—another constricting impact of segregation—even though the demand of the debt commanded one to persist regardless. I'd admit that my depressive stupors for much of my early twenties had consisted of little but my certainty that I was an oppressor of some sort. I fixated on very small things and personal, minute displays of ignorance, and understood them as profound racist injury. My best intentions had resulted in fierce mental immobility, rendering me confused, ineffective, useless, and convinced of my own racial bigotry—no help to anyone but to people who wanted things to remain exactly as they were.

This was a trap as well. I found myself putting outsized significance onto smaller, more individualistic things at the expense of thinking about how to build power to alter the communities and systems that we inhabited and create a future where this did not weigh as repressively on us as it did. That was a perversion much like the flaws of psychiatry. As madness was taken out of communal settings and viewed as a pathology of the individual, racism was taken out of its wider context, analyzed as a character flaw of individuals, and isolated through stigma, shaming, and ostracizing. This thinking permeated my media and the cultural moment of my young adulthood. I worried with amazing sensitivity about statements that could be read as ambiguously offensive, problematic, and racist, and questioned myself for implicit bias in every last thing I did, so much so that it made interactions with actual black people disingenuous and contrived. I remember working on a piece of writing related to race and talking about it with a black man about my age. I blurted out, without any suggestion from him that he was interested, that I'd need readers to check for the minutiae of acceptable representation and appropriation and whatnot. He was quietly nonplussed. He processed the statement, and after some time of thinking, said, politely, "Sure, I can help."

Afterward, I was embarrassed, even deeply ashamed. What about him as an individual suggested he gave a damn about what my writing consisted of, or was concerned that I was guilty about any of these things, or even had strong opinions about white authors addressing race? Yet these were things that I was realistically called to ask for—to speak about race only with the approval of someone who had experienced racism—yet which reproduced racial relationships in a new way. Based on the false virtue of complexion, or lack of authenticity, I deemed myself incapable of actively reaching justifiable conclusions about America on my own, and I deemed him one who could serve the purpose of correcting them for me, thus anointing him as a tour guide through a foreign land. I had taken us out of the realm of two individuals coming from our unique places, who were sharing ideas and having an ordinary conversation, and into a place with roles predetermined on how things should be talked about. Only instead of asserting race by promoting racism, I had asserted race, with vanity, through naïve anti-racism.

I wasn't always like this. I used to not think about this at all. Then it preoccupied me, and I was not alone in this. I often saw white left-liberal types surround themselves in multicultural politics and ask countless questions about identity, culture, and oppression, down to the most trivial detail. It was often very marginal and focused on the ins and outs of ordinary life. "Here are ten common idioms with racist origins, and you should not use them." "Remember when you celebrate your team's championship in public that anti-brutality organizers are called thugs for their public demonstrations." "Remember when you talk about historical figures, even Abraham Lincoln, that they were racists." It was a piety that served to simultaneously reduce the insights of history to condemnation, to reduce culture to a political agenda, and to remove harmless joys from the equation of life in the present, all within a very confused, posturing set of early twenty-first-century social justice politics. And yet this was what my generation was immersed in. The prevalence of this thinking told me much about checking and second-guessing myself, but much less about how I could be an agent to shape a world in which these questions were impertinent. I saw countless editorials and testimonies of white people that bore a strong resemblance to what Baldwin called the "Be Nice to the Negro" novel of the 1950s, consisting of hashtags and oh-so-precious confessionals about the author's white privilege and how hard the average African-American had it. This type of racial arrangement emerged as yet another philosophical trap in which the dimensions of culture, identity, and segregation reasserted themselves, only in different language and clothing. Distinctions of race were still not relieved. They were refashioned in cuddlier lines, according to the whims and predilections of liberals and leftists of the era.

It was all too consuming and too self-defeating. I had to learn how to ignore it and trust myself. For this reason, when posed with the question that my uncle's date asked my father at

Christmas — "What is the problem with the South Side?" to which my father said "Black on Black Crime" — I practiced my answer, taking all of the weight off the personal and the cultural and placing it onto community structures, resource access, and policy:

"Neoliberal triple-segregation by race, place, and class, combined with escalated, harsh systems of incarceration, punishment and policing, political and economic powerlessness; historically stark economic inequality and economic isolation; iniquitous design and access in systems such as housing, transportation, education, and healthcare, delegating large parts of Chicago's South and Westside to the status of a resource desert. These structures sustained a chronic standard of racial segregation, disinvestment, and a more contemporary one of ethnic displacement through poverty and gentrification. This standard originated in an era of starker racial intolerance and discrimination, though were even then sustained by considerable anti-Black thought and racism."

As with other things, it was a definition in progress, and which could be fought over with encyclopedic length, but one that was more fitting for attention and action than the intellectual sand traps of white guilt and hostility. The restrictions on freedom embedded in that definition were where I learned to place the gravity of my debt. The little things I learned to brush away, along with the casual accusations of bigotry or self-importance. My sanity was always tenuous, I was an imperfect individual, and the power of the debt could to drive me to suicide if I mishandled it. Therefore, I'd save my death for the place where it is best spent: aligning whatever power of resources and action I had toward the abolition of systems of punishment and towards the development of full, thriving resources in Chicago's most mistreated neighborhoods. As for all of the other complications within this, what with me being a white person and all, those would undoubtedly remain. I'd simply have to be generous to others and hope to learn to be generous to myself.

As I lost myself in the blizzard of this setting, life outside went on all around me, and I had to remind myself that I only arrived at this position by the coincidence of my insane biography. The likely scenario for everyone else was that relatively few people from where I came from thought about it in this level of concern or had a point of revelation that made it exigent for them to do so. At most, one out of three white people were sincerely anti-racist. Of that fraction, only a small minority understood themselves as urgent actors within their lifetime. How great that minority was, I did not know. Could the rest of that third be radicalized? Some, probably. Would the resistance of the other two-thirds be too imposing to overcome? That was also hypothetical. It was likeliest that my ranting only made sense to myself, and to most of everyone else appeared either as a petulant, entitled white child trying to appease guilt, be it from a drained spirit in Lawndale or a brash businessman father in Kenilworth. But if there was ever to be a utopian Chicago, eventually people like myself would have to place themselves outside of their upbringing and be willing to withstand that sort of insult. When I reflect on the time that I did not care, at every moment of my life there were a dozen things offered to me that were more convenient and convincing than this question: the party, the job, the television, the hangout, the economics major. It all suppressed critical faculties and made this level of analysis impossible. Maybe that was how my parents' generation got sucked into Reaganism and Clintonism—the appeal to turn the other way was too intoxicating and too easy, no matter how poor other people got in the process nor how brutally they were policed and incarcerated. That was the racial aggression of the North Shore: the tamed hostility of looking the other way, not the warmongering of a street mob. Maybe that was why my peers did not acknowledge that the spiritual world unfolding around them was informed by the debt: it did not exist in the culture, and rarely, if ever, did animus reveal itself.

My friend Diana once noted that there was something that spiritually happened to a person when they walked by a homeless person on the street and ignored them. By intuition, one was drawn to stop and do something, for what sick soul takes pleasure in seeing someone hungry? But we taught ourselves to keep walking and to tolerate their hunger as the facts of life, as some must become executioners and say that they were only looking out to provide for their family. While one moved past that homeless person on that street while they died, one felt a part of themselves die. Not a total death, but a partial death. This was practiced over and over and a tolerance accrued, as addicts become used to the unreality of their drug. It became habitual. One became conditioned into it. But what was the impact over time? What was the culmination of those partial deaths? Did they cease to have an impact, or did one merely become accustomed to living that way? Did you medicate it? Did you console it with new purchases? The addict eventually found anomie, anxiety, and suicide in his new reality, and suddenly the whole world became backward. Life was death, death was life. Truth, untruth, both for the man on the street and for oneself. Those closest to pain were closest to self-actualization. Those furthest from it were barely human at all. Where did those little deaths go, and how did one face it?

To come from obscene privilege was, in a way, to be conditioned into this on a tremendous scale, which may have accounted for the fact that so many children of the wealthy appeared to be the least mature, the most self-deluded, and the most unwell. To walk away from less-than was to simultaneously accept a challenge of better-than, and flee into a world of businessman kings and self-medicating queens, using children as a competition in status as one might do with a salary or an exclusive piece of clothing or furniture. The reality of the homeless person was confined away from the setting of a home. Not only were there looming realities of injustice in our near vicinity, but much of our goods came from someone else's blood in the first place, through the blood of the working class, food picked from broken hands. While some may tout ours as the good life, the sheer number of privileged people on antidepressants suggested a more insidious underbelly to the prestige. In what type of system could education and a nice home produce despair like this? And who was correct to call themselves the owner when they may only be slaves to something else, such as their work or the perception that others had of them? The morning after the spoils turned material privilege from a feast to a wailing, forlorn hangover.

One of the redeeming aspects of the severity of my Depression was that the old version of me died. Or, rather, she woke up and was allowed a rebirth, a resurrection. She saw things for what they were. Once she was rejected as Mad, she had no temptation to be deluded. For madness too was expendable to whiteness and the bourgeoisie, and therefore the terms of solidarity changed entirely. Truth and untruth reversed. The truths of America revealed themselves to be institutionalized. We promoted a version of our country as a manic promoted a delusion of grandeur, running all over the place with babbling with certainty about its views and its system, covering itself with half-truths and platitudes about exceptionalism, democracy, and defeating fascism across the world. There may well be a time when we are brought to trial, and plead the insanity defense.

The culmination of those little deaths was madness and brutality. It was the inhumanity of being able to look at a world heading toward mass extermination and tolerate it as a normal state of affairs. It had been years since I'd been in that Depression in total, faced with the vision of my death. That was my blessing. I had faced it once, and I did not have to face it anymore. I could dissent and dance towards wild ideas of solidarity. For a while, everyone said my benefit was in the joys of accumulation, therein that solidarity lay my actual salvation. I did not need to fear or to be conflicted about this choice: one side has already revealed itself to be synonymous with suicide, and there was no alternative except for what I had to create for myself. There was no natural divide amongst one another that was not an illusion at the core. On the Titanic, the class in the dining hall and the class in the basement existed in conflict, but they ultimately hit the same iceberg. Despite immense pressure to stay in the space that conflict had designated for me, I could remove myself from this conflict in sincere faith and try to divert course. Or, at least, jump off and swim away.

The others were not so lucky. They remained tied to their place, waiting for someone else to allow them to abolish the terms outlined by their money, their genital composition, or their complexion, each of which had varying aspects of freedom or the lack thereof. Conventional wisdom in many places would say that I was most limited by the conditions of my diagnosis or my gender, yet these were also the places in which I was often most free. The moral power of a scorned soul was profound, and the freedom not to be tied to the values of the crowd was amongst the purest and most beautiful human freedoms there were, as the Doc said. As much as I was enraged by the silence expected of me, I was empowered by the force of my voice, which grew despite silence, as the most elaborate flowers grow in long rains. I did not have to view myself as one who was merely limited, nor merely privileged. To have understood oneself too heavily by the conditions that harm them was to agree to a victimized, self-fulfilling contract. Somewhere amidst all of the blather, I heard about how precious and special women are in spite of men, and I was allowed to step outside of this narrow he/her thinking and investigate who a pure Boo would have been had none of this dross existed. In the same vein, in being drugged and shunned for my madness, I was able to reject the thinking that enabled this shunning altogether, and in so doing pursue new possibilities that were far more fulfilling than what I had before. I also knew this world was not available to others in the same way, and that was my gain, and their loss.

The irony was that in the absence of these experiences, the terms of freedom would be different. It did not work the same way with debt: I would only be truly allowed to escape the burden of debt once the debt was paid. There was no depersonalized oppressor class to mock: I was the subject of that mockery. Until final payment, I would always be responsible to understand myself as "white," whatever that was, and interact with the world as such. I was responsible to understand myself as "rich," though I had earned none of that, either. And until those terms reached their point of insignificance, I could not absolve myself of their limits, lest I absolve myself of a necessary debt.

There was no exit. It is always reasserted. So very much was categorized into class or ethnic stripes: your neighborhood, your church, your school, your family, you. I said Winnetka, you said cake-eater. I said Englewood, you said gang-banger. Divisions come along grand lines of White and Black or Brown, yet smaller subdivisions exist within these lands. Kevin and his high school friends all referred to one another by the slurs related to their European heritages: mick, kraut, diego and wop, and, alas, pollack. And they were able to sustain this with some level of cohesion throughout their adolescence. Not that I cared — friends should be allowed to be perverse amongst themselves. There wasn't a black kid in the mix, however, so who knows if they would have called him nigger as remorselessly and confidently as they derided one another with their respective slurs. That question remained entirely hypothetical, as they had never introduced a black friend into their ranks.

On the other side, too, you could still hear blacks complaining about illegal immigrants and referencing "oriental corner stores," and Hispanics complaining about black gang-bangers. And that was Chicago as I observed it, where the illusion of racial difference and separation was presented as a real, out in the open, pedestrian way of life. There was a lot of intermingling, sure, and I participated in it, but almost everyone woke up and went home amongst their own. "That's simply how things are," one might have said, rather conservatively, and there was no pretense of sensitivity about the matter whatsoever. Sometimes these attitudes existed within the bounds of friendship, and other times they did not. Other times, one would be brought to murderous rage over it. I imagined—and I could have been dead wrong—working men bringing the same brazenness and irreverence to their workspaces that Kevin and his friends shared, where it was all tossed together in an insensitive, blue-collar machismo, in which nobody gave a damn and everyone returned home to their own spaces afterward. I imagined a city where one could start a conversation with sentences like, "Man, these fucking Bridgeport Irish Catholics," and where the Bridgeport Irish Catholics returned the favor prolifically, and where I—a supposedly a conscientious observer—was oddly comfortable acknowledging all of this, acquiescent to the ridiculousness of stratification. It was fascinating how gritty and matter-of-fact the racism could feel. And also diverse: it was not a tale of two cities, but a tale of seventy-seven cities, of which I had known only a few intimately. And each had its unique style of tension, like a local spice. In normal times, though, rarely would I get the sense that someone was plotting racial terror. I got the sense that people were different, apart, and treated accordingly, and that was simply life. Race, class, and geography shaped the person, and she should stay where she belongs and act within that space.

And it was also fascinating how some grew out of it, questioned it, and broke with it—what did their path look like?—and how some clung to it as a right, seeing it as a part of their way of life, a personal characteristic that had no actual significance nor required any compromise. Like my brother, once more, when it was suggested to him that there was a problem with him saying "nigger" in private settings. Why did he remain stubborn and reject that anyone would ever suggest a restraint on this word? And why did his old friends mature to reject this thinking and confront him, while others avoided conflict with this question? Segregation, no doubt, enabled this. As did a clear devaluation of life and history. The illuminating experiences were out of consciousness, upheld by a conservative skew in culture that erased as many of those illuminating experiences as possible. The most incendiary word in the American-English dictionary registered as little more than a low-level cuss word, no more relevant than fuck or shit, because Kevin was genuinely ignorant of how far the problem extended into the present.

Comparatively, on the North Shore, people did become highly defensive when accused of racism. I suspect it was because they felt attacked, or because it implied a more brutal state of affairs that did not reflect their values; one of du jour segregation, blatant discrimination, and open public intolerance. I also suspected that some had always referred to the harsher standards of the past to downplay the depth of problems in the present. It was true that this kind of racism was not around the North Shore in noticeable currents, at least not to me. Aside from Kevin and his Notre Dame friends, I did not know anyone who condoned blithe use of the n-word, nor anyone who aggressively belittled expressions of black outrage. Even Kevin and his friends cared too much about their image to say this anywhere but in behind-closed-doors settings, always hiding behind a supposedly respectable conservative front. The racism of the North Shore was racism that most did not see, or was too dim to register. It was soft, like the pillows you did not properly wash. Dr. King said the racism of the North was an air of unease: it was quiet and unwelcoming, kind of like how I felt the need not to say too much about madness when I was home, for one never knew when they would be pushed away for speaking about an inconvenience like that.

Regarding the unease, little tipoffs were there. I felt its uptightness at almost all times. Read the police blotter in the local press and you'll find petty traffic offenses and Hispanic names. My father—both aware of the bias at play and in disagreement with it—referred to it disparagingly as "D.W.H.: Driving While Hispanic." Once, at the library by my parents' house, there was a Puerto Rican woman checking out material after two white women did the same. The librarian asked the woman to show her ID along with her library card, to which the woman responded with offense, as neither of the other women before her had been asked to show identification to borrow an education. "I've been coming to this library for years! I've brought my children to every event! I've taught them how to live in here! You didn't ask for any of the other IDs, did you?" she said. I asked one of the librarians what was happening as I watched it, and she rolled her eyes and kept walking. A few days later, I saw a young black girl at the same library. She was probably about thirteen or fourteen years old and sat alone. She was hunched over the table, and she looked nervous, if not frightened. We made eye contact. She said, "Excuse me?" I acknowledged her. She said, "Are they going to arrest me here?" I smiled at her as though her question was the stuff of childish fantasy. "Of course not, you aren't doing anything." She smiled back in relief. I don't know where she came from, but then, I often felt psychologically inferior in Winnetka, and it was my own home. How could she, in her age, not feel that a police officer may question her simply for showing up? That sort of profiling certainly happened to others.

I did not see brutal displays of discrimination, but I understood the discreetness of unease, how there were public morals and private perversions of those morals, and how one's true soul was always concealed from other people. I understood the air of unease and its capacity to stifle, how it felt like a form of repression. Supplemented by the reduction of American racism to a matter of interpersonal manners, it could never properly be spoken to or exposed. The people of my home believed they were tolerant, but race, like mental illness, was one of those unpleasant, too-serious topics that got sectioned to another place and time when it was more acceptable to talk about, a place and time that ultimately never came. The "don't disturb dinner" material. Like the fickle liberal, the suburban conservative ultimately also understood racism as a matter of etiquette and required no political action beyond the bare minimum of picking the right words. Yet segregation persisted regardless of the words one chose and who was on your bookshelf. Beneath the niceness, social outrage was selective. I had heard murders by cops excused away, and killings at the hands of young black men condemned to no end. I had heard welfare condemned as greediness, and the hardships of poverty brushed off with, "deal with it, it's better here than anywhere else." Or, "Oh, I suppose people are so poor and have it so bad here?"

My father, when commenting on Obama's presidency, reminded people that Barack was also a white man, as though we whites were being subjected to a double standard when we talk about the first black president. I liked to point out that men like him—rich North Shore men—paid for Obama's rise in the first place, but he denied it. Too extreme, he would say of Obama, ignorant to both the man's modestly conservative disposition toward American institutions and his flagrant extremity of opinion. A woman in my parish, when people rioted after Michael Brown's killer was not indicted, wondered, "So let me understand: we save the neighborhood by burning it down?" I also listened to a couple excuse the non-indictment of the cop that killed Tamir Rice. They said the internal workings of the office were off; the dispatcher was negligent, the officers were acting on their information. The couple hadn't seen the video. They hadn't seen how quickly they pulled up to the boy and shot him, and how they held his sister to the ground as she ran to him, stopping her yards away from his body. At least my brother had the honesty to say, "I don't care, stop talking about it," when one brought up race. Same for his friends, who said police killings and said, "So what? So a criminal was killed. Should I cry?"

Any one of these remarks was deserving of examination, but when challenged, they diverted the conversation elsewhere with the same tired lines: "Too serious," "Not the right place," "Why must you be so angry?" "Politics does not need to be like this; agree to disagree," "I don't want to talk about it." The troublesome remarks stood, not as a conscientious part of any commitment to act, but as another part of the dinner conversation in between "How was work today?" "Did you hear what the new president did at Loyola Academy?" and "Pass the chardonnay." Not only was it not understood as racist, but it was not even racial. They were merely words, and words, they might say, exist in the realm of the inconsequential. Racism was hard, legalized, and physical, they would say. These were just observations, not acts of discrimination, and therefore nothing to be concerned with.

In close juxtaposition, I would overhear fathers offering wisdom to their teenage children. "You hear kids say these things," they would say, "And none of it is real. I'm depressed because I'm oppressed and I'm oppressed because I'm depressed. Take down the 1 percent. The whole mindset of dealing with hardship is going to waste, and you're seeing the rise of anti-American ideologies go along with it. They're calling themselves socialists and gender breakers, but they are going to wind up victims of nothing but their mindset and of their idea that somebody else is going to take care of them. I don't want to see that in you.

Think positively, think smartly. Do the work. Provide for people something that they want in their life. That's the way to a
meaningful existence. If you can cover that much, America will
work for you, and you will make something of yourself." And
mothers would discuss the lifestyles of their adult children, what
jobs they were taking and what neighborhoods they would move
into. "He wanted to do the do-gooder route, but it got so hard,
so Jim got him a job at Bank of America. He's got such a good
heart, though. He's the type of person they need in the banks
so he can set an altruistic culture. He and his wife are getting
a place in Pilsen. The neighborhood could use their resources,
it's been poor for so long."

The trick here was to simultaneously instill in youth a can-do
individualism combined with an inflated sense of self-importance,
all within a belief system that held that the world should develop
around wealthy people showing up and making it happen. The
way to improve Pilsen was to send people with money there prior
to sending resources to the people who exist there already. There
was no theory of social development that did not first divert the
power of investment to the rich, and treat all other concerns as
secondary. And, evidently, the way to edify capitalism's propensity for selfishness and destruction was to have the good, selfless
son at the helms, as though he had the power or the will to do
anything about it.

I wonder what event could have sparked the point of revelation. All of this occurred within a Midwestern ghettoization
scheme of turbulent cities and quasi-peaceful suburbs, where
many carried a loose fear of criminals coming to hijack their cars
and thugs moving out of the city and into the suburbs and collar
counties, who would take their habits with them wherever they
went. It was an occupier's mentality by another name: civilization
existed on one side, barbarity on the other. And the way to treat
barbarians was through attacks on dignity. Actual contact with

the communities spoken of was limited or non-existent. I was only in Chicago's South or West side infrequently; the conduct I observed was banal, hardly worthy of this alien obsession, nor the punishing use of the cage. Whatever exotic fantasies one may have held about black neighborhoods were quickly discounted when one realized that life everywhere consisted of trivialities like playing children, neighborly discussion, commuting to errands, and so forth. Humanity was the input, and humanity was the same everywhere. Yet segregation did not promote this simple realization. It was the system and the environment that provoked difference, and that was where life most diverged. Why was it that a classroom of fourteen-year-olds in one school hypothesized a future in Ivy Leagues, while another had accepted that the system was never going to progress them beyond high school? Why did the students in New Trier Township struggle with severe anxiety disorders while students in Englewood had post-traumatic stress disorder? This was a question neither of bad attitude nor an imbalance in merit. It was the birth lottery in America and little more. That alone shaped the environment that would develop in one's mind.

The rest of life formed from there. In isolated neighborhoods in the city, cigarettes were sold loosely, not in taxed packets. Broad areas of poverty covered about half of the territory. There were spates of abandoned homes across a majority of residential blocks, open street commerce, and huddles of unoccupied men on the corner with no apparent agenda to spend their time elsewhere. There were comparable huddles of younger men on the stoops of their block, who I was told were the inheritors of futurelessness, those closest to death and confinement in Chicago, the subject of national morbid attention. For many of them, life had been hijacked by the criminal justice system. Conventional wisdom said to stay inside after dark. If you asked where to get food, you were told that you were technically in a food desert. And a healthcare desert. And a job desert. There were not enough local savings for most new businesses to have an enduring customer base, but there was a powerful enough liquor store lobby to capitalize on the spare cash that was there and offer a convenient fix to eternal problems. Taken together, there were as many cracks to fall into as there was ground to stand on. That was intended by the design of Chicago: socialism for the rich, rugged individualism for everyone else.

None of this existed where I had ever lived. And other times, anecdotally, mostly, I heard how that poverty was policed. The stories I heard were of life under state surveillance. Police were experienced as an invasive presence who did too little prior to the moment of the crime, and who were understood and treated as an oppressive force known for, I repeat, harassment, bullying, assault, extortion, unlawful invasion, crime fabrication, torture, murder, and impunity. They could attack at any moment: in a matter of minutes, a driver could become quarantined on the road by three police vans, removed from his car, handcuffed, searched, and, after nothing incriminating had been found, returned to his vehicle to carry about his business as usual. In Winnetka, by comparison, when you went out of town, you could call the police and arrange for them to gather your mail for you, and they did not complain about it.

On the other side of the wall, we identified punishment not as an enabler of poverty, but as the solution to it. Where I lived, you would sooner hear $5,000,000 allotted to a super-maximum prison than a fraction of that given to health or educational resources. You would sooner hear that police were the good guys who had the rough job—our finest boys were taking care of the social disturbances, those people, the social problem. Nowhere in this mix was it said that the average black family had between a nickel and dime to the white dollar, nor was it interrogated how that came to be so. "My Irish ancestors did it, so why can't they?" seemed to be a sufficient explanation for many, or a fitting deflection for the moment. This was where the debt became more than a pretty moral rumination about America. It was a stern, real, endless conflict, between myself and my home, and between my home and the city that gave it context. It burdened me each day that I had accepted it. I would have been happier having never known.

Of the books I had kept beside my bed, I had been consistently changed by *Silence* by John Cage, not that this had anything to do with race. Half of the time I was not sure what I was reading. The other half brought me into a mindset of spectacular possibility. "More and more I feel as though we are getting nowhere," he said, without context. I repeated that in so many ways in so many situations, and not once has anyone ever picked up on it. This dinner table discussion was one of those times: another racially iniquitous outcome deemed race-neutral, another episode I would have to repress or deal with, another compromise for my home. It was an interesting concept, silence. In Cage, and other artists, silence was a musical tool reflecting a natural state of peace, in between which the life of music danced. Or, silence was the music itself. But here, in occupied Chicago, silence was a nervous force. It was an unnatural, manmade silence. It was the air of unease. It was the material of that abstract center of gravity that corrals people back into their neighborhoods, where they would be most understood and accepted and free of mental rattling. Silence as in, "nothing can change because we don't even have the words to address it." And within that silence there were noisy, disturbed minds. I yearned for that natural state of quietude, free of indebted history and free of every tense mental symptom of that. Oh, to sit next to a stranger and feel nothing but peace, and to know that there was nothing that we needed to resolve amongst ourselves. That was where freedom existed. Between that world and mine, the only way to achieve that state of peace was to confront the disease head-on and replace it with historical resolution.

Around a year after the LaQuan Macdonald shooting, Jude and I attended a Department of Justice testimonial at a disability rights office in the city. During this testimony, Jude got her voice in first as well as last. "I called the hotline from the local chapter of the National Alliance for Mental Illness because I was unwell," she said. "I told them I was thinking about killing myself and I wanted someone to talk to. Then they told me that they were obligated to call the authorities because I indicated that I wanted to harm myself. But I never wanted to be involved with an authority. I wanted to talk. They called the cops on me anyway, and I got terrified and left my home for the rest of the day. Because the cops only have two options: they can arrest me, or they can put me in a hospital. Or, they can shoot me. I don't want any of that, so I went far away and saw a movie, and only came back hours later. I don't know how to reconcile this. Despite many cops being my friends, despite the fact that cops have been good to me for most of my life, I am nevertheless terrified of the police."

At the time, I was careless about the severity of Jude's statement. I could not see how this constituted the testimony of a justice investigation, which, I thought, was a place to prioritize people who were more directly threatened. Meaning, black people, not Jude and me. There had been no injustice, for there had been no interaction and therefore no harm. The entire testimony consisted of Jude's fear of the police, and it was not their fault that they were the default line of aid for mental health crises. Jude's gripe was with bigger things, not the conduct of the police department. Eventually, however, I changed this position and rejected it as a narrow framing. For when did a problem become a problem: when it happened to you or when you had to plan for the possibility that it would?

I remembered a comparable episode of panic I'd had a couple of years earlier. Mark was still in Chicago, and I was on his couch in his apartment in Old Town, reading about mental health calls to the police. I expected to read what was by then an all-too-normal journalistic account of a black man being killed by police — there was a point in my life where for several months the only thing I saw on the internet were police killings — but the image I found instead was much closer to my own skin: white, suburban, deemed mentally ill. I'd previously thought I was immune to this form of violence by the sheer and perhaps uneducated assumptions I held about complexion or my ignorance about how exposable people with psychiatric disabilities could be. What I read that night was about the shootings of people who had been in situations exactly like ones I'd been in many times before, only someone close to them made the mistake of calling the police. A mother would call the police on a suicidal son, and the police would then arrive, presume the cup of tea beside the suicidal individual to be poison, and shoot the young man before he killed himself.

I'd never thought that I was merely one variable away from this death, yet there I was: frightened, solemn, and eerily unprotected. I got paranoid. Though, like Jude, there was no interaction. Realistically, it was always one call away, and that required a different approach to police, both in private and in public. How would I describe this to the people close to me? How would I have to cover my tics and distressed appearances in public? I tried to explain to Mark that I was only a slim matter of circumstances away from being one of the people on the newsfeed. "In the wrong setting, Mark, that could very easily be me. Very easily. Please take precautions. Please don't call the police. I know you've never seen me like that, but if you do, just please let it be. Or don't call them. Anything but that," I told him. He didn't seem worried or changed in any way. "Is

there something you'd like me to do?" he asked. At the time I
wanted him to experience my fear, to uncover what I had just
uncovered, and place himself in my own skin at the moment I
learned I'd have to reacquaint myself to account for bad cops.
But I could not say it, nor could he do it. I didn't yet have the
words. "No, there's nothing you can do. I'll sleep it off. Just
respect my plea if it ever comes to it," I said. It ended like that,
and I never talked about it with anyone again. At the Department
of Justice testimony, however, I nevertheless considered myself
an intrusion in the conversation. It would take a long time to
undo that. A police encounter gone tragic was within the realm
of possibility in my life, and I would often retreat into private,
withheld places because of it. What options would I have if the
police came for me? In a Mad state, I could try to remain still
with paralysis and hope that nothing happened. Or, like Jude,
I could run away. Thankfully, for me, there were only a few,
mostly avoidable scenarios in which this would be necessary.
The same could not be said if those scenarios were as quotidian
as the street corner, the local park, or the traffic stop.

Jude and I were on the top floor of the disability rights building at a round table by ourselves. About two dozen members
of the disability advocacy community were present, while four
representatives from the DOJ sat at the front of the room. Each
table had papers organized at the center, along with stimulation
toys. I took one and held it flimsily in front of me. It was a standard
black and white page of pictures copied from Google images.
The headline read: "People with disabilities killed by police." The
pictures, no bigger than yearbook photos for one's wallet, were
arranged unevenly across the page, some blurred opaquely due
to a poor quality available on the internet. They were captioned,
". . . Quintonio Legrier, Terrance Harris, Korryn Gaines, Alfred
Olango, Lashano Gilbert, Laquan McDonald, Sandra Bland, Eric
Garner, Matthew Ajibade, Mario Woods, Tiffani Jacobs, Miriam

Carey, Jeremy McDole, Ezell Ford, Stephon Watts, Keith Vidal, Natasha McKenna, Tanisha Anderson, Phillip Coleman, Barry Montgomery, Kajime Powell, Ethan Saylor, Kaydon Clarke, Leundeu Keunang, Marcus Abrams, Angel Cruz, Freddie Grey, Reginald Kevin, Michelle Cusseux, Keith Scott . . ."

The facilitator of the event rose and introduced the federal investigators, who were dressed for professional litigation amongst a crowd otherwise dressed in street attire, Jude and I included. The investigation outlined the background of their aims succinctly—to see if the conduct of the Chicago Police Department was abusive, racially discriminatory, and discriminatory toward people with disabilities—and opened the floor for commentary. An older man took the microphone first and quickly dictated a list of flaws about the police department in his community. I tried to notate his response as well as I was able to, but often lost him in his speech. "This union is a blood fraternity," I heard him say, pointing toward no concrete action, but a cultural trait. "They teach you how to coerce, they teach you how to lie. There is something going on with these men. There is something going on within them. There is no way you can empty a whole clip into somebody and be all right. They target people. They prey on the weak. It's a bully tactic. They're dealing with something, and so long as they have the backing of the Fraternal Order of Police, they have the strength to do what they do. Police accountability is in the hands of the Mayor's Office, and it goes all of the way up to him. The same people that are pushing all of this on us are the ones responsible for reviewing it. Alright? You understand that? We're told that the people fail the city. No. The city fails the people."

In that final sentiment, I recalled one of the mantras of anti-psychiatry: madness is a sane response to an insane world. Or, as a rapper might say in my own time, Good Kid, M.A.A.D. City. My critical inquiries of biomedical psychiatry had then brought me to understand the experience of madness as a phenomenon that was both induced and sustained by a corrupted world and the social concept of mental illness was malleable for the ends of that corruption. To be "mentally ill" at various moments in history could mean traumatized, depressed, manic, and psychotic, as well as it could mean being defiant of the prevailing order, be it for sexual expression, drug experimentation, political protest, or the domestic angst of housewives in a sternly patriarchal era. Psychiatry served the dual function of whitewashing social harm—that is, by diverting the impact of an oppressive order on people away from its origins and onto the person—and of censoring social and political dissent, resulting in what Kate Millett provocatively called the most sophisticated system of oppression ever created. My readings into the history of racism in the US revealed strains of that arrangement. Baldwin had caustically noted that a black man who carried himself like John Wayne was doomed to be seen as a lunatic. Psychiatry during the Civil Rights era identified protest psychosis as a form of schizophrenia—a range against the order that was deemed a mental illness. Such politically repressive uses undoubtedly remind one of Stalinism, only it was not as often in vogue to talk about the repressive forces in one's backyard as it was to talk about the repressive forces in Russia. A country that equated a yearning for freedom and recognition with insanity had essentially organized itself as an asylum society.

That sophisticated tool of oppression—that interplay between the person, the world, madness, and psychiatry—persisted under the modern guises of policing and punishment. Chicago's jail, the ominous Cook County jail, had assumed the dubious honor of "America's Largest Mental Health Facility." People rightly said this as a point of concern, pointing to rates of insanity and psychiatric diagnosis in jails and prisons and to the horrid ways in which prisoners were treated. They were "The New

Asylums," they said, where those who once would have been in psychiatric hospitals were now in chains or units of solitary confinement. In this analysis, the problem of mental illness in jails and prisons was often presented as a failure to provide a mental health system and to treat the individual. But if the onset of illness came from forces outside of the mental health system, such as in the prison itself—which were designed to psychologically ruin people—or in the conditions of the communities from which prisoners so often came—poor, disinvested, and at the bottom of the hope gap—then was mental healthcare capable of reaching the problem effectively enough? Rarely did I hear anyone identify hallucination as the logical outcome of solitary confinement or depression and paranoia as the logical symptom of a policed life in poor areas. No, these were spoken of as medical issues. Rather than neoliberal racial segregation and punishment, the heart of the problem was called mental illness. In the micro context, mental illness was a matter of life and death, appearing—with great justification—to be the source of all of an individual's problems. In the macro context, mental illness was in many cases only the symptom. Symptoms could be managed and addressed. This was the assigned role of both the mental health system and the criminal justice system. Thus the debate between mental healthcare and criminal justice could well be understood as a debate over how to handle the unwell, rather than as a debate of addressing the primary causes of madness in the first place. In the short term, I believed people should be let out of jail through whatever means could release them, including psychiatry. In the long term, psychiatry would be a chronically inadequate response to the truest roots of the problems of mental illness and imprisonment.

When I was twenty-three, maybe twenty-four—age, after it stopped being tracked to an academic year, had become a singular, undefined, uninterrupted concept in my memory; I had no age or social identity, just a long sequence of moments amounting to a lifetime — I transferred my college credits to DePaul University and enrolled in a general psychology program. I had spent a couple of terms taking courses at community college through palpable dysfunction, driving out at 6:00 A.M. to campus and driving back after class with visions of Christlike persecution, to spend the rest of my day just as infirm in my parents' house. The hope at that juncture of my education was that my previous university would accept these new credits and grant me a degree while my family negotiated the mental health circumstances of my college years. The administration, however, had remained stubborn on this point, and I never received a degree from it. During my time at DePaul, I was introduced to the story of Norman Finkelstein, a scholar who was denied tenure at DePaul. His scholarship on the Israeli occupation of the Palestinians was out of favor with academia, if not America at large. For being honest and truthful, he was isolated and smeared. My professor recounted his time in her department. She said, "They pressured him to leave, and he didn't. Then they sent him accusations of sexual misconduct, one from a female student, and one from a male, because they didn't know anything about his personal life. He called bullshit on them. Then they came at him with everything. We tried to tell him that they would ruin him. We told him to wait until he was tenured, and then report his research. He wasn't having it. He tried to hold his people accountable for their crimes against Palestine, and he was ruined for it." This was all driven, I was told, by a renowned, politically connected criminal defense lawyer who shall not be named. I subsequently read deeply into Finkelstein's work, which exposed the lies built around the occupation, and the "savagery" of the Palestinians. It was the most important discovery I had while at DePaul, and one of the most formative of my entire life.

I appreciated having access to a university library. I spent much of my spare time researching the stigma of mental illness, or attempting to, which was then the best phrase I had for the phenomenon I was trying to challenge. I found almost nothing on the subject. Comparably, there was a vast collection of literature on racism, sexism, and heterosexism, as well as movements against them, from which I hoped to infer lessons and weave together an analysis of mental illness in society. I was younger then, still very dumb, and only a fraction of the person I'd be a few years later. And I was often bitter and understood myself as a failure. My response was to try to build social movement out of nothing, because a movement is what I thought I needed, while nothing was what I had. How could one person take this responsibility upon themselves? It required both great desperation and great grandiosity, the perfect pair for revolutionary and messianic fervor. And because there was so little on mental illness and so very much on race, racial justice became the foundation of my life after college. Whether or not I could speak to it or do anything about it, it was indicted in my near vicinity every day.

One of my classes at DePaul mandated service work at a Chicago community agency. During a lecture early in the quarter, representatives from the university presented fifteen different agencies in which the students could work, most of them in Wicker Park, Logan Square, Humboldt Park, Lakeview, and Lincoln Park. There was only one organization from the South Side, in Englewood, and of the fifty to sixty students in the class, I was the only one who raised my hand to say I wanted to work there. I accepted the position and started a week later. On the first day I went to my assignment, I remember my mother being afraid for my safety, for the only thing that anyone on the North Shore had ever told me about going to Englewood was not to do it. I traveled on the Red Line, observing how the train steadily shifted from all-white to all-black while traveling from North to South along the stops of Chicago's Loop. By the time I was south of Roosevelt, the passengers were almost all black or brown, the near antithesis of the Fullerton stop to the North, on which almost everyone was white. I got off at the sixty-third street station on a platform in the middle of the highway and hurried up a narrow, crowded stairwell. At the top of the station, I watched the highway run into the distance. The city rested on its edges, as though looking at itself from split ends of a deliberate chasm. A crowd was huddled in the grey space of the CTA station for warmth, waiting for a bus to arrive. It felt more congested than other train stations in the city, though that perception may have just been the trick of a segregated mind.

The crowd kept to themselves. They stood with their hands packed into heavy jackets, a couple with Bulls logos, some wearing hats and uniforms for service industry jobs. A young boy next to me, probably no more than ten or eleven years of age, looked grown a few years older in his composure, able to navigate the city and public transportation on his own. The crowd looked quietly before themselves, neutralized by the cold. The street directly in front of them had five one-way lanes on each side, connected by a walkway running over the highway in a concrete I-formation over the earth, and there were caged fences on top of the cement bearings between the road and the highway. When the bus came, a line two dozen people deep formed in front of the entrance. I sat stiffly, with my limbs close to one another, and looked directly ahead. The bus passed a row of streets named after Ivy League colleges. I thought to myself that this might have been a joke that urban planners had made a long time ago; a taunt about dreams put out of reach. Later I would realize it was designed for the dreamers before the great evacuation of the middle 20th Century.

My mother texted to be sure I was all right. I ignored the message and watched my surroundings. My understanding of the neighborhood before coming was a litany of statistics on social decay, mostly in formal, academic analyses. RCAP: Racially Concentrated Area of Poverty, in which the breadth of life is a clinical chart in the middle of the map of Chicago; a separate "they" to observe and analyze as opposed to an "us" to participate amongst. On the ground, some of the streets were colored with murals of past icons, figures like Richard Wright, Malcolm X, or Gwendolyn Brooks. I got off the bus three blocks from where my organization was located and walked through slush to the agency. The street was beaten up with potholes, and to my side, there was about half of an acre of unoccupied, undeveloped land. When I arrived at the address, it wasn't clear to me which door to enter. They were all locked. I banged on one, and a woman opened it and looked through. I introduced myself as a student from DePaul, and she let me in. The space was modest, with an old, boxed TV, a collection of books, and crayons and construction paper lying across a couple of tables. I was introduced to an older woman working on an early home computer, a model that we had in our homes and schools at the turn of the millennium, before flat-screen computers replaced them. The leader of the organization, Jean, greeted me and showed her the office, and told me about a young man she wanted me to tutor. Jean said he could do well himself, or he could trail off, and it wasn't clear what way he was going to go. She asked me to work with him when he came in after school and assist him with his homework. In the meanwhile, I sat at one of the tables, read, and waited for students to arrive.

Around 3:30 a group of girls showed up and chattered amongst themselves. I admired their bluntness with one another and the frivolity with which they spoke about school, their teachers, their adolescent love interests. It reminded me of my own high school, before maturity dictated the terms of my honesty. Later, boys came, including the one I was supposed to tutor. His name was Robert. He was tall, sullen, and brooding, and didn't say anything to me for the first few minutes of my meeting him beyond mumbling and one-word responses. I sat down and supervised the crowd, trying to keep my attention amidst a degrading depression. An older teacher arrived, a smiling, wrinkled Australian woman who for reasons unknown to me was working in this part of Chicago. The teacher worked on writing with the kids and asked students to share their material. One of the boys volunteered his writing. It started with the phrase, "The chaos of the city tramples the mind," and I thought he was eloquent for his age, or any age. Jean then asked me to tutor Robert individually, and we walked to a dark corner of the room and worked on an old computer. I tried to work with him, but he remained reserved and recalcitrant. I asked what he had to work on. He said, "Math and writing," while scrolling through Facebook on the computer. His name on social media wasn't his own, nor was it anything that I had ever heard before, some slang name that didn't make sense to me. I asked about his family, and he said his mom and dad lived apart. His mom was a cop, and he didn't say what his dad did. He said his mom was usually working, and he spent most of his time at home watching TV. I redirected attention to school and tried to work with him on his assignments. He looked at the page and sighed, and fidgeted in his chair, then tossed his pen down and went on Facebook again. I quickly put his pencil back in his hand and told him he wasn't getting out of it that easily, then worked through his sentences with him. The pencil moved slowly, in crinkly script. I questioned if he knew how to write at his grade level. Robert tried to give up any time he could not decide which letter to write next, which was often, and to help him, I dictated the letters to him.

After an hour, he got weary, as did I. We put schoolwork aside and sat and talked about his social life. He mentioned some kids in his class had started drinking, only he didn't call them kids. He called them niggas. I didn't know what to say about that word choice. I felt that it was wrong, but did I have a right to question his vocabulary? I asked about the drinking instead. He said that their business was their business and his was his, and he shouldn't concern himself with what other kids were doing.

It got dark early and the kids either went home on the bus or walked home. I stayed to help close the building. This was the first time in months I had been able to stay out for long periods at a time, and the Depression got heavier toward the day's end. When I was finished cleaning up, I went outside to wait for the bus. Noticing that I was getting spaced out, a seventeen-year-old told me that he would wait with me, as I should not be out alone. The street was empty. On the other side, there was an open yard with patches of snow and hard dirt in front of a building with wooden stoops. A police jeep drove slowly by. The driver, with a bulletproof vest, looked at me as he passed, and turned a corner. We stood in silence for another two minutes. A second police jeep slowly drove by, and again the driver looked at me. The jeep drove forward another block and slowed even further, shining a light on a row of parked cars. It came to a halt in front of one of the cars. The officer got out and shined the light in the car. Another man, independent of the car, was walking by in a hooded jacket and was stopped by the officer. The flashlight was now on him. Then my bus arrived, covering my view of the police and the pedestrian. I got on the bus and rode away.

I'd continue to go to this organization several times more and complete my work. My mother remained worried that I would be harmed until I scolded her for it. "We are not having this conversation again, I am going to work there," I told her. I gave a report about it in class about what the organization did, what issues they worked on. I wouldn't have any sort of presence on the South Side for several months, as I never had any reason to. And most of what I was learning was making me believe that due to the distance in reality between myself and them, my presence as a white person could only make matters more difficult and be interpreted that way, regardless of my intentions. I opted instead for studious silence and observation, trying to understand the dimensions of segregation, to better equip myself to break them down. Speaking or acting too soon would be akin to shooting too quickly, or so I thought. The reality was that I lacked the means to take part in critical work, and would have to either hunt to find it or create it myself in the future.

At the Department of Justice Investigation in early 2016, the federal lawyers, all in business suits, took diligent notes on community accounts of abuse. The microphone passed from person to person, mostly African-American speakers, each recounting a public incident of misconduct, harassment, or violence. "I don't like what these cops are doing to the kids in Lawndale," a young woman said. "They pull them aside, try to get them to rat on their parents, try to get information on drug dealers out of them, and then they bully them when they don't comply. Just last week I saw a cop make fun of a kid for being fat, and that's how these guys conduct themselves on our streets and in our schools. My brother is an A student at his school, and one day when he left school last year, there were two cops smoking cigarettes by the wall of the building. They heckled him and said, 'So what gang are you joining?' And my brother said he wasn't in any gang. The cops then blew smoke in his face and laughed at him. Now my brother understands cops as people who will only try to do him harm. And that's how most kids are. They're more afraid of the police than they are of the gangs."

Solemnly, the lawyers documented this on their notepads and raised their heads when they were ready to listen again. A man took the microphone. He looked about fifty years old and seemed intimidated to speak. "About ten years ago, I was returning to my car after work, and two police officers were searching the inside. I asked them, 'Can I help you with something?' They talk to me a little bit, don't tell me anything too specific, and back away from the car. As I drive home, I see the cop cars are driving behind me, and I'm nervous that something is going to happen. I pull into an alleyway by my building, and there's already a police car waiting in front of me. The one that was driving behind me pulls in after, and now I'm trapped. I get out of the car and ask if anything is happening, and one of the police officers says, 'Get out, nigger,' and hits me to the ground. And then I got beaten almost to unconsciousness. The head cop of the district arrived and said I should be taken to the hospital. As they're taking me there, the officer who assaulted me told me, 'We know where you live, and you know what will happen to you if you tell anyone.' So we lied to the hospital and said I was mugged, and I never told anything to anyone. I've got PTSD and bipolar disorder ever since, and I've only recently started getting therapy for it."

As my knowledge of accounts like this accrued—accounts of detainment, brutality, and shooting, along with blunt racist invective from standing police officers—I realized that the Chicago Police served a parallel role to the white gangs of the past. They would shoot a man in the back of the neck and plant a gun on his corpse to justify the murder, and much of the public then bestowed them with the honor of protecting the world from harm. While many would take offense to this assessment, objecting to a generalized representation of the police force, there was a substantial population of officers who were active abusers, who were actively recruited from white supremacist backgrounds, and who were empowered and protected by the institution of policing. Yet my role in this remained indiscernible from that of a voyeur, a passive observer occasionally getting access to a world where young men were detained and tortured, only not from an independent lynch mob but state-authorized authorities. That privacy was in the genetics of the system: every aspect of humanity was atomized and placed at a distance. What I was left with was a flux of images and expressions rooted in brutality and righteous anger, while actual day-to-day relationships remained stratified, and the depth of terror was largely concealed. Without an extravagant effort to cross lines, it was close to impossible for new forms of understanding to develop, leaving us with many of the same problems, the same tilt in society's eye, asking the same questions in slightly edited forms.

Somewhere on social media, when I was still a student at DePaul, I heard about a group called The Mental Health Movement, grown out of Woodlawn. The Mayor, in a twist of Orwellian logic, had decided that the city could not afford to maintain six community mental health clinics, mostly on the South and West sides of the city, which operated at an annual cost of about one million dollars. This was around the time that he was closing dozens of public schools as well, and around the time that the Chicago Teacher's Union went on strike. The city's defense was simple: "We have no money." As I looked more into that reasoning, it seemed more and more a bald lie, though I had never looked at the fine print before to realize just how insignificant one million dollars is to a city, nor how the burden of that million dollars would be shifted fivefold into prison and emergency room costs. The city housing authority alone had diverted about half of a billion dollars from its budget into less transparent places, and whenever the Mayor needed tens of millions for private development, he was able to find it. The city did not say they were broke then, and the city never questioned where the money would come from.

Amid the rankness of Chicago politicking, a small group of mental health consumers organized and named themselves the Mental Health Movement. When the city closed a clinic, the Mental Health Movement occupied it for a month in resistance. Though they tried to shame the Mayor on several occasions, he had demonstrated that he was shameless. There was a lot of anger, outrage, and consciousness-raising going amongst my era—most of my peers espoused values of non-discrimination of race, gender, and sexuality—yet prior to the Mental Health Movement, I could not identify anyone who was treating mental health as a political issue and applying movement principles to it. I wrote to the group instantly but did not get a response. Then I saw that they were having a meeting in their office in Woodlawn, and drove down Lake Shore Drive on a Thursday evening to attend. I parked near the University of Chicago and walked to their building. The first thing I noticed was how strikingly the lines of segregation made themselves apparent between the University and the neighborhoods to the immediate south. The walk to the office made me nervous, I admit. I had only heard ominous stories about the South Side and kept a skeptical, defensive eye at every corner. For having this clear discomfort, I was not proud. For hardening myself in neighborhoods where I would eventually be perfectly comfortable, I was not proud. But the path I was on involved messy means toward clean ends, and it was necessary at the time to work through that point. The distance would have to dissolve one way or the other.

I knocked on the office door, but nobody answered. I stepped away from the building and put my hands in my pockets, my eyes still squinting with the suspicion that I was somehow unsafe. It was quiet, and I saw maybe one or two cars come by in the time I waited. I knocked on the door again, and still, nobody came. Eventually, a bus arrived, and an older woman, a grey, grandmotherly figure wearing loose sweatpants, got off and approached the door. I asked her if she represented the Mental Health Movement. She said she did and introduced herself as Dorothea before explaining to me that the meeting had been canceled. She apologized sweetly, and I left. I remember it was dusk when I got back to my car, and the setting by the parks at the University of Chicago had a natural grandeur of red, orange, green, and brown, all in the heart of an unloving city.

Some time passed before I sought them out again. In the interim, I remained bookish, sober — I had quit drinking for almost three years after college — and accepting of the fact that I would die young. One day, I saw that the Mental Health Movement had organized a demonstration outside of the closed mental health clinic in Logan Square. The occasion was for a mayoral runoff. In the event no single candidate received over half of the votes in an election, the top two candidates had a runoff election in the spring; a virtual impossibility in a Chicago, where only a detested Mayor would ever lose electoral dominance. The Mental Health Movement was speaking against the Mayor's disinvestment from their communities and was organizing a march to the voting booth at the nearby library to cast an early ballot. It was a beautiful day when I arrived, one of those breezy afternoons that made the city look like a mix of joy, character, and culture that cities were supposed to be. Across the street, a community brewery had opened its windows, and the patrons inside were laughing with pint glasses in front of them. This was a distorted judgment, however, since gentrification was the underlying source of this moment. The old mental health clinic at which we gathered had been halfway turned into a macaroni restaurant, while the other half was another bar in development. The life of that brewery I was watching with such glee had likely only opened through the displacement of something else, something poorer, and less white.

A crowd formed around the clinic, passing out flyers for the challenging mayoral candidate and sharing information about the history of the city's mental healthcare. Upon first encounter, the crowd seemed older and more modest than the neighborhood across the street. A van arrived with speakers and a microphone and the organizers started playing music. Parts of the crowd danced lightly over a Latin and electronic fusion beat, as cool and effortless as the spring day. My feeling of acceptance within this community amplified, my awkwardness waned. As I started to feel comfortable enough to talk to somebody, a young man took the mic. He was thin and Caucasian and introduced himself as Joe Scalia. He made a brief introduction in Spanish and then repeated his statement in English. "Thank you all for coming," he said. "As you know, this used to be the site of the Logan Square mental health clinic, which the Mayor heartlessly shut down three years ago. We knew it was a cold decision, we knew that it was a shortsighted decision, and we knew that it would cause a lot of pain. And we still know it today. As we see this mayoral race come down to a runoff, we need to remember who this Mayor sides with and who he is willing to cut off. Let us remember the words of Helen Morley, who looked the Mayor directly in the eye and told him, 'If you close my clinic, I will die. I will lose my support, I will lose my community, I will go off of my medications, and I will die.' Within three months - three months - of closing the clinic, we found our friend Helen dead in her apartment. We need to take this message straight to the Mayor; you closed our clinics and people are dying. People are losing their healthcare. They're losing their jobs. They're disappearing into the shadows, they're living under the highway on the South Side, and they're in Cook County Jail. Thousands are unaccounted for. It's ludicrous that the Mayor would try to risk this to save . . . how much was it again?"

A woman from the crowd shouted, "Less than two million dollars!"

"Not even two million dollars!" Joe continued. "We need to go to the ballot box and make a statement—that this city belongs to us, not the bankers that the Mayor works for, who paid him twenty million dollars on a sinecure to be their Mayor. Our clinics belong to us, and our schools belong to us! We need to tell him that he is not going to be able to get away with bullying us anymore, because we are going to vote him out!"

The crowd of about thirty people erupted in affirmation. He opened the microphone up to the audience. An old woman with a hunch a t-shirt donning the phrase *I Am One of Those People* took the microphone. Her voice was hoarse, and she spoke carefully, with concern for punctuation.

"Hello, my name is Jude Freedman," she said. "You may be wondering what my t-shirt means. Well, I'll tell you what it means. It means that I am a person who suffers from a chronic, serious, persistent mental illness. I've dealt with it my whole life. Several years ago, I got ill. In fact, I got so seriously ill that I started to retreat from my work. Then I lost my job. Then my husband left me. I spent half of a year sleeping on my couch, losing a battle for dominance with my dog. Then I lost my home and spent a year living in a homeless shelter. After that, I was put in a nursing home for two years, and when I got out, I made it my life's work to advocate for people with lived experience of mental illness and homelessness to make sure that they get the services they need to lead full, happy, and productive lives. This hasn't always been easy in Chicago. The previous mayor threatened to close many of our mental health clinics, and I took to city hall with many of the people here today to stage a sit-in to protest this decision. By the time it was over, Daley decided not to close the clinics. I look back at this as one of the greatest, proudest moments of my life. This current mayor threatened to close the clinics on us, and we did another sit-in in City Hall. While we did so, he turned off the lights and shut off the bathrooms, and we had to leave. Even beyond that, he has proven himself to be extraordinarily comfortable with removing us from his vision of the city. He treats us with outright contempt. I've never seen this level of disregard before. I implore every one of you to get as many people as you can to the voting booth next Tuesday."

The primary reason I could recall this speech so clearly was that I'd hear Jude repeat it verbatim one hundred more times. It became ingrained in me. During the demonstration, passing cars would honk at us. I assumed it was because we were waving signs for the challenger to the Mayor, and not because they recognized this as an action about mental health. The next woman to take the microphone was the same woman who greeted me at the office in Woodlawn.

"Good afternoon, my name is Dorothea Moore, and I was a consumer at the Woodlawn clinic for twenty years. Every week, I went there for counseling, and it gave me space to connect with someone and to be honest about who I am and why I feel the way they do. But that's been taken from my life, and I haven't gone a day where I don't try to get it back. There were people I saw all of the time when the clinics were open, and I have seen them less and less ever since. They don't get out in public, and they've stopped answering my calls. They're at home, too depressed to come out. I had a friend from the clinic, Gloria, who I had been calling for two months, trying to get a hold of her. She was in the grocery aisle, and I was so, so relieved to see her. As I looked more closely at her, I was beginning to think something awful was happening to her, and as I looked into her eyes, it was clear that something had tormented her. It was as though she had her life taken out of her, and she hardly said anything to me at all. This is what started happening to people once the city took their supports away. They retreated from having a life in public altogether. Laura Campuzano, a dear friend and a member of our movement, watched her son die in the street to gun violence. She used to be able to walk to her clinic, and when it closed down, her care was transferred several neighborhoods away. It took her over an hour on public transport to get there, and another hour to get back. Even the Mayor's Office has said that say they want to keep us in care, but they know that they're pushing us out. Since when did working people with families have the time to spend an extra two hours getting to an appointment? While the Mayor has been trying to save face now that he has to put effort into keeping his seat, we had an encounter with him at a meeting in Wicker Park. Laura and Joe interrupted him to ask him about why he closed our clinics—because when a powerful man shafts you and expects you to play nice as he lies to you, sometimes these little bursts of impoliteness come into play. He took them aside after the meeting and yelled at them, and I quote this thin-skinned man, he told them, 'You will show respect for me.' I must tell him in response, Mayor, you must give respect to get respect."

The crowd applauded, more drivers blew their horns. "And I'm not even talking about my own issues, yet," she said. "I need help for my PTSD more than I ever have, and everything I hear about this administration just furthers my trauma. Our children had their schools moved, and now they have to cross gang lines just to get an elementary education. There are more of us who have gone off the radar. They're homeless or they're in jail, or they're on the streets. They can't speak for themselves because we have no idea where they are. Above all of this, I see something in the paper every day about the Mayor mingling with bankers and private developers, and I just...I just do not give a damn for him. We need to go down to that voting booth and get this man out of office."

The speeches concluded, and we marched towards the voting booth, spread out across two blocks of Milwaukee Avenue and chanted, led by a nasally, irascible, indefatigable voice from a man named Chuy.

"Whose city?"

"OUR CITY!"

"Whose city?"

"OUR CITY!"

"Whose clinics?"

"OUR CLINICS!"

"Whose clinics?"

"OUR CLINICS!"

There was a CPD car driving slowly beside them for a bit, with no semblance of threat. They continued with a chant.

"Fight, fight, fight! Cuz healthcare is a human right!"

"Fight, fight, fight! Cuz healthcare is a human right!"

I fell back amongst the crowd and introduced myself to Jude. She was towards the far end of the march.

"I liked your statement," I told her. "What sort of work do you do with your advocacy?"

"Are you familiar with Harvard's Kennedy school?" she said.

"I am not," I said.

"Then we'll have to find some time to meet and I can introduce you to all of this," Jude said.

"Have you been with the mental health movement for long?" I asked.

"Since they started, yes," she said.

"Oh yes, you mentioned that in your speech. Can I ask you why the city closed the clinics?" I said.

"You can," Jude said, "but I don't think I have an answer you'd like to hear."

"Try me," I said.

"The city's rationale is that they're closing the clinics to make care better, which is an obvious lie. If you ask people here, they'll tell you that there are two forces at play that contribute to it. First, they believe the mayor wants to be able to prove to his banker friends that he's capable of making the quote-unquote tough budget decisions. Second, they believe that he wants to take resources out of the South Side to encourage people to leave it. Then people can buy and refurbish old real estate, and somebody else can move in," she said.

"Do you think that's true?" I asked.

"It's as plausible as anything else, probably the most realistic view. When the Mayor took office, he said that Chicago was falling behind places like New York and San Francisco, and he would like to tailor the city to attract people who view those destinations as ideal. He's vying to make Chicago a competitive city in the global economy, and that requires municipal politics to be open to large amounts of capital. So he tries to rid the city of certain elements, namely poor folks, black and brown folks, and mental health consumers. There isn't a rationale for closing the clinics that is based on the quality of care. All the city has told us is that it has saved money and that the state of mental healthcare in Chicago has never been better, and we know that's a lie. There used to be a wide, public social services system in Chicago. As recently as the 90s, there were almost thirty community mental health clinics in Chicago and a fairly robust set of social service workers. Now there's almost none at all. All I hear from the people now is that there are a lot more schizophrenics huddled by the train tracks than there used to be," she said.

"I don't see the fiscal logic, though," I said. "In the long-term, one dollar put into community supports saves five to ten dollars that would otherwise be spent on emergency rooms or prisons. All you have to do is forecast a few years ahead and the fiscal problem is much, much worse. What do these people think is going to happen?" I said.

"As Keynes said: In the long-term, we're all dead. The neo-liberals rewrite that statement and use it for their agenda. The short-term is the only life there is. Neither fiscal stability nor responsibility have anything to do with it," she said.

We kept walking, and I noticed the smirks and laughter from cars driving by, mostly from clean-cut white men and women wearing brand-name sunglasses. One of the women marching with us sighed. "Every time we come out here, they look at us like we're crazy," she said to me with mild resignation. "And when we actually talk to them, and they realize we're talking about mental illness, they look at us like we're really, really crazy."

We voted, and days later the Mayor handily won reelection. An activist told me the Mayor had utilized the old machine network, where ward and union operatives instated a block-by-block presence to secure victory.

That spring I finished my studies, finally got a college degree, and applied for graduate school. There was a school of psychology in the city that offered a program in urban mental health policy. I did not have to take any testing for admission, and it was the only school I applied for. I was accepted with a social justice scholarship. Mark, who I had been dating through much of this, also got into school at the University of Washington and was moving in the following August. I had taken up Jude's offer for coffee, and she quickly coaxed me into being her chauffeur and assistant. Generally, I wouldn't let people treat me like she treated me—always asking me to go out of my way to do everything for her, insulting me when I did not, demeaning me for no reason, threatening suicide when I disappointed her—but Jude had all of the insight that I had been desperate for, and I would suffer any expense to get access to it. I became her sidekick at meetings, where she was always the first to talk and the longest to do so. Sometimes people changed their minds because of her, sometimes they didn't. The numbers were largely stacked against her: everywhere she went, she was talking to providers, social worker unions, academics, psychiatrists, and nursing home representatives. I suspected that many of them only saw her as a token, or as an inspiration story. I suspected that they saw her as a means to validate their compassion, while their firmer commitments lied elsewhere. Jude, to them, was someone to be tolerated, but not to be followed.

In the fall of 2015, an activist and investigative journalist effort forced the city into releasing the camera footage of the shooting of LaQuan MacDonald. A lot of people suspected that the Mayor's Office had suppressed the video to win reelection. MacDonald's family, I recall, had asked that his death not be publicized. The young, irritable side of me then would have screamed, "Release the video and screw the Mayor's Office!" though later I'd grow to think that a family's request for what happens to their deceased child trumped all other concerns. In other words, Mamie Till's consent came before anything else. In a few years' time, I'd endorse a different belief altogether, and my loudest political convictions would again be proven transient and pointless.

The city did eventually release the video under very tight circumstances. Only a handful of journalists were granted access to the file, and only for a very brief period. When it went public, I watched it as soon as it was made available over the Internet. There were probably thousands of people sitting anxiously, for their own reasons, to see what the killing of this boy looked like. That was one year after Ferguson, and this experience of watching a black man's killing had turned into a public ritual. The image of the crime was made commonplace, replicating over and over amongst the footage as digital resistance graffiti. The audience watches as bystanders to a public execution. Over a black-and-white police camera, I watched seven cops restrain a frightened youth holding a pocket knife from a distance. It was not physical restraint but distant restraint, with a pointed stance and firearms in their hands. The boy had a knife and, barring a superhuman leap toward an officer, was out of the range of inflicting harm. Then I watched an eighth cop arrive and, within too brief of a time to register, shoot sixteen bullets into his wiry, terrified body. And then he lied there, dead. Car lights moved in the far backdrop of the footage amidst the standstill of a city in the middle of the morning.

The immediate fall-out in my personal life was heated. In addition to going to graduate school at night, I was working at a brunch restaurant during days and weekends. The video was released on the Tuesday evening before Thanksgiving, and on Wednesday, my manager revealed to me that the Mayor would be having Thanksgiving brunch with his family at the restaurant. Our owner was once a prominent Chicago Democrat, one who did leave for control of the White House with Barack Obama, and had started this restaurant after his family bank defaulted and he a lost campaign to be a Senator.

I took a trans-historical approach to this scenario, seeing myself as an agent in a modern-day civil rights struggle, and asked myself what should I do with this information. But I only had a few hours to deliberate it. I felt this information required attention, a notice to local activists or organizers. I had no concept of what a good action should or should not be, or whether it was tactically wise to confront the Mayor on a day like Thanksgiving. The rule was that family is off-limits, I had said, but what concern did the Mayor ever have for any of the families I knew? Does the aggressor maintain a right not to be aggressed without repentance? It was an honest question, as a history of violence must be ceased somewhere, though I did not actually care about that. I was not strong enough to parse the ethics out of the moment, nor did I have enough time. My conviction was too strong. Common sense indicated that the mayor had protected himself from consequence by repressing evidence of the police killing of LaQuan McDonald, so what claim did he have to the sanctity of private life, especially if he would only manipulate privacy towards impunity? I messaged a few groups over social media on the night before Thanksgiving, giving them the details of his reservation if they wanted to do anything. They thanked me and said no more. Maybe they had their own ethical struggles. My mind fired at a restless pace, and I consulted Jude to ask if I did the right thing. She thought I did.

I remained restless on Thanksgiving morning, obsessing over what might have happened at my restaurant. I went for a jog to Gilson Park by the lakefront in Wilmette, where my cousins played an annual football game. They used to call it the Turkey Bowl, but once the Doc passed, they started calling it the Doc Bowl. I stopped and watched the boys fight with one another over inconsequential bullshit, and it took my mind off of the press that might be coming to me if there was a confrontation at the restaurant. Afterward, we went to a local bar for beers and Bloody Marys. I had a couple of each, and I checked social media on my phone every few minutes to see if anything happened, or if activist groups had posted anything about an encounter. There was nothing. When I was back at my parents' house, I blurted to my parents about what I had done. My mother seemed pleased, or at least not disturbed. My father, less so. He left the room silently and with a sour face, and returned minutes later to tell me he thought I did the wrong thing. "When you have a contract with an employer, you have a fiduciary responsibility to honor that."

"I made my decision, Dad, and I'll own it," I said. "The Mayor has been screwing people over, and I think I had to do this."

As I said that, I flung my arms open. I had made a pot of coffee to sober up before Thanksgiving dinner, and I hit a French press off of the counter. It broke on the ground, the black tar of the coffee grinds spreading over the marble, and I scrambled to clean it up. I said a bunch of mean-spirited things about my father taking cues from the wrong sources, such as the Cato Institute or the Heritage Foundation, being influenced too much by right-wing propaganda, and not being critical enough about what was happening. I reiterated that this was a modern-day civil rights movement, and things like this had to be done. He said he understood the circumstances of the moment. It continued like that until we were both flustered and could not sit with one another without tension. I told him I was disappointed in him, and that was the only time I had said that to anyone in my family. We spent the drive to my uncle's house discussing lighter things, like the music on the radio and the Thanksgiving Day football games.

Subsequently, the Department of Justice then started its investigation into the Chicago Police Department. At that disability hearing, another activist spoke of a police raid on a protest. "We had an action on May Day," the man said, "and it turned into a police riot. We had sixty people, and we walked from Douglas Park to the federal prison. There were ten officers following us. We were on the sidewalk. About twenty of our marchers left, and as we got to a bus stop by the prison, the police officers transferred. The ten switched out, and eighty came back. They peddled us against the building. They took our legal observer and threw him into the back of the bus. The crowd fell back. My friend was pushed onto the ground. When I went to help her up, a cop threw me against a car. I showed him my medical card so he knew I had a disability. He didn't care. My friend started having an acute panic attack. There was a woman nearby having a seizure on the ground, and the cops cuffed her. They arrested twenty people just for walking down the sidewalk. This was completely disregarded in the press. I can't be around the police anymore. They've burnt out any concern I have for free speech."

I continued graduate school in public policy, formed a stronger set of politics, and became more involved with activist work in the city, mostly in disability rights work. Trump ran for President and everyone lost their minds. Elements of segregation that were previously withheld were made public. Factions of open white hostility emerged, demonstrating the persistence of unalloyed racism as an organizing force in my world. I was once a firsthand witness to such a display. My friends who worked in organizing for housing justice had worked to get an affordable housing building developed in Jefferson Park, a neighborhood on the Northwest side of Chicago, a neighborhood with a high residency of municipal workers and police families, mostly people of Irish and German descent. A neighborhood group staged a protest against the building, and my friends organized a counterprotest. It was on a February night, near zero degrees. I skipped class to attend. The protest was set at a church where the local alderman and other community representatives were meeting to discuss the development. A crowd extended around the church, encompassing about a block of space on each side of the entrance. I slipped anonymously into the back and asked an old man what was happening.

"They're trying to bring Section 8 housing into the neighborhood," he said.

I asked him, pretending to be ignorant, "Is there an issue with that?"

He looked back, "Are you joking?"

I looked for my friends amidst the scene and eventually found them huddled near a wall of the church, surrounded by a mob ten times their size. I settled in with them, and a man jeered at me from behind, "Hey honey, how much is George Soros paying you to be here?" I snapped back at him and one of the organizers, Henrietta, told me to keep my composure. I looked at my friends, and they looked silenced and defenseless, some of them in wheelchairs. I surveyed the crowd and looked at about 150 people with enraged mouths and fierce glares. There were about fifteen of us, and we stayed in a tight circle in front of them. What proceeded could only be described as a belligerent white riot, reminiscent of the reaction to the Chicago Freedom Movement for fair housing in Chicago. It was possibly the most disheartening thing I'd ever seen.

A tall, middle-aged man toward the center of a lawn lifted a bullhorn and led a chant against the alderman in the church, "You're a liar! You're a liar! You're a liar!" The audience screamed with him in unison. They were holding signs that read, "No Up-Zoning," and "Cabrini Green Started as Housing for Vets."

Others were taunting us, "Go Back to Rogers Park! Go Back to Rogers Park!" Another man tried to bait me with taunts, "Hey, where do you come from? Lakeview? Lincoln Park? Go back! Take it to your own neighborhood, you phonies! Who paid for your signs?"

One of the protestors in our huddle argued with a man in front of her, who identified himself as a cop. She tried to explain to him that his salary was socialized. "No it isn't," he said stubbornly, looking over her.

"Yes, it is!" she yelled.

"No," he said, this time looking into her face, certain of his position. "It isn't. I work. I get paid. That's not socialism. Socialism is when you put a building for criminal do-nothings in an honest, hard-working neighborhood."

She shouted at him once more, and this time he ignored her.

Several feet away, the same conversation was happening between two other people. The crowd had consolidated and moved closer toward us. Our space enclosed. Someone from the mob had grabbed my friend's wheelchair, shook it, and was then pulled away. By now I was almost alone in front of half a dozen people interrogating me. "Housing is a human right, huh?" a man laughed at me. "Where is it a human right?"

"Everywhere!" I shouted back. My friend Ruthie was nearly ripping her hair out. "I can't believe you people! You people are fucking ridiculous!"

"Where? Here?" the man said.

"Everywhere! Everywhere! Everywhere!" she shouted.

We started chanting, "Housing is a human right! Housing

is a human right!" while Ruthie interjected, "Everywhere! Everywhere!" A brawny middle-aged man counter-chanted, "You guys are retarded! You guys are retarded!"

The man who was questioning me stepped into me. He leaned over me. I could smell his body odor and his breath. His chest pressed into my shoulder. "Who's going to pay for that, huh?"

"You," I said.

"Yeah, because you said so?" he said.

"For that, and other reasons," I said.

"I suppose you think healthcare is a human right, too," he jeered.

"Yes, I do," I said.

The man stopped talking.

A man behind him yelled, "How much do you get paid to do this?" I made a zero sign with my hand.

"That's how much she earns, too!" They all laughed.

One of my friends, Javier, was in an altercation of his own. "Welcome to capitalism," a man shouted at him.

"Fuck capitalism!" Javier shouted back. "Fuck capitalism!"

"Get a job and get out of my neighborhood!"

I stepped away to find any semblance of civility. With each pocket of the crowd I fell into, there was more confrontation.

"Racist!" we shouted.

"Who said anything about race?" they shouted back.

"Racism has got to go! Racism has got to go!" we shouted.

"I don't see race here," they shouted.

"My mom is Irish, my dad is German. That's diversity, and that's Jefferson Park," one man said.

"Don't bring them here! They'll dilute their crime all over the city! We've had three robberies this month already! Put them in Glenview!" one woman said.

"Why can't we just pay for housing and education where they already live! But, no, that would make too much sense, wouldn't it?" one man said.

"I'm not paying for any of this for anyone, not unless you're like her," said one man, pointing at my friend in a wheelchair.

A woman put an iPhone to my face. "Why did you push me?" she said.

"I didn't," I said.

"Why did your friend push me?" she said.

"She didn't either," I said.

"Why are you being so divisive? This is our neighborhood!" she said.

There was a sweet young high school boy named Ryan, a Lane Tech student, who crossed sides to talk to us. I shook his hand. He said that he thought that talking was more civil than shouting, and wanted to hear about our positions. We talked about politics and public services, how to get housing for people with disabilities, why they are often unable to find work, along with the merits of socialism and capitalism. I tried to tell him how extreme inequality shapes our country, subverts democracy, and makes us fight over things like housing in our neighborhoods. I recommended a book, and before he left he came back to shake my hand and take note of the book.

I tried to shake other people's hands, and I was called scum, commie, or told, "Don't fucking touch me."

There was a man who said he worked for CPS for fifteen years. He was telling a story about gunshots on an ordinary Tuesday morning in one of the neighborhoods where he worked and talked about four men in an armored car near the incident. "What do you think they had in that car, huh?" I came late to the conversation and didn't hear the context.

"I'm telling you, this is a choice these people make. I've been in the schools, I see it all of the time. They drop out and sell weed, and we don't have the police presence to handle that here," the man said.

"Don't you think that crime is a consequence of a lack of opportunity?" I replied, "A hopelessness thing?"

"Opportunity?" he laughed. "There are countless minority scholarships. The South Side is loaded with them. It's a choice they make," he yelled.

"But the city systems are designed to shortchange black Chicago and keep them in a geographic place," my ally said.

"You think we make them live there? You think we make them drop out?" he shouted.

A woman on my side challenged his statement that he worked at CPS. "Where do you work?"

"Marshall, Parker, Baird, wonderful places, just the best," he said mockingly. "Nah, these people, they shoot themselves. How do you expect anyone to get out of a situation like that? Jesus fucking Christ."

The crowd started Trump chants. I lost feeling in my toes. I wanted to leave but did not want to abandon my friends out of concern for their safety. I got weary and disheartened. I had to go. I trusted my friends to be well. Before I left I made one last effort to be civil with the other side and was treated with outright contempt. It was a five-block walk to my car, and I was alone. I sprinted and drove away as quickly as I could.

✳ ✳ ✳

My friends spent the months after that trying to see that the development went through. They were harassed, stalked, and had their whereabouts documented and shared by Jefferson Park cops and people with neo-Nazi affiliations on their social media accounts. Henrietta disclosed to me that after months of this, she had a series of five nights without sleep, and attempted suicide on the morning of the sixth day. I should have been more active with them, but I wasn't. I had my excuses: work, suicidal ideation, writing, trying to keep Jude and her work together. I had the comfort to step away, be it to my bed, to my parents' home, or any space outside of the ire of organized, executed bigotry. The organizers documented over three hundred pages of slurs and invectives posted on the Internet by the Jefferson Park backlash and presented it to the Mayor's Office. When the ordinance was brought to the city council, the alderman voted unanimously in favor of building the development. When it was brought to the Mayor's Office, he vetoed it and it didn't happen.

I started developing a more coherent, critical outlook on power in Chicago, how it operated, who it respected, what color it was, both physically and ideologically. I saw more and heard more from the ground level and illuminated blind spots, though many undoubtedly remained. I'd take on a more proactive organizing role with Jude, and would learn that Jude was too ill to work about half of her time. In carrying some of her work, I'd get overwhelmed by the gravity of pleas for assistance I received, and with my inability to offer anything substantive to work with. Each day, somebody called me with a new tragedy and asked what they could do. A teenager diagnosed with schizophrenia was shot by an off-duty cop in Morgan Park; a radical pastor tried to kill himself and admitted himself into the psych ward; someone's brother had a manic episode and drove their car 500 miles to nowhere and had to be bailed out of jail. Everyone saw Jude—and by extension, me—as an authority when someone went mad, and yet there was nothing we could do. We called ourselves organizers, but we did not actually run programs, create safe havens, or put our bodies on the line. We advocated at the table, and that was it. There weren't services for any of these people, though we'd be seen as the point of contact for services anyway. I drank more and yearned for someone to rest on. By default, that was Mark, though he'd stopped responding to my messages, which I only sent every few weeks. I got to a point where I never saw Jude anywhere but on the Internet, where all she did was ask people why she should live. People asked me where she was. I said, "I don't know. She's sick, as far as I can tell."

The city announced a plan to close another mental health clinic, this time in the neighborhood of Roseland. The Mental Health Movement staged a protest on the floor of City Hall outside the Mayor's Office—a body bag demonstration to commemorate those who had been killed by police during a mental health crisis, and those who they said would be killed if the city continued to disinvest resources. I arrived at the event an hour late. Dorothea Moore was speaking before a circle of demonstrators, recounting her arrest when she occupied the Woodlawn Mental Health clinic after her closing.

"As the officers arrested us, they stood us up and patted us down, one by one. One of the officers there was named Officer Smith, and everyone in the neighborhood knew him. Everyone in the neighborhood knew to be careful around him. And as he's patting me down, he came as close to me as possible, so that his chest was pressing against mine, and he reached behind me and squeezed my buttocks in front of everyone else there. We were taken to jail and had to spend the evening there. We were prepared for it and had our medications on hand, and we came out of that part of the experience relatively unharmed. Yet that incident with Officer Smith traumatized me. I have PTSD to begin with, and after he groped me, I was so disturbed that I could not sleep for a month. It reminds me of our history, and of how we are still living with it today. I don't often read about slavery. It's very difficult for me. I have a book on Harriet Tubman that has taken me months to get through. It tends to be a painful experience. But one thing I learned from that era is that in the slave trade, when black women would act out, the slaveholders would rape them in front of the rest of the ship and then kill them to show everyone else what happened when a black woman got out of line. Still today, black women are going through similar rituals at the hands of white men to put them in their place. In 2012, in 2013, in 2014, in 2015 . . ."

I quietly greeted the individuals along the circle while Dorothea continued with her story. "We filed a complaint of misconduct against the officer and were later interrogated for it. All of the women there testified to what had happened, and when the department got back to us, they told us that they were unable to identify the officer in question. Now, there were only three officers on the scene. One black, one Latino, and one white. Who else could it have been?"

I was hoping to see Jude at the event. She wasn't there. Dorothea ended her speech, and a man took to the heart of the circle to speak. "What we are dealing with here in this movement is broken heart syndrome," he said. "Some don't die of broken heart syndrome, others do. We've lost a place to rest our spirits. We've lost our place to be comfortable. We are constantly being taken out of our comfort zones and told to go somewhere else. We need to know that we will be able to come someplace and it will be safe for us, and that it will be our comfort zone, and we can be ourselves, and that it will be fully staffed. I don't want to say that all of this is about mental illness. It isn't. The environment we live in dictates what we do with our lives. A lot of this is something else. It's not mental illness, it's where we grow up. We've lost a lot when we lost these clinics. I miss the presence of the counselors who could teach our young men about conflict resolution, and anger, and love, and all of the things that are necessary for a young man to be himself. We've got some real despair here, kids who have been through some nasty things . . ."

Unexpectedly, the Mayor left his office with an entourage around him. I called them "the goons" — men in suits who looked like people you'd find in Old Chicago around the Boss. Dorothea and another old woman Dianne approached to confront him about the clinics, and he turned his shoulder and pulled out his phone to keep busy. One of his attendants met Dorothea and Dianne where they stood and tried to talk them down and prevent them from going any further, telling them the Mayor was very busy. The elevator arrived and the Mayor and his people huddled in it, and the man standing before Dorothea and Dianne backed into the last open space before it closed. The circle observed this event calmly, and then returned to the man in the center of the hall.

"He always does that," Dorothea said. "We look him eye to eye, posing no harm, just asking him questions about things he has done to us and our communities, and he runs away. Every time."

My phone buzzed in my pocket. Jude. I put it on silent. The phone buzzed again, this time for a text message. *Boo, I need you to come to Swedish Covenant Hospital. I complained to a friend and she called an ambulance on me.* I put the phone down. The man in the circle was talking about $16 million that the city was planning to use to subsidize private development in Uptown and how poor whites and poor blacks have more in common than they have differences. I stepped into the elevator and jabbed the button to the lobby five times over.

CHAPTER 8

2011–2012

I started what was supposed to be my final year of college with four consecutive nights of memory-erasing intoxication. During the summer, I'd gotten accustomed to binging. Convinced of my laziness in work and my lack of direction, I worked a ten-hour-per-day retail job at a department store for little reason but to prove to others that I wasn't a slouch. It was like a hamster wheel: I'd wake up hating the world, sprint through the hours, and come home and drink wine. First, two glasses per night, then half a bottle. Then, for the last two weeks of summer, a bottle per night.

People at home often asked, "How do you enjoy California?"

"It's great, I love it!" I'd yell, often with a drink in hand at an afternoon Chicago beach event or a street festival. Or, at a fine restaurant, being introduced to one of my parents' friends, or at a black-tie gala in the city for one of my parents' causes.

"What are you going to do after college?" they'd ask.

"I'm thinking I'll work for a year and then go to business school!" I'd say.

"Great!" they'd say. "Good for you!"

Or, before I could respond, Dad would interrupt and say, "She's getting an economics degree and is thinking about working for a year in the Jesuit Volunteer Corps before coming to a Chicago firm."

"Ah, well isn't that great?" they'd say. "I'm sure you're going to be successful at whatever you do!"

I'd smile and thank them, my parents would talk with the other couples, and I'd leave for the open bar. At the philanthropic events, teenage girls a class wealthier than me — blond-haired,

figureless girls in dresses that would bankrupt most families —
accompany their parents in a hall full of investors and their wives,
who auction a $25,000 weekend at a Tuscan country home, and
encourage others to bid for more.

On weekends, I'd go out to Lincoln Park bars with high
school friends and waste my paychecks on the tabs, $110 at
a time. Usually, I found my way home all right, sometimes I
woke in someone else's apartment in sweltering Chicago heat,
and sometimes I found little scratches and bruises on my legs
with no memory of how they got there. When I did not sleep
through the night, I'd either not sleep at all or wake up at 2:00
A.M. in sweating panics, and carry that toxicity through the
rest of my day.

In the middle of the afternoon on my fifth day of senior year,
Tina called to tell me that the Doc had a stroke, and was at risk
of dying within a few days. I was hungover at the time, watching
reruns of *The Simpsons* on my computer.

"Oh," I said with a pause, unready for such an unvarnished
message.

"Yeah," Tina said, also with a pause, evoking the solemnity
I now found too sudden and too complicated to speak about.

The night before I was up until 4:00 A.M. with Charlotte,
my one-time lesbian encounter who I ran away from. There may
have been other nights too, all of which I teased her. The end of
junior year involved possibly a dozen blackouts, and I suspect
she was there for a couple of them. We were at a party at which
I, nearing blackout, bounced coquettishly from person to person.
It was quite a high — I was devilishly forward and smooth with
my tongue, enough so to leave many guys speechless in response.
I also openly declared my alcoholism. "Oh, and I'm an alcoholic
now. So, fill it up, please!"

After the party, Charlotte and I went to her place and drank
white wine on her back porch. It was a lovely backyard with

spherical bulb lights hanging overhead and bugs squeaking in the yard. "Boo," she says to me, "you worry all of the time. And you've said some very nasty things to me, but I know where it comes from. I know why some girls say bitter things to lesbians." She pours me more wine and flips her leg over her knee, one thigh over the other, toned like a runner's legs, and her shin is grazing against mine.

"I won't lie to you, I'm probably bisexual," I blurt, all while dismissing her coy advances, with my head dallying away from her. We keep talking and drinking, refilling our glasses, listening to music. Every twenty minutes until 4:00 A.M., Charlotte propositions me. Each time, I decline. When she finally goes to bed, she turns around and calls my name.

"Boo?" she says.

"Yes?" I say, collapsed on her couch.

"You're a trifling whore," she says.

The call from Tina came mere hours later, while I was missing class. I'd been in such delirium I didn't even know what courses I was enrolled in. When Tina hung up I sat, dazed, and told myself, *Well, we all know I'm going to get wine for this one.* Nobody else was home. I purchased a large bottle of Woodbridge chardonnay from Safeway and drank most of it myself.

That night, I consumed enough to incapacitate me, if not kill me, beginning with that bottle of wine, and continuing with half-glasses of whiskey.

To be this far into a bender and stand is to be like Natalie Portman in *Black Swan*—risking death before an audience, exposing oneself totally, only without grace. Oh, how charismatic and loquacious I think I am, how they laugh at my act. We all go out to a Light Side house. It is still summertime in Northern California, and the lawns are packed with people drinking and laughing. At the end of the night, we return home (we now have a larger house on Dark Side) and stay up drinking with a couple of friends Katie and Carla have brought home. I am blathering about lord knows what, pouring wine into everyone's glass. Then, on a quick turn, my babble becomes grotesque and cryptic. I'm making sexually explicit remarks about the guys at the party, and then detouring into grand, religious rants about the Kingdom of Heaven and the Kingdom of Lucifer, and who belongs to which, and why. I don't really have full consciousness of it, it just comes out. Some old impulse from my childhood in the church has been brought out of me. Katie and Carla seem to be thinking very carefully about what is happening. They do not look scared, but they do not look relaxed, either.

I wake up the next morning and shoot out of bed, feeling ecstatically intoxicated. A maddening tactile sensation runs through my arms, like red ants crawling inside my skin. I rub my forearms vigorously to remove this feeling, to no success, then run to the bathroom, open the faucet, and slap water against my face. Heaving, panting, dripping with water, I raise my vision to the mirror and see my image looking at me with total disdain. It does not belong to me. It is apart from me, judging me, condemning me, removing itself from me forever. It is a disgrace. Resentment and folly have perverted my life, and I no longer have a self.

I hasten out of the house and stagger toward the campus mission, following a mystical urge toward repentance. My vision of the world is as penetrating and extraordinary as the colors and scenes of my acid trip; an unreal, substance-induced supernatural land. Overhead there is a swarm of bugs that follows me for blocks, like locusts in Exodus. Their buzzing and flapping consume my hearing, as though they are implementing a form of torture. On the sidewalk, I step over a dead pigeon with its neck snapped. Its purple collar radiates in the morning sun. I view this with the seriousness of an omen, a symbol of forthcoming plague.

It's frigid in the mission, and I kneel before the cross, raising my head to a thin, ascetic Christ who endured a prolonged, austere death for my sins. I ask for forgiveness but feel impure and ungodly. Vertigo ensues. The crucifix dizzies and circles in my perception. If there is a god, I am convinced God wants nothing to do with me. In place of holiness, I have apocalyptic pandemonium and the remorseless end of my time on earth.

I get up from my embittered genuflect, stumble outside, collapse in the neighboring rose gardens, and vomit into them. For a moment, I feel cleansed. The vomit purges some of the sicknesses out of me, and I am again sane on earth. I pant, breathe, and wipe the liquid off my lips.

The moment of clarity, however, is brief. While I walk home, my legs cramp, and I move as though pulled by a puppeteer, with awkward, disjointed limbs. When indoors, I collapse onto the couch and yearn for solace in the living room, a dark, warm room of an old craftsman house. In isolation, alarm resumes. First, I fear the presence of other voices. They call my name and trail off into random English. I cannot tell if they are within me or without me, whether I am inside my head or outside of it, or whether I am hearing things or simply imagining it. This thought echoes inwardly as a roll into the cushion of my couch, curled in a fetal position for safety.

I call Tina, frantic to have somebody to talk to. My mental speed retards, and I cannot communicate a single phrase.

Tina senses emergency—that is clear in how she is ordering me. "Boo, stay where you are. Stay safe. I'm going to call you right back."

She doesn't actually call. Dad does, and he sounds infuriated. "What the hell is wrong? Have you even been going to class?" I apologize and hang up.

That's it, I think, *I've become the idiot.* I've slipped into a state of permanent childishness. I envision the next generation of children in the family talking about Boo the Cautionary Tale, the one who didn't make it like the rest, who could never manage on her own, who lives by herself and does chores at her parents' house for a living.

I search the Internet for symptoms of alcohol withdrawal. I meet all the criteria, and tests tell me I'm severely alcoholic. Then I read about deeper alcoholic problems, such as delirium tremens.

In a moment of sensibility, I text Katie and Carla for help.

Something happened, I screwed up, I need to be taken to the emergency room, I've been in all day and I don't know what's going on. Please come, I'm very sorry.

Within ten minutes, both of them are in the living room.

"It's going to be okay," Carla tells me calmly. "You're going to be all right. You're going to be okay."

Katie prepares her car and looks up directions to the nearest hospital. I enter the backseat, fold my arms over my chest, tuck my shoulders in, and roll back and forth. Carla talks to me at every moment of the drive. They wait with me in the emergency room while I check myself in. I'm still convinced my life is over.

The doctor sees me and asks what the problem is. Frantically, I explain the last few months to him — my work, my drinking, my depression. I rattle off some of the symptoms I read on the online checklist: "high heart rate, vomiting, hypotension."

"Hypotension? What do you mean?" he asks.

"Like, really severe, um, tightness in my muscles. Like a grip around my body. It never leaves. You know what I mean?" I say.

"Okay. I'll write you a prescription for something," he says.

A nurse returns with a sheet of paper. Primary diagnosis: alcoholism. Secondary diagnosis: anxiety. This comes with a prescription for Librium.

"Nurse," I say, "I'm going to have delirium tremens. I know

I've gone off the edge permanently this time. What am I going to do about it? Who is going to help me?"

The nurse smiles and tells me, "I think you should stop thinking about it."

Katie takes us to a pharmacy to pick up my drugs. I'm less mortified now, standing in the aisle, behaving as a somewhat functional person. At home, I have a light dinner in my living room. The glow of the chandelier hangs over me like an interrogation lamp. As I eat, Katie approaches me with some trepidation. "Are you feeling . . . better?" I nod. After dinner, I take two Librium pills and lie in bed, my back to the room and my face to the wall. The Internet tells me not to expect sleep. Alcoholic withdrawals last for weeks. *Tough it out,* I tell myself.

On my back, I stare into the stale room like a bug caught in a pod of glue. Around 4:00 A.M. I sleep, only to experience a series of dreams that come to me as waking hallucinations. Each vision takes place in my room, exactly as it appears to me while alert, real, and unblemished by imagination. I rise from my bed, yet I'm pulled to the floor, and then I start spinning on my side like a child in a horror movie about demonic possession. In the next moment, I am in my bed. I rise again and move to the living room, only to find decrepit, unclothed bodies staring at me and then assaulting me. Then, again, I am in my bed. The sun rises, light enters my room, and the morning settles peacefully.

I call my parents and explain to them what I did in whimpering English. They are ready to forgive me and tell me everything is all right.

"How is the Doc?" I ask.

"He'll live, we are told," Mom tells me.

"Can I call?" I say.

"Perhaps next week," Mom says.

I call him as soon as he is semi-cognizant, about two weeks

later. Oddly, his is the only authority I trust. I am able to get through to him in his hospital room.

"Boo!" he heaves. He sounds delighted to hear from me. "Como ca va?"

"Ca va bien, Doc... Actually, that's not true."

"No?" he asks.

"I drink too much. I think I'm an alcoholic," I say.

"You do?"

"Yeah. I blacked out five nights in a row and got taken to the hospital."

"Do you enjoy it?" he asks.

"Sometimes, yeah."

"Then don't beat yourself up for enjoying it, and don't keep doing anything you don't want to," he says.

"Sometimes I have anxiety. I don't talk about it with anyone, though. Do you know what I'm talking about? Were you like that at all?"

"Oh, God. When I was in school I used to have the worst panic attacks."

"Did you drink?"

"I'd drink while I worked. But I didn't go out much. I only studied," he says.

"I don't really know what to do with myself, Doc."

"You do whatever you want to do."

At this time, the Doc loses composure. My aunt takes the phone from him and asks me all about my life in California. I move out of this conversation on white lies.

My community is generally supportive. I told them all I was an alcoholic as a part of a thoughtless confession ritual. It was the only way I knew how to explain myself. What else do you call someone who drinks too much and gets in trouble for it? They've got these little phrases for me. "I'm so proud of you!" they'll say, for example, before they go off on a binge of their own. Or they'll question me about hiding drinks, as though that is something I've actually done before. I haven't. Everything about my drinking is out in the open and always has been. Jeremy jokingly signed on to be my sponsor and has carried himself like a dopey older brother ever since.

Dad put $900 into my bank account and told me to buy a bike with it. He says that his additive friends always became bikers, and since I was expecting to have withdrawals well into the future, I accepted his generosity. The withdrawals, as I understand them, consist of deep cynicism, sleeplessness, fatigue, ineffable tension, and general dysfunction in academic and social life. The stagnation following the bender never ceases. My back aches, I hunch and hack empty coughs from gas in my stomach. My eyebrows are permanently clenched, and I am angry over everything I interact with and everybody I have to speak to. And the fear is constant. I hope that biking will offer refuge from this, much like running before it.

There is a trail that runs between a spate of corporate lots and the highway. More proximately, there is a cement waterway next to the trail, which tucks under the edge of the highway. I ride it up to the southern tip of the San Francisco Bay and pull my bike up to a pebbly border along the water. Every time I am there, I have the same experience. An existential crisis, if you will. A trick of alienation. I question reality. I see what everyone else sees: mountains behind heat strokes, a still body of water, azure sky. But it is not real, and why that is I cannot totally say. It doesn't carry the same substance that it used to, nor does it hold the same depth. I perceive it as a Hollywood backdrop: a single, two-dimensional façade that can be broken, removed, and replaced with something more horrifying. The road, too, is unstable. I vaguely suspect it could fall apart at any moment, sending me into a universe I can't predict. The beauty is a façade, everything around me is just a fraud that conceals a much bleaker existence.

Upon returning from biking, I am thinly layered in a cold sweat, and on the inside I feel petrified. Part of me thinks it is because I am toned and muscular, but the truth is, I am neither. It's another trick. In actuality I'm emaciated since I don't really eat anymore. Tina sends several emails asking if I am doing well. She is on a vacation on the East Coast and says that she cannot relax until she hears that I am stabilized. I respond.

Don't worry, Tina, I just wanted to experience it all: the senseless highs and the pointless lows. That's where insight comes from, no? Knowing it all? Maybe I've gone off track a bit, but you've got to integrate all of that into your worldview. But I've learned now. Do not fret about me, because I'm already better.

Not long after sending, I regret every word, create a new email account, and never check if Tina replied to my note in the old one.

My days consist mainly of drinking coffee and procrastinating, dodging work with television programs on my computer, and with unrelated reading. I found a word in a piece of David Foster Wallace's writing, *acedia*, that describes my situation well: "spiritual or mental sloth." Only I'd go deeper than that. It's total listlessness, total lack of spark, total waste. I pick up little words like this to make myself look smarter, so people do not know that when I am at the library for four hours, I spend almost all of that time staring at my books and accomplishing nothing. The vocabulary and the references to authors make me seem educated. Makes it seem like my time here isn't in vain, like I'm actually learning things. Twenty, thirty, forty minutes pass at a time, and I do little but scroll through articles and drift into hypotheticals, giggle to myself as the fear turns giddy and childish. Entire hours pass in the library without anything getting done. I reread the same pages over and over, processing nothing, and doubting the validity of the concepts I do grasp.

During the first week of the quarter, I charmed my professors. I made little jokes in the middle of the lecture, complimented their clothing, asked about their personal lives, but that very soon turned around. If only I could get by on flattering, then there would be no problem. I enrolled in statistics and a logic class, and out of courteousness, I go to my logic professor's office hours. He is a sardonic, self-deprecating man in his late thirties, and makes a lot of jokes about his unfulfilling love life. He's on his computer in his office, and I greet him and wisecrack about his San Francisco Giants hat. "Too bad you aren't winning the World Series again this year," I smile, and he laughs. I then ask about my midterm grade, "Have you gotten around to it yet?"

"What's your name again?" he says.

"Ellen Harvey," I say.

"I can look at it now," he says.

He pulls a stack of papers from his desk and finds my name. There are six pages in the exam. The first two are empty. "So that one is easy to grade," he says and marks a red zero over it. The next two have a few lines of reasoning. He marks some checks over my errors and gives me a couple of points, but ultimately, I fail. The next two pages are also empty. Again, a zero. Quickly, he rotates his chair to his computer and lets the exam fall onto my lap.

I see my old professors on campus too. The ones I have failed. They look over me every single time. Or maybe I just see it that way.

"It's okay," Dad says once I've told him I dropped the course. "You'll still graduate. We don't care about the grades anymore. It's about getting through." I haven't yet told him that I'm going to fail another.

Sleep, the little that I get, is an existential dilemma. It doesn't happen easily, my dreams are terrible, and I always wake up feeling worse than I did the night before. In the early morning hours, I've started watching classic cinema scenes, particularly the closing scenes of *2001: A Space Odyssey*, with the spaceman rushing through fields of madness and winding up confined to a one-man zoo. He has no idea what he is chasing, no purpose to his mission, yet he goes to the outermost extremes and finds himself detached, lifeless, and controlled. In the long, inorganic hours of the night, I watch his downfall.

As a younger person, I was happiest in the moments just before sleep. I can remember how tranquilizing it was to be alone and out of life. Oh, the thoughts I had then—wishing my family was dead, wishing I had no life at all, so I could be free from anyone else's pressures. Prayer was my morphine. Ten Hail Marys, Five Our Fathers, a blessing toward the souls of all the saints, and toward all of the poor. Now, I don't believe in God. I lie by the glow of a laptop and write screeds into a journal. There is no solitude here, nor any escape to yearn for.

I hear chatter in the living room, and check the time on my alarm clock. It is 3:17 A.M. and since I am not tired, I creak the door open, wearing a loose bedtime t-shirt and tennis shorts, and enter the living room. Rachel is slouched in an armchair, her eyes red, sleepy, and happy, and Katie is lying on the couch beside her with a similar look on her face. Without announcing myself, I take a seat on the floor and tilt my head back against the wall. My face is pouting out of fatigue. I rub my eyes and say, "Hello."

"Oh, hello," Rachel says, smiling bigger. I shrug. She is stoned and grinning and says, "Are you, like, trying to hang out?"

"Sure," I say, and then the two of them bellow into prolonged laughter. Insulted, I leer at them and leave. In the kitchen, I prepare hot water for a cup of calming tea and then grab a pack of cigarettes that Katie has left in the drawer. I wrap myself in a blanket and walk to the back porch, flip the lights on, and hug myself in a dirty plastic chair. I am resentful about my life and my body is shaking, particularly in the back of my head, where the neck muscle meets the scalp. There is an animal rustling in the bush at the side of the yard, and I look in its direction and blow smoke into my vision in the night, rocking back and forth in the half-broken chair for comfort. Shortly before five in the morning, I fall asleep with the taste of smoke on the walls of my mouth.

After dropping my logic class, my mornings are free to squander. I bike, I jog, I take long, meandering walks. There's always some pretentious piece of literature in my backpack. Today, it's another Virginia Woolf book, which I have checked out only because I'm told it deals with suicide in some way. I find a bench at the edge of campus, sit the long way across it with my knees up and my backpack propped up as a backrest. Every few pages, a passage resonates with me and sparks a moment of creative thought, which I then forget a moment later. Attention is fleeting — I think neither of the past or the future. All that exists is in a myopic, destructive now, with no link forward or behind.

I read, I twitch and tick, and I pretend these movements are not happening. A creepy restless sensation takes hold of my neck, and I go haywire. I hear an old woman screaming in the caverns of my mind, and moan. Students divert themselves from the sidewalk in front of me and walk to the other side of the lawn. I do things indirectly and with uncertainty. For instance, as I do dishes, I remove one cup from the washer, walk toward the cupboard, return the cup to the washer, wash my hands, close the washer, and then make a meal. Contact with people is comparably strange — I never know what to say, how to stand upright and look others in the eye, or how to move easily in the presence of others.

The guys come over in the night with an old speaker set. They play the Talking Heads while they smoke, and I curl up on the edge of the couch with my used textbook resting on my thighs, pressed within inches of my face. I lack even the faintest expression of pleasure or presence. The equations on the page look back at me without any meaning. Tired of my stiffness and my languor, I try a hit of the guys' weed. The strain is called "crystal blue" or "crystal purple," or something like that. I don't care either way, but the distinction means a lot to them. Time slows within moments of my exhale, and thereafter I hallucinate. Jeremy is ranting in front of me. His face moves spastically, but his words come slowly, moments behind the point of impact. Then, as though hearing the music of dread, a black wave covers my vision, accompanied by a string orchestra bending its pitches toward lower and lower frequencies. I recognize that I am dying, again, and excuse myself to bed. In my room, my body is calcified, and I hear a great chamber door crashing shut. The lights are on in my room, since I am scared of the dark, as children are. I watch cautiously at my door, for I fear that a hideous creature is just outside. After twenty minutes, I let my guard down, clench my eyes shut, and cling tightly to my sheets. I wake through the night with the same fears at the same degree of intensity. The next morning, my roommates joke about how stoned I got while I feign normality.

A friend from high school, Francelia, who is studying music composition in Boston, sends me a set of piano variations the composer Robert Schumann wrote amidst visions of angels and devils. The music came from the angels — arranged as a choir, he transcribed their song. The devils threatened to drag him to hell and, possibly at their behest, he threw himself into the Rhine in wintertime. He didn't die. Not then, at least. His body was recovered and he was put into an asylum, where his wife left him and he died. I listen to these piano pieces repeatedly on long walks on campus and talk to myself about the lives of insane artists. I try to imagine Schumann's mind, torn between his heaven and hell, an apparition to life on earth around him.

By November, I am drinking again. The first two to three drinks have no effect on me. My tolerance must have never dropped from its peak only a couple of months earlier. The drinks do not get me high. Instead, they disrupt my temperament, make me jaded and spiteful toward those around me, so much so that I could lash out and rhetorically cut someone at any moment. We are in the guys' living room for a pregame, passing around a hookah, a joint, and listening to glitzy, misogynistic pop songs. The girls are all done up in designer jeans and shirts that cut off at their shoulders, and the guys, who show no more substance, are in glossy shirts and crafted haircuts. All are fabricated. No real person presents themselves as cleanly as these people. The guys are drinking whiskey on the rocks while they smoke, and the girls huddle together around the one gay guy in the room and close themselves off to the rest. They are all going to black out later, which is normal. I don't think they accept me. I am only here because they don't know how to drop me yet. I'm already a part of their network, and they cannot simply pull me out and leave me. Smoking could be my entryway to acceptance, but it would make me go insane. I drink whiskey, the next best thing, and have four in quick sequence. The oddness holds sway again once the drink has taken full effect. Objects take on more meaning as I capture them in my attention: for instance, the single glass on the table before me, isolated in my vision, reflected against the wood, glimmering with alcohol, its contours sharply defined against the background. Oh, all the amazing things something as simple as this can represent if you look at it a certain way.

But I cannot spend all of my time alone like this. *Enough*, I tell myself. *Fuck it all*. I'm helpless before the conformity of the moment. They all talk to one another, but never to me. They have endless positivity, and I am sure they are full of it. There is no sincerity in any of it. I leave early and walk home halfway in a rage, looking at the palm trees with the same delirious attention and the same otherworldly glow that I gave the glass. At home, I blister my journal with lines of ugliness and disgust, even for the slightest, most passing encounters with the world.

I loathe the shallowness of the world. I loathe them all. I walk through campus like this, with heightened sensitivity and boggled consciousness, taking in all of the colors and the amazing vividness of the world around me. But what do I ever learn from it? Nothing. Like a drug experience, like passing through a sedated heaven where the natural world makes itself more awesome, ending — as I imagine life does — with unbridled fear and mental decay. I did not wish this short-lived, suicidal fascination with the world upon anyone, because of the instability and the damage to the nerves that it requires to get there. There is a long, long hell to pay for not being sound in the mind.

I am in bed as they get back, all loudly. I've got poetry to bide my time, old Europeans who share my distaste for everything. Nothing obliges me to talk to anyone else. As predicted, the next morning is brutal. There is a great conflict for my soul. On one hand, I panic, and this spurs me into physical action. On the other, despair overrides me as soon as I exert too much energy, and I halt and collapse to the floor. When my roommates leave the house in the afternoon (I assume, of course, that it's to find time away from me), I play the house keyboard, singing old Cole Porter songs. Generally, I sing softly to myself, so as not to be heard, but now there is too much to release to get away with singing softly. My voice is coarse, and my vocal cords scrape together like rocks against bricks. Then the music bores me. A great, frozen hole rests behind my eyes — a dissociated vacancy of soul and conscience. The vapor is in my veins. In its flow, life drains from the body and I am left only with sloth and incompetence, like a lobotomized patient. I run into bed, crawl under my sheets, and close my eyes to visions of barren fields. This disturbed, antisocial dimness approaches nihilism   sociopathically unmotivated and uncaring. My insignificance to the world is obvious. All others appear vapid, monolithic, and superior to me. Speaking to others emboldens my dissociation. I am too slow to say anything worthwhile, and though I see their discomfort and strained efforts to connect with me, I cannot respond to it. With each encounter people speak to me more and more like a child, more and more in simple, cowardly platitudes—the sort of meaningless, fake talk that everyone hates having to participate in. The world becomes a murky dream in which I can only smile, feign languorous social pleasantries, and become more isolated and susceptible to more vicious triggering. Environment and psyche collude toward the ends of mental degradation and madness, and I am the only one privy to it.

The home is quiet in the evening. Carla makes pasta, Katie listens to music on her computer, Rachel watches a movie in her room. I am talking to them less and less. I have no idea what they are doing with their lives and feel to be in no position to talk to them—not with the horror always riding on my back, compelling me to go away. Somewhat discomforted by their presence, I go for a long walk by myself while bitter moments from my past berate my mind. On impulse, I voice the inane, vulgar thoughts as they come to me. *Fuck 'em. I mean what do they even do? You feel me? They don't know shit. I don't care. I'm not dealing with it.*

I see my shadow in front of me and it startles me. It is personified: a being apart from me with its own agency and its own intentions. It is coming for me. I look away, trying to ignore it. The trees in front of me and around me are brooding over me, too. The surveillance of my environment is total. Everything is paying attention to me, leaning towards me, mocking me deviously. I keep as much distance between myself and other objects as possible and walk into the middle of the road to be farther away from the trees, lampposts, and homes.

There is smoke somewhere in the distance. I cannot see it,

but I can smell it, and its richness calms me and grounds me. I think, *It's all right, it's all right, it's not your fault, it's all right, it's not your fault, it's all right, it's not your fault,* time and again. When I get home, I drink vodka tonics for comfort and watch Comedy Central with Rachel, who is sleepless. We don't talk and I am uptight, sipping casually, asking questions every few seconds. Rachel gets irritated by these tactless nuisance quips, I can see, and after so much pestering she sighs, looking upset, and leaves me on my own. I continue to drink in my room past midnight, reading John Ashbery poetry and pacing before my bed, at times putting him down and reading passages of other texts I have collected and arranged on my shelves. I go to sleep once my sight blurs, only the horror grows too great to allow me that. I hyperventilate, then get on the floor and aggressively do sit-ups until the horror is mitigated and I have tired myself.

I wake without checking the time and with no appetite. I pour bland cereal, thinking it's something I should do for my health. It rests queasily in my stomach and makes me want to return to sleep. I look at myself in the mirror in the restroom. My head and shoulders are sagging, my arms have no discernible fat on them, my facial affect is that of a stroke survivor. In the shower, I sit and hug my knees. The water strikes the top of my head from the front, and the horror is devouring me from the inside. The shower is long and likely a waste of resources. While drying, I ruminate and write in self-admonishing bursts. *I was a loner who never learned the rules of the game, and was therefore never loved or respected. The world gave me chances, lord knows I had plenty of those, but I was too dumb to make good on them, being the fuckup that I am...* I fantasize about self-harm—just a quick slash up the wrist—and am relieved for a passing moment of sanity. Then the hatred grows more pointed and writhing, and I write a difficult, uncentered run of stream-of-consciousness sentences. It starts with a thought from the classics, then trails off into one from Mary Oliver. After about a thousand words I jog, the horror and the hate still with me. The light of day shames me, and I want to shout. I run away from campus, first in sprints that last one block at a time, and then in lighter jogs. The mind quiets and I listen to the wind hush and the leaves tussle. It's as though I lose consciousness — I feel that the hushing and tussling are happening within me, and I am one with my environment. I cannot tell anyone what I think and what I feel.

At night, I put everything that could potentially kill me in a complicated place of reach, out of fear that in an unconscious state I'll use it against myself. I am rattled, disconnected, and loveless at all times. Food repels me, and I go many nights without it. I always feel like I need to vomit. To get rid of this feeling, I force my finger deeply down my throat and wrench it against my insides. Nothing comes of it but a few coughs of blood. I don't have the energy to get myself out of bed. I wonder if one can die by doing nothing but being in bed. There's a stabbing pain in the front of my head. If I get up to face the day, I expect horrible things to happen. My stomach is twisted. I want to scream it all out of me — what better way to prove my sanity? A valium would help, or five. The worst part is that I know there's no discernible way out of it. I'm stuck with myself, which for some time has been the psychological equivalent of being surrounded by hyenas, always mocking, threatening, attacking. There is no exit. I am pathetic. When I see people, I want to tell them how sorry I am. I want to weep and tell them I'm sorry for everything, the whole mess of it. I want to fall onto them and cry on their shoulder, and say, "I didn't mean for it to be like this, I really didn't, and I'm so, so sorry." They'd have no idea what I'm talking about, which is fair, because neither do I.

This has gotten me nowhere. I get out of bed and join people in my living room, a lounging ensemble of students on a Sunday who flipping through movies on television and recounting their

exploits from the weekend. They are talking amongst themselves in low, Sunday afternoon voices. Off in the corner by myself, I run my fingers around my lips and think to myself again. The crowd gets tired. Half of them fall asleep, and the others watch a movie. I mutter something unintelligible, and one of the boys, Tim, who had started hanging out with Katie and had been coming over regularly, glances at me oddly, and then at Katie, who does not regard my noise. Without context I say aloud, "No." Now Katie listens, and in a strong, directed voice, says, "No, Boo? No, what?"

"Nothing," I say.

Enter a surreal, colorless world. It feels like the middle of September. The temperature is crisp, and the surface of the pool is as flat and still as the stone beside it. The home and the plants are without their color, and the clouds move sideways overhead. I am alone, wearing a thin dress of white cloth and nothing else. Despite a breeze, nothing around me moves, not even the leaves or the papers of trash. I am now in the pool, gliding through it, inhaling its miniature waves and motions as they roll and trickle by my ears. Then I am standing at the edge of the property, facing the rest of the neighborhood. The homes are vacant and have lost most of their color. Their windows are covered in black, and there is no interior nor any reflection to see. The atmosphere is dead, and I believe I am standing on earth sometime after the end of civilization, in my grandparents' neighborhood. Something has acted on earth and changed the nature of seeing, feeling, and breathing.

The brush of my bare feet against the stone amplifies amidst the gentle freeze of the wind. My grandparents' pool has felt like this before, at the end of summer, just before school. Do I have school in a week? Why has everyone left? I am in the pool again, floating listlessly on my back. Next, I am naked, and entering the property from the cabana. I am outside of my body, looking

at my own face. It is statuesque, inhuman, and emotionless. My hair is wet, and it has gotten colder around me. The air is insipid and removed. The briskness sticks to my skin, heightening my sense of touch, and my attention to the cold. I am on the ground, head, shoulders, arm, hips, and legs lying harshly against the stone, scraping my skin where my ribs and hipbones make contact with the earth. My right forearm sags limply over my chest and touches my ribcage. My left forearm, pinched beneath the other side of my chest, extends perpendicularly from my torso. The freeze is strongest on the underside of my wrist, which is facing upwards and expelling an unidentifiable liquid. The ooze is moving along my arm and into my chest. I am breathing heavier, feeling heavier, and losing warmth in my face.

In my bed in California, I awake from this dream in the middle of a violent flip from my back to my chest, hacking at my left wrist with the nails of my right hand. Lines of red develop across my skin, yet there is no blood drawn. When I am conscious of what I am doing, I tighten my blanket around me like a straitjacket and try to will myself into a comfortable sleep, protected. Enter, again, the land of the surreal. I am talking on my phone in a vast white space. When I try to speak, I cannot enunciate anything. My elocutions are long, ugly blurs of vowel sounds. Whoever I am talking to on the phone doesn't agree with me, and I am enraged. I groan into the telephone until the other party hangs up, and I toss the phone into oblivion. My mouth is in pain, and out of nothing I retrieve a hand mirror and examine my face. Teeth protrude several inches from my lips. One even pierces a bloody hole through the side of my mouth, and my jaw twists towards my shoulder.

The alarm rings at 7:45 A.M. My room is bright, the wind breezes through my slightly opened window, and the hubbub of morning traffic rolls in the background. The fear convinces me my mind is going to cave in on itself, and I want to shout

so hoarsely and vociferously it would ruin me. I shut the alarm off. I do not get out of bed for class. Instead, I go back to sleep and read from a collection of American plays for distraction when I get up.

In the afternoon I take a long, still, warm shower. I am certain my roommates hear me talking to myself as I do so; my voice echoes alongside the streams of water. I dress quickly, putting on extra layers of clothes for warmth; I am cold and afraid at all times. On campus, simple, brief interactions with others dull my livelihood, bringing me toward catatonia. When faced with ordinary questions such as, "How are you?" and "Where are you going?" I either shake where I stand or react many seconds later once I have processed the questions. The longer I stay in interactions like this, the more worried others become. And in some instances, they are outright contemptuous and eager to get away from me. Some, I fear, have written me off as a mental invalid, and stopped regarding me altogether. When I am intoxicated, others poke fun at my fear and my cowardice and remind me of my incompetence. "You're pathetic with people. Just pathetic."

I get as far away from them as I can, now, and spend my days either in dysfunction in my bed, chain-smoking during long walks through town, or trying to study in the corner of the library, breathing frantically into the top of my chest. My GPA for Fall Quarter, once it's determined, is my lowest yet: below a 2.0. My parents agree that the emphasis for the remainder of college is damage control. So long as I graduate in June, that's enough. Over winter break, I barely speak at Christmas parties. The stressors of the environment lock me inside myself. When asked how California is, I force a smile lamely and say, "Great!" Though unlike in California, nobody suspects anything is off nor views me differently.

The Doc is in the hospital again after a fall. It's the first holiday I have ever had when he is not present. In the lull between

Christmas and the New Year, my family arranges a visit to his room at Evanston Hospital. He is sleeping with his mouth is open, and his body is hooked up with wires to machines. His veins are more visible than before, and his skin folds over his arms. Grandma is reading magazines in a bedside chair. We ask Grandma how Doc has been, and she tells us he has been more delusional and has been put on higher doses of antidepressants. The Doc speaks, though he is still sleeping.

"I'm missing school," he whines. "Have you seen my uniform?"

"What?" Grandma shouts, leaning into his ear.

"I think Al took it," he says. "I need it or I'm going to be late, and if I show up without my uniform I'll be in trouble."

"Al is not here!" Grandma shouts at him. "And you don't have school! You're in the hospital!"

"Who is Al?" I ask.

"Al was the Doc's brother," Grandma says. "He was a bit older than the Doc, old enough to go to the war. But he didn't want to fight, and when he enlisted, they assigned him to clean up bodies in the Pacific. He came home shell-shocked."

"Oh," I say, glancing at the Doc. He seems even more withered.

Grandma continues, "When I started dating the Doc, I'd go to his family's apartment in the city. Al would be there talking to the refrigerator while we ate, and the whole family would just ignore it. I'd look around the table, and they all pretended it wasn't there. Meanwhile, I'm thinking, what am I doing with this family? After some time of this, Al walks into another family dinner and talks nonsense to himself, and the Doc gets up and shouts, 'Enough!' and committed him to a hospital the next day. It caused a lot of tension in the family, and when he got out, he was always a little odd."

The Doc coughs and sniffles.

"It was the war that did him in," Grandma says. "War does

that The Doc never had to go to war. He spent some time in the Navy, but never was in combat. Al could have been in combat, but he was also a conscientious objector. And I don't know how it was sorted out exactly, but they put him in the South Pacific, and he spent his time shoveling up the limbs after battles. He was always a little weird before that, from what I heard, but that was enough to take him a level deeper. And they never got him back."

The story unsettles me. I ask Mom if we can leave for dinner, and Mom says it's all right to leave early for a cocktail. We kiss my grandparents goodbye and leave. Kevin and Dad meet us at the restaurant. It's an Italian diner owned by a man who the Doc once treated and who always had outstanding psychiatric bills owed to the Doc. As a rule, the family is never allowed to eat here, and if we do so, we do so in secret. We share wine at dinner, and it makes me quiet, scared, and dumb. I am tense in the presence of alcohol and all in that doltish, slow place in which the world moves faster than I can react to it. I am dressed beautifully and look beautiful, but don't speak my mind beyond basic pleasantries, thanking the waiter excessively and demurely for her service. I do the same to my parents, never saying anything more than, "Thank you," and smiling to be nice. It is the etiquette of one who cannot think for themself.

Dad puts a lot of effort into engaging with me. I do not feel the same about Mom. She's onto something. The look she gives me is the same look of examination that people at school did: realizing me to be unwell. Mom stops talking to me during dinner. Her eyes are at first disheartened, then disappointed, then distant and unemotional. Then she doesn't acknowledge me at all. At home, we light a fire in the gas fireplace and watch *Casablanca*. I lay on a blanket on the ground next to the fire and cuddle with the dogs. Dad is in his armchair, and Mom is on the edge of the couch across from him. We watch the film in its entirety. Afterward, we each disassemble to either prepare for bed or watch another program. I pass Mom in the kitchen while on my way to bed and approach her to hug her goodnight. She stops walking and looks past me. As I hug her and say, "I love you," she is motionless, her arms at her sides, and offers nothing back to me physically or verbally as I tuck my head into the shoulder of her robe. I go to bed.

The remainder of the winter is gray, and my pitiable disposition toward myself takes full hold over my life. My schoolwork consists of half-finished nonsense, and when I try to "work" with other students, they notice my jumbled thinking and ask if I even read the material. When asked about my plans for life after graduation, I offer prepackaged answers. "Oh, you know, I think I'm going to get an entry-level job and work my way up." In what setting, they ask. I flutter off into more evasion, and they look confused. The charm, if you could call it that, is wearing off. More likely, the patience of others has run out.

I am blacking out again, taking drinks from wherever they come from. Katie and Carla take me out, doing their best to keep me talking to people. They introduce me to boys at the party who in turn look concerned or say something rude. Or more commonly, others see my palpable self-loathing, my impotence before the world, and take it in themselves. When my friends are tired of holding my hand, I am out alone, a frightened pinball amongst more confident people.

The DJ plays electronic music in the back of a dark and crowded party, and I have a panic attack. In a disorienting pit of people, someone grabs my shoulder, then my waist, and I scream and jolt outside for fresh air. The people on the lawn sense my terror. They step back, rotate away from me, and whisper. At home, I hyperventilate and try to sleep. After midnight, my roommates come home. Katie lights herself a small spliff before bed and shares it with me, and I make a number of low remarks about what others think of me, and how incompetent I am. "Uh huh," Katie says, blowing smoke past my face. The weed takes effect. My vision is distorted and goes blank for several seconds at a time. When consciousness returns, I am in a different part of the house. Voices call my name throughout the night and I fall asleep near dawn. Upon waking, near noon, I barely have the strength to rise from bed. I make a small breakfast of toast and orange juice. My arm shakes while I butter the toast, and drop my knife onto the plate. It rings shrilly and harms my ears. The thought of cutting myself is close to the mind, so I throw the knife into the sink and take my phone into my room. I distract myself with my phone, yet the metal of the product feels keenly sharp, another object for the deed. I sit on the floor, dazed, and press it into the side of my wrist, just for a light tempting.

Before going to the library, I drink a small glass of red wine from a box to steady my fear and pack a Gabriel García-Marquez novella in case I need an escape. On the top floor of the library, I sit by myself and hallucinate a juggling clown in a chair across from me. On my way out, I imagine myself slipping on the steps of the library and falling three flights down to the bottom.

My roommates have dinner parties and the guests are sneering and inhospitable to me in my own home. I emerge from my seclusion in my room with a face that looks drugged and the gait of a zombie. "Yeah, hey Boo," they say curtly before shouldering me away. I sit on the floor absently and the more sympathetic guests pat me on the head.

I maintain vigorous exercise, which consists of long runs and bike rides to places where I can walk and ponder in my delusions, far away from everything—alongside the cemeteries, or to the library, or at the face of a weeping orange sunset on a Sunday evening in the Bay Area. This is where I get respite from the crowd, and from the alcoholic evenings I am too spineless to refuse and which I can never escape. It keeps up a good image, too. I look fit in body, therefore I must also be fit in mind. I'm enrolled in three classes, all of which I must pass to graduate. I keep lying to myself that I'm going to do so. The weight of the charade—four years at a private college in California with no paper to show for it—would be too much to bear. The noises I hear at the end of nights are the classic, cartoonish depictions of insanity, full of ringing clocks and banging pots. An indefinable madness squirms over my scalp like electric eels and strangles my back. My dreams remain nightmarish and grotesquely sexual.

My need for counseling or pharmaceutical intervention is undeniable, so I seek help. The counseling center is characteristically booked, though I do get a single cursory meeting with a counselor, a younger woman who doesn't seem long out of grad school. I try to explain my issues to her. She gives me one of those "introvert or extrovert" personality tests and asks me about my career aspirations. After twenty minutes of fruitless conversation, I leave. I get an appointment with a doctor next, thinking that drugs will be easier and more effective. It's with the same doctor I saw freshman year for depression. Again, I get Zoloft and take a full dose as soon as I can, along with a beer. My chest loosens. I breathe easier; if only slightly, I let go. For the next week, I take about twice as much Zoloft as prescribed, hoping it will relieve me sooner.

The family comes to school for graduation: Mom, Dad, Kevin, the Doc, and my two grandmothers. They all think I am great at everything, and I've always bought into it, despite the lack of evidence that I've ever been anything but ordinary. My roommates and I have a graduation party the night before we walk, with a keg and a potluck. My family tends to the Doc, for he needs aid all of the time. Dementia has onset in him, and he never remembers anything anyone has said to him. I talk to him all night, anyway. In the early morning, we observe a "drinks with dads" tradition at a local dive bar before sunrise. Dad and I drink Bloody Marys before going to campus for the ceremony.

The students are lined across campus according to their degrees and their names and are held until it's safe to march them into the soccer stadium for the affair. I pass by my doctor, who asks me if things have turned out alright. "Yes, they have," I say. It is baking hot in the stadium, and I am drunk, blathering, and wise-cracking for most of it. I when called to the podium, and asked to write the pronunciation of my name on the card, I change my middle name to "Gah-dam," so that the speaker will announce me to the crowd as, "Ellen God Damn Harvey."

At the reception, I am dancing like a singing lady for a win-ery advertisement. To everyone else, I am a wayward mess at a family affair. The reflection of the heat off the turf makes the event almost inhospitable for my grandmothers and for the Doc. The family leaves after about forty minutes. The celebrations continue throughout the evening, marking a twenty-four hour spurt of little rest and nearly constant consumption. My friends remark that they have never seen me this drunk before. Sometime after midnight, I regain consciousness in a neighborhood I do not recognize. I must have left home and wandered, as I have done on hard nights before. One of my shoes is missing, and dirt from the pavement is compiling on the side of my foot. I approach street signs and put a hand over my eye to straighten my vision, and then walk several blocks until I find a street I recognize. The town is asleep. The streets are empty. Eventually, I find one that leads to campus. When I return to campus, it's also vacant. I sit in the center of the lawn and take a final, 360-degree look at the world around me. I hobble past the mission, across the academic buildings, and take the campus exit closest to my house.

CHAPTER 9

March 2016

Like many of the fallouts of my life, I subconsciously understood this evening was going to happen. And like the other fallouts, I tolerated this knowledge and set it aside, even as inertia was taking me toward a head-on confrontation and my dread became unmanageable.

Prior to hospitalization, the last time I'd seen Jude she was in her apartment complaining about heart pains. Generally, I ignored Jude's problems, as they were too vast and labyrinthian to get caught up in. But her complaints about pains across her body suggested the need for medical intervention. I called her one evening from my bed, consumed with the idea that she was going to die on my watch.

"Jude, I'm concerned about your health."

"There's good reason for that."

"Be serious with me. You said that you had pain in your arms and legs. Those are the symptoms of a heart attack."

"I'm fine, Boo."

"Do you think you had a heart attack?"

"The last time I had a heart attack, I didn't know for weeks. So I don't know. I might have had a heart attack."

"But you may die."

"And I'd like that."

"For fuck's sake, Jude."

"You knew this."

"So why don't you, then?"

"I lack the gumption to kill myself."

"If you were dying passively, would you just let it happen?"

"If I laid down and died, I'd ask that you respect my wishes."

"Jude, be honest with me: do you think you're dying?"

"No, I don't. I think God is playing a cruel joke and I will be alive for another thirty years."

"Let me take you to a hospital to be sure."

"The last time I had a heart attack, my friend forced me to the hospital, and it screwed up my finances. I still owe thousands of dollars."

"But your finances aren't as important as your life."

"That's not true."

"It is, damn it!"

"It may be true for someone on the other end, but not for me."

I hung up on her and dwelled on the conversation for the rest of the night, wondering whether or not I should allow Jude the right to exercise the ultimate freedom: to lay down and die, or, in other circumstances, to will herself headfirst into death.

When she alerted me to her eventual hospitalization, I left City Hall with haste and took the train to a hospital on the North Side. The two people on the train both appeared Mad. One was a palpably downtrodden woman with frizzled hair and body odor I could sense from half a car away. Her head swayed while she mumbled, and she fell into a sleep. The other was a man with dusted sweatpants and a scar underneath his eye. He looked meanly at an empty seat across from him. He planted his elbow on his chin and pressed his chin on his fist, looking like a person in determined contemplation. He pointed his finger at an empty seat across from him and shook it. His eyes squinted to a boiling point as he shouted, "But that's not what it's about! You can't—you can't—you—don't play me like that, don't you play me. That's not what I said! This isn't what that's about!" He covered his mouth with his hand, glaring at the seat, and shook his head in disbelief. I, too, was getting manic. Everything that followed seemed to happen very quickly, in splats, without connection. And then it ended.

I got off the train, ran toward the hospital, and requested to see Jude Freedman at the ER. I lied to the check-in nurse and said that I was her daughter. Another nurse escorted me to Jude's room, where I found her berating the hospital staff.

"Ms. Freedman, I'm only here to help you," the attending nurse said, mid-altercation with Jude. It reminded me of the many times I saw the Doc chiding the nurses when he was in the hospital. It must have been a supreme insult to have to sign your last years of independence to other people and have them tell you it's in your best interests. The Doc lost his mind in those hospitals. At one moment he'd be sweet-talking the nurses, and in that same afternoon, he'd be reporting his dreams and hallucinations to his family.

Jude was lying in bed in a hospital gown. I said hello, and she seemed relieved to see me. "Finally!" she said, lifting her arm toward me. "Someone who understands me!"

"Jude, please don't be dismissive of the nurse," I pleaded.

"I'm only taking control of my own decision making in the health system!"

"Ms. Freedman, the doctor will be in shortly to ask you some questions," the nurse said. "It's in your best interests if you respond honestly."

I sat uncomfortably in the corner of the room. If the paternalism did not enervate, the interior design of the hospital did, with its colorless tiling, its bureaucracy, and robotic beeping of the various life support machines. I understood the reasons a medical institution has to be stale, clean, and technical, but it truly did feel like a good place to die in.

The doctor entered the room, and Jude was predictably curt with him. He asked Jude about any preexisting health conditions.

"I have so much bullshit acting on me at once that it's impossible for me to articulate my health to you," Jude sneered at him.

"Ms. Freedman, can you tell me if you have any preexisting health conditions?" the doctor asked.

"I have anglia spondylitis, sleep apnea, diabetes, cholesterol, high blood pressure, and poverty."

The doctor checked her breathing and then asked her to sit

up. Jude grabbed the handles of the bed and strenuously lifted herself up about half a foot off the bed.

"Ma'am, can you move up any further?" the doctor asked.

This infuriated Jude. Her face went red, and her arms were shaking as she held herself up just a few inches above the backrest of her hospital bed.

"This is as far as I can go!" she said to the doctor.

"Ms. Freedman, is there any reason why your heart might not be well?" the doctor asked.

"I haven't been taking my meds," Jude said.

"And why haven't you been doing that?" the doctor asked.

"Because I've been depressed," Jude said.

"Did you take your meds today?" the doctor asked.

"Yes, I took them today."

"Have you been diagnosed with depression?"

"I've been mentally ill for forty-five years."

"Do you take any medications for it?"

"I have in the past."

"Which medication?"

"It's inconsequential."

"Why did you stop taking it?"

"It made my symptoms worse."

"Which symptom is that?"

"One of the symptoms of my depression is somnolence. I spent too much time in bed, and once I started taking the drug it increased my somnolence."

"Would you like to talk to one of our psychiatrists?"

"In my forty-five years of experience with this, I have absolutely no reason to believe that would do me any good."

"Ma'am, we have a psychiatrist who could assess you and talk to you."

Jude looked at me and waved her arm. "What did I just say?" she shouted.

"Don't take this up with me," I said, not wanting to tolerate any of Jude's complaints. "He's the one you're pitching to."

The doctor breathed and spoke to Jude carefully. "Ma'am, I'm not the enemy. I'm here to help you, alright?" Jude did not respond to him. "Now, because you said you've been depressed," the doctor continued, "I have to ask you—do you have any thoughts of hurting yourself or others?"

"If I did, I wouldn't tell you."

He looked flatly at Jude and asked, "Ma'am, do you have any thoughts of hurting yourself or others?"

"If I did, I wouldn't tell you."

The doctor looked at me, possibly for clarification or assistance. I shrugged, then Jude responded, "I can tell you unequivocally that I do not intend to harm anyone else."

"Do you intend to harm yourself?" the doctor asked.

"I will not harm myself," Jude said.

The doctor left the room, and the nurse fiddled with the chords hanging over the machine next to Jude's bed. She tried to make small talk with Jude and reassure her of the good things she had. "It looks like you have family who cares about you, ma'am," she said.

I stayed with Jude for about thirty or forty minutes, mostly in silence. I asked her who called an ambulance for her, and she said, "Nobody you know."

I paused and scrutinized her with a direct, interrogative glare. "Did you call yourself into the hospital? Did you do this for attention?" I asked.

She didn't say anything and stared into the ceiling. I let it go. I stayed with her for another hour until Jude was transported to a cardiologist. While she was under evaluation, I walked to a convenience store a block away and bought a pack of American Spirits and a bar of chocolate, and then returned to the plaza outside the hospital. I reclined onto a bench underneath a streetlight and lit a cigarette to calm the pace of my mind. Very little of what Jude had said made sense when examined against what I had seen of her. Why would she not take her drugs for weeks, but have taken them on this day? Did she slam them down her throat to appear stable once an ambulance was called for her? And why did she not tell the doctor about her psychiatric background? I coughed after a clumsy inhale, hacked for another ten seconds, and then spit and threw the cigarette at the ground. "Shit," I said to myself. "This is the world's slowest suicide attempt."

I got off the bench, kicked the air, hyperventilated, screamed, and thought about bruising myself into the hospital to demand attention to Jude. "She may be a crude, ungrateful bitch, but she's a VIP, and you cannot let her die! Not on my watch!" I leaned against the wall of the hospital until I was collapsed on the concrete. "My God, fuck that woman. Fuck her, fuck her, fuck her," I said again, punching the brick until my knuckles bled. I could not feel anything but a light burn. Then I laughed and cleaned a tear off my eye with the end of my sweater's sleeve. I hadn't eaten all day except for the chocolate, and felt hollow, nauseous, and irate. My vision started to black out. I went inside the hospital for water and rested in the waiting room. Soon after, I took a cab home and slept on a small meal of fruit, whiskey, and NyQuil.

The next day I spent my morning doing schoolwork. Jude called me and asked for a ride from the hospital. I skipped class to pick her up, pulled into the entrance lane of the hospital, helped Jude out of her wheelchair and into my car, and drove off. During the drive, she explained that she had a heart attack, and the hospital had put three stents in her heart.

"Anything else?" I asked.

"I have to take pills for my stents. If I miss a dose, I'm liable to have another heart attack," she said.

"Meaning you'll die if you don't take one," I said.

"Possibly," she said.

I was rarely able to say or ask what I actually meant. I've always been that way. What I actually felt had been repressed long ago, and usually was unrecognizable in the moment. The right articulation of the moment only came to me days later, when the memory revisited me. Such as how someone's death only felt like a death to me a week after it happened. In the present, all I get to is politeness and small talk.

"So it's every day now, a simple yes or no with the pill," I said, deadpanned.

"My mood is much better. I'm glad I was brought to the hospital," Jude said.

"But the question remains," I said.

"Yes, it's every day now," Jude said.

I pulled the car over onto the roadside. "Look, Jude, I know you can tell other people whatever you want, and you can post whatever you want on the Internet, and everyone will take you at your word. But you cannot do that with me. This right here was a suicide attempt," I said.

Jude sat stubbornly, silently. I awaited a response. I continued, "And you know what else? The issue isn't with doctors. The issue isn't with the people who leave you. It's you, man. It's been you all along."

She sighed, looking through the windshield. "I know."

"You want to go?" I said, "You want to leave? Fine. Go out the backdoor. Pretend it was a heart thing. Tell people you don't have the gumption to kill yourself, even as you literally sign off on your own death and deny that you had any agency in it. Go ahead. And I know that you've got ideas in your head that if you go, someone else will just pick up your work where you left off. But that's not how it is. Hell no. When you go, this whole thing disappears. You're it. You're the whole thing. The vision falls apart, and I'm left again with nobody to teach me a damned thing about how people like us might get out of this rut. Nobody else to even talk to. When you go, this doesn't go on. That's it, Jude. That's it. It's over."

Her lower lip trembled; her eyes wetted. I turned on the radio and drove her home.

I brought her dinner later that evening, along with some pre-made meals for the days thereafter. I did not check in on her for some time. When she returned to her work, she alerted me to political happenings. She had not been checking her emails, and when she did, she learned that one of the agencies that she was a board member of was voting to reorganize their board structure. The organization received substantial federal funding to coordinate mental health services, and Jude had been a mainstay at their meetings, always railing against the flaws of the system and the neglect of the people who used it. When Jude was getting out of the mental health system, she had earned a board seat not just for herself, but also for five other individuals with lived experience of the system, constituting a whole power block at the table. The net impact of the proposed restructuring would be to reduce "lived experience" seats and shift board representation toward service providers, the Mayor's Office, and state officials.

Jude panicked and explained to me that everything about the proposal was hasty and secretive. What a precarious world we had, where you woke up every day to find something else has been apart while you weren't watching.

This is my life's work they're fucking with, Jude wrote in an email to me, sent at 3:17 A.M. along with a memo from the agency head that voting would take place in less than one week. *Organize everyone you know. I want them there. They can't kick us away. Not again.*

Jude, I politely wrote back, *I don't know anyone else.*
Sigh.
But I'll come.

Thank you.

We wrote to journalists, homelessness activists, housing activists, peer groups, rabble-rousers at large in the hopes they'd come and stand with Jude. We explained that the little influence the people who used the mental health system had in shaping it was being voted away, and that we had to oppose it. Mostly, people didn't respond to me.

On the day of the meeting, I picked Jude up and asked her how she was doing. "Not well. Not well at all."

My health had also been missing, I'd had felt no joy in weeks, and I'd been eschewing that fact on a daily basis just to persist. My first thought out of bed in the morning was "Kill me," and it took two coffees to penetrate my depression and think at least somewhat clearly. And it was a foregone certainty that we'd get dismissed and ignored at the meeting. It felt like another bottoming-out before I once more had to decide on a different life philosophy.

Jude wasn't wearing her token t-shirt, the one that read *I'm One of Those People.* I asked her why, and she said, "I don't have to remind myself that I'm one of those people when it is obvious that my life is a mess."

We were running late to the meeting, with under forty-five minutes to arrive before it began. I sped through traffic. Jude yelled in pain as we ran over potholes. "Sorry, Jude, sorry!" I said, braking just feet before the car ahead of me. "Who all is going to be there?"

"A lot of people who don't want to hear from us."

"Where do they stand on the system?"

"They think I lack insight into my own condition. They want all cops trained and involved in all mental health crises. They want to save money through drug treatment."

"Every meeting we go to, the talk is about access to medications and increasing the scope of police presence."

"I've told them this before and it doesn't change."

"So why do you keep doing it?"

"We have to expose the inadequacy of deinstitutionalization and the premises of mental healthcare. Mental illness is its own horizon of American life, and while it's possible for many to avoid it, it's not possible for us."

"And I think this whole conversation is a sign of our powerlessness."

"It's true. And I've nothing left to put into it but to pass it onto you. I'm going to die in this fight. You have a future with it."

"God fucking dammit you can be so manipulative when you are down!"

"That the board shouldn't disempower people with lived experience of the mental health system. We are going to say we are the only people who should speak for ourselves," she said.

"And what are they going to say?" I said.

"That consumer voice is corrupting the system and that people with mental illness shouldn't have any influence on it," she said.

"But that's not where the thinking of the literal mental health system is at."

"It's not where anyone is at, Boo. Our conversations are very limited, and they're designed in accordance with that limited understanding of mental health. Even on our side, Boo, we select our experiences to fit our narrative. We don't look too much at people who say they liked their inpatient visit or who are grateful for their antipsychotics. The politics of the matter will mostly divide that reality and make it difficult to unify a consumer base around any given narrative of mental health. It's too complicated, and we do not have enough knowledge for that conversation as it exists. We're years from any of this taking off. For now, we can only move from where we are at," Jude said.

"But it is also true that there are reactionary forces in disability," I said.

"Yes. What's much more urgent," Jude said, "is that people like Tate are getting closer and closer to a victory, and the forces of the advocacy community are lining up behind them. Their message is much softer now than what it used to be. I can remember a time when they openly advocated for sneaking drugs into people for experimentation, bringing back the asylums, reducing commitment standards to nothing, and allowing parents to put their children into treatment. They haven't been successful in this, so they've gradually made concessions on their policy goals. Now they talk about much softer forms of coercion, while other trends are piling up around our people. Mass community disinvestment, privatization, a move away from private prisons, where many of our people are kept, gun violence, drug addiction, suicide. All of these things contribute to a vacuum you might call 'the mental illness problem.' And as there is big business in warehousing people and treating people, and as America becomes more plutocratic, the political agenda around our suffering is going to be set by those with the power to lobby. Nursing homes, private hospitals, pharmaceutical companies. If you can take away the restriction on keeping people in hospitals, then you open up the door for institutionalization. These places can make a lot of money. They're ready to inject that into the vacuum we are in. Even if they watered down their agenda to nothing, I would oppose them. And if they can push people like us out of the table, then they effectively erase their fiercest critics and biggest stalling points. I've lost everything, and I maintain this as my last right to be able to speak against them when they evacuate me."

We arrived at a church in the Loop where the meeting was held. I dropped Jude off and spent another twenty minutes looking for parking, settling upon a garage that charged me fifty dollars for a two-hour stay. I ran through the sidewalks and contorted myself around bystanders until I got to the church. I signed in, assembled the requisite paperwork for the event, and quietly entered the back of the auditorium where the meeting was being held. There were about two-dozen rows of chairs arranged, half of which were occupied, and within which I could not identify Jude. I creeped along the side of the building in search of her while a panel of emcees finished an address:

"We will now open up the floor for statements. We will limit your statements to a three-minute maximum. Please be conscientious of your time," said the facilitator — a short, serious woman with a stopwatch and notepad on her desk.

Campbell Tate was the first person to request and receive the floor. Tate was an old man with long, thinning hair and an overgrown chin beard. He spoke in a hoarse, pedantic voice devoid of intonation. While I thought his delivery was contrived, he presented his statement with an upright posture and an expert's sense of seriousness. "I've sat on this board for ten years, and I've only seen things get worse. The system has been dissembling, and our advocacy response has been diluted by interest groups who have no interest in helping the people who are most impacted: individuals with serious, untreated mental illness. These are the people who are in our streets, our jails, and our emergency rooms with no attention and no means for help. We have the same conversations at each meeting, and the result is the same: nothing gets done. What we are talking about most of the time is either administrative mush or a symptom of a problem. We end up with these tragedies like the LaQuan MacDonald shooting, and we talk about the politics of policing and mental health, and the debate is reframed into a story about who the bad cops are shooting at, when in fact the story should be about how people wind up dead after a crisis or a psychotic episode because the mental health system is not doing anything for them. It's been taken over by corrupted interests who advocate for closing hospitals and then take the community reinvestment funds for programs that don't work, and this board is no exception. Therapy is a fix for the worried well. Crisis Intervention Training is a downstream intervention. Will it help officers gain the skills to deal with these confrontations better? Yes, I believe it will. But it shouldn't be the center of the discussion, because the criminal justice system should never be the first point of contact for a problem with serious mental illness, and it won't stop these confrontations from happening. And it won't help the people who are most in need of treatment, who are most unable to recognize that they need treatment, and who are most likely to become violent without treatment avoid confrontation with a police officer. We are giving them nothing and getting tragedy in return."

"Excuse me Tate, who is getting violent?" Jude interrupted. Her shout echoed through the church, and the crowd turned toward her.

"Ms. Freedman, please respect Robert's Rules of Orders. You will have your chance to speak," the facilitator said.

"People with untreated serious mental illnesses, Jude," Tate addressed her, unshaken by Jude's interruption.

"Did you by chance happen to see the man in Michigan who was noncompliant with officers and who was shot by a firing squad? Without any weapon?" Jude shouted again.

"You will have your chance to speak," the facilitator stated again. She wasted as little time on Jude as she could and barely looked at her.

"Officers do not want to shoot. They are on our side," Tate said, growing a bit more confrontational with Jude.

"They are on your side insofar as they want a mental health system and think you have the answers. But they're not on my side. The more they agree with you, the less they are on my side," Jude said.

"They are on our side. I worry that our current social climate is so charged about the nature of policing that we forget that these guys are on our team and that they want the same things for our people that we want." Tate was now hurried and his body tensed with frustration.

"They're the ones who have the most contact with mental illness and are the ones who most want us to invest in treatment for the mentally ill. While I think it would do modest good to invest in police training for the mentally ill, we shouldn't let it turn into a celebrity cause that distracts us from our bigger mission of fixing the system to get treatment for our mentally ill citizens and family members. We need more hospital beds and more reasonable commitment standards. We need to accept the biological reality of serious mental illness, with all that it entails: lack of insight, psychosis, and total obstinacy in the face of what works. The last few decades have shown us a repeated pattern of shunning the most seriously ill while promoting policies that sound benign and integrative on the surface, but ultimately do nothing to help those most in need. We need a board that is ready to address that without getting distracted in secondary concerns for modernity's discontents and political correctness advocates. Thank you," Tate said.

Tate retreated from the microphone, and Jude stood up behind him for her turn to speak. "As usual there are some things about that which I agree with, and many things where I strongly disagree. You're correct that the system doesn't help those most in need, and that police training won't solve violence. You're incorrect in insinuating that drugging us and locking us up is the solution, or that kicking me off of the board will solve anything."

"You're being incendiary. I advocate treatment according to a least restrictive standard," Tate objected. He clenched his papers and slapped them on his knee.

"You advocate for restrictive standards in all of their forms, Tate, and you throw people like me under the bus by linking us with serial killers over and over, and then push in policy through the backdoor that is far more restrictive than what your rhetoric suggests."

"I have never linked violence to serious mental illness when violence was not caused by serious mental illness," Tate objected again, pointing at Jude.

"Are you going to tell him not to interrupt?" Jude begged the panel. "No?" They did not respond to her, and she turned and spoke directly to Tate. "I follow your website, you do so all of the time. Any time there is a violent news story, you share it and link it to serious mental illness, even when there's nothing about mental health in the context of the story. Then when people die, be it by police or by their own hand, you assert that treatment would have stopped it."

Tate interrupted Jude, "That's what I'm talking about. Your only option shouldn't be police officers. I've known police all over the country who are advocates for treatment. They're victims of this too. Nobody trained them to be mental health professionals. It's not what they got into this line of work to do. We have two mental health systems today: the community system is for the 'worried well,' the people with problems in living, the people with quote-unquote mental health conditions like trauma and poverty. Then we have the system for people with serious mental illnesses, who are too sick to accept treatment voluntarily or who are pushed away from the community system because they are too difficult to treat, who are served by the criminal justice system, or are not served at all. I repeat: the focus on policing only comes in several steps beyond the root. We think everyone with a mental illness is able to live in the community, and we selectively ignore the evidence that proves otherwise…"

Jude laughed. "Who is included in this population of invalids? The half of us that you say lack insight into our conditions? A concept you shoehorned into mental health solely to justify forced treatment? Or is it those of us who you say constitute half of all mass shooters?"

"Ms. Freedman, you have thirty seconds left," the facilitator said.

"Are you serious?" Jude shouted. I could see her losing her composure. She lifted her arm up to her chest, as high as they could go, and shook them. Her facial muscles were twitching.

"I don't say that everyone with a serious mental illness is violent," Tate said. "I say that serious mental illness like schizophrenia and bipolar disorder are real, that they are proven to be physiologically based, and that if untreated, then individuals with these diseases are at least ten times more prone to violence than the rest of the world. And consumer voice has gone so far off the deep end that we cannot build a system that accounts for this."

"I've lived with your serious mental illness for decades, I've been compliant and noncompliant, and I have hardly put a hand on a butterfly. And if I ever did, it was only because the butterfly deserved it," Jude said.

"Time! Allow the next speaker to take the floor, Jude."

"I was promised three minutes to speak, and I'm going to get my three minutes to speak!" Jude said.

"Ms. Freedman, please remove yourself from the floor!" the facilitator said. She showed no sympathy as she said this.

"No! This is a battle we have been fighting for three decades! There used to be no consumer voice in mental health policy at all. Today, this is the only board like it in the country that has this large of a constituency of consumers! This board is going to vote to take away my voice, and I have my right to the voice!"

Tate scolded Jude as a father might scold an unruly adolescent. "The police are dealing with the homeless population, the hallucinating population, and the people who need psychiatric beds and medicated treatment and who aren't getting them because the system does not serve their needs. It's obvious to them and to anyone on the streets that the people who are smearing their feces under the viaduct and shouting to the sky are going to be more violent than the rest, and it should be obvious to you!"

Jude replied, "Tate, I've had only had one friend who ever killed anyone in a delusional state. She was a doctor who had a diagnosis of schizophrenia, and she was fully compliant with her medication. She had two little children and joked to her friends, 'Do you ever think about killing your kids?' The friends laughed because they thought it was just something people said. She went home and drowned her children in a bathtub and has been in a forensic unit ever since. I know that if there was anything in the world that she could have done to prevent herself from killing her kids, she would have done it. But her issue was not her lack of compliance. She did everything that her psychiatrist said she should have done. Maybe, Tate, it's misguided to think that what you call serious mental illness is enough to predict a murder, but rather violence comes from many things happening at once in ways you are not capable of addressing, but you only want to understand it in terms of what suits your desire for psychiatric institutionalization."

A tall, gentle man from the audience approached Jude to get her to sit down. "Get your hands off me!" Jude shouted.

"The studies show that violence is reduced with treatment, the studies show that incarceration is reduced when we have court-ordered treatment on the books," Tate responded.

"And how, Mr. Tate, are we to trust your solutions when you preface your arguments with the pseudoscience of a hate group?" Jude said.

"I am not speaking from an ideology of hate! My sister died of schizophrenia after leaving home in a psychosis! These are the stories of people's lives and families who are being ignored and thrown away! I will not let you defame my work like that!"

"Order!" the facilitator said. Jude and Tate quieted. The

audience murmured, some with laughter and some with exasperation. A woman took the floor and introduced herself from a charitable foundation. "I understand that it's not an untroubled solution, but things weren't working before. We have to try something new, which is why I support the planned restructuring," she said.

"Are you fucking serious?" I heard Jude murmur. The facilitator glared at her. Jude looked at the people around her mistrustfully. None of them returned her astonishment. Two more speakers gave similarly bland endorsements of the restructuring, without any criticism. "I can't believe this," Jude said.

"If we have no other speakers, we will put the proposal to a vote," the administrator quickly said.

"I have to speak again! If everyone else is finished speaking, then I can speak again!" Jude said.

"You have three minutes," the facilitator said.

"You want to say you're keeping people out of jail? Then end the war on drugs. End broken windows policing. Provide independent, safe housing for people with mental illness. Employ them or provide them with a livable amount of welfare. That's how they all get there, anyway. But we won't be talking about this if people like me are off the board! You don't want to address root causes, and you only want to use people like myself as sympathy points. If we kick people with lived experience off the board, we will only end up with people like Tate, who want to take us back to the system we had a century ago."

"This is defamation!" Tate interjected. "I want 150,000 hospital beds, I want reasonable commitment standards, I want HIPPA laws changed so loved ones can get help for their sick relatives!"

"I've been in this as long as you have, and I remember you advocating for things far more severe than that!" Jude said. "I remember your doctor pal going into the hospitals, trying new antipsychotics on them without their consent, allowing family members to put their loved ones away."

"Time!" the facilitator said.

"This has not been three minutes! I have friends who saw it firsthand! You want, without a doubt in my mind, to take us back to the time when people like me had no rights in society whatsoever, and no matter how benign you seem, I am not allowing you any victory, because I know you'll just get back to work to build on it," Jude said.

"Ms. Freedman, half of a million people with serious mental illness are in jails and prisons! How can you be outraged by putting them in a hospital but all right with them being in the criminal justice system?" Tate said.

"That is an outright lie! You think I put those people there? And you think I'm all right with it? Your whole operation is a lie! You're not an advocate, you're a PR machine for Nurse Ratched! And this whole board is complicit in it!" Jude said.

"Time!" the facilitator shouted again.

Tate was enraged now. "I'm an advocate for the people who cannot speak for themselves! I'm an advocate for the people who are being tossed into penury and homelessness in the name of civil liberties! I am standing up for people with serious mental illness in face of people like you, who are totally functioning but don't actually have a mental illness!"

"Let me teach you something about this phrase 'mental illness!'" Jude said. "When I'm with my friends who have been in the system, I piss them off because I identify as a person who experiences symptoms of mental illness. They hate this type of language. 'Illness.' 'Symptoms.' They say the term schizophrenic is a slur of the worst order. Words such as 'schizophrenic' and 'mental illness' take the hope out of things, and they're probably right. A lot of them hate the phrase so much they don't talk to me. I won't deny it, a lot of us are difficult. But what they can't

answer me is why I never get better and they do. So, I say someone who feels unwell is allowed to call herself ill. Someone who
gets better may one day see it as something else. I don't know.
I'm not here to tell people what to call themselves. All that said,
while I allow my friends to call themselves mentally ill, I have
tremendous objections to providers telling me I have an illness,
because if they tell me I have an illness then it means they're
going to treat me."

All through this, the crowd grew frustrated, and the facilitator told Jude to be quiet until she eventually gave up. The man
next to her tried to set her down again, and the administrators
tried to move toward a vote. "Let me finish! Now let me ask,
who here has ever been on antipsychotic medication before?"

Jude raised her hand, nobody else in the room did. Only
half were paying attention to her.

"Come on, let me see. Nobody? Very well. I'll assume some
authority on the matter and tell you a little bit about the system
of psychiatry. For decades, they've been telling me the drugs are
getting better, and for decades all of my people in the system
have told me that it isn't true. A lot of them look like zombies
— they have less of a mind today than they did before they ever
got involved with the system. Their jaws move around without
control. They get diseases they never should have had. And when
the previous generation of drugs don't work, the companies just
create a new one and say that things are better. Maybe they will
find something that's what they say it is, but why should I believe
it? It's like the boy who cried wolf, only my brain and body are
at stake. And yet with every generation, it is always the same
people pushing the system — shrinks, parents, and police. They
always talk like they know what's best for people."

"I resent that," Tate laughed.

"And you know what Tate? I resent you. You call yourself
an advocate for us, but you listen to nothing we say, and you

dehumanize us at every turn so you can force us into a system nobody wants to be a part of. Now this young guy comes into Newton, Connecticut and shoots a room of kindergarteners. And what do you and Representative Culhane do? You blame it on us! Two months later, you're saying these kids died because of untreated serious mental illness, and you're pushing a bill for drugging mandates and looser commitment standards that would have brought it back fifty years!" Jude said.

"Go on, keep talking to yourself. Keeping distorting the facts," Tate jeered at her. He was now reclined and smiling with his arms crossed.

"The only reason I talk to myself is because no one else will! It's not insanity, it's just that I'm the only person I have to talk to!" Jude said.

I burst out laughing at this statement.

"I did not think I'd have to request that anyone be forcibly removed from this hearing," the facilitator snarked.

"The irony," Jude scoffed.

"Does anyone else have a statement to make?" the facilitator said.

Tate rose. "The intent of my agenda is to prevent tragedy, and the purpose of common-sense policies like Assisted Outpatient Treatment is to get care for people with serious mental illness who have historically failed to comply with treatment to keep them out of jail. We need to center and advance mental health policy like this."

"Compliance?" Jude said. "We've been through this. I've had people call me noncompliant for forty years. All it means is that I don't agree with the way they assess my life and tell me how I should run it. By the way, it's not assisted treatment. It's forced treatment."

The facilitator made a motion toward the security in the room. The crowd grunted and some of them left the meeting.

"It's not forced. It's the least invasive treatment available, and eighty percent of people who have been through it in the State of New York are grateful for it," Tate said.

"You're looking to expand the bureaucracy to control our lives, just as you always have. This is all you have left, and I'm not giving it to you. You've never meant us well and you never will!" Jude said.

"I do mean well, I want people off the streets. I want to help the people the system has neglected," Tate said.

"I'm one of the people the system has neglected and I think your solutions are dead wrong!" Jude said.

"Nonsense! Absolute nonsense! You deny everything! The way the mental health system is run today, they deny the very existence of mental illness!" Tate said.

"That's because there isn't proof for the biochemical origins of mental illness upon which the near entirety of the system rests!" Jude said.

"Stop this 1960s smearing! Mental illness is real and denying it is the heart of the poison of the system! You said they were real yourself!" Tate said.

"I said I felt a certain way and call it mental illness to certain company, but I don't think anyone has proven to me that it's all in my brain like you say it is! I can read off a litany of reasons I have for the psychological life I live, starting from the day of my birth and coming right up to this exchange with you. How do you test for it? You can't, can you? I don't want more of the same-old mental health system. They say the treatment of the mind consists of bio-psycho-social-spiritual, but all I've ever gotten is just bio-bio-bio-bio. My life is too precious to give it to people who want to treat me like that. Give us some space where we can sort this all out. I don't want to be somebody's patient. I want to be somebody's neighbor," Jude said.

"Jude, I agree with that," Tate said.

"But you push for the exact opposite! And you say you are funded independently of pharmaceutical companies, but none of this is true! I know how it works. The whole world of advocacy takes funding from pharmaceutical companies! I read that individuals with my experiences in developing countries live with less severe pain than I do. And it's not like these people have drugs or psychiatry. They go about their lives in their communities, and the state of development in these places is such that they have something to do with their lives that contributes to the community. Fancy that—having a community and contributing to it! I'm a damned expendable in America, and I know it!" Jude said.

The security guards had been waiting on the edge of Jude's row and nodded to one another to intervene. Jude railed on anyway. "I'm expendable to its economy and I'm expendable to its social life! I've seen some of my strongest friends end up as modern-day lepers. They don't want us anywhere. Our lives are defined by having a label of serious mental illness, and yet if we want a chance to be integrated, either we've got to be lucky enough to find the handful of people who don't care, or we've got to hide it forever!"

The security guard grabbed Jude by the arm and started to usher her away. "Have at it, sir! It's nothing new! And it's not like I wasn't able to get along in the world. I could have done perfectly well. So my father beat me up a little, and I was a bit too into the spirit of the sixties, and I got a little reckless in the head—go figure! I guess I had to be locked up. And they put me in the ward and I lived in the hospital for a bit. Then one day I got out, and the people I knew before didn't want anything to do with me. The shame of being in the institution was too much for them to look at. I was a nobody. And that's been the story to this day! My spouse left. I live on public assistance, and they give me less and less of it each year. I can never have more than two thousand dollars in my account or they'll kick me off of supports."

By now Jude was resolutely ignored, and willfully escorting herself out alongside the guards. The board was moving forward with a vote. "All in favor," the administrator started.

Jude persisted. "I'm always on drugs, and they've made me fat and slow. Oh yes, I used to be thin…"

She squirmed from the guards' grip and faced the room for one last grandstand.

"Oh, I've had decisions made for me. ECT: that made me less sad, sure, but it also made me a lot dumber. Haldol: the chemical straightjacket, like pouring cement into your veins. The padded room, the physical straightjacket. And you'd never take into account that I know this better than you do. And now we're out here and you're still trying to find ways to control us. Forty years of psychiatry and I've never been made better, nor do I think it has learned anything about itself.

As though in a mania, Jude exited the hall faster than I've ever seen her move. I followed behind and grabbed her bag.

"Jude, we are going to miss the results of the vote," I said.

"It doesn't matter. There are sixty of them and two of us. The vote is counted for."

We went outside, the wind hitting Jude and blowing her jacket open. "Jesus Christ, the whole world hates me," she said.

"Be still, Jude, I'll get the car." I jogged to the parking lot, paid the fifty-dollar fee, and sped back to get Jude. I helped her into the car, and then laughed when I got back in the driver's seat.

"At least that felt good, though, right?" I asked.

"I admit that it was fun at parts," she said.

"I've never seen that side of you before! And to think just this morning you wanted to die!" I said.

"Your old Jude is still here. I'm still certain I'll still take death over this however."

"But you're laughing."

"It's a bizarre world when you're caught in the mental health system. You may as well have a laugh about it."

"Do you think you changed anyone's mind at all?"

"No dear, we're screwed. Everyone in that room is in agreement. I know it. They'll vote to send us away and then fight over how to get money for their agencies while Tate sets his agenda."

"All of them?"

"Every last one."

"So, what's next?"

"Next? I die and hold you responsible for changing the world."

"Don't be callous."

"Just drive me home. We'll get back to work tomorrow."

I pulled up to the curb in front of Jude's apartment, and said to her on her way out, "You know your work is going to carry on, right? You may not see it, but we'll take it one day and do something with it. You set a precedent, you set principles. I'm going to follow that, and others will catch the fire."

"I don't believe that's true at all. I'll go and I'll leave nothing behind me. It's predetermined, we've known it for a long time."

"That's not true."

She got out of the car and walked to her door. An unexpected cold front came through the afternoon over sunless, incurable Chicago, and the light rain had turned into sleet. I watched her walk against the welts of the downfall until she fidgeted her way through the old door into the lobby of her apartment. Then I drove away.

I somewhat expected her to be dead the next morning, but then I had long felt death to be hours away, and a new morning has always come. I knew she wouldn't be convinced that her life was not a waste. In an abstract, transhistorical way, I know that her existence would influence life in ways she could not recognize, even generations into the future. There was nothing I could do to help her see that.

When I watched Jude burst from that hall, I opted on near impulse to get off my psychiatric drugs and pursue a freer life, one that did not feel consistently dependent on a product that made me feel hollow. My first attempts were unsuccessful. I panicked and I hallucinated. I spent hours in bed and missed assignments, and I had to get back on my dose. It took a couple of months of pill-cutting and gradual weaning before I was finally off. When I had no more drugs to take, it was like stepping into my original madness and understanding it in a different way. It was like I could have gone back to age nineteen and everything would have been different, if I had only had a different set of ideas about it, a different response, a different world. While I was creeping back into that place, I wrote a lot of long rants onto my computer, because warm people cannot truly know what it was like to be freezing, and there would be a time when I'd have to remember what instability felt like. I revisit those sometimes, when I need to be reminded of what it was once like to be resentful, defeatist, utopian, dystopian, suicidal, grandiose, bold, ecstatic, contradictory, fickle, and paranoid, all in a psychic conglomerate. It reminded me that there were still days after certain death, and the unseen hope in seemingly hopeless settings. What Jude always said was that there are false promises and false prophets, but there is no such thing as false hope. She clearly didn't actually believe it herself. It was a lie she told herself to keep moving. And very few believed it of her. But she said it anyway. Probably for reassurance, to convince herself not to die when life seemed vain. I've used these long rants as a similar form, to remind myself of the sense of possibility and spontaneity that is concealed in pointless suffering, and the potential it holds to change the individual. Every time I think it is the end, I come back to the writing. Much of it I later delete in embarrassment and never wish to see again. Some I edit, and some I even send to others. And some I let sit, because doses of unalloyed insanity can be redemptive and life-affirming, and do not always need intervention from an ostensibly rational force.

What a life. My loneliness is getting severe, and most of the people in my life who I see don't change this fact. I cannot determine whether the fault is theirs or mine. The likeliest case is that it's nobody's fault. It just is, and we weren't meant to be around one another at this given time. It's sorrowful. My most regular social encounters consist of the banalities of American life—the luster of reality television, the dimness of a bar on Friday, where one of my old acquaintances prattles on about her problems and doesn't particularly care to hear any of mine, withstanding advances from simple, unfunny men.

I tune out from my fantasies of a kinder world and try to play the game along with the rest, and I often wind up more disheartened than before, bordering on dysfunction, with spite on my mind and pain in my stomach. What's most striking is how little they really know about me, how dual-consciousness exists so covertly nobody has to identify it unless I am visibly insane. I talk about mental health and they think it's out of sympathy for crazy people. They don't properly understand me as crazy myself. I wonder what things would be like if they did. Without some grand, elaborate outing, I suppose the full details of madness will always be out of perception for them, just as their versions of insanity are tightly concealed from me, and any latent prejudices or fantasies they carry about the matter will never strike me with their true force. Anything beyond a superficial identification would probably seem to them like garden-variety depression, not the truly psychotic form. They always look confused when I suggest otherwise, and they correct me, "No, you are not crazy like them." Like them, bah. Who is this ominous "they" you are setting aside? Who is this part of humanity that is not like us? And to what ends? But yes. I know who I am, and I am most certainly one of them. And whether you acknowledge it or not, I am one of you as well. And there ought to be nothing I should have to explain to you about it, nor anything to have hidden from you for so long. And yet here we are: me standing nakedly before you under a light on a dark stage, a posed model vulnerable both to pelting and reverence, and you confused about what to think of it. Because perhaps nobody has ever told you that you can decide for yourself where to draw the line on what you do and do not look at, and you can look at the whole of a person, and not just the parts of her you are comfortable with. Not just what you see selectively, or how you want to see her, but for who she is in whole. And for how she understands herself.

At least I am at a place where I feel I have personally transcended this part of my identity, and these lingering social bothers have less and less meaning to me. Once it seemed loaded with negativity, because that is what the world put into it, and when I became aware of it, I could not see anything but hostility in other people. I became separatist and reclusive. Then, in formulating a response to this psychologically benighted hand, madness seemed loaded with super-human possibility. I believed that my suffering somehow elevated my humanity in a way that others could not achieve, that it gave me insight into the world others could not access by their own experience. But that is a merely a lie the frustrated and the unwell tell themselves to cope with their misery and restore themselves to a more stable state, a way to glamorize misery and make oneself more important than they actually are. But now none of that is significant. I am Ellen "Boo" Harvey because that is who I am. And you are who you are, and that is a fine starting point for our interaction. Unless you give me a reason to, I'd like to read no more complexity into it.

If not for my parents' money, I would be anywhere, probably on a commune close to nature or in a simple life. Because of the money, and because of its power, I am tied to something else. Something in the loose genre of a Robin Hood life; there was never any rationale to a trust fund but to be born into it, no claim to affluence by worth or merit, only by the happenstance of birth. And in an epidemic of debilitating loneliness and compromised dreams, in a planet that appears fated to become unlivable, I have a choice to make that wealth a point of resistance and work with others to create an existence in which peace is politically possible. I choose to who and to what that goes to. There is a three-hundred-trillion-dollar transfer of wealth from boomer to millennial transpiring over the coming decades, and the inheritors should understand themselves as actors within a world degrading to spiritual and ecological death. The decision of who to align with and why is a crucial one, and I do not dismiss that responsibility even slightly. I have chosen this tragic American city as the place to let that life play out; building community, provoking new possibilities for social engagement across truculent boundaries, claiming the offensive for the soul of my country in a way that has so far been the exclusive craft of false patriots. My primary role in this affair will be that of a coincidental patron to would-be revolution, if I am welcomed as such. Or a cultural warrior, or even a genuine leader of people. Or, perhaps, there is an even greater role I cannot envision right now, or none at all. Whatever the future may be, for the present, I am here, even if the city seems to be crushing me, and there is no exit but to toil over these questions.

I stare into my apartment often thinking about all of this. The books are stacking higher and higher. They used to be how I kept myself interested in life, the library being my place of respite, the only place kind enough for me to feel healed. As I write this, I realize this sounds like the child without friends. Perhaps it's why so many adults read more with age. Community stretches apart, life becomes a solitary venture, and the depressives who could never command your interest in youth suddenly speak to your experience of the world. What does it say of me that I've already outgrown the depressives? How old am I? Am I approaching a way out?

I've had a nearly constant feeling of apocalypse for months now. Not only do I see the end of my own life, I see the end of life for everyone close to me. I see the dead end of humanity and the fall of the American empire. It's with me almost all of the time. In my earliest depressions, I imagined myself dying young, and I was incapable of contemplating an alternative and believing it to be possible. I knew I would not live beyond the age of thirty, and imagining grandchildren, green pastures, and blue skies was a virtual impossibility. Now I have the same premonition of destruction, only on a larger scale. We're all in for tremendous downfall, and I cannot imagine a world beyond 2050 that has not devolved into some combination of barbarity, political extremism, mass migration, corporate feudalism, and chaotic anarchism. I cannot ignore it. I want to escape, but I understand this is more futile than anything else, so I accept it and, for the time being, carry on as usual.

I have been ranting and repeating myself because I've been trying to wean off my meds. I've decided to walk into the world free of drugs and accept the disorientation for what it is. I embrace the erratic aspects of living without any form of psychiatric regulation. If my thinking isn't clear to the world, then the world will have to learn to deal with it. It would only be the reciprocation of a principle, what with me putting up with it for so long. If I seem loopy, then I don't need to feel like an Other for it. No need to let the consciousness of dual-consciousness disturb me from appreciating what is right in front of me. Rather, I can assure them they're missing out on something I find tremendous value in. Madness gives me a cultural voice anyway. Something human, something for a country of pluralist difference and varieties of minds. Have I argued to the opposite before? Ah well, all is contradiction.

Normal is nothing. It has no significance, no flavor, nor any bend toward an ideal other than itself. It is bastardized of soul and ecstasy. And yet, paradoxically, normal is everywhere; it's at once an unreal concept and a core organizing point for reality. What if there was a reality where normal ceases to have meaning? Might madness be a disturbing point to assumptions of "normal"? Jude comes from a Jewish tradition that seeks truth, and I can see that in the way she discusses her family and what they stand for. Yet I have no such tradition to rest on, save that of commerce — the reduction of children's creative interests and unalloyed joys to an input into business. In pointless scenarios, madness allows me an exit from the anomie underneath that existence, to reclaim imagination and feeling where the air is insipid and the mind is stodgy.

Sometimes the feeling is refreshing in a sadistic way. It reminds me of all of the useless years and the nervous, vulgar hours I spent between the ages of nineteen and twenty-four, often dumb, disabled, drunk, or all those things at the same time. It reminds me of those days when the depression was thick and soporific, and I could feel it running through my veins. I would take total refuge in the public library, bemused by the art and the knowledge I was surrounded by. I've become so political and concerned with the world on the ground that I've forgotten what it is like to let a mind wander through the world of fiction, how those idle joys are purer than anything I get from human contact or fighting with the flaws of my time.

This evening I went to the art institute and took asylum there, and then did the same in Millennium Park. Both of them are safeguards from the inward-looking, thwarted lens that has been threatening me and compelling me to shout obscenities in the street. I loved the expressions in the photographs in the basement of the museum, full of more history and intention than the unsuspecting subject intends, and the way the buildings on Michigan Avenue look when the sun is setting beyond them, glowing with a ferocious streak of the sun's paintbrush across their fronts. I love the music of the children's choir at the park, singing rhythm and blues as though it were a cosmic realization of God, with a warm organ guiding the homily. The sounds of the families in the park had me feeling that pockets of heaven are attainable and that I can be an occasional participant in the sublime. I love how my senses are so responsive I can just sit and stop thinking and feel to be a part of a singular being with these actors. I can't forget this is also a part of my nature, that there are gentle voices alongside the rabid ones, and we carry the propensity to nurture and be exuberant as well as the capacity for avarice and violence. The art brings that out of my madness and reminds me how pleasant it can be to depart from reality.

Sometimes I have moments of ease like this, as I imagine dying people experience a state of flow even as their life dissipates before them, much like that sweet shot of the Pacific Ocean before my hallucinated death, before the confinement of eternity ensues. Then my contentment falls apart, and I'm pulled toward one of the many poles of the mind; either into bursting, meaningless laughter or into all-consuming, self-deprecating shame. It's a light, mercurial, inconsequential life I lead when I am like this. I get back into the world of dirty social glances and avoidant behavior, with everyone looking at me for a peculiar, hostile reason. I am constantly looked at, always being inspected for something trivial I cannot figure out. I feel the need to get away from all of them, to have nothing to do with them, and get back with the books and the music and be safe, protected.

Someone asked me the other day if I was single. I laughed at them and said, "Single is such a cute euphemism. I'm alone." Sometimes I forget about Mark and sometimes I do not. He treats me like I don't exist, and that makes me feel insignificant in a way that I only thought children could be broken when they are rejected. I sometimes wonder what he is doing on the West Coast. He doesn't have a roommate or friends, and he could barely keep his orders neat when I dated him. When I do think of him, my guess is he's for the most part living in isolated squalor and drinking more casually, much like myself. I can picture him having drinks and laughing with some girl who isn't worth half of her weight; an easy type, soft on the eyes, unchallenging on the mind, and invariably much better at sex than me. And he tells her that every time they fuck, "You're much better than Boo." But then, I knew who he was, and I knew he was leaving. The reason our time went as well as it did, while we had it, was because we had no future together, and could therefore forfeit any anxieties about responsibility, accountability, and whatever else it is that keeps people from participating in life in the present with one another. Perhaps I should do that far more in my life — accept there is no present without abandoning a concept of the future, in which we will all inevitably be dead and, perhaps very soon, burnt out.

I have dated a few men recently, all of whom are technically interesting, yet almost none whom I feel very interested in, or have even spent a night with. One is a musician, a violinist from Harvard who works in financial analytics or some other well-paying buzzword industry to support his musical career. He's lavishly well versed, and when he speaks he alludes to philosophy and literature. Maybe I'm prone to this fantastical type of seduction, but he does not strike me as too pretentious. I'd usually think of men who lead with this kind of intelligence as taking themselves too seriously. It's very quick and often exhilarating — even through my fog — and with him I often feel like I'm being intellectually lifted from the lewd, weary earth on which I live. He's bisexual and confident, and as I keep describing him he sounds like a symbol of free love, beauty, and art for art's sake. In many ways, he's the ideal. And yet, I don't really give a shit about him. It's strange. The feeling I get from him is more like that feeling I get from being in a museum. He's an artistic escape, and I know I cannot live in that space in the longer-term. He appears apart from the people who inhabit our era in its most honest expressions, and those are the people I want to be with. You could say he's the poetic, and my concept of beauty in less insane times is prosaic: grounded, raunchy, struggling, fighting, imperfect, brilliant, and tragic. I don't fall in love with "the art" or "the artist." My beauty is a teacher who stays in a benighted place and does so with poise. And I'll lurk this grungy earth until I find that.

It's not just romance. I feel this way about everything. The further from the ground, the less I'm inclined to feel comfortable with it. It's a little prejudice I've picked up. I see my peers from the North Shore and from college go into various high-end sectors, all of them seemingly influential, and they talk about weekends in LA and contracts in San Francisco and trips to East Asia. Yet when I converse with them, I don't feel as though anything is being done. I easily forget the soul of the people as they reveal it to me, outside of buildings with lanyards, research, and market exchanges. I mostly see self-aggrandizement in it—a harsh bias of mine, no doubt. The young people in these lucrative settings seem disconnected from any sense of humility and realness. They talk about themselves incessantly, who they saw, where they saw them, the concerts they went to, their teams, their alma maters, their jobs, their assessment of the global economy, and their bizarre confidence that things will turn out all right. Almost like professional teenagers, always straining about how to be perceived the right way. It's all perfectly human, I suppose, but I also observe there is an eternal Jones to keep up with, and that is half the reason for my insanity in the first place. How does the outsider fit in? Of course, the mere concept of an outsider implies that someone is not supposed to fit in. The only universal community is one in which everyone accepts their own status as an outsider and solidarity amongst outsiders.

I despair often, in many settings, because one person is only capable of small deeds, and small deeds feel hopeless before large systems. Until that is changed, until there is something more peaceful, less self-interested in place with that Mad community, I'll probably always feel comforted by the idea of drowning. I need love, honestly, and I need it incorporated into all parts of my life. In its absence, I invoke these exhausting high ideals to guide my time: continuing a tradition of my home, education in a new land, political identification with mental illness, intoxicated disaffection, work and advocacy, mindless conformity, finding restoration with the crimes of my heritage, total abjection, mockery of the ignorance of power. And I do it all terribly. But all of that is a vacuous farce if there is no love, all of it is but a masturbatory touch to make life seem more important than it is.

I spend most of my time in isolation, but I am grateful for it. People are corrupting. When you spend time with them, you become corrupted. You pick up their standards, their distaste for others, and their arrogance. You look away from the things they look away from and care about what they care about. No, I take that back. Isolation is miserable. It's like an afterlife. You spend all of your time thinking about how you've carried yourself, always reaching into the past and saying, "Everything would be different, if only . . ." my schooling had been different, I'd had a first boyfriend earlier, or I wasn't so heavily influenced by the Church. It's endless self-reflection. I need other people. I've got thoughts stampeding within me, and I'm not sure which ones to believe. They come from every dimension of the mind in no logical order. At least I have my independence. I may be miserable, but at least I am not an ass. Ah, getting off meds. I'm getting there again. I wonder how long I'll be there. I never tell anyone just how often I think of dying. I don't think many people understand a mindset where this happens, and don't know how to respond to it. I fear a response of hysteria. I fear that my autonomy will be questioned and my personal control may be taken away. I fear that others believe that when I question whether life is worth living, I prove to them that I do not understand life, and that I am therefore not worthy of having a free one. But if suicide is the fundamental question of philosophy, then by now I must have garnered some insight. Maybe she who has not dealt with the question suicide does not appropriately understand what makes life worth living, though that may be another statement of overcompensation.

I cannot fault anyone for not knowing what it's like to be me. I can only fault them when I try to tell them what my world is like and they treat me with one-sided interrogation and abuse anyway, or when they willfully deny the reality of my pain, or treat me as an afterthought while simultaneously treating others with fawning interest. It is neither a crime to experience madness nor to have not experienced it. From the standpoint of a person's character, these are neutral qualities that only become positive or negative once we apply social and personal meaning to them. They tell you nothing about the individual other than that she feels one way or does not feel it, or that through some combination of personal predisposition, environment, and experience, she became Mad. This should garner your sympathy and attention, for it could tell you very important things about the world. Instead, we often treat it as though it does not exist, and as though Mad individuals are to be ignored and cut out of social life. Because of this, I've been drifting toward ideas of psychiatric abolition. I used to not know what people meant when they talked about abolition, but I'm beginning to comprehend it. In abolishing psychiatry, we abolish other people's ability to claim authority over other people's suffering and shape lives of isolation and dependency around it. That's a fundamentally backward way to deal with distress, and there's little reason to trust a social institution that makes these qualities a part of its bedrock. People get locked away, disrespected, denied love, put into "treatments" that are said to be safe but often turn harmful, and returned into a world in which they understand that speaking carries the risk of further discrimination. By abolishing psychiatry, I wish to rearrange society to integrate people deemed "mentally ill" like anyone else, lest we wish to keep them in a position parallel to that of asylum patients. The folly of deinstitutionalization was that while many were set free, too many were cast into a comparable marginality, either by communities that wouldn't accept them or by other institutions that would, like nursing homes or jails or prisons. The community project is not complete, and I don't want to be a part of any of this. I have been close to its crosshairs long enough. I'm getting off the drugs to get away from the disease model, because I don't have a disease. I have a life.

There are times when I feel like being bitter, but I am too old for that now. Bitterness is a trap that evil wants you to fall into. It blurs everyone who I view as luckier than me into a single hostile entity, and in this part of the mind, one will always feel slighted, ignored, patronized, and cheated. I was often bitter when I was younger, sometimes with good reason. The people on TV said I was going to shoot schoolchildren. Neighbors thought I was a fuckup. Old friends would not even look at me. People told me that the only jobs I could manage were those of menial labor and pitiful financial compensation. I was angry and scorned, but if I did not learn to grow beyond that personally then it was remarkably difficult to hold the life I needed for survival. But here I am, bound up in a hyper-delicate state, made worse by a large, accessible memory bank. Individual, neutral words bring me back to moments when I said something ignorant, backward, or offensive; and I mean truly meaningless words, without any inherent invective. When I hear them today, I'm often brought right back to the moment of humiliation. I've been punishing myself for years for statements that others have forgiven and forgotten, and I don't know how to get rid of them. I'm always in this crooked space of memory in which I understand myself by my dumbest and most reprehensible minutes. I don't know what to do but rebel against them in whatever form that may take. Resentment and bitterness offer no exit. At best they bear testament to my anger, but beyond that, little can be accomplished with them.

I want a space where I can think freely and listen freely, and where others aren't talking over me, where I never have to hide my pain for their comfort. I want a space where the impulses toward kindness and creativity are felt in the air, and where the responsibility of being a have in a world of have-nots isn't stretching my guilt toward numerous severe places at once. In this space, my past stops ridiculing me. Work is done for the craft of it and for constructive social reproduction—an Aristotelian simple life defined equally by deriving as much meaning from one's profession as from one's relationships. I can simply be and nobody will try to disturb me under the thought that their need for entertainment and attention demands my foremost concern. And if I need to shout, I can run into a field and bellow the weeds out of the ground. We will stop pretending the wealthy nations of the world don't owe rest a sweeping, long-term commitment to reparations, nor that our own nation doesn't owe it to the ancestors of slaves and to the indigenous populations of this land. There will be no human without a home, nor without the needed care for their ailments. All places hold access and recognition of both body, mind, and feeling, and love without shame or discrimination. There will be redemption for past harms and the understanding to prevent future ones. Note that none of this can happen without a reorganization of power and forgiveness for the wrongs of the past, and a bold vision pursued without apology or the compromise of dignity.

Alas, when anyone else says I am a hopeless, Mad idealist, they are correct. In an honest mania, I have an obnoxiously quixotic emotional life, but feel as though I must pack it into a tight, limited space in order to speak to anyone. When it is released, it comes in quick spurts and quickly returns to dirt. My hands shake. I am always moving. I go on ten-mile runs without thinking, write two thousand words in a single breath, never motionless. While many generations have believed themselves to be the last, ours may make it true. I could stand from the mountaintop and speak truth to power today. Tomorrow, I cower in weakness. A changed world would save me from this fate, but they tell me this is too much to ask for. Instead, I became addicted to drugs. In return, I get a marginally better emotional state, but I can never get off the drugs without hell to pay. If I try to get off, I face confusion, agitation, violently suicidal thoughts, nightmares, tremors, sweating, vertigo, fatigue, anxiety, physical imbalance, brain zaps, sensory disturbances, and nausea, with few other means for emotional release. I see things that aren't there and I entertain delusion. And in less oppressive moments, I feel weightless and fantasize of utopia. The grandeur takes me to cosmic places. The impermanence of everything I do and everything I say is made bare by the possibility that we may not even have a habitable world by the end of my life. What is all of my internecine squabbling compared to the ultimate question of suicide? And how can all of these conflicts be resolved at once?

All of this considered, to hell with the cynics. There is a fine line between saying "things cannot be changed" and "do not bother trying." I understand why they think this way because I was once amongst them. "The problem is too big," I'd say. "There's no hope, no chance, don't bother." In between then and now I've been branded with the meaning of "no hope." Unlike the cynics, I understand how much better the effort is than the alternative. I ramble in mania, but I also have to keep asking about things like this, even if I feel like I am the only one. I must ask what fearing and shaming suicide and suicidal thoughts reflect about society. The truth may be too damning—that we are willing to avoid confrontation with our own mortality because it is too depressing, and we are too craven to handle reality. It may be that our collective interest isn't about what makes life worth living, but is something entirely detached from that question—a more basic, Darwinian approach to survival, like preserving power and wealth in a struggle against others who are doing the same. I may even go as far to say that if we cut off respect to another person beyond an arbitrary point of suffering, particularly psychological suffering, then this reflects that we don't actually care about life and about being human. But at the present moment, I don't know how to explain that in depth. Like many things, I feel it to be true without knowing how to adequately say so.

I must ask what it says about a society that deals with mental sufferers this abjectly. This truth too may be too damning. Is it a crime to be in pain? Do we only know how to punish? These aren't easy questions to ask. The structure of sanism has long gone largely unacknowledged and unquestioned, except for by a relative underground of individuals who call themselves survivors. Even as I go through various radical texts, I hear almost nothing about these people, nor the word sanism. And that's a great loss. What sanism reveals about the world are central questions about spirituality in our world, about reason and rationality, how we treat those who are in more pain than us, or who deviate from us ideologically. Are these not some of the most important issues of a community—how a variety of minds can contribute to a single human, aspirational whole? I've learned that once you are diagnosed in the system, a part of you is defined by it. You can never lay a valid claim to sanity again, for even a single episode makes that suspect. You must learn to carry the social weight of being in the mental health system. And in whatever part you're in, be it in drugs, therapy, or nursing homes, it never really wants to let you out.

Some of us are told that we will never get out and never get better. Contrary to what they said, we do, and it has little to do with their prescriptions and their treatment. We find other paths. We detour. We look for answers in unconventional places, and we find them. I read of a town in a faraway country, in which they are welcoming of the mentally atypical and hospitable to those we call "mad." The Mad there are tolerated, recognized, and spoken to—far from the shunning that occurs here, where we cannot talk of it for what it is. And that keeps us Mad in perpetuity, when all that is required is reconciliation between one another. This is how we deal with the deviants, and this is what we call civilization. We don't know what they can teach us. We don't realize how we are limiting ourselves.

I still don't know where madness comes from. Some may say it is the natural result of a world that values power and wealth over love and community, while the individual existence becomes both more alone and more depersonalized. I have said that often, but it is narrow to consider that alone. I don't profess to know the mind, or the soul, or the heart. Even as I know anguish firsthand, I can only conjecture. I cannot know the origin of these things. I don't know why people suffer. I don't know where it is rooted: in the body, in the home, in the school, in the country. In obstinate rant, I have decided that it comes from the fundamental structure of society and a person's experience within it: how that person has been beaten and shaped, either in a few large blows or in several little blows over a long period of time. It could also be rooted in the mere fact that we exist. I do not know what all of this is about, and I do not know what the best system for the mind looks like. I'd say we shouldn't have a system at all, but a community where aberrance is not a point of drastic consequence. But that's hardly a practical approach.

You may say, "Outline to me the alternative or do not criticize the present." I cannot always do this. My imagination for a new world is a work in development, and the present is too imposing not to be screamed at. I lack the spare hours to develop an alternative, and I admit I'm intimidated by what is before me. It reproduces endless defeatism. As the great bomb warped the psyche of an entire generation toward immediate, compulsive anxiety — trading long-term trust and safety for short, ceaseless pleasures — so the prospects of the extinctions in my time is altering the scope of our minds. We grow older as individuals, but the duration of the future decreases. For every day we live, the expected end of times happens a day sooner. Like a portrait burning on all perimeters, the magnificence is destined for disappearance from the memory of the universe. And it is difficult to move and think within these constraints. At some point those two meet at history's greatest contradiction: there is no future to inhabit, no memory of what came before, but there is life nonetheless, and humanity will cope. And what awaits us there may well create new, pervasive forms of madness that we have never experienced.

It is not important in the moment that I do not know what a world after this looks like. It is important that I pursue it anyway, and that I and everyone else with a stake in a new world take part in shaping a system they want to live in. When we don't ask, that is when we die. If I'm being honest with myself, what I advocate for is Revolution. Although "Revolution" is a rhetorical ploy. I do not know how to paint with detail a sustainable vision of a world in which all life flourishes. Partly this is due to a shortcoming of conviction, and partly because humanity seems locked into so many trends that we cannot escape from flourishing's opposite.

We have long been driven by imperatives of production and competition, and reprioritizing these imperatives against those of connection and sustenance is too radical to implement. And that is part of the bind: the way of the world as we know it has always been there, and it has been the burden of posterity to inherit and solve what their ancestors could not reconcile. It has been the burden of the young to give meaning to historical suffering, to amend for historical atrocity, and to transfer mass disaffection into a sustainable way of life for all. So far, none have accomplished this, and all have eventually accepted selfishness and resignation. Whatever amendment comes will not come in total, only in art, personal testament, and the reparations and relationships of the few individuals stubborn enough to resist the intransigence of history. That is all that is realistic to expect, lest the hallucination of an unidentifiable afterlife allow us a deeper peace with our tragedies.

Of course, as a depressive, that's all I'm going to see in my future. I see a world in which a majority of the human species lives on either nothing, in indentured corporate servitude, or in a makeshift bohemia, as surplus wealth asserts that it is a luxury for just a chosen few. The slums of the second or third world will grow to amazing proportions, with the military presence of the declining American empire overseeing its business in the near background and radicalizing young men into terrorism. America will then have to deal with the consequences of its aggression against these people with homeland attacks, and America, like a true abuser, will go in for more war. Cities will go underwater, both at home and abroad. Disease the likes of which we have never encountered will spread through our health infrastructures like handshakes. And so cataclysmically on, and so cataclysmically forth.

Meanwhile, many of us will persist in solipsistic localities in which the only problems and the only life are those that are most immediate, and revolutionary fervor never gets more practical or fulfilling than an embarrassing coffee date. Our corruption and our wounds are interminable facets of our lives and perpetuate an environment that overrides our capacity to even speak to new forms of socio-political-economic organization, or to the insurmountability of mass death within our lifetimes. Barring transformation, it will continue to devolve that way. We will try to maintain some semblance of a good life, even as we understood that this had long ago been compromised for us by forces that placed us wholly outside of consideration. To pass this onto my child would be to assume for her the responsibility of saving humanity against multiple leviathans, each with the capacity to induce the end of civilization before she is old enough to have a child. I would do everything to maintain for her areas of respite and love, so as to mitigate the angst of the fractured, impaired consciousness we expected her to carry on our behalf. Anything less would be selfish and unforgivable.

Yes, the prospect of the future as I see it is mercilessly violent, and in return I cannot imagine a violent response to the systems binding us to it that will not be suppressed by stronger, more brutal forces. Another reason I say "Revolution" is because I believe that the mass human despair in the face of these morbid ends is as good of a fact to organize humanity around as any. It is like asking, once more, the central question of philosophy — to be or not to be — on a profound level: is it better to give into the slow-death suicide of the world, or can we reclaim the potential for human flourishing? The depressive realist in me says that we are already the living dead, always being pushed inside our- selves, and conversing with our own trivial personal phantoms as life and history dissipate around us. As the prophets say, the apocalypse is easier to envision than any fundamental change in how humans coexist, and the point when that became definite is when we became a haunted species, the cerebral dinosaurs of the solar system. If my personal saving is my best interest, I'd remove myself from the fate of the world altogether, laugh and drink as I'm lit to fire, pursue sublimity through sex and art and intimate camaraderie, and wash myself of any sense of obligation to postpone the downfall. On some days, however, I live outside of this gloom, and I hypothesize glorious movement against our collective suicide, in which we complete the mass spiritual epiphany and realize the location of our distress, their madness, and their psychosis in the death of the world—a condition that is mutual in any relationship. This then sets new principles: to confirm life with a secure future, liberty with social recognition and accountability, and the pursuit of happiness amounting to spiritual flourishing as inalienable human rights, and to achieve this through the revelation of a common human soul and a civilization organized around those principles. To do this requires the abolition of bourgeoisie influence over human life, the release of human relationships from the apathy of commodity, and the replacement of them with relationships of nurturing and equity. Such a world is neither dependent on coercion, nor overburdened with dispositions that sneer at the notion that individuals should not live in neglect nor in necessary detachment from one other. To do as much would be to realize a shared fate amongst bitter, segmented factions, and perhaps translate into a real upheaval of social priorities and lasting comfort. The cure, if you can call it that, becomes the pursuit of great happiness in spite of the end of times and the erosion of human bonds to abysmal alienation. If such a thing is remotely possible, that is my revolution of the mind. Anything else will be but another fantasy to pass my time.

CHAPTER 10

A Long Time After

Contrary to the insinuations of colloquial American English, I do not feel sorry for myself. Rather, I believe that life is too painful to live, which isn't the same thing.

I cannot bear this. It is all around me. I'm sleepless and jaded all of the time. Everything is a hammer ready to pound me, every encounter I interpret through jaundiced eyes. I sincerely cannot look at anything without wanting to withdraw and run away. With every act, there is a mental backlash exponentially greater that fills me with disgust, shame, and anguish. How is one to live if even cleaning the dishes is a psychologically disabling chore, over which the ghosts of my life haunt me?

For months now, too many months to count, I feel as if I have been looking into a wall. All is malignant, all is without hope. I don't know where I learned the good faith to keep living, as though trying to act against it will accomplish anything.

I am often called a pessimist because I say things like this: that things are hopeless. I'm told I'm looking at life the wrong way, but I don't think those who say this understand the rightful context of what I am talking about. They must see that I am not a pessimist because I feel that I am walking into a wall. They must see that I am an optimist because I keep moving anyway.

I've learned a lot about the toils of the mind and the spirit. I was never prepared for it, never schooled in it. It's futile, Sisyphean. But I persist, for there is no alternative from it. Except to choose to die, which would be both to opt for the ultimate freedom and accept the ultimate defeat.

I drain myself in my efforts. Everything is exhausting, so, so damned exhausting. It's difficult to see if even trying will get me any closer to a normal place again. But then, it was a lie that trying was enough. The soul and the mind don't work the same as the body. If I did twenty sit-ups today, I would know tomorrow that I did it. But the mind isn't the same. Concentration is important. Retention is important. Comprehension is important. And too often all of this is disabled for me, and my thinking is cracked and fleeting. There is no way to communicate at an adult standard like this. How am I ever going to have work that requires thought? Though I may read twenty pages, it may feel tomorrow as though I've read none at all. Even as I read, there is little but a blot of meaningless words in front of me, and it takes all of my scarce energy to maintain attention on them. I remain disabled, only able to jot my thoughts when the maelstrom settles for some time at the end of the day and my setting is peaceful. Often this is with music, and without having to deal with anyone else.

Everything I see, feel, think, and say must be permeated through the thickness of my psyche and the hold it has on my body. I have come this far, railing and willing myself against this thickness to learn this: it is impermeable. Like the American Dream of the mind, trying does not guarantee any outcome. The conditions upon me are too great to be overcome by will, and I often worsen myself when I insist otherwise.

My Depression is psychotic at most times. In waking hours, as in the visions that haunt me in sleep, I feel consummately worthless, unloved, invalidated, and unrecognized. None of that is at all true, yet I'm bound to revisionism in memory that rescripts the whole of my past, to interpret myself as both a tremendous personal failure and a stain on humanity in general.

I don't know how to keep "passing," a concept I have borrowed from queer language, as none of this is apparent to others without disclosing as much. And what would I gain if I did so? It would only make things more troublesome, and make the double-consciousness, a concept I have borrowed from race langue, more neurotic. I'm already in a hard, separatist place as it is, as I cannot trust anyone to be moved into sympathy for me, let alone acknowledge me. The personal work involved in managing a sane front with an insane interior grates me to obliteration, and often I want to submit into a ditch and call it to rest.

I don't know what else to do but keep moving and say as much to somebody, anybody who can be trusted.

I've had to accept that psychological hell is neither a result of my character or my choices, nor can it be undone by such means. This hell is beyond one's choosing. What's worse, I have made a wretched failure of myself trying to prove otherwise.

I live at home with my parents now. For a while, it was not clear whether or not I would receive a college degree. Because my grades were so low during senior year, my major GPA fell below the 2.0 threshold required to receive a degree. I failed all of my classes during those last Mad months, getting a 0.0 for the term. Without discarding the Fs I received in that last quarter, I will not be able to pull my GPA above that level with the university. My parents have been negotiating with the university about dropping the grades from my transcript. The hope is that they will allow for extenuating circumstances based on mental illness, and pardon the 0.0 quarter so I can make up the requirements at local universities and get a degree.

It's a complicated, political question. The university's policy is that courses can be excused if a student had mental health issues that significantly hindered her ability to be a full-time student, but this request is only possible during the quarter in which the student was ill. If a student approaches the university before, say, halfway through the quarter and has proof of serious mental health problems, the university will allow the student to withdraw from the course and her transcript will not be impacted. If she continues through the class with a mental health problem and then receives grades such as the ones I have, those grades will not be pardoned, because she did not reach out to the university soon enough. I laugh at this, sometimes. Whatever happened on campus where I would have been wise to tell anyone that? For personal, social, or ideological reasons that I'm still trying to sort out, I would have never reached out to do this.

I'm very hard on myself for it. I accept full responsibility and full agency for how college happened, and I don't believe the university should be required to make an exception for me. I'm a rich kid—the world has always been making exceptions for me, even when I am a failure. Often that seems to be the only way to start the conversation—to say there were no factors at play outside of those I had command over. The university had its rules, and by choosing to attend the university, I agreed to them, even if there was so much I didn't know about the university's disability policy and mental health, or about mental health at all.

My father thinks that the university is being unsympathetic. Clearly, I was going through something beyond my control, he says, and this is probably true. Even with all of the poor decisions I made, they were made within the context of mental illness, which we are now calling Depression. Obviously, something was happening, he pleads. First I was an A student. Then a B student. Then a C student. Then a D student. And then a 0.0 student. The decline was steady and clear. Because I do not respect myself—or because the prison of my psyche inclines me to be this way—I look at that decline and I feel I should have intervened earlier. I accept that the university has no obligation to revise my record. Mom asks if I would consider going back to school to do one more term. I cannot, I say. Everyone else thinks I graduated. I cannot go back nor look back. "But Boo, I don't understand," Dad says.

I also understand that all I was trying to do was avoid being "Crazy," even if I'd be much better off accepting that I was. And to be honest, I can recall few times when saying as much would have been to my advantage. I had artificial needs. For example, the need to avoid having a crutch, the need to be seen as sane, even if it was against my long-term interests. These are matters of pride which, if I had neglected at the time, would have marred my sense of self and made me feel inferior. So I avoided this at all costs, even though my life has been made drastically worse because of it, as this insanity I was repressing was far more serious—even lethal, possibly—than I gave it credit for. I just wanted to be normal. Better to be sane and dead than crazy and alive. I believed that, and now I wonder where I learned it. Even today, I don't know what I am living with.

Ah, well. The university does not care that there are reasons why I didn't disclose my condition earlier, nor do they care why there was such a wide drop-off in my standing. It's their policy, and they're upholding it, and I allow them to, even if I sometimes resent them for it.

My father is hurt. He thinks they're cheating us and they have no heart. Of the kids he has sent to college—poor kids I've never met or talked to, many from neighborhoods I've never even been to on the South and Southwest Side—some have had similar problems and have gotten their university to excuse aberrant semesters because of mental health situations. He can't understand why a Catholic university is so unsympathetic, especially since he's given so much money to the Jesuits. I don't know what to tell him. Why should money give us preferential treatment, and how could money be the solution when it was so much of the problem in the first place? I do not say that, though. I tell him, "It's all right, Dad. We'll make it somehow. You can still become a perfectly well-adjusted person without a degree from Santa Clara University."

At times, however, I find an upside to my plight. My college years were a bit like my asylum years: spent in a big, beautiful building on a big, beautiful plot of land where children go to become normal. And, for that matter, where most people are insane. I left as a babe with the pretense of sanity, and now I have lost it. Now my social position is permanently altered, and yet in this loss, I've been made free from much of what constrained me in the first place. I don't have to fake anything for anyone. I am the 0.0 student: the one who drank her wits out in California and went off the deep end, the one who left home innocent and came back seeing things through the bottom. That was my education, and it may be the best one I'll ever get. I don't have to define my intelligence by scores, letters, or degrees. I'll have to work to let it speak for itself—develop the informal smarts of those who were never credentialed or protected by institutions. That was never my place before, but it will have to be my place going forward. I'll have to learn how to be myself.

Once discarded from the game, there is nothing to own up to. I have no obligations to all the little social deadlines to which I once felt vainly tied, nor the allures of the economy or the cheap ways people evaluate one another. "What are you studying next? What are your career plans? Have you been thinking about business? Who are you seeing this weekend?" People don't want me as I am. I'm not attractive to them, and I'm not attractive to the system. I'm not attractive as a friend. There's no temptation on my end to go along with anyone else whatsoever. I'm cut loose from it all and can stand for whatever I choose. The only person I have to listen to is myself, the only values I hold are whatever I want to. There's no false sense of belonging I stand to get from pretending otherwise, and no incentive to put on a mask or go passively with the flow. I'm miserable, but in a way, I'm also freer. Why did I have to be a screw-up to come to this conclusion?

There are layers of deception in my situation. First, there is a drastic miscommunication about mental illness regarding its depth, severity, disability, and the character of those who experience it. Then the experience is received with second-class social treatment. These two coexist and reiterate the same messages: self-loathing, hatred, assumptions of inferiority, dangerousness, ignorance, incompetence, and failure. And that nobody is to blame for this condition but me.

I've been very introspective about this. I think about my miseducation and I suspect something very wicked is at play. Firstly, I have been forced to accept that I am capable of experiencing major psychological disability and horror. I call it Depression, a diagnosis I don't totally trust. I also call it antiquated terms like Melancholia, the Black Bile, or by slang names such as The Beast or The Shit. Whatever it is, it is real, very real, and now that it's been removed from my blind spot, I cannot brush it off as "being fine," or, "not a problem." Nor can I endorse "tough it out" as a sound response. No. I was taught my whole life to either underestimate it or not acknowledge it at all, and that is how it gets me.

Secondly, I have been forced to accept that what a depressed mind has me believe of myself—my infirmity, my incompetence, my failure, my ignorance—is more or less reiterated in my social world by virtue of being associated with Depression, of being Depressed, of being Mentally Ill. Treat one like they are stupid, and they will be stupid. Treat one like they are insane, and they will be insane. An abysmal paradox. This, as much as anything else, makes it difficult to emerge to higher mental ground. Even in my shit, I know this isn't even the worst of Madness—imagine where I would be with schizophrenia.

Before, I could avoid it. Though Depression was always there in some capacity, I was able to keep it concealed while dressing as normal. I could deftly slip it into a pocket of my past—"it's an issue I once had for a season,"—or simply choose not to speak of it. Though I felt on some unconscious level that I needed to do this to protect myself, I understand this was a complacent choice. I do not have that option anymore. It is not merely a fact of my mind—out of sight and out of social consideration. It is a fact of my whole life. I have the body of a Depressed person—drooping, slow, frail, deathlike—and I cannot avoid anything by pretending it isn't there. There's no closet anymore, it's all out in the open. I have the clothes to fit the part.

First people see me for who I am, and then they choose not to see me.

Some can hardly restrain themselves from laughing when they look at me in this state—oh, how their mouths shoot open, and how they rush their hands over them to cover their vast laugh from exploding. Others deliberately distance themselves, cold-shoulder me, turn their backs, run away. They do not even look at me. They look around me, past me, over me. They isolate me. They quiver when I get too close, and get frustrated they have to speak to me, as if it is hard labor. I can hear their voices shake as they try to make trite, polite conversation, as though I'm now a danger and they haven't known me for years. As though there's something they're trying very hard not to talk about. Mothers on the sidewalk step in between me and their children as I pass, shield the little ones from me, and hurry by. Coffee shop patrons give me looks of disgust when I walk in. Others coldly dictate to me the realities of emotions and life to me and especially me, telling me how I ought to think and feel—stop being so sensitive, get your shit together, take better care of yourself—as though they know exactly what it is I am going through in my inner world, which is known to nobody but myself.

Actual conversations with people are increasingly rare. I cannot think of the last time anyone touched me. I have become an Other.

How many people will deal with me like this? One out of every three? One out of every two? I cannot tell, but it seems like a lot. The sore thumbs stick out, and I am one of them. It becomes harder and harder for me to distinguish safe people from unsafe people. The whole world is a stern, contemptible Nurse Ratched, and the individuals within it are painted together into a single inimical mass. Everywhere I go, the world exercises petty displays of power over me, solely because I am weaker than other people and it can identify this instantly. All the while I remain alone, returning again and again to fits of mental violence that render me helpless, useless, and suicidal, desperate to escape.

They all probably like to believe that they have nothing to do with it, that it's all within me — a medical condition. That's their excuse for my suffering. But it is a lie. They have quite a bit to do with it. Everyone is in some way involved in this. I try to explain this to some, yet they deny it. They tell me it is in my head, that I'm reading into things and taking other people's personalities too sensitively. Am I?

I don't think I was ever discriminated against too aggressively. In little ways, sure. And yet I was ruined anyway. There must be a broader culture implicated: one of exclusion and fear of mental illness as a life-threatening monstrosity. Downstream from this fear there is a culture of shame and moralism. After shame, avoidance. With avoidance, silence, repression, and inactivity. It creates unexamined social standards for youth, which children then respond to thoughtlessly and carry with them into adulthood. Left without a response, the burden of the disease is placed on the individual, where it grows uninhibited and ruins the person's ability to cope. Beyond this unbearable amount of madness, the individual lives in debility and disability. There, isolation, incompetence, and unemployability compound both the discriminatory patterns of the world and the individual's catatonia and psychosis. The walls cave in — you are caged within yourself. And now I am the very invalid I did not want to turn into, and all the negativity, fear, that I was once safe from cannot be escaped. It is the public I exist in. I once shunned the nega-tive side of the mind. Now the world shuns me. The negativity subverts my sense of self and deceives me into believing my lack of worth and the hell of my universe.

There is no way I am the only one. There is no way this is merely a personal complaint. I believe my misfortunes flow from a vast, historical, sinister wellspring. I'm starting to believe that mental health exists within a form of social oppression. I'm hesitant to use that phrase—it sounds insensitive to others. As I am white and rich, to lay a claim to this inherently minimizes the suffering of others. And the second the phrase comes up, it connotes an order of violent, physical suppression, and a full-scale denial of rights and liberties. The American temperament as I experience it loathes the idea that anything is degrading enough in our climate to constitute oppression, and when I say as much, others assume the role of prosecutor and try to dismiss me as quickly as they can.

Nonetheless, it seems that many of the core attributes are there: assumptions of inferiority, prejudice, discrimination, a social position of silence, isolation, exclusion, paternalism, and total misinformation about my personhood and of mental illness. It culminates in and perpetrates a deep and seemingly insurmountable state of depersonalization and dysfunction for me, the "crazy" individual within these crosshairs. And psy-chologically, I am not just inferior, but psychotically detached from who I actually am: a sweet, honest person. It's as though the asylums were abolished, but their standards remained. They didn't disappear but rather evolved to take form in more invisible ways in everyday life. And in at least one use of the term, this is oppressive.

And yet, I am generally wordless to identify what this phenom-enon is called. I feel quite strongly that the gestures of contempt and fear that now outline the boundaries of my existence are all connected to this idea of mental illness. They are far too common and far too similar to be coincidental. It's a bigger, systematic problem — a problem of the country and how it's arranged. And I am the only person I know who sees it this way. Others cannot see inside me, nor read my mind or inhabit my spiritual space. They cannot identify anything oppressive at play, for by being primarily psychological it is too abstract to identify. My life seems normal. No, not just normal — exceptionally privileged. The things I say are killing me are all invisible to them, and the things they do see discredit the concept of a burden. They do not see me as someone facing a constant, unjust, and cruel power. Rather, they see it as pathetic, entitled, or crazy.

Is this all not adding humiliation to an already humiliated individual? Is this not further incapacitating the incapacitated? Is it only considered oppression if someone forces another underwater, or is it also oppression to deny a life vest to a drowning body? This is why speaking to it is a loaded conversation. No individual has forced anything on me, and yet, through the sly collusion of cultural, institutional flaws and personal misfortune, I have been destroyed. I've lost my future, my sense of self, the respect of others, and my basic dignity. I've lost the ability to see why life is worth living. Does this mean I am just ill, or am I also oppressed?

I'm not put down with police and batons. It's the abundance of petty gestures that do me in and keep me down — the alienation, society's scorn, its fear and condescension, the code of silence around the unpleasant side of the mind, amongst other things. They act upon me regularly, with the effect of keeping me in a suppressed, voiceless, second-class state of mind. In this place, I am capable only of being a fraction of my proper self. For my daily persistence, I learn to accept being easily delimited, and the possibility of being ostracized or made "less than" is a part of my participation in social life. I accept my place of inferiority as the default starting point of my day, because there are no other options available, and lately I have been taught little else.

And this is how I feel, as one who is, by conventional standards, otherwise well-off. For those who are not, I imagine the situation is much nastier. I am convinced that my parents' wealth is the only thing keeping me from homelessness, police brutality, an institution, or jail. Or death. And the most damning statement may be this: before reaching my nadir, the entirety of this was hidden.

Dad assures me often: "There is nothing we will not cover financially for your health and happiness. You have unlimited resources." As such, I have been in and out of therapies and treatments. At first, I did a long series of questionnaires with a psychologist, who then determined I had issues with anxiety and depression. He referred me to a separate psychologist for counseling. I could not put my own words to anything I was feeling and he got frustrated with having to work with me. Much of our sessions were spent on him talking about himself. Then I went to a psychiatrist to try drugs. He was actually an ex-student of the Doc's from Northwestern and recalls having dinners at his house by the lake. He has put me on Mirtazapine. It knocks me out at night but also unleashes the harsher elements of the subconscious. In books I have checked out from the library, I have learned that psychosis is the point where the subconscious overrides the conscious. This comes out in emotional extremes, but also in daily settings, like just before sleep and just as I wake up. Each morning is a mental barrage of scenes from my unresolved past, which lasts for about two hours. I have no choice but to work through them and try to be normal. There is also a theory that when psychiatric drugs are first taken, they activate these latent impulses and take hold on the mind. For three weeks, I was virulently suicidal because of the drug. Then it settled and I am mildly better off. I have tried talk therapy with the doctor, too. For two sessions my parents have been present. They are absolutely speechless in a very helpless, flabbergasted way, and seem desperate for the doctor to guide them. They want to say something but are too intimidated, or too daft, and wait on his every word. Whatever culture I complain of has evidently constrained their ability to confront this as well. They too have no tools.

At home, it is as usual. I read every night. It's the only hope I have to make any sense of this — where words do not exist, read those of others and make some for yourself. And I am happiest alone with books. Any other stressor could incapacitate me. I fear I may never hold steady work. Creative outlets may be my only choice, but what voice do I have? Who would pay for me to be a creative, and why? Mom, who watches TV every night, doesn't always seem to understand why I do this work. She would like me to lighten up, enjoy my time more, and stop being so serious. Dad is also having difficulty understanding what I am doing. Dad comes home in his Porsche and sees me debilitated in his home. "I just don't understand, Boo. What isn't working?" I'm aware that there is very much he does not understand. I tell him he'll just have to believe me that this is real. Another day, he stops into my room after a deal did not go as well as he hoped. "We got $60 million less than we could have, I'm a little bummed," he says. Does he want sympathy? I also do not understand. If we were able to engage with these questions more then I would spend more time with them. But they aren't willing to do that, perhaps because of old age. I deem this work too important to set aside to do anything else. It's too much a matter of life and death for me.

As one might expect, I only think about these things alone. I dig through the library and get what I can on mental illness. Anything is better than nothing. Certain authors jump out as bigger than others: Kay Jamison, Elyn Saks, Oliver Sacks,

Thomas Szasz, E. Fuller Torrey. There's a lot of information here, but none get quite to the heart of my question. What is the place of mental health socially? Politically? Can I place it in a history and system as others have done for, say, race or gender, and in so doing make it a site of movement, class identification, and social change? That was what I never had, and that would have plausibly saved me. I have been following a long, convoluted trail through library stacks, references, and footnotes, but depressingly I cannot identify anything in our culture that takes this analysis.

I have scraped together a few terms that might be helpful. "Sanism." "Ableism." "Mentalism." Even as I write them into Microsoft Word, a squiggly red line develops underneath each of those words, saying to me that this is not a part of our dictionary. "Stigma" is a bit more helpful, but yields few results. Every so often, a psychiatric book may have a few paragraphs on this phenomenon, but I am hard-pressed to find anything that interrogates it as length. Why is there nobody who speaks to this? Why does nobody challenge this bane? Where is my great movement for rights that soars through history? By comparison, the library at DePaul has entire stacks devoted to race or gender. This becomes my default site of study, and I borrow what I can and see how it might apply.

I've gotten into African-American literature, as the movement against racism seems like the logical starting point for examining models of superiority and inferiority in America. And very much of what is said in critical race theory and the psychosocial impact between black and white is relevant to my own experience, where dual consciousness, the secrecy of my mentally ill nature, and negotiation with blithe yet completely tolerated gestures of disrespect shape my perspective. James Baldwin has become particularly instructive. I regularly rephrase his observations to describe my plight, such as in the look of "bland ignorance" that he finds in a certain type of white gaze, or "phantom normalcy"—the way someone pretends to see you as an equal when it is obvious in their behavior that they do not actually believe that. How often do I find myself standing before an empty gawker, a raised eyebrow, or a confused tone of voice, all of which ask me, "Who is this alien being, and what is she doing here?" Or how expectations have been lowered so that maintaining basic responsibilities are now seen as major accomplishments, and I'm applauded in the way that parents reward a child for learning to do things on their own.

And though I am hesitant to say as much, for aforementioned reasons of class and complexion, I theorize more or less everything off of critical race literature. Nowhere else is the psyche of social inferiority expressed quite as clearly, and nowhere else gives me so much material to hypothesize what sanism might entail, or how to describe it maturely and accurately within my time and place. This is ultimately too great of a task for one person, especially since I don't know anyone who has done it before, but that's precisely why I feel compelled to understand it in total. The education about a spectrum of racism, ranging from explicit, fundamental racism—"I dismiss someone on principle because of their complexion or heritage"—to more nuanced forms of the disease. It comes in layers, too. More than being a flaw in the white mind, it is a multidimensional, psycho-social-politico-economic arrangement. History is whitewashed, structures of policy are arranged iniquitously by race, place, and geography, all undergirded by a cultural enterprise of moral handwringing towards the poor. "Lazy," "fatherless," criminals," "welfare cheats," "hustlers." "Mentally ill," "incompetent," "dangerous," "psycho killer," "drain on the system," "failure to launch," "cannot make decisions for herself." I see all of these pop up in the world, in places of varying respectability.

The more fundamental form of sanism is surprisingly public. I can see it now that I'm paying attention to it. I often hear people dismissed on principle as being "mentally ill," "crazy," or "off the deep end," which is then the rationale for social exclusion and the end of relationships. Cut-and-dried, no argument required, Q.E.D. The discrimination is transparent, but without robust studies into the matter, all I know are anecdotes. Just the other day, I overheard a debate about gun control, and an older liberal at a coffee shop was talking about how we need to ban the mentally ill from gun ownership. I interjected and told her that I have a mental illness and that I've also never been dangerous, and her desire would probably only stigmatize me further. "I think you're just making negative assumptions about the people you're talking about," I told her. She responded like I had offended her, "Oh my, for the sake of yourself and your family, I hope you get the spiritual and psychological help you need. And please, for everyone else's sake, do not register for a carry card. Goodbye." And then she stopped looking at me.

More often though the rebukes I receive are a step removed from fundamental disdain. They are based on a perception of me that is related to my Madness but not wholly attributed to it. I lose presence in the classroom at DePaul, and the teacher questions my direction and ambition. I got a C on a paper and told her I had mental health issues. She reprimands me, "We have accommodation resources for this!" and shakes her head as she would to a disorderly child. I'd never identified with a disability before, so it did not occur to me to place different standards on myself because of it. I am still learning it. That wasn't a part of me. I also told her I had once gone to school in California, but that it was, "a total disaster." "Ah," she says. "And are you better now?" I said yes, but if I wasn't, would she treat me differently? Would my recognition depend on the correct answer? So much weighs on the answer to the question of, "Are you well?" Mind you, this is a gender studies professor, and an avowed "intersectional feminist," whatever that is. For anyone else, this would be a minor incident, but she had spent most of her class talking about language and representation of gender, race, sexuality, and class, all with stringent injunctions towards analyzing everything and correcting behavioral mistakes. I don't think she realized that by her own standards she was betraying the practices that she was trying to implement in her students. I totally doubt that my specific quest for liberation had ever occurred to her.

Fatigue and Depression set in at my waitress job, I'm scoffed at as a "bad worker," and the higher-ups crack jokes while I balance the demands of my work against my patent incapacity. My obsession with my suffering is proof of selfishness and immaturity, not a logical response to a raw deal. Admittedly, I am often out of it much of the time. I feel depersonalized and can easily be made weaker by outside stimuli. My head swirls when I listen to others. There is an impediment between them and me, a woozy onset of depletion from which I instantly need rest. They become impatient, upset, and incredulous. Oh, they must deal with me again.

There are also honest, well-meaning people who joke, "At least it's not the 1950s. They'd have locked you in the loony bin," as though I should be grateful not to be thrown away. They say this to me lightly, yet the statement of course does not apply to them in quite the same way. They can be grateful for the freedom not to be in an asylum, as they should be, but I am not arguing against 1950. I am arguing the present, where we exist now, and what I would like them to understand is how the asylum mentality lingers in the real world in less concrete ways, creating a psychological asylum for me that continues to be a repressive force. It's nice, I suppose, that they can understand the restrictions of the past. What I want for them is to understand the restrictions of the present, because today is where they actually have the power to help me and to expand social freedoms for others. It's so easy for people to look down on their ancestor's worlds, but there is power in this position to absolve people from acting in the present, unaware that one day their children will be treating them with the same condescension.

I would not be thinking like this had someone not already challenged the statement, "At least it's not Jim Crow," but that's an acknowledgment I keep to myself. When people in my life — namely, white people — tell others that they take part of their lifestyle from France, Spain, or Japan, they make it sound interesting and cultured. When I try to explain to many of these same people that I admire black resistance or black culture — for reasons I'm not yet bold enough to state in person — I get smirked at. Oh, white girl. It becomes a punch line for our relationship. A parallel tendency holds true in more multicultural crowds. It's not patronizing in the same ways, but there's genuine pushback. Without an appreciation for the ins and outs of mental illness, this confession risks being seen as privileged naivety, or a form of cultural theft, or an obscene equivalence between black Americans and white Americans. "So, what? You're telling me white people aren't happy?" No, it's not that simple. It's not about similarities between black and white, it's about the stigmatization of race and mental illness, and how they are both are treated. Thus, I've learned it is best not to talk about it, even if the story of my life cannot be accurately told without it.

I engage with the literature of the oppressed on the sly. One day we may be able to talk about what it means that Baldwin's writing is that which speaks most to how I experience the world, but I don't think that day is today. I worry too much about being a flash-in-the-pan white liberal or some other fraud to talk about this openly. I need my own movement. I need my own tradition to speak from. I see the issue woven into the fabric of everyday life. Sanism, that is. With mental illness, there is a world of

unrecognized resentment. Slurs have a respected place in colloquial American English. Prejudice is just as quotidian. Fear-
mongering after school shootings is by now a modern American
ritual. Many employers turn away from "mental illness" as soon
as they see it, and the burden of unemployability entails its own
complications, which lead directly to welfare, invisibility, and
more mental illness. Neighborhood demonstrations to housing
come with picket signs that read, "No Schizophrenic Shall Live
On My Block." I am told up-front, by people who otherwise pride
tolerance, that they would never have a child with someone with
serious mental illness in their family. The presumed toxicity of
friendship, or motherhood, and of romance is the most painful
reality with this label—it's okay to see me as undeserving of these
timeless, essential bonds. As much as mental illness dominates
my mind, their fear of it dominates theirs. I see this, and I am
aware of it. It only fuels my despair, like attacking the wounds
of an invalid for humor.

The investigation into inequality in America also enlightens
me to a number of matters that were previously out of sight.
Criminal justice matters, geographic concentration, political
dog-whistling, all of these things that float around me, though so
far I have never analyzed them. Economic inequality, too—I've
read that the average black family has between a nickel and a
dime to the dollar of the average white family. And households
like the one I grew up in have far, far more than the average,
like in the top tenth of one percent. I never talk about it in terms
of color, though. At least not black or white. That never gets
me anywhere, people here are too sensitive to accusations of
racism, and the talk gets shut down. Guilt is a hell of a drug. I
talk in numbers, in the color green. That's Dad's logic—always
talking about the world in dollars, almost never in the quality
of human lives.

His view of the world posits that his class—the investing

class—is best equipped to manage the economy's resources. From there, opportunity for the rest will follow. I ask him if he actually believes the rich are capable of acting responsibly enough to justify the transfer of our world's wealth into their hands. Is the power of their investment that great? Can private philanthropy meet the world's needs? His answer is indirect. "You'd be surprised how generous the rich can be," he says. "Your mother and I do a lot with our wealth for the poor, and we expect you and Kevin to continue that."

"But what about the structure? Why does so much need to first make a pit stop through the rich? What is this logic supposed to accomplish?" I say.

At this point, he has had a Manhattan too many and does not address the question. He turns up the volume on golf programming, and again complains about how hard people were on Mitt Romney, and he says that a lot of the people he knows with money care very deeply about doing good with it. This still dodges the question: how does he simultaneously laud people for their charity while cosigning a world that tolerates poverty in the first place? It is futile. Conversations with conservative businessmen like him are designed to push attention away from the root, and this is only a gentle example. It takes a rhetorical contortionist to get through it. In less filtered moments, he gets irate over what he sees as the persecution of the rich in politics and has taken moments when we are together to insist upon me how the system is being gamed from below, hardly allowing me any space to talk. Is there any immediate context for it? No, not really, but my budding skepticism of how wealth is distributed— perhaps the only thing he believes in uncompromisingly—has evidently provoked something defensive in his mind and deluded him into understanding himself as a victim.

This environment has a strict conservative slant, and it's laborious to communicate and maintain humanitarian values, as they are always under scrutiny. The capitalist holds the power, and he chooses what does and does not get acknowledged. Any discussion that does not center on his profit is treated with trenchant skepticism. I've attempted several approaches to change this. First, to educate myself, and speak to the conversation on those terms—understand the premise of his view, and speak to that, and offer a critical question. But he has the power to ignore me, or to deny whatever I say, or to run me in circles with tangential clarifying questions. "What about x, y, z?" he says, in direct response to, "a, b, c." I then take a more militant stance, only to be accused of attacking him, or rashness. Or of "speaking emotionally." Then I lose my aplomb and get accused of being the very adolescent stereotype the old conservative believes his critics to be, and he laughs at me. It is worse after alcohol, and therefore, I try not to be alone with him at night. After the third Manhattan, there's no hope for talking to him without resorting to a rehearsal of this conversation. He never exits business mode, and family hangouts very often turn into rehearsals of the twenty-four-hour news cycle of rightwing media. He will use it as an opportunity to, without any provocation, tell me how I'm wrong about the rich, wrong about policy, interrupt me each time I rebut, and peg me as a hapless, naïve radical, so as to disregard my views completely and keep things his way. It is no different than being a guest on Fox News. Then, after the steamrolling has finished, he says, "Good night, Boo. It's been nice talking to you." To which I wonder, "Doesn't a conversation consist of more than one person?" I would have to spend years rhetorically slitting my wrist just to make a single point. And even in that event, I don't know if he would be able to hold a real discussion.

Acknowledgment is unattainable. He is far too concerned with uncritical acceptance of what is and the self-preservation of wealth than in recognizing the limits of what is and what harm that entails. Even in matters about the life and death of his own child. His head bursts when people suggest the rich get too much and give back too little, and he accuses them of working and doing less than him. He derides Barrack Obama as an "anti-rich" demagogue, and yet in Obama's rule to date, my parents have probably accumulated eight figures of wealth, and have bought a second mansion in Florida. If the world and the president weren't so vicious toward them, maybe they would have bought a third.

In general, Mom and Dad manage as many aspects of my life as they can, although I don't think they realize it. Parents never realize it. They do it first because it is their job, they make it a habit, and then they let it carry on into adulthood. Though they don't consider it management. They consider it parenting. I tell Mom I need to leave and she says, "What makes you think you would be better off somewhere else? Wouldn't it just be the same thing?"

"No, I need to leave," I say.

"But I'm concerned that you are going to hurt yourself if you do," she says.

"I am not going to. I am going to be better in a different environment," I say.

"I know that you know more about this than I do, but I think there are treatments out there that you have not considered before," she says.

The two of them do all of the talking in almost every conversation we have. Dad talks about Notre Dame and his business life. One of his friends, who is one of the wealthiest individuals in Illinois, also moved to Florida. He says that the man and his wife make several hundred million dollars per year, and they decided that the income tax in Illinois wasn't worth their stay. Mom, on the other hand, talks about movies, television, and her family. Sometimes I think I can't get two honest words through, not least of which about Depression. It's work. The other family conversations feel the same way. Most of the content consists of nostalgia and material acquisition — a story about high school in the 1970s, the condition of a new sofa, salacious gossip about another North Shore family's drug problem, trips to Europe, which cities their children and other people's children are working in.

Dad flips back and forth between good sense and no sense whatsoever. His attachment to his wealth and his sense of victimhood as a rich man is a bit strange, given how well he is faring in the bigger scheme of things. I cannot say that I'd be different in his situation. I don't know how decades in private equity would shape me. The way Kevin is turning out makes me queasy. He's gotten brash and entitled in college. He says he wants to become a business owner, he lauds himself for the superior career path he has chosen, and he chides and mocks anyone who "whines" about it though it is unclear whether anyone does. At the same time, he is paranoid about being vilified as a racist. Unfortunately, he looks like the next generation of American arrogance in training. This is where my father's exclusive business views do harm. He's given my brother the idea that strict business logic comes before all else, and now my young brother sees questions about life outside of that as a personal attack on him and his ambition, denying him a future he believes he is owed. Therefore, he laughs and browbeats them away.

That's where I stand with the two of them, looking at the same world from the same household, yet from entirely opposite positions. Their idea of common sense is, to me, no sense at all, and vice versa. What they call, "left," I call, "right." What they call, "right," I call, "extreme," as the agenda of the radical right has excelled in making new political intensities possible. My family is, in terms I do not doubt, politically extreme. Their American Dream is my American coma, and nothing short of my own suicide would release them from their convictions. I've tried to engage and tried to reason, but I've resigned myself into believing that whether or not they change is entirely up to them. Remove them from their fortunes, and I wonder what they would believe, or what they would think about and feel. What would they think of business? And our neighbors? And our neighbors' neighbors?

I get out sometimes. I see kids from high school, we go to Lincoln Park bars together. At these events, the girls go to one side, and the guys go to the other. It's a bit too much like a high school dance, only I think the guys have gotten more immature since those days. I'm not drinking anymore, and everyone who I still see knows that and is fine with it. People who don't know aren't as easy. When I meet people, they ask why I don't drink (people are inclined to have the abnormal quality explained). This question, like many others, puts me in a bind. If I say mental illness, it scares people away. It's like there's a creature on my back that jumps out with those words, and I get to look at everyone's reactions. Only it's more hurtful than that, since in reality, I am the object of fear. Then they ask me what I'm doing, which I also cannot answer without detouring through "mental illness." Because what I am doing is recovering. And it's taking a damned long time. I didn't graduate from college because of insanity, and I don't know if I ever will. I have to find ways to sidestep the conversation and broach some avenue to a normal interaction. The perception of dangerousness makes me a liability. It puts risk into social contact. Many therefore disengage and place me at a distance. This secondary discrimination — separation after examination — is common.

Even those I expect to know better end up being tough. I tried telling PsyD students and medical students, thinking that at least they would be decent and enlightened. Turns out they are about as prejudiced as anyone else, if not more so. I make jokes about it to disarm people. If I show them that I am aware of their fears (and therefore of the risk that being with me entails), then they are more apt to interact with me. It's a subordinated position, but sometimes I think it's the better option to total withdrawal. Neither is desirable, but you have to have a social life somehow. We all make compromises.

I am like an ex-patient. I simply cannot explain my life without explaining mental illness, and my culture simply isn't prepared to respond to that in an adult, accepting way.

It's not too different with the family either. Mom, though she ought to know everything, closes off when I bring up mental illness. It looks like she's showing disapproval, the way she furrows her eyebrows and takes a sip of her drink, the way she turns her head away from me at the dinner table. I perceive it as deliberate silencing, but I can't say for sure. It's just ambiguous and unspoken enough that I don't know what her motives or feelings are. Yet the result is always the same: I don't talk about it. I am silenced.

That's a contradiction of its own. I always perceive these slight motions of discomfort in an emotional state near despair, and they are barely open-ended enough to be either innocuous or subtly malicious. Who's to say how much of it is in my head and how much is genuine contempt? I don't think I'll ever be able to disentangle this, and that's what makes psychiatric exclusion impossible to validate, like how boys fight with punches, but the quieter, relational tactics of girls are much harder to spot as aggression, and much more harmful because of it.

The family parties carry on in the same manner. Sometimes they drive me to rage. I'm feeble to begin with, but am made more so by subtle negligence of my position. And I repeat, it's all ambiguous. I become distraught in their presence. Frankly, this happens anywhere where I can't be "myself," where I cannot talk frankly about the experiences that have defined my life in the last few years. It is a weight I carry alone, and I'm too desperate to have to suck it up and listen to them talk about nothing in the name of being a good niece or a good daughter.

Between me and them there is ever an unasked question: unasked by some through feelings of delicacy; by others through the difficulty of rightly framing it. My family gathers for their party around me. As they stand in line by me for food, my aunt and uncle sag their sides and shoulders and look lifelessly downwards, as though my presence has punched the gusto out of them. They ask light questions about my mood, and say, "I'm glad you're well," when I say that I'm all right. Then they talk about more pleasant things.

All, nevertheless, flutter round it. They approach me in a half-hesitant sort of way, eye me curiously or compassionately. It's the small acts that destroy me. It's the way my mother hides her face in her glass of wine and turns away after she makes eye contact with me at a social event and the way my aunts do the same. It's the way I sit down at the dinner table, sullen and morbid, nerves damaged and muscles chipped to atrophy, and people shift uncomfortably away from me. It's how they notice that they are monopolizing the conversation and pose a minor question toward me, to give me some recognition, and then become tired of listening as I answer, and do not say anything to me when I am finished, but instead return to discussing their own interests. This isn't home. There is no home for me. Is it cultural appropriation if I wonder to myself, *how does it feel to be a problem?*

Eating is a forced exercise. I don't want to do it, and I get no joy from it. I do it only because I know I need to. When I swallow, I don't feel any more or less full. It's as though the food falls into a hole and disappears, and when I am finished eating, I feel sicker than before. Afterward, I lie down, and the faces of my life haunt in my mind and sneer at me, humiliate me, prevent me from thinking of myself as someone better and instead I am the same, less honorable version of myself that existed a long time ago. I exert as little effort as possible. Any exertion would aggravate the faces further, having them actively shout towards my failure and jeer when I screw up, turning the simplest tasks of my day into trials of torment, innocuous tasks like putting dishes away and tying my shoes. The nastiest and most unsubstantiated things people have said to me come to mind, and I can't help but think there is a lot of truth to them, even when there is not.

Every afternoon is like this, for hours at a time. Suicide is the only comforting thought. Every linear trail of thought is obstructed immediately by some other nuisance or a black obstruction of doom and dread. My sleep consists of nightmares and imagery from Christian depictions of hell; my ascetic, naked body alone in barren caves, huddled around dimming fires. I see from an out-of-body experience, and from a cold, huddled position, it turns its head up to me. Then I wake, and the intensity of that fear remains with me throughout my day. That which is real and that which is unreal blend into a singular, distorted world. In more anxious times, I am certain that my awareness of a cohesive and stable reality is going to fall apart altogether, and I'll find myself spinning through an empty, imagined dimension. It's a black hole psyche. Mom comes and asks how I'm doing. I say, "All right," then lie down again. I'm most consoled when it rains. The harder the better. My heart breaks over nothing. I have everything to express yet no means to do so beyond slapdash, grammatically juvenile screeds into Microsoft Word.

In the evenings I have dinner with my parents, and we talk about the city, the Cubs, the relatives. One night, Dad comments about hostility to Goldman Sachs. They hire freakishly smart people, he says. Every single one of them went to Harvard, Princeton, or Yale. Demonizing them is to take the economy out of the hands of people who actually understand it. Mom smartly adds, "They don't understand. They think we need more representative people in government, but it is just the opposite:

we need more one-percenters." Then I go to bed reading about the Civil Rights Movement.

I keep to myself a lot. I have too much social shame and suspect that others see me the way I see myself. It's a Catholic pathology, always understanding myself on the "sinner" side of morality. I am too tightly wound thinking about how I will next be derided, and always assume it in others. My fear with other people is that they will not accommodate my pain, this large part of my life that is now central to who I am, and that I will be left even more feeble and disoriented than before. I curl into an armchair by the window and listen to the silence. That is what is best for me. I don't need to hear other people talking about themselves. I'll never find peace that way. The further from technology, from obligation, and from keeping a schedule, the better. I need to return to a simpler form and just be. That is how I will heal.

I don't know if this will ever end. I have a harder and harder time imagining a future for myself. It seems cut short, and it's beyond my capacity to see green fields and grandchildren in the years ahead. Usually, I see myself alone and dead by age 30, sprawled along the wooden floor of a solo apartment, and it goes no further. I have some faith this mindset won't last forever, but there's always a possibility that it will. That's how the mindset feels: eternal. I'm in a haze known only to myself.

When I get bad, it's toxic. A livid poison runs through me. I can only describe it in cosmic, pretentious terms. I become transformed into nothingness and chaos, experiencing life without the decencies of the mind that allow us to make the world beautiful. Misery is enraptured within me, flowing through my body while I lay motionless, waiting in helpless vanity for sleep. It is like descriptions of a biblical possession. I am neither frightened nor sad, but I am furious. Fury, held in this tender, innocent body, unwilling to act on its primitive impulses. She who spends a lifetime being bent may ultimately break.

The other night, after three hours in a manic rage, I turned my bedside lamp on, a long and tall lamp, grabbed it by the neck, and thrust it against the wall. The light went out and will never be fixed. I walked to the bathroom, venting over the toilet, and punched the wall three times. Pacing in circles back in my room, I dropped quickly to the floor and got up again, before displacing enough energy to be well again for the time being. I went downstairs and filled a mug with three bags of chamomile—better this than alcohol—and returned upstairs to my couch, where I drank the tea and streamed an episode of Carl Sagan's *Cosmos* on Netflix and eventually fell asleep.

These violent outbursts have been more and more common. I made a hole in my bedroom wall when I threw a water bottle I use for collecting spare change into it, and I've also broken a few garden tools by smashing them against the ground. After I broke the last one, Mom sat me down and said, "Stop doing this." I tell my parents that I do this because I have impassable feelings of wanting to harm myself, and this is how I dispel them. More than that, I say that I want to kill myself. "Boo, do you have any idea how devastating it is to hear that?" Though she masterfully restrains the severity of the emotion in telling me this. In turn, they think it is a bad idea if I move out. They think I will act on these thoughts if given more independence. The reasoning is ironic—as though with more freedom, I will destroy myself.

I take long walks to clear my head, sometimes alone, sometimes with the dogs. The muggy summer air is not nearly as heavy as the lead on my mind. There are a couple of destinations where I stroll away to and fantasize about suicide. The first is at the lakefront at Northwestern University, where the rocks are painted by thespians with their favorite lines of poetry or the initials of the people they fell in love with at school. I imagine stepping down from these rocks and swimming out until the current takes me outward, and then I'll duck under and release the air from my body, and let the muffled sound of waves of Lake Michigan calm my thoughts as I depart. Once, in my parents' pool, I sank to the bottom and sat with my legs crossed. My internal vision went black, the spirit was exiting from the body, and all was divine. Then I opened my eyes and came above water.

Another fantasy suicide is along the Metra tracks at Green Bay Road and Winnetka Avenue, where a bridge stands about fifteen feet over the road. I'll stand off the edge, and slip my feet off and fall backward onto the concrete, snaping my head in a pool of my blood. The world goes on all of the same. The next morning I imagine that young girls will come and hang a banner over the place where my body lied, and it will read: *Good Luck At State, New Trier High School Field Hockey!*

My ode to home, its ode to me.

I hold myself well enough given the circumstances. And compared to people in similar situations. I try romance, again, with humiliating results. The last guy I dated was like a nineteen-year-old boy: impetuous, aloof, and full of contradicting biases. Only he was twenty-seven, so sooner rather than later I stopped putting up with it.

A month later, Michael Daniels stayed at my parents' house while he was in town for a wedding for a graduate school classmate of his. He told me about a manic episode that got him hospitalized. I wouldn't have suspected him of having a psychotic break, but then again, the faces of madness are as boring and ordinary as anything else. "They treat you like an animal," he told me, recalling his hours on the psych ward. "They keep you in a room without light for a week. It's like being a prisoner. I actually was with an ex-prisoner, and he said that the staff on the psychiatric ward treats people worse than correctional officers do. I've done that five times by now, and each time they put me on a different drug. What really creeps me out is that my delusion is coming true. I mean, what I was committed for. Something switched in my brain after work one day and I called my family and told them I was leaving because Google was spying on everyone through eyeglasses in a plot to take over the world. I had my luggage packed and was ready to run into the woods when they came and intervened. Up until recently, it sounded like nonsense, but the Snowden documents said that Google is spying on everyone. And guess what their new big product is? Google eyeglasses."

We sat in my parents' backyard drinking tea and listening to music, an idyllic Midwestern summer night. Being with him was like having the clouds within me part and evaporate into a light mist. The tautness of my face released, and I smiled. It was a couple of hours after dusk and the crickets were vibrating in every branch of every part of the wide, forested yard. He told me that he was proud of me for continuing to be who I was despite being sick.

We walked inside, and as he closed the back door I stopped in front of him and put my hand between his chest and his shoulder, and kissed him. Then we went upstairs and continued this quiet caress, and I heard somebody come home. I hurried to the kitchen and saw Kevin, whose eyes were glazed red. I asked him if he was drunk, he said he was not. I asked him if he was high, he said yes. We talked while he gathered a late meal, but mostly I was thinking that I needed to go upstairs and disappear with Michael before anyone saw anything. I went upstairs, kissed him again, and said, "We need to either go to my room or to the pool house," and he grabbed my hand and pulled me into my room. We undressed one another and I teased him about having trouble taking off my bra, and he squinted cynically at me. We made love, and that's the first time I'd call it that, mawkish as it may be. I felt for him and felt a rightness and solitude to the act of being with him that I had never felt before. We laid next to one another afterward, and he almost immediately asked me if I had gotten there, and what it was that he did that made me get there. Then he went into my family room to sleep on my couch. I laid in bed and felt a swirl of Depression and a great sense of assurance and belonging, galaxies within me colliding, as though light came through the cracks of my chamber.

When Michael left I felt drawn to reconnect with my piffling romantic past. I called Luca, who I saw only once every two to three months at college after freshman year. I felt he never allowed me to outgrow his idea of me as a lost soul, and perhaps I did the same to him, and every encounter with him centered around the obnoxious question, "But how are you really feeling?" As though I wasn't allowed to be all right sometimes, and was always hiding my real, awful self. It got in the way of us getting to know one another as anything but miserable nineteen-year-olds.

I told him about what I was doing and gave him my "coming out as Mad" spiel. Surprisingly, he told me that his life was no different. He had manic episodes throughout college, and in his gloom his interest in Dylan became obsessive, and then became a full-on delusion of grandeur. He thought he could spend his college years farting around and then one day "go off" and be some modern Dylan-esque figure, but later realized that his temperament was too self-destructive and that he needed treat-ment. "I don't judge, Luca. That's what Dylan was with Woodie Guthrie," I said. He said at first he thought he was absorbed in the world of fiction, but had since stopped using the word "fiction" and replaced it with the phrase "embellished reality" – a fanciful notion of what is presently unlikely but could one day be made possible. He decided to take this Dylan obsession and pursue songwriting and performance on his weekends and evenings. He understood everything I tried to say about sanism and how it was a subtly repressive norm in American life and told me that he wanted to get an audience of any sort and use culture as a means to subvert that. He alluded to the reality that socialization in our day and age was centered in entertainment and media, and that entertainment and media had become more open to the power of amateurs. Therefore, he was putting faith in the one talent he felt he had, with the hopes of back-dooring into a position of notoriety, and then using his cunning to catalyze movement and identification around mental illness. "People like us are bound by common grievances, and what's stopping us from doing something about it is the fact that our conditions are invisible. We're disunited from one another, and we're in a closet about it. So what if I want to preach from the mountaintop? It's better to do something rather than nothing. Let me be a preacher. Let me be someone people can come to." I told him that this was all very bold and exciting to hear, but expressed my uncertainties. He said he knew what odds he was against, and that it didn't deter him. "I have the right to claim my white whale and kill it. You and I, we are looking at things that people are refusing to see. We have to do something to popularize our vision. Besides, only a few of us are lucky enough to develop a delusion of grandeur and then audacious enough to pursue it in clear consciousness."

He then played for me one of his songs, which he called "The Pitiful Catch-22 of Depression," a simple two-minute song for an acoustic guitar with a keen pentatonic melody, like an old Irish folk song. His voice was still rough and untrained, and technically very bad, and his words teetered between eloquence and pedestrian conversation, leaving out clauses and words that would smoothly transition one thought to the next if he weren't singing it. But since when was good syntax a prerequisite for singing? He started with a reference to a Dickinson poem I recognized:

Much madness is divinest Sense
To a discerning Eye

Much Sense—the starkest Madness
'Tis the Majority
In this, as all, prevail
Assent—and you are sane
Demur—you're straightaway dangerous
And handled with a Chain

He was playing on the opening line, indicting the "divinest sense" of madness with an irritated croon about the confinement of depression. This is what he sang to me:

I wonder how she meant it, "Much madness is divinest sense,"
For I've basically forgotten what it means to feel blessed
And all my money for just an evening's rest
For just a moment of sanity from this strangle around my chest
My past is always backward, I feel guilty of any crime
There's hollowness and error where once I held my life
And at my lowest, it's like a riot against the mind
And still I'm at my bravest when I'm alone in bed
And there's nothing all that fearful—and yet I'm full of dread
With the less they're saying, the more I believe to be said
Ah, but life for us, the living, is no better for the dead

Afterward, he said, "And remember, Johnny Cash sang for the prisoners, not the warden," and then hung up. I left thinking that of the countless readings into Dylan one could toss around, the value of singing while ugly is the most important to me. I also left thinking about art, Madness, and exuberance. I thought of Nijinsky dancing across the clouds, Nina Simone quaking the earth with her voice, Beethoven striking thunder in an orchestra hall, and, in my own life, a feeling of utopian possibility for my world that I doubt I'd ever had if I cared about being sane. There is a real possibility of genius in madness—just the other day I was reading about Robert Lowell's insistence that things noticed in darkness are seen only to those who live in darkness themselves, allowing for originality of insight. This is appealing to mania, though, and I try to ground that excitement, as though mental illness has to be brilliant and romanticized. There is indeed a long history of arts and letters in which genius and Madness are synonymous. Yet of all of the poets and the lives of Mad people who have been dramatized endlessly, why do so few, if any, grasp that this has been a second-class condition in our history? Who has dared to be the political genius of the Mad? Who has dared to be the social champion of the mentally ill and ignite the heart of a nation toward its spiritual potential, and challenge the assumptions of a society that renders this potential invisible?

Aside from them, I do not have communication much with the people I went to school with. They live on the coasts and have good lives from what I can tell. Katie Reynolds did call once, sobbing about how awful her depression after college was. She couldn't talk clearly and I had to leave the call quickly for other reasons.

It is November now. I've been taking psychology classes at DePaul and volunteering at Evanston Hospital's psych ward, where the Doc used to work. Some of the current doctors and nurses remember him fondly as a rule-bender of a bygone era. They ask me how he's doing. I say, "Terrible."

I got up early this morning during a grisly dream and felt lamentably unrested. This happens often, probably because of Mirtazapine. In the morning I am blitzed by old memories. It makes me feel like a loathsome miscreant, and I have to charge through suicidal impulses just to get out of bed. From the instant I wake, my failures and mistakes are with me at every moment. It's a waste, really, since they are so, so unimportant.

I was in the kitchen trying to shake off the thought of a

kerfuffle in California that I'm almost certain nobody else involved remembers. I cursed at myself as I made breakfast, and Dad rushed into the kitchen with a look of heartbreak. He asked what was wrong, and I said, "Nothing, just an old something I did that I wish I hadn't been a part of."

"Well, Jesus Christ, Boo," he said, as though my illness was also making him sleepless. "You're too good to be using the F-bomb on yourself." He comprehends my predicament at times, but he also does not. We have the same conversations. "I need to leave," I say.

I apologized and tried to forget it happened, and then drove to Evanston Hospital, where I volunteered as the concierge at Evanston Five South. The psych ward has been busy, with all 21 beds occupied on most days and twice as many people on a waiting list to get one. The night before, some nineteen-year-old had overdosed on something—benzos, I think—and was awaiting discharge as I arrived. He was stocky and looked older than nineteen. Didn't look the slightest bit uneasy, either, unlike the other patients, who were either without affect or had their arms crossed, standing nervously against the wall, looking back and forth, taking too many sips of their cup, as anxious people do at crowded parties. Only there was no party.

The doctors were loose. I eavesdropped on one conversation when the doctor said, "You know, I'm trying to get him to smile, talk; those little things that we take for granted that for Jonathan are very difficult." Another doctor stormed in with news of an overdose, and the perpetrator either refused hospitalization or wanted a copy of her mental health rights, which evidently makes checking the patient in much more effortful. Everyone was stressing out but me, and they probably hated me for it. The doctor came in panting about the woman who took all of those painkillers and anti-anxiety meds and then said, "Oh! And guess who else is here—Jerry! Remember the guy who cut off his testicles about two years ago because some passage of the Bible said that he should be a eunuch?" The professional space of the hospital staff is a very telling place, but like me, they must need humor to cope.

I was going to go to the gym when I got off, but then my father called and told me to go to the Doc's house. A nurse said that the Doc was going to die in the night, and the family was gathering for a vigil. I went to his home where much of my family was already waiting. They didn't seem different at first. It was a typical gathering of cheap wine and flippant conversation. The Doc was on a cot in his office with tubes tangled over his body and a ghastly white hospital sheet for clothing. If you spoke to him he might say dimly, "Who is that?" but his eyes were never open and his few cogent remarks were shortly drowned out by his moaning and phlegmatic breathing. I held his hand with both of mine and leaned over his chest to tell him about what he taught me and the childhood he made for me and made sure my last words were, "I love you, guy."

We called a priest from Saint Francis Xavier Parish in Wilmette to say final blessings. One of my aunts was madly frenzied, as it constantly appeared that the Doc was dying at any moment. My Uncle Harry was delirious for being at his bedside for many nights and subsisting on scotch. My grand-mother watched calmly and serenely over his body. Everyone else maintained relative aplomb, with a solemn drink in hand. We learned the next day, and the day after, and the day after that the nurse was wrong. He lived a bit longer. Just as it had been for many years, the end wasn't as close as predicted. He didn't pass for another five days, and the family spent all of their available hours at his house. We had his wake and funeral on a Friday. His body was displayed for the church, thinned nearly to the bone in a spotless white suit. He looked like he was dressed to meet a God, before whom he would be shameless.

My cousin Rico delivered a eulogy that was a character study of philosophy and lewd retorts, explaining all of the Doc's maxims and the meaning behind them. Not every comment requires a response. You don't always have to believe what you think. I guess they don't always sound meaningful if you just write them out like that, but at one point they were worth a lot to me. I do, however, remember Rico's final lines, word for word: "One final Doc-ism I would like to share: we are in control of our disposition toward the world. We as free human beings are in full control of our relation to the world, and consequently, our feelings about the world. It is the one freedom inherent in all of us, and is the last thing we should give away."

My male cousins pulled his casket down the aisle, each wearing one of his hats. They pushed him into the hearse and when the door of the car slammed, each of them was sobbing. At his home, we had a reception. My family drank while I brooded and wished to drink. His image was shared on eight-inch paper cards, giving a toast in a velvet jacket. We spent the evening talking about his life, his shrug at what was thought of him, his humor with his wife, and his boundless list of gripes before his death. I drove my parents home near 11:00 P.M. and then drove back to the house to be with my cousins. On the drive back I lowered the windows on Sheridan Road and played Sinatra's "My Way" as loudly as was possible.

In the meanwhile, life goes on. I think about dying, and I continue to develop magical ideas of social movements about the mind and society, even as I have little participation in any of it. It is while I am reading Baldwin late at night on his visit to Tallahassee to cover a student protest at a Black university called F.A.M.U. that I had the most poignant revelation about my days as a student, mired in Depression, struggling to find any meaning in life at all. For a time much longer than what was appropriate, I debated whether it was even worth facing the possibility that I should be thinking about Madness, or considering a drastic reconsidering of my life path. At this time, one did not take precedence over the other. I coated myself in alcohol and spent long hours during this time in gruesome hangover; the kind that feels like something is jabbing at your skin from the inside, mostly bothered and thoroughly forlorn. My sense of time was gone. I would recall fragments of memory, while a sudden alteration in thought would erase it from understanding completely, and I would then be thinking of a different point in life. There was a touch of chemical tide about me then. There was a legitimate feeling of being imbalanced—undoubtedly aided by alcohol abuse—and that my fate could go to heaven or hell. It never did; I only felt bad, not good.

My body, though healthy, was strained and tired, and there was a feeling of deadness behind my eyes: a hypothermic, bare deadness. "You look as tired as I feel," sweet old women would say to me. I had a heightened—or shall I say altered—sense of sight and touch. Images took on more significance. Not the images as symbols, but as things with colors and shapes, set against other things with colors and shapes, auspicious for the brush of a manic Van Gogh. Those emblems stood out as though beholden to a world more awakened than my own. The air felt incisive and smelled unblemished. Often I thought it best to nestle myself in a blanket with a jug of water—how redemptive that water felt—and try for sleep, sometimes succeeding. The coolness of the sheets against my body provided some comfort and seized all of my attention. Other times memory had its way—the twisted and backward abysm of time, according to Shakespeare's Tempest—the rats coming through the trenches, according to Bukowski at his typewriter, his machine gun. It wasn't uncommon to hold visions of dystopia as I lied in that half-waking, half-escaping predicament.

I had lost myself, and I knew it. I searched desperately for a figure to emulate who could help me reclaim my wholeness once more, if I ever had it. Someone who, through their voice and empowerment, could stand me upright once more. I was so derelict that I performed the same internet searches over and over, dreaming that they would produce a different result. And invariably, they never did.

It was in this disorder that I carried on, fully to my own detriment, too afraid to test the air of unease that my condition had, by my estimation, now created amongst as much as one-half of my social network. But that may be a biased estimation. Quick attempts to mention mental illness amongst this supposedly progressive crowd were met with patronization or pity. There are few things more enraging to me than to be addressed with pity by someone who, by all other accounts, ought to be my equal. I do believe these interpretations deserve analysis and that the experiences that I am referring to are more than a fever dream or a perverted memory. The sad part is that any time I may try to defend myself by suggesting as much, that is what I get: subjective, made up. That is, all in my head.

Baldwin's observation is that these students in 1960 — students who risked their lives and welfare, as well as the status of their university and education to revise the racial order of America — were also long eager for a powerful platform, and they received such leadership in the emergence of the Civil Rights Movement. There is more to be said about these students than I am willing to offer in a single draft late at night. Frankly, I would have thought that they would have felt such scarcity for voice and leadership in the year 1960, but then, I don't know much about it, and the history I have learned has only made pit stops through race, never lived in it. It goes to show just how long an inauspicious situation can endure before somebody resists it in a method that inspires the conviction and aspiration of others. And these particular situations were enforced by far more social power and terror than anything I face. Though of the rest of the mentally ill world, I am not certain that is true.

When Dr. King spoke, you will notice that he spoke often of spiritual and psychological despair. While delivering an address after the signing of the Civil Rights Act, he talked about how this changed not only the external circumstances of black Americans, but more importantly, it changed their internal circumstances. He breaches the separation between the spirit and the world. There is no separation. The evils contaminate the soul and disarrange one's assessment of both the world and of oneself. And in my own way, that is where I sit: without a personal polemic or an inner light. And I know others feel the same.

I full-body-cringe after drawing a comparison between them and me. It feels impudent, but why should it? It's all one ambit of life, and there shouldn't be any restraint to what the freedom of one person can incite in others. Currently, I have nothing else to study, and I must make what I can with what is available to me. The lesson here is replicable: how many students have gone Mad and taken the defeat of their situation upon themselves? How many have lost their dreams and their futures and never been bold enough to speak to it in public? For how many decades have they been doing this in reticence, and what leadership could compel them into a life that generates more respect, both from society and from themselves? How do they know the degree to which they are removed from being themselves if they have never known anyone to dispute the particulars of their repression? An estranged mind is a dangerous instrument—I don't deny it. And there is power here to turn toward acidity over a world that isn't permissive enough to see you for who you are, a world that assumes less of you for wholly capricious qualities. Having seen analogous models play out in history before, how does one transfer these lessons into a different place and time?

It seems that in settings, crisis precedes confrontation, and it can be a slow, unchanging drift before a complaint is declared a crisis. In fact, it may have been a crisis several times over, only nobody termed it so. Certain suppressions take an abundance of courage to trouble, and it can take a long time before one finds the right crowd to work with, the right person to follow. And perhaps one does not recognize the problem until it reveals itself in full, and you realize both what you are fighting and why you must fight it.

There are still many people who desire separation from Madness, and for the most part, they have it. When they don't have it, they have the power of not having to recognize it or talk about it, even when it may be imperative to do so. When this arrangement is challenged, one is usually treated as though they have broken a rule. The system of sanism today that influences relations between people, their mental illness, and other people is nowhere near as terror-addled as the system of racism that ran old America. One would surely not risk death or assassination by protesting the order, I hope. But then, this system of sanism is more understated. And I don't know what guides it most. Silence? Isolation? Paternalism? Control? Fear? When not in the open, it is not easy to say just how violent its perpetrators can be, nor how virulently they detest this attribute of humanity. Previously, when people wished for separation from madness, they were granted that separation thanks to the asylum, what sociologists called a "total institution", in which each aspect of a person's life was confined, controlled, and segregated. The hypothetical terror that seethed underneath the asylum was never threatened in the way that the terror underlying racial segregation did. Who today understands the "mental patient" as part of America's pluralist fabric? When asylums were abandoned, many patients were transferred to other margins, or other institutions, where they were again made invisible and controlled in other ways. They never had the tragic mass confrontation that demanded, "We belong here too," which could never be detached from memory. We were let go, a Ship of Fools of national memory. I cannot know how America may have responded to them. That history has not yet been shared with me. This confrontation will come soon — I insist that it happens. The world will presumably treat it with less violence than it did in that infamous era. But that does not mean that it will be a venture without violence. Those conditions are still there, the phobia and the separation, the punishment and the prejudice, and they are expressed perhaps more unabashedly towards madness than they are for any other quality, and I cannot identify any individual who will get up and say, This Will Not Stand, as is done for others. While the people who understand this are numerous, I worry that, like the recipients of Dr. King's address, they have internally resigned themselves to a second-class mindset. Disheartenment is the hallmark of their inclination, and it is intimately linked with their social position as mentally ill people. They live with it, partnerless, without sorority, fraternity, or leadership. And if they are like me, they will think about killing themselves one or two more times, choose a superior regiment for life, and become a person worth emulating.

I don't know what is feasible. I strive for the impossible escape, and if nothing else, that mandates questioning, as I currently hold no other power. Questioning of myself and my world. And what I have learned is that since the world is depressing, many don't have the strength to look at it for what it is. In Depression, however, the folly of the world cannot disrupt my mood as it would if I was pleased with myself. I have nothing to abandon by staring directly into reality. And thus, because I am able to question without concern for my comfort, there is space for me to establish a life predicated on reality. Brutish, risible, winsome reality. The life-breath of antiracist thinking evolves into an extensive, interconnected mesh of subaltern life—indigenous, anti-imperial, queer, trans—all of those with whom I have no dialogue, and yet who I can never fully understand myself, nor my country, without. It is an overgrown path, extending across time and terrain, ever-winding, ever-revealing, ever-damning.

Recently I have learned of the military occupation of Palestine—an unmissable moral abomination, an apartheid state applied by merciless military force, all with unanimous, uncritical endorsement from my government, and a thorough absence in our culture and media. On its own, it is a site of revelation, but in conjunction with my education on my home, it reveals the underbelly of the local, and it has illuminated my backyard in ways I have never heard spoken of. The people of Chicago and its suburban outskirts are bedfellows with the Israelis in creating and maintaining a locality of ethnic segregation, with gated mansions alongside occupied ghettos. There are parallels that I cannot unlearn: the Israelis had an ethnic cleansing and moved the Palestinians into occupied territories through a military raid. Chicago whites fled from the city when blacks came from the South, and while some say they left for economic security, others marked the borders of neighborhood living with riots, stones, and vitriol, which the leaders of the Civil Rights Movement referred to as the worst racism they saw in America. Israel restricts Palestinian life through bombs and bulldozers. We do so through politics, police, and prisons. They built a wall to divide, we built a highway. They euphemize their abuse with bromides like, "national security," and "democracy." We say, "tough on crime," and "balancing the budget." They settle, we gentrify. They occupy, we patrol. They detain and torture, we detain and torture—just last month journalists and activists exposed Homan Square as a site to torture hundreds of black youth. They whitewash their past, and we do the same to ours.

What, then, am I supposed to do with this fable of the "Good

North" and the "Bad South" that I have always lived with? The more I uncover about Chicago, the more I see that this idea of the "tolerant North" is a carefully crafted façade. Mayor Daley understood that if he avoided saying the n-word in public and instead arranged segregation through the backdoor mechanisms of public policy and the covert actions of a racist police force, he could fulfill the same outcomes as an explicitly racist society. We cover for freakishness in private with prudence in public. We pass our condemnation onto the police dogs and the plantations of the South, and don ourselves the Land of Lincoln. I now believe that the Devil's greatest trick was making you believe that he spoke only in a Southern drawl. The North was a devil by a different name. Cicero was a Selma that the Civil Rights Movement deemed too dangerous to march on. And I know that I am closer to the crime than I have been led to believe, because I have read the books on Daley and I see the names of the Irishmen in his machine, and I know that I went to Catholic school with their grandchildren. I know that much of the membership of South Shore Country Club, the pre-flight affluent Irish, settled in North Shore Country Club after white flight, one of the scenes of my youth, a club to which much of my social network belongs. Chicago's black ghetto is an American model of carefully structured encampment, so ingenious that decades later the consequences of underdevelopment and isolation could be publicized as deliberate self-destruction. Young black men shoot other black men on a regular basis, and we watch it in the news in the North Suburbs after drinking wine and watching second-rate crime dramas, shake our heads, and wonder how they can't take care of their own home without resorting to violence. Oh, the savagery! But this is just another extension of the Northern plot. Here is the question: how does one make the beneficiaries of the scheme look passive and helpless, and the victims of it look like the perpetrators? I object. But Boo, we did not decide this. Someone else did. Now pass the wine and flip to Conan, please.

I understand it is difficult to look beyond the material advantages that I hold in this world and say that I have been cheated of anything. Hopefully, those who cannot conceive of a rich life in this way will grow to appreciate more nuance in my world. I may be bottoming out, and I may be disabled for much of my time, but I will still come out of it with countless opportunities for rebirth. Thus, I can be easily ridiculed for claiming an unfair deal, as it is wrapped in the finest gold and silver. Yet what I experience inside that wrapping is the absolute antithesis of fulfillment, and I wish it upon nobody. Much of my Depression comes from the specific biological makeup of Me, but another part of it—possibly a much greater part—comes from the divorce between myself and my world, in which I am peerless. This divorce comes somewhat from the delusion of being quote-unquote better than it; the natural, unchecked mindset of the bourgeoisie. And yet I am neither better nor necessarily freer, since every day I contemplate that life might not be worth living. It also comes from sitting in a manor by the lake, being confronted with policed poverty, and proclaiming, "Life is not fair, there have always been masters and there have always been slaves. That's just how it is."

One can downplay the magnitude of the Depression in my life if they so choose. But this is a mistake. Depression reveals the spiritual ties of humanity. There is only one history and one spiritual conclusion within it. And here I am: young, angry, and resolute to bridge ideas of race, wealth, and history into a new Chicago, and to excavate this confidence from others from their madness. And I do so without irony, from the mouth of the silver spoon. Depression in someone of my background is at first paradoxical: those who come from success and privilege should not also be terminally unwell. But I now accept that this logic is myopic. Depression in affluence is not a paradox. It is necessary affliction to restore equilibrium when people drift into pretentious fantasy, full of status insecurity, masturbatory hedonism, and callous dispositions towards the rest of humanity. It is easy to see how the hardships of poverty amount to psychological debility. It is less clear, however, how having everything does not make for a sound spiritual base, and no degree of privilege, self-importance, or looking-the-other-way can safeguard or rescue anyone from this.

These are not the lessons one picks up in a place like the North Shore. Everything is pushed a step closer toward commerce, and a step away from solidarity and relationships of depth outside the bubble. The best that exorbitant wealth can attain on its own is the illusion of fulfillment.

Such as my brother, who I love. I want to attest to the fact that it is all right to let all of this collapse. Though we are tempted to see dystopia in the fall of the world as it is, perhaps its rebirth will release us from needless dependence on hidden violence and greed. For our lives as they exist can only be upheld on the distant subordination of other people, who are expected to value their livelihood less than our most insignificant opinions. It is all right to fall into the so-called abyss, which is a false metaphor, anyway. In a real abyss, one never returns. That is not how the spirit works. And now that I have a keener appreciation for the resilience of the human spirit, I do not expect those people to abide by this forever. Nor shall I abide.

Can that change? I do not know. Movements consisting of millions barely receive mention in the North Shore. What possibility do I have to change anything as just one person? The conservatism of my home would overtake me time and time again, and nothing short of my suicide would prick their consciences into revelation, no matter how thorough and astute my efforts may be. I was raised within this dreamlike existence, and now two and a half decades into my life I am refusing it, and trying to decipher its intricacies. This much I know: people do not understand the illusion that we live in by ourselves. The nature of ignorance is not to understand itself. Only in context to who I am not will I understand who I am, and only through relationships with them will I know my life.

The body of African-American input illuminates the details of my community, the white bourgeoisie in the post-Civil Rights era. Followed to its furthest extent, it illuminates my death, just as I imagine feminist input would illuminate the conditions of my brother's death, if he ever paid attention to it. And voices from abroad reveal the soul of America to itself. Suicide and homicide are two halves of the same bifurcated world. One day my ravings may help others know themselves in ways I cannot foresee, but which nonetheless have great value to them, even if they do not consider themselves insane in the way that I do. I am lucky to escape it, this reverie, though it has been incalculably unpleasant, and it may not truly feel blessed until I am closest to dying. I cannot go back to the childish, ignorant happiness I once had, if I ever had it. Once this illusion has been disillusioned, it cannot be returned to. The children of the rich must learn that a greater reality exists for them if they will rearrange their lives to accept it—but alas, it is not easy to show things to those who see through sleeping eyes.

I think about Doctor King moralizing, "Indeed, let us say it bluntly and candidly, many Southern leaders are pathetically trapped by their own devices. They know that the perpetuation of this archaic, dying order is hindering the rapid growth of the South. Yet they cannot speak this truth—when Negroes win their struggle to be free, those who have held them down will themselves be freed for the first time." Alas, that is the paradox of the North. This is my bane, too, and only through correcting this will my salvation be enabled.

As for the money—fuck it, give it all away. I have no need

for it. Poor kids ought to be as entitled to screw up with my father's wealth as I was.

Finally, let me digress to contemplate the Doc once more. The Doc said that there is no happiness in life. Happiness is only attainable in death — the best we can achieve in life is momentary contentment. Within my present reality, he is correct. But my present reality is also myopic and unimaginative. For the most part, it does not speak to the spiritual plummet of Depression. It knows the middling emotional grounds, the finely scheduled work, the inherited social mores that demarcate our relationships, the artificial social deadlines, the circumscribed, inhumane politics, and the drab, inundated notion of culture to which my people give too much of their time.

But that is only present reality. A higher ground within this world is possible through the triumph of the mind. It is possible through the courage to recognize that one's suffering is joined with the suffering of all, and to rearrange the terms of how one lives according to that recognition. This higher ground is built on the need for spiritual belongingness with individuals who have learned and contemplated the way of the world, who have been burnt by it, and who will lay down their lives to compel it towards its most uncontaminated purpose: Love. I anticipate that this pursuit is lonely yet noble. I anticipate that it is routinely disappointing, due to people who reject its promise, to the people who invoke its promise but live it selfishly, and to the often-fruitless toil it involves. I admit that it is not a sensible pursuit. It is a pursuit based on a contract one has to make with the world out of faith. One must say, "I will prepare myself for a new future if you will too, and together we may achieve a fraction of that possibility."

I do not believe the rewards of this pursuit are constant or in any way guaranteed. But I will wager that to know for only a moment that there are others who excel in this pursuit is to experience something much bolder than mere contentment. For that reason, I believe the Doc was selling us all short.

Acknowledgments and Call to Action

I'd like to acknowledge Emily Johnson for her preliminary edits, Erik Hane for his line edits, Anna Paustenbach for her advice and knowledge of the literary business, Lisa Bess Kramer for her prolonged literary services, Joel Bahr for his proofreading and editing, and my mother and father for their unconditional love and support.

Small presses and self-published authors rely on online reviews to generate awareness of their work. If you write book reviews, please consider writing a review on websites like Amazon, Goodreads, Edelweiss, LibraryThing, or r/books. Your contribution is valuable and vital to maintaining a strong culture of independent publishing.

Please follow @HeelerBooks on Twitter or visit heelerbooks. com for news and future book projects.